"[A] confection that brims with kindness and heartfelt sincerity. . . . You can't do much better than Anne Gracie, who offers her share of daring escapes, stolen kisses and heartfelt romance in a tale that carries the effervescent charm of the best Disney fairy tales."　—*Entertainment Weekly*

"I never miss an Anne Gracie book."
　　　　　—*New York Times* bestselling author Julia Quinn

"For fabulous Regency flavor, witty and addictive, you can't go past Anne Gracie."
　　　　　—*New York Times* bestselling author Stephanie Laurens

"With her signature superbly nuanced characters, subtle sense of wit and richly emotional writing, Gracie puts her distinctive stamp on a classic Regency plot."
　　　　　　　　　　　　　　　　—*Chicago Tribune*

"The always terrific Anne Gracie outdoes herself with *Bride by Mistake*. . . . Gracie created two great characters, a high-tension relationship and a wonderfully satisfying ending. Not to be missed!"
　　　　　—*New York Times* bestselling author Mary Jo Putney

"A fascinating twist on the girl-in-disguise plot. . . . With its wildly romantic last chapter, this novel is a great antidote to the end of summer."
　　　　　—*New York Times* bestselling author Eloisa James

"Anne Gracie's writing dances that thin line between always familiar and fresh. . . . *The Accidental Wedding* is warm and sweet, tempered with bursts of piquancy and a dash or three of spice."　　—New York Journal of Books

THE
HEIRESS'S
DAUGHTER

ANNE GRACIE

BERKLEY ROMANCE
New York

BERKLEY ROMANCE
Published by Berkley
An imprint of Penguin Random House LLC
penguinrandomhouse.com

Copyright © 2024 by Anne Gracie
Penguin Random House supports copyright. Copyright fuels creativity, encourages
diverse voices, promotes free speech, and creates a vibrant culture. Thank you for buying
an authorized edition of this book and for complying with copyright laws by not
reproducing, scanning, or distributing any part of it in any form without permission.
You are supporting writers and allowing Penguin Random House to continue to
publish books for every reader.

BERKLEY and the BERKLEY & B colophon are
registered trademarks of Penguin Random House LLC.

ISBN: 9780593549681

First Edition: May 2024

Printed in the United States of America
1   3   5   7   9   10   8   6   4   2

Book design by George Towne

*This book is for all the lovely readers
who have bought and read my books and
who have generously shared their
reading pleasure with me and online.
You are the wind beneath my writing wings.
Thank you.*

Prologue

**Studley Park Manor
Hampshire, England
1806**

Don't wiggle around like that, child," Nanny said. "You want to look nice on your birthday, don't you? The more you wriggle the longer it will take."

Clarissa Studley did her best to keep still, but it was very hard. It was her birthday.

"Mama said that now I'm seven I'm a young lady."

"Well, behave like one, and let me finish this hair," Nanny said severely, unwinding another long rag and setting it aside.

Clarissa's hair was a trial, Nanny often said. It was plain brown and straight, and a little bit bushy, and if she wanted any hint of a curl, she had to sleep with rags, which wasn't very comfortable, but was necessary if she wanted ringlets. And ringlets were essential if she wanted to look pretty, Mama said.

And today of all days, Clarissa wanted to look pretty.

Mama had ordered her a new dress, pink and white, to match Mama's new dress—also pink and white—Clarissa's favorite colors. The only difference was that Clarissa's dress had shiny pink satin bows sewn around the hem.

Mama had also bought her a pair of new shoes, white

kidskin slippers with a cluster of tiny pink velvet roses on each toe. Clarissa loved them, but she hadn't been allowed to wear them yet. "Not until your birthday," Nanny had told her. "And never outside."

"There, that's it, you can move now," Nanny announced when she had fastened the last pink satin bow in Clarissa's hair. There were three, and they matched those on her dress exactly. "Don't you look nice?"

Clarissa gazed at her reflection in the looking glass, twirling happily this way and that, watching the bows dance as she moved. She felt like a princess.

"Your mama wants to see you downstairs," Nanny told her, and then added, "She has a surprise for you."

"What kind of a surprise?" Clarissa asked eagerly. She already knew Mama had ordered a special dinner, with all Clarissa's favorite food—wonderful smells had been coming from the kitchen all the previous day—and there was a splendid pink and white cake with her name iced in an elegant script. And tiny icing rosebuds.

And now, another surprise.

Nanny laughed. "If I told you, it wouldn't be a surprise, now, would it? Now run along—no, walk, don't run. You're a young lady now."

Clarissa walked carefully downstairs. The new shoes were a little tight, but she didn't mind. They would stretch, Nanny said. She was a growing girl.

She had just reached the landing when she heard the sound of carriage wheels out front. Who could that be? They didn't get many visitors. Was this Mama's surprise?

"I won't be long," a man's voice said.

"Papa!" she shrieked happily, and ran down the remaining stairs. Papa hardly ever visited, but here he was, on her birthday. He must be Mama's surprise.

Papa handed his hat to Maddox, the butler, just as Clarissa bounded down the last step and rushed to greet him. "Oh, Papa, Papa, you came!" He made no move to embrace her—

Papa never embraced people—so she hugged him around the legs.

"What the devil! Get your sticky hands off me." He bent and pried her fingers open and pushed her back. "And look, you've crushed my trousers, you wretched brat."

"My hands aren't sticky, Papa, truly they're not. I just washed them. I'm sorry about the wrinkles." She tried to smooth them out but he shoved her roughly away and raised his voice.

"Will somebody remove this brat?" And then to her he said, "Get to the nursery, child, where you belong."

"But it's my birthday, Papa."

Ignoring her, he strode to the room they called "Papa's office" even though he hardly ever used it. Clarissa followed, saying uncertainly, "I thought you'd come to celebrate it."

He searched through some papers in one of the desk drawers. "Celebrate what?" he said impatiently.

"My birthday. I'm seven."

He snorted. "Expect me to celebrate that? Commiserate, more like."

Clarissa didn't know what *commiserate* meant, but it didn't sound good. "I've got a new dress," she said in a small voice. "And pretty new shoes, Papa—see?" She showed him.

He didn't even glance at her. "Waste of money. Nothing will ever make you look pretty."

Clarissa swallowed.

Mama said from the doorway, "She's just a child, Bartleby. Must you be so harsh? It's her birthday."

He snorted again. "What's to celebrate? A useless girl child, and plain as a stick."

Mama came forward and took Clarissa's hand. "I'm sorry, Bartleby. I have tried and tried for a son, and I've failed you, I know. But it's not the child's fault."

"There's nothing of me in that child."

Mama gasped. "Bartleby! I swear to you I never ever—"

"I know that, you stupid woman. Who'd have you? If it

wasn't for the money—Ah, here it is." He pulled a document out of the drawer, folded it and slipped it into his pocket. He turned, glanced at the two of them standing side by side in their matching dresses and made a scornful noise. "Look at you—both as ugly and useless as each other. Now get out of my way, I have a party to get to."

Clarissa glanced up at her mother. Mama's mouth quivered. She stretched out a hand to him. "Take me with you. Please, Bartleby, I haven't been away from this house for years."

Papa snorted again. "Take *you*? To a stylish ton party? Don't be ridiculous! As well take a barnyard sow to a soirée. Now, out of my way, woman." He brushed roughly past Mama, snatched his hat from Maddox, climbed into the waiting carriage and drove off.

Mama stood as if frozen. "A barnyard sow," she whispered. A tear rolled down her cheek.

Clarissa squeezed her mother's hand. "I think you look lovely, Mama."

But Mama just shook her head. "There's a present for you in the library, Clarissa. I'm going to bed. I have a headache." She turned and climbed the stairs slowly, as if every bone in her body ached.

Clarissa watched, wishing she knew what to do. Mama was always like this after Papa had been home.

After a while she went into the library. She found a wrapped box on the table under the window. In it was a doll, a beautiful doll with golden hair and bright blue eyes. She was wearing a dress that matched Clarissa's, even down to the tiny pink bows around the hem of the dress, and the little white slippers with tiny roses on the toes.

Clarissa stared at the doll. Golden hair in perfect ringlets. Blue eyes. Clarissa's hair was plain dull brown and her eyes weren't even a proper color; they were a strange greenish brown, that sometimes looked green and sometimes brown.

The doll was beautiful. Clarissa wasn't. She looked just like Mama, everybody said so.

A useless girl child, and plain as a stick . . . both as ugly and useless as each other.

She put the doll back in the box and went outside. It didn't matter if she got her shoes dirty now. Her birthday was over.

Chapter One

London 1818

Clarissa Studley sat in the summerhouse, gazing out through windows blurry with rain. It had been raining all night and the garden was soaked, the air filled with the fragrance of rich earth and drenched flowers. If only she could make a perfume as magical as that . . .

She sighed. The paper in front of her was still blank. She'd come out to the summerhouse in the garden, intending to pen her regular weekly letter to her old nanny, who lived retired in the country, but her mind simply wouldn't settle to it.

It was the morning after her sister's wedding to Leo, Lord Salcott, and Clarissa had passed a sleepless night.

She and her sister would no longer be together—not in the same way—ever again. Of course, they'd see each other frequently: when she returned from her honeymoon, Izzy would live in Leo's house, which was just across the garden.

But at the end of the season, Izzy and Leo would go to live on Leo's country estate in Hampshire, and then who knew how often Clarissa would see her sister? Oh, she was sure they would invite her to come with them, but Clarissa had no intention of playing gooseberry in her beloved sister's marriage.

No, face facts. From now on she was essentially on her own. Of course there was old Lady Scattergood, Leo's aunt, with whom she currently lived, and Mrs. Price-Jones, the chaperone Leo had hired for her, and Betty, her maidservant, whom she'd known from childhood. But fond as she was of them, they weren't the same as a sister.

So, her old life was over and a new way of going forward had to be embraced.

Embraced? Accepted, anyway.

No, she told herself firmly, *embraced* was the word. If she had learned one thing in her life it was that if you wanted something to happen, there was no point in sitting around wishing and hoping and dreaming. Because nobody would do it for you. You had to *make* things happen yourself.

She had made Papa accept, however reluctantly and resentfully, that Izzy was her sister and would live with her. And it had changed her life.

And when they'd come to London after Papa's death, she and Izzy had made Leo, her guardian, accept Izzy's entry into society along with Clarissa, despite Izzy's illegitimacy and his vigorous opposition. And look how well that had turned out—Leo had fallen in love with Izzy and had married her. So now Clarissa needed to work out what she wanted and try to make it happen.

But what did she want? She twirled her pen meditatively and gazed out of the rain-spattered window and the saturated garden.

First and foremost she wanted a family—children. Not just one child, either. She didn't want any child of hers to be as lonely as she'd been before she'd found Izzy. That had been providential, but purely accidental.

And of course, to have children she needed a husband. Up to now, she'd been waiting for a desirable husband to present himself—but so far no likely candidates had. The fortune hunters kept coming. So she needed to take a more active role.

The idea of husband-hunting repelled her slightly— she'd cringed, observing the blatant tactics used by some of the pushy, matchmaking mamas and their ambitious daughters. She wasn't ambitious in that way: she just wanted her own chance at happiness.

But what sort of husband did she want? She thought for a minute, dipped her pen into the ink and wrote a heading— *Desirable Husbandly Qualities*—and underlined it.

Then she drew a decorative border around the heading. Then some flowers along the border.

Stop procrastinating, she told herself sternly. She dipped her pen in the inkwell again and added the first criterion: *1) A man as unlike Papa as possible.*

That went without saying. But she needed to be more positive. Qualities. What next?

2) Handsome. She looked at it, then crossed it out. She wasn't even pretty, so it would be rather hypocritical to demand good looks in a husband. Besides, Papa had been handsome, dangerously so. So . . . *2) Handsome. Attractive.* And then she added *to me*, and then added, *and interesting.*

3) Fidelity. Really, that should be number one—she wanted a man who would be faithful to her. Unlike Papa, who had repeatedly broken Mama's heart with his blatant affairs. But the list was in no particular order.

She glanced out at the wind tossing the branches of the trees, and considered their neighbor, Lord Tarrant, and how he adored his three little tree-climbing daughters. Yes, that was another really important quality.

4) Kindness, especially to children. Because she dearly wanted children and wanted them to have a kind and affectionate father. Which was, when she thought about it, covered in number one. But this was a specific quality, whereas number one was general.

And then she thought of Lady Scattergood's little dogs and how the first time she'd seen the first chink in her brother-in-law's hard exterior was when he'd been so gentle with little Biddy, who'd been abused and injured and was so frightened. To number four she added, *and animals.*

What else? A gust of wind sent a flurry of raindrops spattering against the glass of the summerhouse. She snuggled back in her chair. It was so cozy in here when it rained. She and Izzy had spent many happy hours here, reading, writing letters or just talking. Perhaps she could have a summerhouse of her own after she was married. Assuming she married a man who paid attention to her, who listened to her views and respected them.

5) Respects me.

Paid attention *to her*, not her fortune.

That thought prompted the next on her list. *6) No fortune hunters.* That was crucial. Papa had married Mama for her money, and the minute they were married he stopped being charming and attentive—and later, once he realized her fortune came with strings and trustees and was not wholly his to spend as he liked, he had become downright nasty.

Clarissa had inherited that same fortune. Grandfather Iverley had set it up that way—from mother to child, with only a limited amount going to the husband—and her trustees would control it until she married.

What happened after that? Would it be the same for her as it was for Mama? She had no idea. She made a mental note to find out exactly what the terms of her inheritance were. She wouldn't deceive any potential husband. And if the conditions put off someone then it would show they cared more about the money than her.

Thinking of Papa, she made a seventh notation: *7) No rakes.* It really should have gone under *Fidelity*, but rakes were the kind of men who were habitually unfaithful, and she doubted one could change.

Was that all? She regarded her list critically.

There was one quality missing, the most important one. But it wasn't something you could put on a shopping list like this. Nevertheless it was what she wanted in a husband, so she wrote it down: *8) Love.*

Then she crossed it off. *8) Love.*

It wasn't possible to *make* love happen. And as long as she could remember, Mama had told her that her life would be easier if she never expected love, that women like them— plain and plump and dull, and of undistinguished birth— weren't the kind of women that a gentleman could love.

Papa, too, had said the same—repeatedly—and though Clarissa tried hard not to believe him, a small niggling voice deep inside her kept popping up to remind her: *Plain as a stick. Ugly and useless. If it wasn't for the money . . .*

She stared out through the gray blur of the windows, feeling blue. She knew how that ended: *If it wasn't for the money . . . no man would want her.* And Mama had agreed.

A spurt of anger made her straighten her back. Mama and Papa were wrong. Everybody deserved to have the chance to be loved and though she could not *make* it happen, she would not deny herself even the possibility. She picked up the pen again and wrote it down in big black letters. And now number eight read: *8) Love.* **Love.**

Horatio, Lord Randall, known to his friends as Race, ran a finger around his stock, which suddenly felt so tight about his neck it was near to strangling him.

It was ridiculous.

He was merely doing a favor for a friend. Leo was, after all, Miss Studley's guardian, and Leo was Race's closest friend. He'd been best man at Leo's wedding.

"It needn't be a hardship," Leo had assured him. "I

know Clarissa's devilish shy and not much of a conversationalist—not your type at all—but you can't deny, the girl can ride. Just take her out on the heath from time to time—you know how she loves a good gallop, and her chaperone doesn't ride."

Race had promised. It wouldn't be a chore to take Clarissa Studley riding—far from it. Besides, she was an excellent horsewoman.

"And I know how much you dislike society events," Leo had continued, "so I won't expect anything of you there. I've told her chaperone, Mrs. Price-Jones, to be especially vigilant for any lurking fortune hunters. I'll deal with them when I return from my honeymoon. Clarissa's fortune makes her a target and according to her sister, she's too softhearted for her own good. I wouldn't put it past some plausible rogue to persuade her into an elopement. So if there are any problems, I've told Mrs. Price-Jones she can call on you for assistance in my place. I hope that's all right."

Of course Race had agreed, and so now here he was, on the front step of Leo's aunt's home, where Clarissa lived, facing Lady Scattergood's butler.

"I'm sorry, Lord Randall, but Lady Scattergood is not at home." The ancient butler delivered the message in a sonorous, faintly smug voice.

Race frowned. "Dash it all, Treadwell, Lady Scattergood is always at home." The old lady had been housebound for several years, and on the rare occasions she ventured out of her home it was inside a covered palanquin with all the curtains drawn—the very palanquin he could see sitting in the hall, unoccupied.

The butler repeated without a blink, "My lady is not at home."

He made to shut the door, but Race shoved his boot in to prevent it. "Then be so good as to inform Miss Studley that Lord Randall is here and wishes to speak to her."

"Miss Studley is not at home."

"Her chaperone, then, Mrs.—" Race couldn't recall the chaperone's name, blast it: something Welsh and hyphenated.

"Mrs. Price-Jones is not at home."

At that moment the sound of female voices followed by a gust of feminine laughter floated from somewhere behind the butler.

"Damn it, Treadwell, I can hear the ladies. They *are* at home." It was too early for morning calls, which for some unknown reason invariably took place in the afternoon, so who else could it be but the ladies of the house?

Through the butler's granitelike mien, a faint smirk was allowed to escape. "Perhaps, my lord, but not to you— ever." He closed the door in Race's face.

Race stared at the door, resisting the impulse to kick it. Not to be admitted, *ever*? Had the butler gone mad? Or was it Lady Scattergood? She was, and always had been, eccentric.

The morning had dawned fine and sunny, and he'd intended to take Clarissa for the first of many rides. But now, thanks to that wretched butler, he couldn't even get past her front door.

Irritated, he returned to his lodgings and swiftly penned her a note, inviting her to come riding with him on Hampstead Heath.

❦

"A note? From *a man*?" Lady Scattergood raised her lorgnette.

"Yes, from Lord Randall." Clarissa looked down at the bold black handwriting. A note from Lord Randall. Personal and handwritten. A shiver of pleasure passed through her. Lord Randall!

Lady Scattergood snorted. "That rake! What does he want?"

"He's invited me to go riding with him this morning," Clarissa said breathlessly. It wasn't the first time she'd gone riding with Lord Randall, but the other two times had been with Leo, her guardian, and her sister Izzy. This time it was an invitation just for her.

"How delightful," Mrs. Price-Jones began, but Lady Scattergood cut her off.

"The rogue! Such cheek! Send the villain a curt refusal."

"Oh, but there's no harm in Lord Randall, surely," Mrs. Price-Jones said.

The old lady snorted. "Have you forgotten his father? 'Rake Randall' they called him, and with good reason. The way that man behaved! Disgraceful. And I hear the son is just as bad."

"Surely not," Mrs. Price-Jones argued. "After all, he's Lord Salcott's best friend."

"Be that as it may, Althea, you've been in the wilds of Wales for the last twenty years. You don't know the dangers of the modern world as I do. And men have no judgment when it comes to suitability."

"But Leo trusts him, and it's such a beautiful morning. I'd love a ride," Clarissa said in a coaxing voice. Hampstead Heath was one of her favorite places. The fresh air, the wide-open spaces. "You know I've been riding with him before."

"Yes, with my nephew there to protect you. Never by himself."

"I won't be by myself. Naturally Addis will accompany us." Addis was the groom Leo, her guardian and now her brother-in-law, had hired to escort them whenever she and her sister rode out.

Lady Scattergood shook her head emphatically. "Addis is also a man! No, Clarissa, before he left for his honeymoon, my nephew specifically asked me to take good care of you and I won't let him down. I've barred that Lord Randall from the house."

"*Barred* him?" Clarissa exclaimed.

"Of course. Let a fox into the chicken house? Over my dead body! So send the fellow to the right-about."

Clarissa sighed. Leo had said to his aunt, *Take good care of Clarissa*, in a casual, farewelling sort of way, but Lady Scattergood had taken it to extremes. It was as if the old lady thought she should lock Clarissa away in a tower.

She'd already issued instructions that Clarissa was to have no single male callers, and was very strict about the events Clarissa was allowed to attend, even with Mrs. Price-Jones in attendance. The events she approved of seemed to depend entirely on what Lady Scattergood recalled of the hostesses involved. But to bar Lord Randall from visiting . . .

Clarissa and her chaperone, Mrs. Price-Jones, exchanged rueful glances. There was no gainsaying Lady Scattergood in this mood.

"Very well," Clarissa said. "I'll decline his invitation." She fetched her little writing desk and wrote a short note, thanking Lord Randall for his kind invitation and explaining that Lady Scattergood felt that it was unseemly for Clarissa to ride out without a female chaperone in attendance, and Mrs. Price-Jones did not ride. She didn't want him to think the refusal was her choice.

Half an hour later another note arrived, this time on lavender writing paper and written in an elegant, decidedly feminine hand. "Oh, how delightful." Clarissa hid her surprise. "It's from Margaret, Lady Frobisher, inviting me to ride out with her this morning." She didn't know Lady Frobisher very well; in fact she'd met her only once, in the company of Lord Randall. He was her cousin.

Clarissa turned a limpid gaze on Lady Scattergood. "I trust that's an acceptable invitation. She says her husband will escort us—and of course, Addis will be with us." Lord Randall must have read between the lines of her note and was trying again. A small thrill ran down her spine. He really did want to go riding with her.

"All these people suddenly wanting you to go riding with them?" Lady Scattergood pursed her lips, considering it. Clarissa held her breath.

"No doubt because it's a beautiful day, and perfect for riding," Mrs. Price-Jones declared. "And a married lady in the company of her husband? Perfectly unexceptional, wouldn't you say, Olive? Lady Frobisher has an excellent reputation."

"I don't know," Lady Scattergood began. "I don't know the younger generation of Frobishers but—"

"Oh, they're nothing like their grandfather. This generation is quite, quite dull. Staid and frightfully conventional," Mrs. Price-Jones said, with a wink at Clarissa. "In fact, are you sure you'd want to go riding with her, Clarissa? It's bound to be quite dull."

Clarissa tried not to smile. Lady Frobisher and her husband, Oliver, had accompanied Lord Randall the night he'd escorted her and Izzy to Astley's Amphitheatre. Lord Frobisher was indeed a quiet, steady sort of gentleman, but *staid* and *conventional* were the last words she'd use to describe Lady Frobisher. "Call me Maggie, everyone does," the lively brunette had said and, under the indulgent eye of her husband, proceeded to laugh and flirt briefly with perfect strangers.

"I would like some exercise and fresh air," Clarissa said hopefully. The preparations for her sister's wedding and the grand ball that same evening had left very little time to go out, let alone to have an invigorating ride in the fresh air.

Lady Scattergood sighed. "Very well then, but be careful. Anything can happen when you venture out into the wilds."

Hampstead Heath was hardly *the wilds*, but Clarissa appreciated the old lady's concern. "Thank you, dear Lady Scattergood," she said, giving her a kiss on her rouged and wrinkled cheek. "I'll write a note of acceptance to Lady

Frobisher right this minute." Before Lady Scattergood changed her mind.

She sent off the note and hurried upstairs to change. Betty, her maid, set out her riding habit and helped her to dress.

"You haven't forgotten, miss, have you?"

"Forgotten what?"

"That we told Miss Izzy—Lady Salcott, I mean—that we'd get a girl from the orphanage and train her up to be Miss Izzy's personal maid."

"I hadn't forgotten," Clarissa said, though it wasn't quite true. She hadn't forgotten, exactly, but Lord Randall's invitation had driven all other thoughts from her mind. "We'll go this afternoon," she promised. "Now, where's my hat?"

Twenty minutes later she'd changed into her riding habit and was waiting downstairs in the front room. Addis, the groom, waited in the street outside with her horse and his.

The restrictions Lady Scattergood had imposed on her were quite frustrating, and if her sister Izzy were here, there would be an explosion. But Clarissa knew the old lady was doing her best to protect her, and she couldn't hold it against her. Lady Scattergood had her own fears about the world, and if they dominated her attitude to Clarissa's social life, well, it would be for only a few weeks. Once Leo and Izzy returned from their honeymoon things would return to normal.

Besides, Clarissa didn't crave social activity the way Izzy and Mrs. Price-Jones did. She did, however, love riding. And getting out of the city into the countryside.

She paced up and down in front of the window, peering out at the street from time to time. Riding with Lord Randall's cousin and her husband. Would Lord Randall come, too?

The sound of hooves clattering on cobblestones brought her to the window again, and she saw Lord and Lady

Frobisher approaching. Lady Frobisher looked very dashing in a habit of vivid cherry red with silver lacings à la hus-
sar. Her hat was pale gray felt and vaguely military looking,
too, rather like a shako. Worn at a rakish angle, it looked
very feminine with a long cherry red scarf floating behind,
while three matching ostrich feathers curled coquettishly
over her left ear.

Clarissa's bosom was filled with envy. She'd been perfectly happy with her own neat outfit five minutes before,
but now it seemed quite dull by comparison. She instantly
decided she needed a new, smarter riding habit. And hat.

She hurried outside to join them, greeted them and
glanced around. There was no sign of Lord Randall. Oh
well. Her spirits sank a little.

"Race is lurking around the corner, like a villain in a
melodrama," Lady Frobisher said from the side of her
mouth as Addis helped Clarissa mount her horse. "I adore
the intrigue—rescuing the maiden from the seraglio—such
fun!" she added as they moved off, her eyes dancing.

Clarissa laughed. "It's not as bad as that. Lady Scattergood
is very good to me. She's just a little bit overprotective,
that's all. I'm still allowed to go places with my chaperone,
but she doesn't ride."

Lady Frobisher gave her a skeptical glance. "Race told
us he was barred from the house."

Clarissa nodded wryly. "As are all single male visitors."

Lady Frobisher pulled a face. "Ridiculous. How are you
ever going to find a husband?" She glanced at her husband
and smiled at him.

Clarissa caught his answering look. It was clear that Lord
Frobisher doted on his vivacious wife.

"Oh, it's not all single males who are not granted entry,"
she explained. "Lady Scattergood seems quite happy to welcome some single gentlemen, as long as they are accompanied by a respectable lady—preferably a relative. And I can

go places with my chaperone, and we have plenty of invitations to balls and parties. Single gentlemen not being allowed to enter the house alone is but a small inconvenience."

"Race didn't think so."

"No, I'm sorry about that. But my brother-in-law, who's also my guardian, will be back from his honeymoon in a few weeks, and everything will return to normal."

"Have you heard from your sister?"

"No, not yet, but they've only been gone a short while." They turned the corner and she saw Lord Randall waiting on Storm, his beautiful smoke gray gelding.

"Ah, there's Race now," Lady Frobisher said.

"Mmm." For a few moments, Clarissa couldn't say a thing. The sight of Lord Randall always left her briefly breathless. He was not precisely handsome, but she found him very arresting with his bold nose, firm chin, chiseled features and casually elegant bearing. On foot, she found his tall, lean frame and loose-limbed, easygoing bearing very attractive, but on horseback, he was even more impressive.

His white cravat and shirt emphasized the faint tan of his skin. It might not be fashionable for a gentleman to be tanned, but to Clarissa it only emphasized his masculinity and his love of the outdoors. Loving the outdoors herself, she appreciated a man who made no attempt to be fashionably pale.

His buff-colored waistcoat and beautifully cut dark blue coat showcased his lean build and the breadth of his shoulders. Fawn buckskin breeches hugged long muscular thighs, and his tan-topped black leather high boots gleamed with polish. He wore fawn pigskin gloves, and a smart curly-brimmed beaver covered his thick dark locks.

His gray eyes lit with faint amusement as they approached. "Well met, Miss Studley. I'm delighted you could join us."

Feeling her cheeks warm, Clarissa dropped her gaze and

murmured a greeting. Somehow, whenever Lord Randall looked at her, she felt foolishly flustered. There was no reason for it, she knew. He didn't mean to unsettle her—his behavior toward her was everything that was polite and gentlemanly—but for some reason his attention was . . . disconcerting.

It was his eyes, she thought. Gray eyes should be cold and hard, like her guardian Leo's could be at times. But Lord Randall's eyes seemed to dance with light and appeared—to her overactive imagination, at least—to contain an invitation, though to what she didn't care to consider. And a man had no business having such long lashes.

He was a rake. Everybody said so, and she needed to take that to heart and stop these foolish fancies. Papa had been a rake, and he'd broken her mother's heart with his callous infidelities. He'd made no attempt to hide them from her, but Mama had loved him anyway. Hopelessly.

Clarissa was a lot like her mother. Softhearted and susceptible, her sister Izzy often said, and Clarissa knew it was true.

And look at the damage Papa had caused to Izzy and her mother. Izzy was illegitimate—oh, it had turned out all right for her in the end, marrying Leo, but for a while they'd lived on a knife-edge. It could have turned out very differently. Illegitimacy was a slur that followed a person all their life. But did Papa care? No, he had carelessly seduced Izzy's poor young mother—barely sixteen she'd been when he ruined, then abandoned her—shattering her life, and leaving a young girl and her baby daughter to face poverty and the condemnation of society.

A rake was a dangerous creature, no matter how charming and handsome he appeared. In fact, the more attractive he seemed, the more dangerous he must be. After all, the ability to charm foolish females was a rake's stock-in-trade, and Clarissa needed to remember that.

Still, it had been thoughtful of him to invite her to go riding on this fine sunny morning, and then to go to the trouble of arranging for his cousin and her husband to collect her so Lady Scattergood would allow it. His unexpected consideration warmed her.

Chapter Two

❧

They rode two by two through the busy London streets; Lord Randall and his cousin, then Clarissa with Lord Frobisher. Addis, the groom Leo employed for her protection, followed behind.

Lady Frobisher and Lord Randall talked and laughed—she was such a confident, vivacious person, Clarissa was a little envious. She always found it hard to make small talk to people she didn't know very well. As a result, she felt so dull, which of course, made it even harder to think of things to say.

She and her partner rode in silence. Luckily Lord Frobisher didn't seem to mind. He was a very comfortable sort of person, Clarissa decided, and seemed happy enough to let his wife be the life of the party, while he looked on. On the surface they seemed an unlikely couple, but it was clear theirs was a love match, and that they were very happy together.

Would a man ever look at her the way Lord Frobisher looked at his wife?

She sighed. Probably not. Lady Frobisher was everything that Clarissa wasn't—pretty, lively, confident, slender and stylish. If Clarissa hadn't been due to inherit a fortune, very few gentlemen would be interested in her at all.

Oh, stop it! she told herself sternly. That was no way to think. She was who she was, and she would be loved for herself—or not at all.

The street traffic thinned out and they rode four abreast for a while, and when they next re-formed into pairs Lord Randall was her partner.

"I'm very glad you were able to join us," he said.

"Yes. Thank you for arranging it."

"Oh, Maggie was delighted to help out. She's always up for a bit of mischief."

"Mischief?"

"Didn't she tell you she was 'rescuing the maiden from the seraglio'?"

Clarissa managed a laugh, though the description was somewhat mortifying coming from him. "Yes, but it's not like that at all." It wasn't quite true, but she didn't want to criticize Lady Scattergood. The old lady meant well, and Clarissa was her guest.

He didn't respond, and when she glanced at him, he raised a dark eyebrow.

"It's not," she repeated. "Lady Scattergood is merely doing what she thinks is best."

"And why is it best that I am not to be admitted to the house? One would think, as Leo's best man . . ."

She felt her cheeks warm. She couldn't possibly tell him what Lady Scattergood had said about him. *Let a fox into the chicken house? Over my dead body!*

"Single gentlemen are admitted, as long as they're accompanied by a female relative that Lady Scattergood knows. And approves of."

"I see. So a respectable aunt or grandmother is the key, eh?"

To her relief, he didn't pursue the matter. Because she was sure Lady Scattergood would forbid him entrance even if he were accompanied by a respectable female relative.

A few minutes later they once again walked four abreast, with Addis in the rear, and then resumed their two by two. Clarissa was relieved to be paired with Lord Frobisher again; she found talking to Lord Randall . . . difficult. Just a glance or a smile from him scattered her thoughts and she quite forgot what to say.

Race's cousin Maggie gave him a sideways glance. "She's a nice enough girl, but not exactly scintillating company, is she?"

Race didn't respond.

"So tell me, cuz, are you finally planning to settle down? Get yourself an heir?"

"Plenty of time for that," he said easily. "My father didn't marry until he was forty, which means I've got a good ten years of freedom before I need to concern myself with securing the succession."

"Then what's your interest in Miss Studley? You don't need her fortune, I know—unless you've lost yours on 'change.'"

"I'm doing a favor for my friend Leo, that's all."

"Keeping an eye on her while he's on his honeymoon, eh? I see. So it's duty rather than pleasure."

He shrugged. "It's always a pleasure to ride out on a fine day."

"Well, you won't get a ride out of her," Maggie said, snickering naughtily.

Race snorted. "You have a wicked mind. Miss Studley is completely respectable—as she should be," he added with a mock quelling look at his mischievous cousin. Maggie had become more outrageous since her marriage, relishing the freedom a married woman had, compared with the restrictions an unmarried young lady was subject to.

Maggie laughed, entirely unquelled. "Well, I didn't think a plain, plump, dull little innocent would be your style at all."

"She's not pl— Look out!" he exclaimed as a ragged urchin darted into the road in front of them, almost under the horses' hooves. Maggie's horse reared and plunged. Race grabbed the bridle and dragged its head down, holding it until it was calm again. The child, apparently unaffected by his close call, disappeared down a side alley.

"Wretched brat nearly got himself killed," Maggie said, her distress masking itself in anger. "What's a child of that age doing running about the streets alone and unsupervised? Where are his parents? It's a disgrace!"

Race shook his head. His cousin knew as well as he did that the streets were full of orphaned, abandoned and unsupervised children. But in recent months she had become very sensitive to the fate of children.

Her husband came up behind them. "Are you all right, my love?" He reached out and took her hand.

"Of course." She smiled at him, all sign of nerves gone. "It was a close call, but the child wasn't hurt. Besides, a little excitement never hurt anyone. Shall we continue?"

They rode on. "What were you saying again?" Maggie asked Race.

"I forget."

"You said Miss Studley is not—what?" When he didn't reply, she repeated, "What is she not?"

Race shrugged and shook his head. "No idea. Excuse me a moment, I might buy some of those." He headed over to a man selling apples and bought a bag.

He had no intention of discussing either his thoughts about Miss Studley, or any future plans he might have. He was very fond of Maggie—she was his favorite relative—but discreet she was not. Besides, he didn't have any future plans, not really. Just . . . possibilities.

He didn't find Miss Studley in the least plain, not with that silken complexion, those expressive, wide-set hazel eyes—

eyes a man could drown in—and that smile, the sweetest he'd ever seen. As for her being plump, *voluptuous* was the word he would have used: he itched to get his hands on her.

Anyone who thought her plain was just . . . blind.

When he returned with the apples it was to find his cousin riding with her husband, and Miss Studley following behind. He joined her.

"Lord Frobisher was concerned about the fright Lady Frobisher had with that little street urchin," she explained.

Race nodded. He doubted Maggie had had much of a fright—nerves of iron, his cousin. "I think she was more worried about that child."

He thought he knew the source of his cousin's increased concern for the fate of street children. Maggie's failure to conceive, after eighteen months of marriage, was eating at her. Oh, she put a brave face on it, but society's view was that the wife of a titled gentleman had but one duty to perform—provide her husband with an heir.

Race himself had been witness to a number of well-meaning female relatives making delicate—and less-than-delicate—inquiries and offering various suggestions for enhancing her fertility. Eat this, drink that. Have you tried . . . ?

Not that Maggie's husband, Oliver, seemed to mind. He'd pointed out on several occasions that he had younger brothers and was in no hurry for an heir. But despite her frivolous appearance, Race knew Maggie took her failure to conceive hard.

He glanced at Miss Studley and caught her gazing with a wistful expression at his cousin and her husband. "A penny for them," he said softly.

She started slightly. "Oh, nothing of any significance." A faint blush colored her cheeks. "I was thinking about the girl we're going to get to be my sister's maid."

She was a very poor liar. It was another of the things Race liked about her. She hadn't been thinking about a maid at all. One didn't get wistful thinking about hiring a maid. But he let her explain how she and her maid were planning to visit an orphanage to find a girl to train up as a lady's maid for her sister Izzy.

"Very commendable," he said when she was finished. "But why not simply get an already-trained lady's maid from an employment agency?"

She hesitated. "My maid, Betty, came from an orphanage, and we thought we'd like to give another orphan a chance. And Izzy liked the idea."

There was more to it than she was saying—there were mysteries in the Studley sisters' background—but though Race was intrigued, he knew better than to push her to explain. In some ways Clarissa Studley was like the sea anemones he'd found in rock pools as a boy; get too near and she closed right up.

Which was why he was taking things slowly.

"My maid and I are going this afternoon to select a girl."

Race nodded. "Not your chaperone, Mrs. um . . . ?"

"Mrs. Price-Jones? No, she has an appointment with our dressmaker. And since Betty will take the main responsibility for training the girl, I want her to help me choose the right sort of girl."

She added defensively, as if he'd said something critical, "My sister and I have known Betty since we were all young girls together. She came with us from our home in the country. I trust her judgment implicitly."

"Sounds like an excellent plan," he said mildly.

They rode on in silence for a while, concentrating on avoiding porters and barrow boys, street sweepers, hawkers, urchins, dogs and more—the usual chaotic London street scene.

Up ahead his cousin Maggie was chatting vivaciously. She said something and Oliver threw back his head and laughed.

"I'm sorry I'm such poor company," Clarissa said abruptly.

He glanced at her. "You're not. I'm perfectly content with the company I have."

She gave him a skeptical glance. "I know my conversational skills are lacking."

"Not everyone can be a chatterbox like my cousin, and I thank goodness for it. Otherwise the rest of us would never get a word in."

Unconvinced, she gave a perfunctory smile. "It's only since we came to London that we've had any experience in social intercourse."

"Really? Why was that?"

She hesitated, then said, "My sister Izzy and I were not permitted to mingle with people in the local area."

He frowned. "Why ever not?"

She shrugged carelessly. "Our father would not permit it. He never did explain why."

She knew why, Race thought, watching her face. She might not find actual conversation easy but her face was very expressive, particularly her eyes. They were her best feature, he thought, wide and clear, and their color seemed to change, which fascinated him. Sometimes they seemed to be a soft greenish hazel, at others they were a honey gold color, like her hair when the sun hit it.

"Conversation is a skill like any other," he said easily. "The more you practice the better you get."

She shook her head. "My sister Izzy enjoys meeting new people and converses easily with strangers, but I find it . . . difficult."

"Oh, but you don't consider me a stranger, do you?" he said in a low, teasing voice. "You can tell me anything. I won't mind."

She blushed, but lifted her chin and gave him a direct look. "I don't flirt, either."

She was warning him off, and he found it delightful. "That's another skill that develops with practice."

"I'm sure it does," she said primly. He was sure she meant it to have a crushing effect on him. It didn't. He enjoyed a challenge.

"You could practice on me," he suggested.

"No thank you."

"You can trust me, you know."

"I'm sure I can. After all, my guardian asked you to keep an eye on me, did he not?" There was a tightness to the way she said it. And it was no coincidence that she used the exact same phrasing that Maggie had used a few moments before.

"Ah, so you heard that, did you?" What else had she heard? He'd been trying to deflect his cousin's curiosity, but maybe Miss Clarissa had taken it the wrong way.

She shrugged as if indifferent, but it only confirmed his thoughts.

"Leo did ask me to take you riding," he said, "but don't be thinking I consider it a duty, because I don't. It's my *pleasure* to accompany you—anywhere you like, in fact—but riding especially, since you're such an excellent horsewoman."

She obviously didn't believe a word of it. "Then thank you for arranging this excursion," she said, polite as a schoolgirl.

They rode on in silence. The countryside opened up before them, buildings dropped behind them; there were fields on either side of them now, here and there a small plot of cabbages or some other crop, but mostly fields of green dotted with sheep and cattle. And new houses being built.

Race glanced sideways at Clarissa, thinking to tease her a little more, and frowned, all desire to tease wiped away. Following her gaze, he watched as Oliver raised Maggie's hand to his lips and kissed it.

Unaware of his observation, Miss Studley bit her lip, her expression a little dreamy, a little wistful, and somehow . . . melancholy.

"Sixpence for them," he said softly.

"Sixpence?" Her head jerked up and she gave him a startled look, as if recalling where they were. She gave a half-hearted, not-very-convincing laugh. "Heavens, they're not worth the penny you first offered me, let alone sixpence. Anyway, I was still thinking about the maid we're going to hire this afternoon."

No maid caused her to look like that. He glanced ahead at his cousin and her husband, riding very close together, hand in hand. "A romantic couple, are they not?"

She nodded.

"To an outsider they might appear to be quicksilver and clay. Certainly nobody predicted they'd make a match of it. Many predicted Maggie would soon get bored with Oliver—he's a very steady chap—and others were sure that he would get impatient with her flightiness." He shook his head. "It hasn't happened yet and I don't believe it ever will."

She tilted her head and eyed him thoughtfully. "Never? You think so?"

"I know so. My cousin is something of a flibbertigibbet, and Ollie is her rock."

She frowned. "You mean he keeps her under control?"

He laughed. "I'd like to see any man try. No. It's hard to explain, but since their marriage, Oliver has been more relaxed, happier. He used to be rather—I don't know—dour. A bit stiff. And she was always a flighty piece, but those who knew her best could see there was always an underlying brittleness. But that brittleness has gone now and she's just . . . happy. Secure. As is he. Together, they balance each other. Ah, we're almost there," he added, as Hampstead town came into view. "In a few minutes you'll be able to have a good gallop. I know you enjoy that."

"Yes, my sister and I always used to race each other."

"Come on then, let's see if we can beat this staid old married couple," he said loudly as he passed his cousin and her husband, and with shouts and laughter the race was on.

After the initial lighthearted race, they slowed, enjoying

the fresh air and sunshine. They dismounted by one of the ponds to eat the apples he'd bought. Race peeled and sliced one for Miss Studley, which she ate absently and thanked him civilly.

Afterward they fed the cores and peels to the horses. Then, before Race realized it, his cousin and her husband had disappeared into the woods, leaving Race and Miss Studley alone, except for Addis, who lounged on the grass a short distance away, minding the horses.

Cursing his cousin under his breath for her blatant matchmaking, he said to Miss Studley, "My cousin is a minx. Would you care for a stroll around the pond?" It was a smallish pond, and they would be under the eye of her groom the whole time.

She hesitated, then said politely, "Thank you, that would be pleasant." But her eyes told a different story. If only he knew what it was.

He itched to strip that veneer of politeness from her, to reveal the woman beneath, with feelings and thoughts and dreams. He knew he could feel them seething under that smooth, calm facade. But how?

Again he was reminded of the sea anemones of his childhood; if he pushed, she would withdraw even more.

Ducks dotted the pond, ducks of several sorts. Race came to a sudden stop. "Good lord, there's an acquaintance of mine," he exclaimed.

She stopped and looked around. "Where?"

"There." He pointed at a large drake waddling through the grass toward the edge of the pond.

"I can't see anyone."

"That pompous-looking fellow over there. Approaching the pond as if he owns it."

"You mean the duck?" she said incredulously.

"Yes," he said completely seriously. "He's an MP. House of Lords."

She gave him a governessy look. "A duck. In the House of Lords."

"Yes, that's him all right, with the ginger hair and the pink waistcoat—Lord Wigeon."

She snorted.

"Large as life and frightfully pompous," he continued. "Look at the way he walks, as if he owns the world. And you should hear his speeches—long, pretentious, repetitive and as boring as— No, on second thoughts, what was I thinking of? You wouldn't want to hear them. Not unless you're in dire need of a nap, and even then I'd avoid them. Nightmares, you know."

"That's very silly," she said. Her smile was trying to escape.

"Oh lord, and there's another one." He pointed at a large drake with a knobbly red beak. "Sir Humphrey Shelduck. He's a member of my club, and believe me, he's another fellow to be avoided. Not that you're likely to visit my club— no ladies allowed, you know, which makes for dreadfully dull company, I can tell you. Do you see him?"

She giggled. "You're being ridiculous."

"No, I'm quite serious," he said earnestly. "You see that large red knobby nose of his? It's because he knocks over at least two or three bottles of port or madeira a night. Ghastly fellow. Talks of nothing but wine and the meals he's eaten. Now I come to think of it, it's a good thing they don't let ladies into the club. A protective measure. Saves you from frightful bores like him."

"I suppose he'd taste quite good then," she said thoughtfully.

He turned, startled. "What?"

"Well, he's obviously well stuffed and thoroughly marinated."

He laughed aloud.

A female duck launched herself onto the water as they approached. She was followed by a small flotilla of slightly scruffy half-grown ducklings. "Ah now, that will be the wife, poor downtrodden thing," he said.

"How do you know she's poor and downtrodden?" Clarissa said indignantly. "She has all those beautiful babies."

"Yes, but how long is it since she had a new dress, eh?"

Clarissa looked at the mottled brown of the duck's feathers. "Perhaps she just likes subtle colors."

"No, he neglects her."

"Why did she choose him, then?" There was an undertone of seriousness beneath the nonsense and Race belatedly recalled that Leo had told him her parents had had such a marriage. He could have kicked himself.

"Oh, no doubt he was quite a handsome fellow in his younger days, and he would have wooed her with impressive gifts."

She tilted her head and looked up at him. "What sort of gifts?"

"Slugs," he said immediately. "Big fat juicy ones."

She laughed. "I don't care, I refuse to believe she's poor and downtrodden. In any case, you don't need fancy clothes when you're caring for so many babies. And they're darling— look at them."

He watched as the little balls of fluff paddled vigorously after their mother. One fell behind and started cheeping urgently. "That will be the baby," he said, "needy and noisy. And that one." He pointed to a little chap ignoring his mother's loud quacks while he investigated something in the reeds. "That little fellow is the adventurous one. He'll give his mother no end of trouble . . . and probably end up breaking her heart."

There was a short pause and Race felt her searching gaze on his face. He pretended not to notice, hoping she wouldn't ask. Eventually she said lightly, "How do you know it's a boy? Girls can be adventurous, too."

"I suppose so. I just think he's a boy." The duckling

cheeped loudly and Race glanced at his companion. "And now I suppose you expect me to wade in, rescue the little devil—ruining my boots in the process—and determine his sex."

"Of course I don't. But could you—determine his or her sex, I mean?"

"I can't but I expect a poultryman could."

The duckling broke free of whatever had detained him and scooted across the water to join his siblings, flapping tiny wings. The duck family sailed off in a small flotilla.

"There, your boots are safe," she said.

"My valet will be relieved. He's very protective of my boots."

They walked on. "Do you have many siblings?" she asked him after a moment.

"No, none."

"Oh, I'm sorry. I just thought, from the way you talked . . . You seemed to know a lot about children."

He shrugged. "Ten years at boarding school."

"Oh." After a moment she asked, "And your parents?"

"Both dead. My mother died when I was eleven and my father a decade or so later." He glanced at her. "And your mother?" He knew when her father had died.

"Died when I was eight." They strolled on and silence fell between them. Race cursed himself for asking about her mother. She'd really started relaxing with him, and now . . .

"You look a little blue-deviled."

She started and gave him a guilty look. "Oh, sorry."

He didn't want to ask about her mother so he changed the subject slightly. "Missing your sister?"

"Yes—well, no," she responded, a little flustered. "She's only been gone a few days."

"Have you two ever been separated?"

She looked at him in surprise. "No, not since we first met."

He raised a quizzical brow. "Met?"

She bit her lip. "I probably shouldn't have said that." She gave him a cautious glance. "But you know about my sister, don't you?"

"I do. And I won't tell a soul." He was one of the few people in London who knew for a fact that Izzy was really her half sister, her father's natural daughter and not the full, legitimate sister they claimed her to be.

She regarded him steadily for a long moment, then nodded. "Very well then. We were almost nine. Her maternal uncle brought her to Studley Park Manor—that was my home then—immediately after her mother's funeral. He didn't want anything to do with her, thought she was Papa's responsibility. Papa didn't so much as look at her, didn't even meet her that time. He gave instructions that she be dumped in the nearest orphan asylum." Her voice shook as she said, "Those were his very words: 'Dump the brat.'"

She paused, remembering, he supposed.

"He changed his mind?" Race prompted after a minute.

Her eyes lightened, and she dimpled enchantingly. "Not exactly."

He leaned closer. "Oh, now I'm intrigued."

"We hid her until Papa went back to London."

"Hid her?" He gave her a shrewd look. "*We* hid her, or *you* hid her?"

She gave a half-embarrassed little shrug. "Well, I knew the best places to hide."

"And when you stopped hiding, nobody objected?"

"Oh, they did. But I insisted on keeping her."

She was clearly uncomfortable explaining, but it was clear to Race that she had played the pivotal role in the adoption of her half sister.

"And when your father returned, he allowed her to stay?"

"Oh no. We had to hide Izzy every time he came home. Luckily he didn't come home very often, so it wasn't difficult. And eventually he gave up."

There was a whole other story there, Race could see.

From all accounts Sir Bartleby Studley had been a nasty customer, a braggart and a bully—except when he was turning on the charm to seduce some young innocent. And yet this quiet, unobtrusive young woman had not only stood up to him, but had somehow won the right to keep her illegitimate half sister with her—at what?—the age of nine?

Maggie was so wrong to write her off as dull; she was . . . fascinating. Quiet, yes, but with a delightful sense of humor and, he was learning, many more hidden facets to her. Another young lady might have boasted of getting the best of her father, but Miss Clarissa had to be coaxed even to admit her part in it. Which she minimized.

It must have taken a deal of courage to defy him like that, but she didn't even seem to realize it.

He thought back to that night at the Arden ball, where that drunken crony of her late father's—Lord Pomphret— had loudly and publicly accused her sister Isobel of being Bart Studley's bastard . . .

If he lived to be a hundred, Race would never forget the way shy, supposedly dull Miss Clarissa Studley, far from shrinking from an ugly and embarrassing public scene, had marched across the deserted dance floor—in full view of a crowd frozen with shock and avid for scandal—and publicly claimed her sister. And refused to leave her side for the rest of the night.

As a demonstration of loyalty, it had rocked Race to the core.

Incredibly, they'd managed to quash the scandal—though exactly how, he still wasn't clear—it hadn't hurt that Pomphret had clearly been drunk at the time, and it helped that he shot himself not long afterward—but there was no doubt in Race's mind that Clarissa's championing of her sister had played a major part.

Had she hesitated, had she shown any doubt or fear or guilt—the accusation was true, after all—the ton would have pounced. And ripped both girls' reputations to shreds.

Society was excellent at ferreting out morsels of gossip and blowing them up into a major scandal.

But Clarissa hadn't hesitated for a second. And the moment had been won.

"Hallooooo there, Race, hurry along, will you?" his cousin called from the other side of the pond. "We need to be heading back. I have an engagement this afternoon."

"Oh, and so do I," Miss Clarissa said. Race glanced at her, and she added, "I'm interviewing for a new maid, remember?"

On the way home, the traffic caused them to separate into pairs again, and this time Clarissa found herself paired with Maggie Frobisher. She felt a little self-conscious, now that Maggie knew about Lord Randall's promise to Leo.

Clarissa had initially been thrilled that Lord Randall had gone to the trouble of arranging his cousin and her husband to collect Clarissa, circumventing Lady Scattergood's decrees. She loved riding, and was so happy that Lord Randall had remembered it and organized an outing just for her. It had made her feel so special.

But he was just keeping a promise to Leo. The realization had taken some of the pleasure out of the outing.

Even when he'd peeled that apple for her, handing her each slice—reminding her of the romantic way Leo had done it for Izzy on a picnic one time—it didn't feel romantic. No doubt it was just part of his "duty." Besides, Lord Frobisher had done the same for his wife, so it was probably the conventional thing to do with apples: Lord Randall was just being polite.

She felt unaccountably low. And rather cross. Keeping an eye on her? It wasn't as if she were some irresponsible child, needing to be watched. And she could peel her own apples—if she had a knife, that is. She made a mental note to acquire a suitable knife.

Though where to keep it? Men's clothing had numerous pockets. Ladies might have a tiny pocket for a small hand-kerchief, but otherwise they were supposed to carry their necessities in a dainty little reticule. It was so unfair.

"So, back to the seraglio?" Maggie said, breaking into Clarissa's thoughts.

"It's not in the least like a seraglio," she said tartly, then apologetically softened her tone. "I can go anywhere I want with my chaperone. And as I said, Lady Scattergood is just doing what she thinks is right."

"The restrictions don't annoy you? They would drive me to distraction."

Clarissa shook her head. "It's only for a month, while my guardian is on his honeymoon."

"And in the meantime you're obliged to receive gentle-men callers in the company of their female relatives." Mag-gie pulled a face. "I don't think much of men who come courting with Mama or Auntie."

Clarissa shrugged. "It's a stratagem, that's all. Like Lord Randall asking you to invite me to go riding."

"I am hardly anyone's aunt!" Maggie exclaimed in faux indignation. After a moment she added more seriously, "Just don't let yourself accept some 'suitable' offer in order to es-cape, will you?"

"I won't." Clarissa gave her a thoughtful glance. "Is that what you did?"

"Heavens no. Quite the opposite—I refused so many eli-gible offers that Mama was getting quite desperate and mak-ing dire predictions that I'd end up on the shelf." She laughed. "But it was worth the wait, because eventually I found my dear Oliver. Poor Mama almost fell on his neck with grati-tude."

They rode on for a few minutes, then Clarissa said, "You

know, I really dislike that expression—'on the shelf.' They never talk about men being left on the shelf, do they?" It came out slightly vehement.

Maggie tilted her head and looked at her. "You're not worried about being left on the shelf, are you?"

"No," Clarissa said glumly. "My inheritance makes that unlikely. There are too many men in need of a fortune." And that annoyed her, too.

"Yes, of course."

"But even if I had no fortune and never married," Clarissa continued, "I'd still refuse to think of myself as being 'on the shelf.' Ladies are not . . . not *apples* to be placed on a shelf, waiting to be picked up at some man's whim! Growing wrinkly while we wait." She paused to let a costermonger cross in front of them, then added, "And if there is any picking to be done, I want to be the one doing it!"

Maggie laughed. "Brava, Clarissa! Yes indeed. We ladies are not apples! We will choose for ourselves."

Clarissa blushed. It wasn't like her to be so adamant and opinionated, especially with people she didn't know well, but Maggie Frobisher was very easy to talk to. She might even become a friend. For most of her life, Izzy had been Clarissa's only friend: now there were several women she felt she could call friends. It was a heartwarming thought.

Women didn't care if she had a fortune or not. They didn't care if she was plump or plain or even shy. Why couldn't men be like that?

A short time later, they changed riding formats again, and Oliver, at his wife's beckoning, pushed forward to accompany Miss Studley, while Maggie dropped back to ride with Race.

"I've decided I like her," Maggie told Race. "I thought she was dull, but she's not, is she? Quiet and a little shy, but quite spirited underneath it all. And a splendid equestrienne."

She cocked her head and regarded Race speculatively. "A case of 'still waters run deep,' don't you think?"

Race arched a brow. "Fishing again, Maggie?"

She laughed. "How do you know I wasn't taking about my darling Ollie? His still waters run very deep. And can be wonderfully exhilarating."

"I know you, minx. And consider this; when the world was speculating about you and your darling Ollie and deciding it was an impossible match, did I join in?"

She sighed. "You did not."

"Well then."

She pouted. "Oh, very well, but you are horridly provoking. I've never seen you paying attention to any innocents, let alone one who has no claim to beauty or any particular charm—and don't look at me like that, I said I liked her. It's just that she's not your usual type."

"I told you, Leo asked me to take her riding."

His cousin sniffed. "And I'm supposed to believe that's all it is, am I? Well, all I will say is that I know you, cousin, and I'm intrigued."

He shrugged. "Your intriguement is not my concern."

She wrinkled her nose at him. "'Intriguement'—is that even a word? You're just trying to put me off."

"Is it working?"

She laughed again. "You are determined to be disagreeable, aren't you? Very well, I'll *try* to be good. I suppose I'm to invite Miss Studley to go riding again soon, am I?"

Race inclined his head. "If you would be so good."

The rode on a few minutes, then Maggie said, "By the way, I asked her why Lady Scattergood refused you entrance."

Race raise a brow. "And?"

"She thinks you're a dangerous rake—the old lady, that is, not Miss Studley."

Race shrugged. "She probably thinks that about every unmarried man. And most married ones. She doesn't exactly have a good opinion of the male sex."

"But plenty of unmarried gentlemen are admitted."

Race turned his head sharply. "What? Plenty, you say? Who?"

Maggie shrugged. "I didn't ask for names, but what I did learn is that those who are admitted are invariably accompanied by some respectable female relative; a mother, grandmother or aunt, usually."

Race pondered that for a minute. That butler's refusal to admit him to the Scattergood house had really irritated him. "I don't suppose Aunt Berenice would consider . . ."

Maggie laughed. "Pry Mama away from her beloved garden at this time of year? To come to London? Not a chance. You know she dislikes the city at the best of times."

Race nodded. It was a vain hope at best. Not to mention somewhat humiliating to have to ask. Dammit, he'd never been refused entrance to any house in the kingdom.

"However, I might be persuaded to accompany you on a morning call."

He blinked. "You? I thought you disliked morning calls. What was it you said about them the other day? 'All inane chitchat and lukewarm tea.'"

"I know. But I'm curious. I admit I'm curious to see all these gentlemen who call with their aunts and grandmothers, but mostly I want to meet Lady Scattergood. I always thought she was a recluse, but Miss Studley said she actually enjoys company; she just never leaves the house. So I'm intrigued. She sounds quite eccentric."

"She is."

"Good. I shall take notes."

He gave her a sideways glance. "I'm almost afraid to ask why."

She chuckled. "I plan to become an eccentric when I'm an old lady. I gather her receiving days are Monday, Wednesday and Friday. So you may collect me on Wednesday at two o'clock. Now here we are in Mayfair, so you may take yourself off, cousin mine, before our little plot is discovered."

Race took himself off, muttering under his breath. How on earth had he allowed his cousin to insinuate herself into his affairs? Fond as he was of her, he'd always kept his personal concerns to himself, taking nobody into his confidence. Not that he'd told Maggie anything; she just assumed her way into his life. Curses.

But what other choice did he have?

If Miss Studley was being pursued by flocks of unknown gentlemen in the supposed security of Lady Scattergood's home, it was Race's duty—was it not?—as her absent guardian's best friend, to protect her.

Chapter Three

❧

"D id you have a pleasant outing with Lady Frobisher and her husband?" Lady Scattergood inquired when Clarissa returned home.

"Yes, it was lovely. The weather was glorious and I feel—oh, I feel as if I've swept all the cobwebs away." And it was true. The combination of the fresh air and the sunshine and the rural surrounds, not to mention the company, had left her feeling wonderfully refreshed. Lord Randall and his cousin had kept them all laughing.

But she'd also come to a decision: somehow, she had to release Lord Randall from the obligation of escorting her. Oh, he put a good face on it, pretending he was enjoying it, but he was only honoring a promise to a friend.

It was mortifying to think of her pleasure this morning when he'd arranged the outing, thinking he'd gone to all that trouble just for her. It was quite depressing to realize she was merely a duty.

"Cobwebs?" Lady Scattergood raised her lorgnette and

peered up at the cornices. "I don't see any cobwebs, but then my eyesight isn't what it used to be."

"No, I meant metaphorical cobwebs."

The old lady frowned and peered harder at the corners of the ceilings. "Metaphorical cobwebs? I don't like the sound of them."

"There are no actual cobwebs," Clarissa explained. "I just meant that I feel wonderfully refreshed."

"Oh, well, why didn't you say so? I expect you're exhausted now, so you'd better go upstairs and lie down."

"Thank you, but I'm not at all tired. In fact, I'm planning to visit an orphanage this afternoon. I'll just go up and change."

"An orphanage?" The old lady trained her lorgnette on her. "Whatever for?"

"I told you about it the other day, remember? After Izzy and Leo left on their honeymoon. My maid and I are going to choose an orphan girl and train her to become Izzy's maid."

Lady Scattergood nodded vaguely. "Oh yes. But you'll have to wait. Althea's gone out. I don't remember where."

Clarissa knew her chaperone would be out. She had an appointment with their dressmaker, Miss Chance, and Clarissa had chosen this time to visit the orphanage precisely for that reason. She was fond of Mrs. Price-Jones, but she did have a tendency to take over, and Clarissa wanted the choice to be hers and Betty's.

"That's all right," she said, "I'll take my maid, Betty, and a footman—perhaps Jeremiah, if he's finished walking the dogs?" The six little dogs were snoozing in small heaps around the room, so they'd already been well walked.

Lady Scattergood pursed her lips. "I don't know. Jeremiah is rather young . . ."

"And of course we'll go in the carriage," Clarissa said hastily, "so we'll have the coachman."

"And a groom."

"Yes, so I'll be well protected," Clarissa said.

The old lady sighed. "I suppose so . . . But I don't like it. Treadwell said that dratted rake had been sniffing around."

"Which rake?"

"That Lord Randall."

"Oh, did he come past while I was out riding?" Clarissa said innocently.

Lady Scattergood waved a pettish hand. "I don't remember. Very well, go off and fetch your orphan maidservant. Though I don't know why you must do it yourself. In my day the housekeeper saw to the staffing. An orphan asylum is no place for a lady."

"Thank you, dear Lady Scattergood." Clarissa rose and kissed the old lady on her rouged and withered cheek, then hurried upstairs to change out of her habit.

I'm really looking forward to this, miss." Betty, Clarissa's maid, bounced on the carriage seat. "Whoever we get will be so grateful. I remember what it was like in the place I was in, and we all thought that going into service—especially as a lady's maid—is that much better than going into one of those dirty manufactories or getting a job scrubbing floors, because that's what they'll get—if they're lucky. There's a lot worse things, too," she ended ominously.

Betty had come from an orphan asylum herself, starting at the age of ten as a lowly scullery maid. But she was much the same age as Clarissa and Izzy, and so when they were allowed to bring one servant with them when they left Clarissa's childhood home, and their elderly nanny didn't want to come, they chose Betty.

But as they drew closer to the orphan asylum, Betty became more and more silent and withdrawn.

"Are you nervous about doing this, Betty?" Clarissa asked.

Betty grimaced. "Not really, miss. I just . . . I don't like these places."

"You don't have to go in if you don't want to."

Betty shook her head and said resolutely, "No, it's all right, miss. I want to help. And I wouldn't leave you to go in there by yourself."

They rang the bell and were shown inside and in a few minutes a tall, severe-looking woman dressed all in gray came to receive them; the matron, who introduced herself as Miss Glass. On their way to her office, they passed a room where a dozen or so girls sat sewing in silence under the supervision of another woman. The girls were all dressed alike, in neat brown fustian.

"These are the exiting class," Miss Glass said. "They will be leaving to take up work as soon as we find them respectable positions. Every one of our gels leaves for employment. Respectable employment." She beckoned Clarissa and Betty in.

As one, the girls rose, curtsied, chanted, "Good afternoon, Miss Glass," in a monotone, and resumed their work, their needles stabbing into cloth while they examined Clarissa and Betty with shrewdly calculating gazes. Their interest was understandable, but Clarissa found it a little unsettling. One of these girls would presumably become Izzy's new maid. They all looked alike. How on earth could she choose?

Miss Glass then showed them to her office.

"Miss, can I wait outside?" Betty whispered, clearly unnerved, and Clarissa nodded.

Over tea and biscuits Miss Glass questioned Clarissa about her exact needs. "I have several gels who might be suitable," she said when Clarissa had finished explaining. "I will arrange for you to interview them." She rose and swept majestically out.

Deciding Betty should sit in on these interviews, Clarissa stepped into the hall, but there was no sign of her. A corridor led off to the right and, thinking Betty might be there, Clarissa went to investigate. But she still couldn't see her.

Just as Clarissa turned back to return to the matron's office, Betty came hurrying up. "Miss, miss, you gotta come and see this." She was bright with excitement.

Clarissa hesitated. "I need to go back to—"

Betty grabbed her arm. "No, it's urgent. You gotta come see. You gotta!"

She led Clarissa back down the corridor, turned left and led her through a rabbit warren of narrow hallways. "I went exploring," she said as she hurried them along. "The front parts of these places are all nice for the visitors, but the back part—that's where you get the real story."

"But—"

"Look!" She stopped and pointed dramatically at a dark-haired girl who was halfheartedly cleaning a bold charcoal caricature off the wall. The girl had her back to them, but it was clear she wasn't making much of an effort to remove the sketch, but cleaning around it instead. The subject of the sketch was unmistakable—the pointy nose, the sharp chin, the severe look—it was Miss Glass, wickedly unflattering, but uncannily like her.

"Yes, very clever," Clarissa murmured, "but we really must get b—"

"Not the picture—the girl!" Betty darted forward, grabbed the girl's arm and swung her around to face Clarissa.

The breath left Clarissa's body. For a moment she felt almost dizzy. It couldn't possibly be . . .

"See, I told you, miss. Unbelievable, ain't it?"

Scowling, the girl shook off Betty's hand. "Leggo of me, you." She glanced at Clarissa, taking in her fine lady clothes, and her lip curled in scorn. "What are you starin' at, lady? Come to gawp at us poor orphans, have you? Well, bugger off."

"No. I'm just—" Clarissa swallowed, took several deep breaths and fought to calm herself.

"D'you see what I mean, miss? It's uncanny, ain't it?" Betty murmured.

Clarissa just stared, unable to think of a thing to say. Unlike the girls in the sewing room, this girl's clothing was patched and worn, and fitted her badly. But it wasn't her dress or the sketch Clarissa cared about: it was the girl herself who fascinated her. "Did you draw that?" she finally managed. "It's very clever."

The girl smirked. "Old Glass don't think so."

"Who are you?" Clarissa blurted.

The girl's green eyes narrowed. "Zoë. What's it to you?"

"You do live here, don't you? You're one of the . . ."

"Orphans, yeah, it's not a dirty word, you know."

"I know," Clarissa said. "Both Betty and I are orphans."

The girl made a rude sound. "Yeah, you look it."

"I'm a foundling, and I started out in a place like this," Betty said. "I hated it. But now I work for miss."

The girl eyed her cynically. "So?"

Clarissa stared. That scowl, those eyes, that cynical curl of the lip; they were as familiar to her as her own reflection. It was Izzy to the life, Izzy as she had been perhaps four or five years ago. But for the age difference, this girl and her sister could be twins.

"Miss Studley, are you there, Miss Studley?" Miss Glass appeared from around a corner, breathing heavily. "Miss Studley, visitors are not permitted in this—" She broke off and glared at the girl. "Susan Bennet, haven't you cleaned that mess off yet? Get rid of it at once and return to your lessons. Miss Studley, if you would care to step this way, I have gels waiting to be interviewed."

Clarissa stepped forward and put a hand on the young girl's arm. "No need, Miss Glass. I have chosen this girl."

The girl called Susan—or was it Zoë?—pulled her arm away, eyeing Clarissa suspiciously. "Chosen? What for?"

"Susan Bennet?" Miss Glass exclaimed. "Oh no, no, no! She is not at all suitable for your needs. She has neither the temperament nor the aptitude to become a lady's maid."

"Lady's maid?" the girl echoed. "I don't want to be a—"

Betty pinched her. "Shut it!" she said in a low voice. Clarissa hoped Miss Glass couldn't hear. "Me and Miss Clarissa are gettin' you out of here."

Susan/Zoë narrowed her eyes.

"There are other, much more suitable gels," Miss Glass began.

"I'm sure there are," Clarissa said pleasantly, "but my mind is made up; this is the girl I want."

"I'm afraid I cannot allow—"

Clarissa raised her brows and said in as cool a voice as she could manage, "I thought you said you wished to place all your charges in respectable employment."

"Yes, but—"

"Then it's settled. I will take Miss Bennet. Immediately, if you please."

"Benoît," the girl muttered.

"You don't understand. That girl will be nothing but trouble; she's unruly, ungovernable, wayward, disobedient and willful. She's headstrong, obstinate—"

"You will not be held responsible for any problems that may arise," Clarissa said briskly, hoping her anxiety didn't show. She turned. "Collect your things, Miss Bennet, you're coming with us."

The girl hesitated, her expression sullen and mistrustful. She looked from Miss Glass to Clarissa to Betty, who nodded in an encouraging way. Then she shrugged, turned and tromped up a narrow staircase Clarissa hadn't noticed, Betty following close behind her.

Clarissa and Miss Glass returned to the front entrance, the matron trying all the time to convince Clarissa that taking this particular orphan was a huge mistake. Clarissa murmured soothing responses, but didn't back down.

She was determined not to let Susan/Zoë out of her grasp.

In a few minutes, Betty and the girl arrived, the latter carrying a small bundle knotted into a cloth and a long cardboard cylinder, and wearing a surly expression. Not overburdened with possessions, then. And judging by her demeanor Betty hadn't managed to convince her that this was a good thing. Oh well, that would change as soon as Clarissa explained.

Which would take some doing. The whole thing was incredible.

Clarissa thanked Miss Glass and the three of them climbed into the waiting carriage. The girl sat silently clutching her bundle and tube to her. She eyed the smart interior with a jaundiced expression but said nothing.

The carriage pulled away, and Clarissa and Betty looked at the girl, then at each other and burst out laughing. "I never thought she'd let her go," Betty began.

"No, I—"

"Who *are* you people?" the girl burst out angrily. She reached for the door handle. "I dunno what you want with me, but I'll tell you now I'm no bloody lady's maid—old Glass was right about that—so I'm warnin' you, if you're white slavers or somethin' I'm jumpin' out of this carriage, right now, and I don't care how fast it's going."

Betty grabbed her arm.

"White slavers?" Clarissa exclaimed, shocked. "Of course we're not. I am Miss Clarissa Studley, and this is my maid, Betty, just as we said. We're perfectly respectable, and you're in no danger whatsoever."

"Quite the opposite," Betty said. "If what we think about you is right."

The green eyes narrowed. "What do you mean, *what you think about me*?"

"I'll explain when we get to my home," Clarissa said hastily. "It's too noisy in the carriage for conversation. But you're perfectly safe with us, I assure you."

The girl sat scrunched in the corner of the carriage, silent and suspicious, clutching her bundle and cardboard tube protectively before her. After a few minutes she said, "But you're gunna try and make me into a lady's maid?"

"As I said, we'll discuss it in private." After a minute, a thought occurred to Clarissa. "Miss Glass called you Susan Bennet, but you said something different."

The girl snorted. "She don't like my real name. She reckons it's outlandish and foreign so she changed it to Susan Bennet, which is more like what she thinks is a proper orphan sort of name."

Clarissa frowned. Was the girl telling the truth or not? "What is your real name, then?"

"It's Zoë. Zoë Benoît." Her narrow green gaze dared Clarissa to dispute it. "Zoë is Greek for 'life.'"

"Zoë Benoît," Clarissa repeated, and gave a brisk nod. "Then of course, that's what we'll call you."

Zoë's mistrustful expression didn't soften. If anything, it hardened.

A few minutes later the carriage pulled up outside Lady Scattergood's house, and they descended. Zoë stood staring up at the house. "This is your house?"

"It belongs to Lady Scattergood, my guardian's aunt," Clarissa explained. "But it's where Betty and I live at the moment. And where you'll live, too." At least she hoped so. Because even if it turned out that she'd been quite wrong about Zoë—not that she believed in her heart that she was wrong—she would still owe the girl some kind of security— a job at least. Though not as a lady's maid, apparently.

The butler, Treadwell, opened the door and, seeing Zoë, blinked. His normally impassive expression vanished and his eyebrows crept up to his long-vanished hairline. He turned to Clarissa. "Miss Studley?" he said in a clear demand to have the situation explained.

But Clarissa had no intention of explaining anything until she'd spoken to Lady Scattergood. "Thank you, Treadwell. Betty, would you take Zoë upstairs, please, and show her where to leave her things? Give her a cup of tea and something to eat and I'll see you both back here when you've finished. Oh, and leave any explanations to me, if you please." The two girls departed and Clarissa sought out Lady Scattergood.

Over tea and biscuits she told the old lady her incredible tale, finishing, "And so you see, when I saw this girl, I knew at once—well, see for yourself and tell me what you think." Clarissa rose and called Zoë and Betty in.

Zoë entered cautiously, gazing around the sitting room with wide eyes. Clarissa had forgotten how the crammed display of colorful and exotic items collected from far-flung corners of the world must look to someone who wasn't used to it, let alone the sight of the skinny old lady swathed in a dozen exquisitely patterned shawls, wearing a large colorful turban and seated in a dramatic peacock chair that looked like some kind of throne.

"Lady Scattergood, I'd like you to meet Miss Zoë Benoît."

The old lady blinked and leaned forward, groping for her lorgnette. "Good gracious me!" She gestured to Zoë. "Come closer, gel."

Zoë glanced at Clarissa and edged warily closer. Lady Scattergood's lorgnette slowly raked her from head to toe and back again, then she gave a brusque nod. "Well, well, well. And you found her in an orphan asylum, you say?" She shook her head and made a disgusted sound. "An absolute disgrace! Should have been drowned at birth."

Zoë gave Clarissa an alarmed look and stepped back as if preparing to flee.

"She doesn't mean you, Zoë," Clarissa said hastily. "Lady Scattergood is talking about my father." If the old lady had said it once within Clarissa's hearing, she'd said it a dozen times.

Lady Scattergood nodded. "A vile, irresponsible rake, he was! Society is full of such appalling reprobates."

"Indeed," Clarissa said soothingly. "Now let us find out a little more about Zoë's background, shall we? Sit down, Zoë. Would you like another cup of tea?"

Zoë's gaze wandered to the plate of biscuits, but she shook

her head. She perched on the edge of the chaise longue and faced Clarissa, her expression guarded. Several of Lady Scattergood's little dogs had come over to sniff around her skirts. Keeping a wary eye on Clarissa and Lady Scattergood, Zoë dropped a hand down, let them sniff and lick it, then began to pat them.

Lady Scattergood nodded approvingly.

"Can you tell us about your mother, Zoë?" Clarissa asked.

Zoë stiffened. For a moment, Clarissa thought she was going to refuse, but then she sighed, and said in a flat little voice, as if repeating a tale she didn't expect to be believed, "Maman was French. She came over here when she was eleven, fleeing from the Terror. She was all on her own. The rest of her family perished on *la guillotine*."

Lady Scattergood tsk-tsked and muttered something uncomplimentary about the French.

"That must have been a terrible time for her," Clarissa said sympathetically. "So young, and all her family lost. However did she manage? Did she have other relatives in England?"

Zoë shook her head. "No relatives. And the other émigrés were . . ." She gave a dismissive shrug. "But Maman could draw. She started out drawing pictures on the footpath in chalk."

Clarissa recalled the clever caricature on the orphanage wall. "And you inherited her talent."

Again Zoë shrugged. After a pause she added with an edge of defensiveness, "Later she became an artist's model. She was beautiful, you see, and it paid better."

"I'm sure," Clarissa said gently, skating over that very thin ice. "How did she die? I presume that's when you went into the orphan asylum."

"I was twelve. She got sick. Cholera, they said."

"I'm so sorry to hear it. So, you're now what, fifteen? Sixteen?"

"Almost sixteen."

Clarissa nodded. "And your father?"

Zoë hunched one shoulder indifferently. "I never met him. I'm a *bastard*." She flung the word down like a challenge.

Clarissa didn't react. "Did your mother ever tell you his name?"

"What does it matter? He never wanted me."

"Humor me."

Zoë wrinkled her nose, and for a moment Clarissa thought she wasn't going to respond, but then she said, "He was a toff, I know that."

"Nothing else?"

She snorted. "A couple of times I heard her call him 'Black Bart, the man with no heart.' He gave her nothing— just a slip on the shoulder." When she saw that Clarissa didn't understand the term, she said, "A baby. Me."

A toff she called Black Bart. Clarissa glanced at Lady Scattergood in barely suppressed triumph. From Sir Bartleby to Bart was no big leap, and Papa's hair had been thick and black. Two stableboys in her former home had been called Harry, and, because of the color of their hair, they were referred to by the other servants as Red Harry and Black Harry.

And if Papa had a heart, Clarissa had never seen any evidence of it. No doubt he'd seduced and abandoned Zoë's mother just as he'd done to Izzy's. He probably would have done the same to her own mother, too, only Mama had the security of Grandfather Iverley's fortune held in trust for her, and Papa had married her for it.

Those few scant facts, combined with Zoë's amazing resemblance to her sister Izzy—and the feeling she got looking at Zoë—were proof enough for Clarissa.

Lady Scattergood nodded thoughtfully and sat back in her peacock chair. "Well, well, well, so we have another one. Well done, Clarissa."

"It was Betty who found her," Clarissa said, beaming at Betty, who blushed and smoothed her skirt proudly.

Zoë shifted uncomfortably. "What's all this about? Another *what*?"

"Yes, I'm sorry. I'll explain." Clarissa took a sip of tea, which was by then lukewarm. "My father was Sir Bartleby Studley. Does that name sound familiar?"

"No."

"You're sure?"

"I'm sure."

"Well, I think he was the man your mother called 'Black Bart.'"

Zoë wrinkled her nose. "Your pa was Black Bart?"

"Yes, at least I think so. I think you and I—and my sister Izzy—had the same father. I believe you're our sister—our half sister, that is."

Zoë's face screwed up incredulously. *"Sister?"* She glanced at Betty. "Is she cracked in the head or summat?"

Betty shook her head. "Just listen."

Clarissa continued, "You'll understand when you see my sister Izzy. You're the living image of her—or rather the way she looked when she was your age."

"What, so she's got black hair and green eyes? That don't make me her sister. Or yours, because I don't look nothing like you, do I?"

"Neither does Izzy," Clarissa said tranquilly, "but you both look a great deal like my father—Izzy's and mine. We had different mothers. And your resemblance to Izzy is more—much more—than hair and eye color."

"So where is this Izzy, then? Not that I believe you or nothing."

"No, I understand." Clarissa gave her a sympathetic smile. "I'm having a little difficulty accepting it myself—the last thing I expected when I left the house this afternoon was to discover a long-lost sister—but the more I see of you, the more certain I am that you *are* Izzy's and my sister. As for where Izzy is, she's away on her honeymoon at the moment, so you won't meet her for a few weeks."

Zoë looked at Lady Scattergood. "And what do you think? You reckon this lady and me are sisters?"

Lady Scattergood nodded. "Your resemblance to Isobel is extraordinary. The material evidence is slight, but I'm sure an investigation into your past will clarify the matter."

Zoë shook her head. "I reckon you're all barmy. I'm a *bastard*. I grew up in the stews and I come from an orphanage. No way am I the sister of a couple of lady toffs."

"My sister Izzy is illegitimate, too," Clarissa said. "And when I met her—we were both almost nine years old—she'd just lost her mother and my father was arranging to have her dumped in the nearest orphan asylum. I heard him say that myself—in those very words. He made no attempt to deny her parentage, he just refused to take any responsibility for her." She gave a satisfied smile. "But I decided to keep her. And so I did."

"Like a stray puppy?" Zoë said sarcastically.

"No, like a beloved sister," Clarissa said softly.

"And you aim to keep me, too?" Said with an air of defiance, it was another challenge.

"I would certainly like to," Clarissa assured her. She turned to Lady Scattergood. "Ma'am?"

The old lady nodded. "Yes, yes, of course we'll give her a home here with us. She's clearly a relative, and the dogs like her. They're very good judges of character."

Clarissa heaved a sigh of relief at that *we*. It was a little awkward bringing home a complete stranger when she was just a guest here herself. "Thank you, ma'am. Then, Zoë, yes, I would certainly like to keep you. But of course it's up to you."

Zoë didn't say a word. She looked from Clarissa to Lady Scattergood and back, her face full of doubt and suspicion.

Clarissa didn't blame her. It was a lot to accept, especially from strangers.

"Give her the little blue room. It's small but she won't mind that, not after being in one of those dreadful places." Lady Scattergood focused her lorgnette on Zoë again and added, "And get her some decent clothing, for goodness' sake. Can't have people mistaking her for my scullery maid—who, I might add, dresses better than that."

"Yes, of course," Clarissa agreed. "She can wear some of Izzy's clothes."

There was a short silence. At last Zoë said, "You want me to live here?"

"Yes."

"And you're not a brothel or nothing?"

"A *brothel*!" Lady Scattergood dropped her lorgnette and let out a bark of laughter. "Good gad, child, is that what you thought?"

"Well, look at all them smutty statues. I never been inside a brothel, but I reckon this is what it'd look like." Zoë gestured to the foreign-looking statues, many of which were of naked people in all kinds of poses. Now that Clarissa looked more closely at them, some were more than suggestive.

Lady Scattergood chuckled. "Gifts from my late husband, child. He traveled the world, sending me back such items as caught his fancy. I've been called many things in my time, but never a brothel keeper." She chuckled again, seeming quite pleased by the shocking accusation.

"And you don't want me for a lady's maid?" Zoë persisted.

"No," Clarissa said firmly. "Not as any kind of maid at all. As my sister."

There was a longer silence. Zoë glanced a silent question at Betty, who gave her an encouraging nod. Betty seemed almost as excited as Clarissa. Betty, too, had come from an orphan asylum, yet she didn't apparently feel any resentment for Zoë's luck.

Clarissa knew it was a common orphan fantasy—that there was a grand family somewhere who would come and rescue them from a life of poverty and obscurity. Betty seemed to have no trouble believing that in Zoë's case it was true.

Zoë, on the other hand, was a skeptic. But she would come around, Clarissa was sure. It was just a matter of time. Once she saw Izzy for herself, she'd feel differently.

Lady Frobisher and Lord Randall to see Lady Scattergood," Race's cousin Maggie said. Lady Scattergood's butler eyed her balefully, but Maggie was well acquainted with the social niceties and had left her card at Lady Scattergood's the previous day. The butler's gaze shifted to Race, standing behind her, and he sniffed. "You can come in, m'lady, but not him. He's forbidden."

"*Forbidden?* Lord Randall is my cousin and my escort," Maggie declared haughtily.

The butler shrugged. "Can't help that. Orders is orders. Are you coming in or not, m'lady?"

"Outrageous!" Maggie huffed. "Very well." She turned to Race and he could see that though her mouth was primmed in apparent disapproval, her eyes were dancing. His cousin was loving this, drat her. "I'll see you back here in twenty minutes, Race," she said. To the butler she added as she sailed into the house, "You would not last a minute in my employ!"

The butler smirked and closed the door on Race.

Race climbed into his curricle, wondering what the punishment would be for butlercide. And decided his plea, if it came to that, would be justifiable butlercide.

Twenty minutes later, after numerous circuits of Hyde Park, he pulled up outside Lady Scattergood's home, and waited. A few minutes later his cousin emerged. He helped her into the curricle and drove off.

"Well?" he said after a minute when she hadn't said a word.

"When we get home. It was as I expected: insipid chit-chat and lukewarm tea. I need a fresh hot cup."

"Insipid?" he queried.

"Yes, but only the visitors. Otherwise it was quite, quite fascinating. Now be patient, Race. Ollie will want to know as well, and I refuse to repeat it all again."

Once they'd arrived at Frobisher House, his cousin kept him waiting even longer while she went upstairs to tidy herself. Finally she returned, having removed her hat and pelisse, which apparently took fifteen minutes.

"Well?" Race asked as she entered the sitting room where he'd been waiting with her husband, chatting about the state of the nation. Ollie was quite a serious chap.

"It was utterly splendid," Maggie said as she plumped down on the sofa beside her husband.

"You said it was inane and the tea was lukewarm."

"I said, the *visitors'* conversation was inane, not my visit— and I've ordered fresh tea and coffee. Lady Scattergood is utterly splendid—I wish you could meet her, Oliver. Did you know she commiserated with me on my marriage"— she laughed—"and advised me to send you off on a long sea voyage from which, with any luck, you would never return." She laughed again. "Which, thinking of some of those men who made me an offer before you, might have been an excellent idea. But you, dearest, are just exactly where I want you." She placed her hand on her husband's thigh and squeezed it gently.

"What about Miss Studley and her suitors?" Race interjected. It was, after all, the purpose of their visit.

"And oh, the house!" Maggie continued as if he hadn't spoken. "It's absolutely crammed with the most amazing stuff—statues and figurines, some of which were quite shockingly erotic, some quite clearly priceless and others cheap things from who knows where, and all crammed in higgledy-piggledy—along with her husband's ashes, which sit in a jar on the mantel between the statue of a person with an elephant's head, and one of a woman with far too many arms to be comfortable—or would it?"

She considered the notion for a few seconds, shook her head, and hurried on. "Lady Scattergood herself is draped with half a dozen fabulously colorful shawls, all clashing brilliantly. And she sits in this huge peacock-tail chair, receiving her visitors like some fantastic empress, delivering pithy judgments. Oh, she is wonderful. I want to be just like her when I am old."

"And the visitors?" Race reminded her.

"There are five—or was it six?—little dogs, all gathered from the gutter, all mongrels, all bitches and quite peculiar looking, but she dotes on them. It's adorable. We must get a little mongrel, Oliver. I predict it will become quite the rage."

"Whatever you wish, my love, but Race here has asked you a question several times."

"Oh, yes, of course." The door opened and the butler and a footman entered bearing a large pot of tea, a coffeepot, cups and saucers, a selection of biscuits on a plate and a cake. "Oh good, here is the tea at last."

Race exchanged an amused glance with Oliver.

"Did you know any of the other visitors?" he asked as Maggie poured coffee for him and Oliver.

"Yes. Young Frencham was there with his grandmother. Ratafia biscuits, ginger nuts or seed cake?" She offered him two plates.

Race took a ginger nut and crunched down hard on it. Frencham was a known fortune hunter, a good-looking, lazy young rattle who'd made no attempt to retrieve his estate from the mess his father had left it in. He'd thought Leo had run him off, but the fellow was back, apparently, now that Leo was away.

"And Taunton was there with an aunt." Maggie frowned.

"Or was she his godmother? I can't recall. Have some of this seed cake. It's Oliver's favorite."

Race took the slice she passed him and set it aside. Taunton? He was another waster whose estates were to let—young, quite good-looking and a shocking gambler whose losses at the tables were well-known. Dammit, that wretched old lady had refused him entrance and allowed two notorious fortune hunters to court Miss Studley while Leo was absent.

"Anyone else?" he grated.

"Sir Jasper Vibart and his grandmother. Can you believe it—Vibart, playing propriety with a stuffy old lady in tow. Hilarious." Maggie glanced at her husband and laughed. "Don't worry, my love, I barely gave him the time of day." To Race, she said, "Sir Jasper did his best to seduce me before I was married." She darted a mischievous glance at her husband and added, "And after." She patted her husband's thigh. "All in vain, of course. My Oliver is quite enough for me."

"But he was showing interest in Clar—Miss Studley?" Race said. Vibart was a conscienceless rake and a scoundrel.

"Apparently. But don't worry. Old Lady Scattergood got his measure pretty quickly and informed him in no uncertain terms that he would not be admitted again—though of course his grandmother was welcome to call anytime." She bit into a ratafia biscuit and sighed. "How wonderful to be as rude to visitors as one wants."

"I've heard that Vibart's grandmother is pressuring him to marry and get an heir," Oliver said, and snorted. "Explains why a fellow of that sort would call on a decent girl."

Race glowered into his coffee cup. Wonderful. Two known fortune hunters and a notorious rake—even if the swine wasn't going to be admitted again. Maybe he'd reconsider butlercide.

Miss Studley needed to be warned.

"Oh," Maggie said, "and there was one fellow I've seen

around but hadn't actually met before. He's not been in London very long, a few weeks, I think."

Race arched an eyebrow at her in query.

"Clayborn. Cuthbert Clayborn. And his aunt, Mrs. Faircloth—or was she his great-aunt? I can't recall. An elderly, white-haired lady, anyway. They arrived mere seconds after I did—I'm surprised you didn't pass them on the steps."

Race shrugged. "I didn't." He'd probably been too annoyed by the butler to notice anyone else.

"Do you know him?" Maggie asked.

"Clayborn?" Race shook his head.

"He seemed to be quite a regular visitor," Maggie said. "More coffee, Race?"

"No thank you. What do you mean 'regular visitor'?"

She topped up her husband's cup. "It was clear that he and Mrs. Faircloth had called several times in the last week. And they both appeared to be very much at home. Quite the favored callers, I gather. Mrs. Faircloth is a childless widow, much like Lady Scattergood, who knew her in their youth, I gather." She darted a look at Race. "If we're talking courting, Mr. Clayborn seems to be a favored contender already."

Race didn't like the sound of that. "What do you know of this Clayborn fellow?"

"Not much. He seems very popular with the dowager set and with very young ladies. You know the type, all pale and angelic yet somehow tragic, golden curls and a manly enough chin." She selected another ratafia biscuit. "And of course there's the heroic limp."

"Limp?"

Maggie nibbled on her biscuit. "Wounded at Waterloo, I understand. Limps. Uses a cane. Still pains him, I gather—winces whenever he moves—but he bears it with noble fortitude. All the females flutter around him."

"All? Not you, I gather."

She snorted. "Not my type. He was a little . . . I don't

know, ostentatiously modest about his heroism. I prefer them a little less tragic and saintly." She winked at her husband, who placidly cut himself another large slice of the seed cake.

"Do you know anything about him, Oliver?" Race asked.

Oliver swallowed a mouthful of cake, washed it down with coffee, and shook his head. "No idea. Seemed to appear from nowhere. One minute he was God knows where—presumably recovering from his injuries—then the next he's being seen everywhere."

"Yes, at all the most select gatherings," Maggie added.

Oliver, having demolished his second slice of cake, began clearing his plate of stray caraway seeds, pressing them one by one onto his fingertip and eating them. Between seeds, he said, "Have noticed, though"—crunch—"that he seems to favor"—crunch—"ladies of fortune." Crunch. "Miss Studley's an heiress, is she not?" Crunch.

"Yes, but his elderly great-aunt happened to mention—several times—that she's leaving him her entire fortune," Maggie reminded him.

Race glowered into the dregs of his coffee. He didn't generally frequent fashionably select gatherings. He preferred more informal, less exclusive entertainments.

That might have to change.

Chapter Four

Clarissa stood in front of the long cheval looking glass, eyed her reflection critically and sighed. It was a lovely dress and fitted her perfectly. The dressmaker, Miss Chance, had done a wonderful job.

The problem wasn't the dress.

"You look very nice, miss," her maid Betty said, hovering at her elbow. "That soft peach color is perfect for you."

"Thank you, Betty." She tried to banish her father's voice: *Can't make a silk purse from a sow's ear.*

"And the dress is beautifully cut."

She sighed. "I know." It was her own shape that was less than beautiful. But try as she might, she could never slim down enough to look as dainty and sylphlike as Izzy. And though Betty had arranged her hair well, nothing could make her beautiful, and she so wished she were beautiful. Or at least pretty.

Might as well sigh for the moon.

"Then why are you frowning?" Zoë said from her perch on the window seat.

"I'm not," Clarissa said. "I'm just a little bit . . . nervous." It wasn't why she'd been frowning at her reflection, but thinking about it, she was feeling quite nervous about tonight's ball. In fact, for two pins she'd cancel.

Surely she'd conquered her nervousness about big social occasions? They'd been in London for weeks now.

"Just missing Miss Izz—Lady Salcott—I'll be bound." Betty laughed. "I'm never going to remember, am I? To think of our Miss Izzy, a countess!" She reached up and adjusted the sprig of tiny silk roses she'd fastened to the back of Clarissa's hair. "But Mrs. Price-Jones will be with you, won't she?"

"Yes, of course." It was the first time in years that Clarissa had attended any social event without her sister—in fact, had she ever gone anywhere without Izzy? No wonder she was feeling a little unsettled. But that was foolish. Now that Izzy was married, Clarissa would have to become more independent. She forced a smile. "You've done a lovely job with my hair, Betty. Thank you."

She turned again to look at her reflection and Betty turned with her. "You look just like your mam, miss. She'd be that proud of you, going out and about, hobnobbing with the highest in the land."

Clarissa swallowed the lump in her throat. Betty was right. Poor Mama would have been thrilled that Clarissa was making a proper come-out in London society. Papa had never even allowed Mama to visit London, let alone attend any society event. Mama wasn't up to Papa's high standards, he used to say, and it would embarrass him to be seen with her, so plain and unsophisticated was she.

And Clarissa was the image of her mother. What was it Papa had said that time, his voice rich with scorn? *You can dress her up all you like; if it wasn't for that blasted fortune, no man would look twice at her.* And variations on it numerous times since.

Her belief in her intrinsic unattractiveness had sunk into her long before she was even aware of it, long before she had found Izzy.

She eyed her image sternly. Plain and unsophisticated she might be, but she had every right to happiness. And like it had been for Mama, Grandfather Iverley's fortune was in trust for her which, for many, made up for any flaws and inadequacies she might have.

Not that she wanted a man who wanted her only for her fortune. That had been Mama's mistake.

The dress Miss Chance had made for her was lovely, and it suited her well, she knew. And what was it Miss Chance said so often? *Every woman is beautiful in her own way . . .*

Clarissa thought of Lady Scattergood, whose face was a mass of wrinkles, and yet intelligence and kindness shone from her eyes. And she wore her odd, unfashionable assortment of clothing with such an air, she looked striking anyway. There was definitely beauty in her.

And the key to bein' beautiful, Miss Chance had added, *is that first you gotta feel beautiful and then people will start to notice that you* are *beautiful. It's all in your attitude.*

Hearing the little dressmaker's voice in her mind, Clarissa straightened. How to feel beautiful when you knew you weren't?

You pretended.

She was good at pretending. For the first eight and a half years she had pretended she had an imaginary sister to share her secrets with and tell her dreams to. And then just before her ninth birthday she'd found Izzy hiding in the shrubbery, eavesdropping on Papa telling someone to dump Izzy in the nearest orphan asylum. A real, flesh-and-blood sister. And so Clarissa had kept her.

Clarissa glanced at her reflection again and lifted her chin. She would pretend then that she was beautiful and confident and all the other things that she was not. And hope that her secret dream would come true.

It was worth a try. Better than feeling plain and unattractive and unwanted except for Grandfather Iverley's fortune.

"Are you ready, my love?" Mrs. Price-Jones said from the doorway. "Look at you! Such a picture you make."

Clarissa smiled. "And you, Mrs. Price-Jones."

Her chaperone chuckled. "We'll dazzle them, will we not?"

"We certainly will." Her chaperone had a penchant for bright colors, and tonight she was dressed in bright yellow silk, with dark red and green piping in rows around the neckline, hem and sleeves. Around her shoulders she'd draped an embroidered, multicolored shawl—one of Lady Scattergood's, Clarissa thought—and on her head she wore a large emerald green turban—another of Lady Scattergood's shawls—with three purple feathers. It shouldn't have worked, but somehow it did. Altogether she looked like a cheerful, multicolored parrot.

Smiling, Clarissa linked her arm with Mrs. Price-Jones's and they proceeded down the stairs to the waiting carriage. With such a blatantly exuberant companion, it was impossible to remain downcast.

Clarissa's nerves were well under control by the time they'd arrived at their destination and had greeted their hosts at the top of the stairs. Pausing at the entrance to the ballroom, they surveyed the room.

"Excellent," Mrs. Price-Jones declared. "Quite a crush, already. Plenty of handsome young men to dance with you, and maybe even a few left over for me." She winked at Clarissa. "Now, I just need to pop into the ladies' withdrawing room for a moment—no, no need to come with me. It's just a quick adjustment I need."

Clarissa looked around, hoping to see her friend and neighbor, Lady Tarrant, and then recalled that she'd temporarily withdrawn from society, awaiting the birth of her baby.

Another neighbor, Milly Harrington, and her mother were standing in an alcove by the window, chatting to an elderly gentleman, but the moment Milly spotted Clarissa she turned her back and pretended not to see her. Milly didn't like competition, and though she had a more aristocratic background than Clarissa, being distantly related to a duke, and was prettier, she didn't have a fortune like Clarissa did.

Mrs. Price-Jones nudged Clarissa. "That nice Lady Peplowe and her daughter Penny are over there, see? You go and sit with them and I'll join you in a trice."

She sailed off and Clarissa began to make her way through the crowd. A group of young men stood talking near a clump of potted palms. Clarissa paused. She often felt quite self-conscious walking past groups of young men, aware they were looking at her and possibly finding her wanting. And sometimes they made lewd comments that utterly discomposed her, even when she didn't always know precisely what they meant.

Usually, unless Izzy or someone else was with her, she did her best to avoid such groups of men, but now she hesitated. She'd resolved to learn to stand on her own two feet. To be braver, and not depend on others.

Pretend you are beautiful and confident, she reminded herself.

Taking a deep breath and stiffening her spine she walked toward the group of young men. But her feet veered away at the last minute, taking her around behind the potted palms, keeping them between herself and the men.

Edging carefully past the palms, Clarissa heard one of them say, "So you're going for it after all?"

Another responded, "Yes, of course. One doesn't whistle a fortune down the wind. The beautiful Studley heiress might be off the market but the little fat plain one is still available. And should be suitably grateful."

She faltered, freezing where she stood. *Little fat plain one? Suitably grateful?*

One of the others said something she didn't quite catch and they all sniggered, then the first one said, "Worth it for the money, I suppose."

And the second one replied, "All cats are the same in the dark." And they sniggered again.

It was a slap in the face out of the blue. She felt sick.

"Take no notice, my love," Mrs. Price-Jones murmured, coming up behind her. "Young men, especially in the company of other young men, are often foolish, mannerless cubs. I didn't hear all that they said, but I heard their nasty laughter and it's clearly upset you."

Clarissa swallowed and forced a smile. "Not at all. I was just thinking about something else. Now, shall we join Lady Peplowe and Penny?"

Turning her head slightly, she glanced back and from the corner of her eye picked out the young man who'd spoken so dismissively about her. As she'd thought, it was Edgar Walmsley, who'd called on her several times at Lady Scattergood's. She'd recognized his voice. At the time she'd thought him good-looking and rather pleasant.

Now she knew better: He was an insensitive beast. And a horrid fortune hunter.

They joined Lady Peplowe for a short while, and then Mrs. Price-Jones found some other friends. They were rather elderly and when their conversation turned to their latest symptoms and comparing ailments, Mrs. Price-Jones screwed up her nose and drew Clarissa away. "Old people," she murmured, "making themselves older before their time. I have no patience with them. Come along, it's time to dance." And indeed, the orchestra had finished tuning up and people began taking their partners for the first dance of the evening.

Behind Clarissa, a man cleared his throat. "Miss Studley?" She turned and her smile froze, half-formed. It was Edgar Walmsley, the pig who'd spoken so rudely about her to his friends. Her eyes ran over him. He was dressed in the first stare of fashion, and his high shirt points were so stiffly starched he could hardly turn his head. His shirt was frilled and his coat tightly molded to his shape. Elegant fobs and seals dangled from a thick gold chain.

He stood before her, smirking, supremely confident of his welcome. *Little fat plain one*, was she? *Suitably grateful*, was she? Resentment spiraled through her. He clearly expected her to be flattered by his attention.

Mr. Walmsley was not as attractive as he'd seemed the other day—certainly not as attractive as he clearly thought himself to be. His good looks were spoiled, she decided, by a weak chin and an affected world-weary expression. And the smugness that oozed from him. Even while he was talking to her, his eyes were roaming past her as if looking for something—or someone—better and more interesting. More worth his attention. Men often did that. Clarissa hated it.

Normally she would swallow her pride and her hurt feelings and pretend to be happy to dance with someone she didn't like. It was the polite thing to do. Or Izzy would step in on her behalf.

She remembered again how he and his friends had sniggered about her.

No, she decided. *I don't like him and I don't want to be polite and dance with him, knowing what he really thinks of me.*

She didn't respond, just let her gaze wander to a point over his shoulder, not looking at anyone in particular, but giving him a taste of his own medicine.

He glanced behind him, frowned and repeated himself. "Miss Studley?"

"Yes?" She gave him a vague look, as if she had no idea who he was.

"We've met at Lady Scattergood's several times."

She raised her brows. "Have we? We get so many visitors. I'm afraid I don't . . ." She lifted her hands in a *no idea* sort of gesture.

He looked a little taken aback, but bowed. "Edgar Walmsley, at your service." His expression was peevish, his voice tinged with reproach.

"Indeed?" she said vaguely, and began to turn back to her companions. She was shaking inside—a mix of nerves and excitement. She was never rude to people, but this man and his contemptuous comments—made in front of his friends, too—had inflamed her temper.

"The first dance, Miss Studley," he said.

"What about it?"

He looked a little annoyed. "Would you do me the honor?" His tone indicated that she must be a little stupid.

A lifetime of training said she should curtsy, thank him prettily and accept his invitation. A lady never refused a gentleman's invitation to dance. No matter who the gentleman was.

Did he expect her to be grateful? His was less an invitation to dance than an assumption. She pretended to consider it for a long moment and when he began to shift impatiently, she said pleasantly, "I don't think so. I only dance with people I like. Goodbye, Mr. Walmsley."

"Goodbye?" he spluttered. "You are refusing me? But, but—" He broke off, his mouth opening and closing like a fish.

Clarissa wanted to laugh, but she'd shocked herself almost as much as she'd shocked him. She was never rude. But this felt wonderful.

Clarissa's chaperone moved forward, looking concerned. "Is there a problem, my dear?"

"No, not at all," Clarissa said. She'd done it. She'd never refused a dance in her life. She was shaking inside, but she felt victorious.

"You realize having refused Mr. Walmsley you will not

be able to dance with anyone else tonight," Mrs. Price-Jones murmured in her ear.

Clarissa nodded. She knew that. It was frustrating—she loved to dance—but an evening spent as a wallflower was worth it to have given this horrid Mr. Smug a set-down.

Little fat plain one indeed. How dare he talk about her like that. Even if it was true. She was more than just her looks. Or her fortune. And she deserved respect, no matter what.

"Ah, Miss Studley, there you are." Lord Randall appeared at her elbow. Clarissa blinked. What was he doing here? He never attended society balls.

Dressed in formal blacks, with a crisp white shirt—without frills—and a gray, watered silk waistcoat that exactly matched his eyes, he looked magnificent.

Her gaze dropped to the elegant silver buttons on his waistcoat: the bottom one was undone. She frowned. That was careless. Should she mention it?

But before she could decide, the orchestra played an opening chord and sets began to form on the dance floor. "Shall we?" Lord Randall held out his arm.

Clarissa hesitated. Another assumption to dance?

"She's not dancing," Smugman said nastily.

Lord Randall gave him a dismissive glance. "Not with you, she isn't, Walmsley. But she promised me this dance earlier."

"She didn't tell me that," Walmsley began, aggrieved. "If she'd explained—

Lord Randall cut him off. "Why should she? Now, Miss Studley, let us make haste lest we ruin the set."

Bemused, a little shaken but enjoying Smugman's confounded expression, Clarissa allowed Lord Randall to lead her onto the dance floor.

"You don't mind, do you?" he murmured. "He's a callow young fool and not worth your time."

"He's a fortune hunter," Clarissa said, "and not a very nice one, either."

Lord Randall gave her a sharp look. "So you knew that, did you? Good for you. You look ravishing in that dress, by the way."

A little of Clarissa's pleasure drained away. Why did men always think they needed to lavish false compliments on her? She was used to that sort of thing from fortune hunters—insincerity was their stock-in-trade, after all. She glanced at Lord Randall's handsome profile. She supposed it was a rake's stock-in-trade also.

But compliments of that sort made her only more aware of her shortcomings. The dress was lovely and she knew she looked quite nice in it, but she was hardly "ravishing."

It was a little disappointing of Lord Randall to indulge in such commonplace and meaningless courtesies. Still, he had rescued her from the consequences of her incivility to Walmsley, which allowed her to dance for the rest of the night.

"I suppose this is more guardian duty on Leo's behalf," she said.

"Good lord no. Leo knows better than to expect me to attend society balls for his sake."

She gave him a puzzled look. "But you came to this one."

He smiled, a dazzling gleam of white under the glittering chandeliers. "I did, didn't I?" Which enlightened her not at all.

The dance commenced and, it being a country dance, there was no more opportunity for conversation.

For the first part of the dance, Clarissa concentrated on her steps: she and Izzy had taken dancing lessons when they first came to London, but even though many of the country dances were made up of familiar movements, they weren't always danced in the same order.

But as her confidence in the dance movements grew, her thoughts drifted back to the way she'd dismissed Mr. Walmsley. And the way she'd felt when she did.

How many times had she danced—or dined with or

walked with—men she didn't like, even some she actively disliked? Simply because it was the polite thing to do.

And while she preferred to be polite, there was no reason she had to be *endlessly* polite, no reason she had to endure the company of men she disliked. Especially men who had no real respect for her.

She thought of what she'd said to Maggie Frobisher. *Ladies are not* apples *to be placed on a shelf, waiting to be picked up at some man's whim! And if there is any picking to be done, I want to be the one doing it!*

At the time she'd surprised herself with what amounted to an outburst, at least from her. It wasn't like her to be so . . . so dramatic. But now, thinking about it, she decided they were words she wanted to live by.

She danced on, lost in thought. She was her own person. She could decide what she did and with whom. And what she said. She didn't need to please everyone. She needed to please herself—oh, not being horridly selfish, but also, not being a doormat.

She had a bit of a tendency to be a doormat, she thought. Like Mama. Izzy never let her get away with it—Izzy was never a doormat. And neither was Clarissa when the issue was important.

Wasn't her own future happiness important?

But tonight she'd stood up for herself. And it felt wonderful.

It wasn't *pretending* that was important—it was taking action, even in a small way.

The dance finished. Lord Randall bowed, she curtsied and he led her off the dance floor. Still deep in thought about the way she wanted to be in the future—the new Clarissa—she hardly noticed what he was saying. Usually she was agonizingly aware of him.

He asked something and, assuming he was inquiring whether she was thirsty and would like something to drink, she murmured agreement.

"Good, and then of course we will take supper together afterward," he said.

She turned her face to him sharply. "What?"

"Well, the second waltz is the supper dance, after all."

"The second waltz?"

"Yes." His eyes danced. "I did wonder whether you were listening. Your thoughts were miles away, weren't they? Nevertheless I'm holding you to it—the second waltz and supper afterward. Consider it a lesson in not listening. Now, shall I fetch you a cool drink? You're looking a little flushed—attractively so, of course."

Without waiting for her response—indeed, she couldn't think of what to say and feared she was imitating Mr. Walmsley's fish—he signaled a waiter to bring her a cool drink, found her a seat and sat down beside her, crossing one long leg over the other, quite relaxed.

And amused. He knew he'd tricked her into agreeing to waltz with him, and felt no compunction whatsoever.

"You do waltz, don't you?"

"Yes," she managed. It had been part of their lessons and she'd even danced it at Almack's a few weeks ago, with one of the patroness's approval.

It was one thing to refuse a dance, it was quite another to retract one. She'd broken one rule tonight; she surely didn't have it in her to break another.

But a waltz with Lord Randall. Followed by supper.

Grasping her fan in a tight grip, she took a deep breath and prepared to grasp the nettle. "Lord Randall—"

"How did your visit to the orphan asylum go?"

She started. "What do you mean?" He couldn't possibly know about Zoë, could he?

"You were going to choose a maidservant. Did you find one?"

"Y— I mean, no. There . . . um. There was nobody suitable."

He raised a darkly elegant brow. "Really?"

She felt her face heating. "Yes. We—that is Betty and I—are going to try another orphanage tomorrow."

"I had no idea choosing a maidservant would be so difficult."

She bit her lip, but the waiter arrived with a long cool drink of lemonade. Glad of the distraction, she seized it with relief and drank thirstily, very aware of those gray eyes watching her. With dancing, knowing devils in them.

"And here comes your chaperone, Mrs. um," he said smoothly as she finished her glass.

"Price-Jones," she said automatically.

"Exactly." He rose. "Good evening, Mrs. Price-Jones, how refreshingly vivid you look this evening. Like a bright ray of sunshine on a gloomy day."

Clarissa's chaperone laughed delightedly. "Such a wicked flirt you are, Lord Randall."

"Wicked? Oh, dear me, no. I assure you, dear lady, I am positively saintly"—he batted those preposterously long lashes—"in my flirting, at least." His smile was pure essence of rogue. "It's in other areas I'm reputed to be wicked."

Mrs. Price-Jones rapped his arm playfully with her fan. "Such nonsense you talk. Go away with you."

He bowed over her hand, bowed again to Clarissa and strolled away.

"Such a divine man!" Mrs. Price-Jones patted Clarissa on the arm, then said, "Oh, there's Lady Bentinck. I want to have a word with her. You'll be all right here on your own, won't you, my dear?" Without waiting for Clarissa's response, she hurried away.

A moment later an elegant lady drifted up to her. "Miss Studley?" The lady, who was approaching thirty, she guessed, was very attractive, slender and dark with vivid features. She was dressed in a dashing, low-cut claret silk gown. "May I sit down?"

"Yes, of course." With a smile and wave of her hand Clarissa indicated the seat beside her, but her mind was racing. Who was this lady? Had they been introduced and Clarissa had forgotten? She couldn't imagine it.

"I saw your face when you were dancing with Rake Randall," the lady said.

Clarissa had no idea how to respond to that. "Oh?" she said.

The lady leaned closer. "Don't get your hopes up, my dear. He's elusive, unreliable and untrustworthy."

Clarissa blinked.

"He's notorious for raising hopes in virgin breasts," the woman went on, "and then dashing them to pieces. So don't be foolish. Keep your dreams for someone worthy." She gave a brisk nod and sailed off, leaving Clarissa staring after her, quite bemused. And deeply embarrassed.

The lady had obviously noticed her secret tendre for Lord Randall, even though she *knew* he was not for her. And if that lady had, who else had noticed? It was a mortifying realization. She swallowed. The idea that people had been watching and pitying her was humiliating.

She glanced across to where Lord Randall was standing in a small semicircle of elegantly dressed ladies, all smiling and laughing up at him. He was the center of their attention.

The lady was right: Lord Randall was a born flirt. Compliments dripped from him like water from a broken pipe. *Clarissa looked ravishing. Mrs. Price-Jones was a ray of sunshine.* And who knew what he was saying now to make those sophisticated ladies giggle and blush. His words meant nothing.

Oh, she wish-wish-*wished* she hadn't let herself be dazzled by him and agreed to dance the waltz with him. And go into supper with him. He was too tall, too handsome, too charming—and it was all false. And even though she *knew* his compliments were meaningless, they flustered her.

One lazy smile from those eyes and all her resolution just . . . dissolved.

And if that lady was to be believed, everyone would be watching.

What was he doing at a ball anyway? she thought aggrievedly. He was well-known to avoid ton events. Why had he chosen to attend this one?

A waltz. The most romantic dance of all. And with Lord Randall. Followed by supper.

It was too late to wriggle out of it now.

Although . . . She could claim to have a headache and go home early.

No, that would be cowardly, and she was determined not to give in to her fears. So she would dance the waltz with him.

Oh, Mama.

Though Mama, even if she weren't long dead, would have been no help at all. Mama had fallen for a tall, handsome, apparently charming but utterly worthless rake who had turned out to be a perfectly dreadful husband. Unfaithful, callous and cruel.

Yet Mama doted on him regardless, making excuses for every vile and cruel thing he did or said . . .

And that, Clarissa told herself, was what she had to keep in the forefront of her mind. She was too much like her mother—in temperament as well as looks—which made it all the more important to avoid fortune hunters. And rakes.

Lord Randall wasn't interested in her fortune. He was rich, everybody said so. And he might not be cruel, but you couldn't really tell, could you, when you met men only on their best public behavior?

It wasn't until after the wedding, when Papa realized most of Mama's fortune was tied up in a trust, that he became so nasty.

But none of that mattered, because she was *not* going to let herself fall for him as Mama had fallen for Papa. It was just a matter of being firm with herself.

Besides, he was only being polite, she was sure of it. No

matter what he claimed, she knew he was here to keep an eye on her for Leo. She'd heard his cousin saying so. And why else had he turned up at this ball, when everyone knew he hardly ever attended society events?

Flirting and charming ladies were second nature to him. She'd seen the way he strolled lazily across the dance floor, his progress followed by the eyes of half the women in the room. She glanced in his direction—yes, there he still was, head and shoulders visible, surrounded by that small cluster of women, all posturing and fluttering and vying for his attention.

Most of them were a good five or more years older than she was—some looked even older than Lord Randall—and all those she recognized were married. Not that it seemed to make any difference to him. He said something that set them all laughing again. He glanced across at her and she averted her gaze.

Don't be foolish. Keep your dreams for someone worthy.

It was also foolish to feel nervous at the prospect of waltzing with him, she told herself. He wasn't serious in the least—he never was, everybody said so. There was no danger from him—and as long as she controlled her ridiculous susceptibility there would be no danger for her.

She watched as one of the ladies placed a hand on Lord Randall's arm and he bent his head to hear what she had to say. They looked quite intimate.

Clarissa made a decision. She would dance the waltz with him. And she would enjoy it. If other ladies could flirt and dance with Lord Randall and enjoy it without any consequence to their peace of mind, so could she.

Playing with fire, a small voice in her head whispered.

Nonsense, she told it. Forewarned was forearmed. She just had to remember: a rake was a rake was a rake.

Was. A. Rake.

And while she had his attention at supper, she would

take the opportunity to confront him, to explain that while she appreciated his protection, she didn't need it, and that any promises he'd made her guardian on her behalf were quite unnecessary.

It was a plan.

M iss Studley, what a pleasure to see you here. And what a pretty color that dress is. It suits you wonderfully well." Clarissa turned. It was one of her most devoted suitors, Cuthbert Clayborn.

She smiled. "Mr. Clayborn, I didn't know you were planning to attend tonight."

He looked very elegant. Over his tastefully frilled shirt, he wore a gold-embroidered blue waistcoat that emphasized his light blue eyes and the gilt of his hair. His curls, tousled and pomaded into appealing disorder, gleamed under the light of the chandeliers. His dark blue pantaloons were tight, and he wore high black boots, which was quite unconventional for a ball. He always wore boots, though, explaining that he needed them to support his bad leg.

"I came solely to see you, dear lady. You mentioned the other day that you would be attending, and my great-aunt and I had invitations, of course. I came especially to ask you for a dance. So, will you grant me the next dance?"

Clarissa hesitated. Surely, with his leg . . .

"You are thinking of my limp," Mr. Clayborn said. "It is cheeky of me, I know, but although I was asking for the dance"—he gave her a droll look—"I was actually hoping to sit it out with you in comfort." He grimaced modestly. "This wretched wound precludes my dancing, you see."

"Of course. I'd be happy to sit out the dance with you, Mr. Clayborn."

He beamed. "How very kind you are. I almost didn't dare to ask, but I told myself, 'Lovely Miss Studley is so

popular that she will naturally be surrounded by gentlemen, but such a kind and gracious young lady might perhaps grant an old soldier—'"

If Mr. Clayborn had one fault, it was perhaps his habit
of giving her fulsome compliments. And perhaps also that
his cologne water—or perhaps it was his pomade—was
rather strong.

She cut him off. "Where would you like to sit? Here?"
She indicated the seat beside her. Mrs. Price-Jones, no
doubt seeing Mr. Clayborn approaching and anticipating
his request, had vacated it a few minutes before. She was
standing a couple of feet away, talking to a silver-haired
gentleman, while keeping an eye on Clarissa.

Mr. Clayborn shook his head. "If you don't mind, I'd
prefer to sit outside, perhaps on the terrace. It's so close in
here, and the breeze outside is delightfully refreshing. I noticed earlier that several chairs have been placed there for
our convenience."

Clarissa glanced at Mrs. Price-Jones, who was standing
close enough to hear his request. She nodded and Clarissa
rose, arranging her shawl around her shoulders. "Outside
would be very nice, thank you. Shall we?"

He stepped forward, winced and offered his arm.

"Are you sure . . ." she began.

"Oh, you mean this?" He indicated his bad leg. "Take no
notice. It's a dashed inconvenience, nothing else." But as he
escorted her across the room to the French doors leading
out to the terrace, she noticed that he limped quite heavily,
and winced frequently, though he tried to hide it.

But he'd made it clear that he disliked sympathy, so she
could hardly show it. He was, she decided, very brave.

And since his great-aunt had told them on several occasions that her darling great-nephew was the apple of her eye
and the sole heir to her fortune, he was that rarity among
her suitors: not a fortune hunter.

They found a spot on the far edge of the terrace where a small wrought iron table and two matching chairs had been placed.

Mr. Clayborn seated Clarissa then said, "Before we get settled, would you like me to fetch you a drink? Some refreshments?" He seemed ready to go off to fetch them, but Clarissa was reluctant to cause him any further pain so she assured him that she needed nothing, thank you.

He sat beside her, so that they both were able to look out over the small, well-manicured garden. A short silence fell. Clarissa racked her mind for something to talk about. "You were right," she said eventually. "The breeze is very pleasant." Hardly an example of sparkling conversation, but her mind was stupidly blank.

He turned to her anxiously. "Are you cold?"

"No, not at all."

There was another short silence, then he said, "It was Waterloo, you know. The injury."

"Yes, I think I heard that." He'd mentioned it several times before.

"I don't like to talk about it."

"No, I understand." She fiddled with her fan. "Have you been to the theat—"

"The worst thing is not the injury, or the constant pain, but the feeling that I let my men down. Leadership is very important in the army, you know, and my men looked up to me."

"Yes, of course."

"I worry that they might have been lost once I was taken off the battlefield. I would have refused to leave them, but I had no choice: I was wounded and insensible."

"That must have been very difficult."

"It was. It haunts me still, not knowing what became of them all."

She frowned a little over that. Did he not make inquiries?

But perhaps he was in no condition to ask until long afterward. The leg might be only one of his wounds.

He heaved a sigh. "Such is life, I suppose."

"Yes."

He turned to her with a smile. "Listen to me, going on about myself. I generally dislike talking about the war, but with you I feel so comfortable. Please forgive me."

"There is nothing to forgive."

"You are too generous. War is not a subject for ladies."

"Have you been to the theater lately?" she tried again.

"No, not recently. I find it difficult, sitting for long periods without moving." He stretched his bad leg and grimaced. "But there are many worse off than I. Are you fond of the theater, Miss Studley?"

"Yes, very. My sister and I never had the opportunity to see any plays when we were growing up, so it is always a great treat for us."

"Your sister, yes. She married your guardian and is on her honeymoon, is she not?"

"Yes. It is a little strange being without her. We have never been separated for long."

"I wouldn't know. I have no siblings—no family at all, except my great-aunt. Who is quite elderly." He heaved a sigh.

Clarissa had no family as well, only her sister Izzy. And now Zoë. Oh, she so hoped that they could prove their relationship to Zoë's satisfaction. The girl was proving quite resistant to the idea, much to Betty's frustration. Betty did love her long-lost-princess story.

Clarissa wasn't so worried. She felt quite certain they would be able to prove it eventually and, in the meantime, she understood that Zoë probably didn't want to get her hopes up. Hope could be painful, and Zoë's experience of life hadn't given her much trust in other people's goodwill.

"Miss Studley?"

Clarissa jumped, recalled to the present. "I'm so sorry, Mr. Clayborn, I was woolgathering. What was it you asked me?" How embarrassing to have let her mind wander off like that. The trouble was, she felt quite comfortable with Mr. Clayborn.

He paid her close attention but it didn't make her feel hot or flustered, like a certain other gentleman, only a little bored at times, which was most ungrateful of her. Men didn't usually pay her such flattering attention, especially handsome wounded heroes. Not unless they were fortune hunters, which he wasn't.

"I'm sorry, I'm boring you," he said, clearly a little miffed. Which was understandable.

"No, no you're not. I was just distracted by a thought. Please repeat your question."

"Are you sure? If you don't want to be seen abroad with a man with my disability, please say so. I won't be offended."

"Your disability?" she repeated, puzzled.

He tapped his leg. Clarissa was horrified. "Of course I wouldn't think any such thing," she said hotly. "I'm not so shallow. Besides, to have been injured in the service of king and country is nothing less than heroic. Now, please repeat your question."

"It was nothing much, just an invitation to go for a drive in Hyde Park with me tomorrow afternoon."

She had planned to go with Betty then, to find another orphan to employ, but after her rudeness in not paying attention, she could hardly refuse. "Of course, I'd be delighted."

He rose stiffly, grimacing as he straightened his bad leg. "Thank you, Miss Studley. At three o'clock, then? Now, I hear the music drawing to a close. Our dance is over. I'd better return you to your chaperone so you can be ready for the next gentleman eager to dance with you. Thank you for so graciously consenting to sit out a dance with a cripple."

Clarissa found that a little offensive—she would have sat out a dance with anyone who asked; his injury had nothing to do with it. Besides, he was hardly a cripple. But he was clearly very sensitive about his condition, poor man, so she wasn't about to argue. She took the arm he offered and they returned to the ballroom.

Chapter Five

Race stalked around the perimeter of the ballroom, greeting this person and that, but not lingering for long. He was well aware of the speculation his appearance at the ball had provoked. This—this was the reason he so rarely attended fashionable society events.

Now it wasn't just bored married ladies seeking him out in the hope of dalliance; he was starting to draw the attention of the matchmaking mamas. His cousin wasn't the only one who'd jumped to the conclusion that he'd finally decided to take a bride.

Curse it. He would leave the instant supper was over and he'd had his talk with Miss Studley.

In the meantime he had to watch the fashionable young drones buzzing around her. In retrospect, he should have sat out that country dance with her, like she had with that yellow-haired coxcomb, Clayborn. War hero be damned; he'd disliked the fellow on sight. A favored and regular visitor to Lady Scattergood's, was he? Pah!

At least Race had secured the waltz with her, and her

company at supper afterward. Not only was he looking forward to holding her in his arms—well, at least as much as propriety allowed—over supper he'd be able to assure her that the attention he was paying her had nothing to do with any promise he'd made to Leo.

Again he wondered how much she'd overheard of the conversation between himself and Maggie.

He hadn't yet decided whether he was going to tell her he was courting her; he had a feeling that announcing it might be too blunt. It might make his shy little flower withdraw, as she had already once or twice.

No, better just to seek out her company at every opportunity and let her draw her own conclusions. Just as long as he made it clear to her that Leo had nothing to do with it.

He glanced across the dance floor and gritted his teeth. He also needed to warn her about those wretched fortune hunters that Lady Scattergood had been allowing to call. And about that villain, Vibart. She was dancing with him now—and what the devil had he said to make her laugh so? *And* make her blush, the swine.

But if he did try to warn her about Vibart and the others, might it strengthen the impression that he was acting the guardian in Leo's place? That would make her withdraw from him even further.

Blast it, he'd never been so indecisive in his life!

Once he held her in his arms and had her twirling about the ballroom, he'd know what to do, he was sure. Follow his instincts.

He glanced at the dance floor and gritted his teeth. His instincts currently urged him to strangle Vibart.

Fed up with the sight of Miss Studley dancing and being charmed by coxcombs, rakes and wastrels—and what the hell was her chaperone doing to allow it?—he took himself off for a brisk walk around the courtyard.

After a time he heard the country dance drawing to a close. The next dance was the waltz she'd promised him.

He reentered the ballroom and glanced around. Ah, there she was—again with that scoundrel Vibart, who was standing far too close to her. And she was blushing again, blast the man.

As he approached, Vibart glanced up and smiled, a sly, knowing smile. "Randall, I understand you have the honor of dancing the next waltz with this delightful young lady."

"Yes, the supper dance," Race said.

"I'm desolate to be so deprived of her charming company," Vibart said. "Truly, I doubt you appreciate the honor she's done you. A dozen men here tonight—myself included—would happily duel you for the chance to sup with the lovely lady," he added with an intimate smile at Miss Studley. Who blushed. Again.

"I do appreciate it," Race said, annoyed. "And she made her own choice."

"*And* I'm right here," Miss Studley said quietly, "and perfectly able to speak for myself. Lord Randall, shall we?"

"Indeed." Race presented his arm and led her onto the dance floor just as the opening chords of the dance sounded. Her lips were pursed tight. She seemed annoyed. Was it because of Vibart's fulsome compliments? Or had she fallen for them? Vibart was held to be very charming. Race couldn't see it himself.

"You know he's a notorious rake, don't you?"

She shot a sideways glance at him. "He's not the only one."

Race blinked. What other rakes had been pursuing her? What the devil did that chaperone think she was doing, letting Clarissa be hounded by rakes?

"Please, I don't wish to discuss it," she added before he could say anything. "Let us just enjoy the dance." Facing him, she placed one hand on his shoulder and presented her other hand. He took it and placed his hand lightly on her waist, waited several beats, then twirled her out among the swirling crowd.

She was a little stiff at first, but her body soon softened, responding easily to his leadership. Her responsiveness delighted him; no doubt she would be equally responsive in other areas. He ached to draw her closer, but knew he must restrain himself. She was so sweetly shy.

But whether it was the effect of the music or his carefully respectful embrace—though he hoped it was his proximity—she almost floated in his arms.

But she neither talked nor looked directly at him; in fact after a few passing glances she seemed to close her eyes. Bashfulness, Race decided. The waltz was a very intimate dance, after all. They danced on, and he felt her relaxing in his embrace. She was his to command—in the dance, at least. Her expression was . . . dreamy. She was light as a feather, soft as a cloud.

He silently cursed the others in the ballroom; he ached to hold her properly in his arms.

He decided to draw her out a little.

"You're very light on your feet," he said.

She blinked, as if startled, and gave him a shy little smile.

He tried again. "A natural dancer, in fact."

"I do enjoy dancing." Her gaze roamed past his shoulder, presumably observing their fellow dancers and, when it returned to him, dropped immediately to his waistcoat.

"You're admiring my waistcoat?" he murmured.

"It's just that the bottom button is undone. It's distracting."

"How shocking. My valet will be mortified." After a moment he added, "Perhaps you could button it for me."

She gave him a prim look. "Indeed I could not."

He lowered his voice. "I wouldn't mind. You're welcome to do whatever you like with my buttons."

She stiffened in his arms and, despite the adorable blush that rose to suffuse her perfect complexion, said with a quiet dignity that impressed him, "Please don't try to flirt with me, Lord Randall."

"Try to? I'm not succeeding?" he said playfully.

"No. You're not."

Race frowned. It was one thing to realize his banter could cause her to close up like a sea anemone, but this serious instruction not to flirt was . . . disconcerting. He always flirted with women.

"Flirting isn't meant to be serious, you know. It's just a bit of fun," he said. "It's like battledore and shuttlecock."

She looked puzzled.

"Flirting is a game," he explained. "Men and women toss the comments back and forth like a shuttlecock in a fun exchange. It's not very serious."

"I've never played battledore and shuttlecock, and I am unskilled at flirting, but I understand what you mean. You have not the reputation of being serious at all, Lord Randall."

Race blinked. "That's not what I meant. I am serious about important things."

She gave him a swift glance. "Really?"

"Yes, I—"

"Like keeping a promise to a friend?"

"Yes." He rarely made promises, and was always very careful about what he promised. He'd never broken a promise in his life.

"Well, you need not keep your promise to Leo—to 'keep an eye on' me, was it not?"

"No, I—"

"I heard you talking with your cousin, but I neither need nor wish to have you, or anyone, 'keep an eye on' me."

Not knowing what to say to that, Race twirled her around and then reversed. When she caught her breath, she continued, "So please desist from this well-meant watchdoggery. I will inform Leo of my request when he and my sister return from their honeymoon."

Race had no intention of discussing this matter here and now. He needed to think. "Why are you talking to my button?"

"Your button?" She looked up at him in surprise.

"The undone one. Still itching to do it up?"

A delicate, delicious flush rose to color her cheeks. "I have no interest in your . . . button." She bit her lip and glanced away.

She was not as indifferent to him as she was pretending. Race wanted to purr.

"I'm flirting." He twirled her around a few more times, then said, "But I will try to be more serious with you."

She looked up at him. "Try?"

"Well, you can't expect a man to be serious all the time—how dull would that be?—so you must allow me an occasional little flirt."

She shrugged. "Who you flirt with is nothing to do with me."

"It's everything to do with you."

She gave him a startled look, then said, "I suppose you're funning me again."

"I promised you I'd be more serious with you, did I not?"

"Yes, but . . . I don't know whether to believe you."

"Why not?"

She pressed her lips together, and after a few more twirls, said, "It's your eyes."

"My eyes? What about them?"

"They're always laughing."

"Not laughing, dancing," he corrected her.

She said nothing, but her expression was skeptical.

"Talking to you makes my eyes want to dance," he explained.

"You are being ridiculous."

"No, I'm entirely serious."

She blinked, her blush intensified and she looked away. "Please don't tease me," she said in a low voice, and he realized she was heading into anemone territory.

He changed the subject. "Have you heard from your sister yet?"

She relaxed slightly. "No, but it's early days yet. She has better things to do than write." She became aware of what she'd said, and the blush returned. It was adorable. He changed the subject again.

"So, will you be going maid-hunting tomorrow?"

"No, I've had to put it off. Mr. Clayborn is taking me for a drive tomorrow afternoon."

"Clayborn? That—" He broke off.

"He's a very fine gentleman," she said with a faint note of reproof. "And a war hero."

Race wanted to curse. You couldn't argue with wounded war heroes, no matter how annoying they were.

He spent the rest of the waltz trying to regain his lost ground. There was no flirting, nothing the slightest bit suggestive; he kept his conversation light, entertaining—he hoped—and innocuous.

But to no avail. She didn't soften toward him again. She wasn't rude, or even cold, but for all the warmth she showed him, she might have been dancing with an octogenarian. Or a perfect stranger. In fact, he decided, she would probably be warmer toward an octogenarian. She was kind like that.

Still, over supper they could talk properly and he could straighten out whatever this little misunderstanding was.

Waltzing in Lord Randall's arms was . . . exhilarating. And exhausting—and not in the physical sense.

He swept her around the floor, holding her with the lightest touch, not the slightest bit too close, or the least bit improper. Even so she could feel the heat of his tall, lean body, his power implicit in the way he led her through the dance.

They both wore gloves, but all that light barrier did was make her wonder what it would be like to have his bare hand on her, skin to skin.

She liked dancing, and she and her sister had practiced the waltz assiduously in preparation for that longed-for first time at Almack's, and since then she'd danced it several times with various partners. But none of those partners had made her feel as light, as graceful, almost fairylike as she felt with Lord Randall.

In the first few minutes she'd asked herself whether she'd made a mistake, accepting his invitation to dance.

Because the waltz, in his arms, was pure seduction.

But she'd crushed her doubts and reminded herself that she was here to enjoy herself, that she was in no danger of losing her heart—her head was stronger than her heart—and that he was a rake for a reason—he made women feel good. More than good.

And it was true: she felt wonderful. And she was determined to let herself relax and enjoy it.

She'd relaxed in his arms, giving herself over to the music and the man. She leaned closer to him and let herself be transported to who knew where.

The others in the ballroom seemed to blur; she was aware of only him. His light touch didn't disguise the leashed strength of him as he whirled her around the room. It was so easy to just let herself be swept away, to trust herself to him entirely, twirling like a leaf in a whirlpool.

After a few moments she closed her eyes, because Lord Randall's compelling gray gaze never shifted from her face. It was warm, like a touch. Far from his eyes wandering about the room to see what others might be doing, he barely seemed to notice anyone else in the room, except that he never bumped into anyone, never made a misstep.

His intense regard was flattering, but also a little overwhelming.

But closing her eyes might have been a mistake, because she became more aware of him than ever.

The warmth of his hands through the fabric of her gloves and the light pressure of his hand at her waist. The subtle scent of him teased her nostrils; the faint masculine tang of his shaving soap, spicy cologne and—she breathed in deeply trying to identify that other elusive scent. She was always fascinated by smells and eventually she realized that the faint, enticing extra layer of fragrance she could smell was masculinity. Specifically Lord Randall's.

Dancing the waltz with him was pure seduction . . . until he'd started to make conversation. It broke the spell. She was hopeless at flirting. His ability to fluster her was as bad as ever. But this time she felt she'd held her own. More or less. She was quite proud of that.

Not that it made much difference. Every move the man made, every word he uttered, every glance he gave was seductive.

It was nothing like her dance with Lord Vibart. He was another notorious rake, darkly handsome and very attractive, but he didn't stir her senses in the least. And his blatant flirting and suggestive remarks only made her laugh or blush. She wasn't at all attracted to him, and so the dance had been easy, lighthearted.

Dancing with Lord Randall had been . . . blissful. Despite his effect on her, she didn't regret it for a minute. She understood, more than ever, why those other ladies pursued him so blatantly.

But despite the magic—or maybe because of it—she knew it would be fatal to succumb. And so she wouldn't.

As he led her off the dance floor and headed toward the supper room, she saw Mrs. Price-Jones on the other side of the room, watching.

Mrs. Price-Jones raised a brow and glanced at Lord Randall, as if asking whether he was taking her in to supper. Clarissa nodded and her chaperone began to bustle her way through the throng entering the supper room.

"Ah, that one will do nicely." Lord Randall led Clarissa to a small table near the window. There were just two chairs. The small table had obviously been brought in from some other part of the house, just for this occasion, but it was too intimate. She'd already told him what she wanted: that she didn't need his protection, especially on Leo's behalf.

She glanced around, hoping to find seats near someone she knew, but there were none.

He seated her, and pulled out his own chair.

"Thank heavens!" Mrs. Price-Jones declared as she pushed past him and sank into it. "I am exhausted. I fear I've danced my feet to stumps." She beamed up at Lord Randall. "Thank you soooo much for procuring me a chair, Lord Randall. My partner seems to have deserted me." She glanced at Clarissa. "Thank goodness for true gentlemen, don't you agree, Clarissa?" She winked.

Clarissa, who was trying not to laugh at her chaperone's barefaced piracy of Lord Randall's seat, managed to make a muffled, agreeing sort of sound.

Lord Randall gave Mrs. Price-Jones a gimlet look that indicated he was quite aware of her tactics, but that being a gentleman, he had no option but to accept them. "Very well, I will find another chair."

"Thank you, dear boy. And perhaps you can make it two chairs—I see my partner approaching. He didn't desert me after all. Nice to know my allure hasn't left me."

Lord Randall, with a long-suffering look, went off to find a couple of chairs.

"You don't mind, do you?" Mrs. Price-Jones murmured to Clarissa.

"Not at all." It was an understatement. What she felt was pure relief.

A few minutes later, when Race returned with a footman carrying two chairs, it was to find the chaperone's partner, an elegant silver-haired gentleman, already seated on the other side of Miss Studley.

"Put it down here," Mrs. Price-Jones instructed. "And we won't need that other one. Dear Sir Henry found his own chair. So clever of him." She beamed. The footman placed one of the chairs beside the chaperone and went off with the other.

Race glanced at the table arrangement. The cunning old duck, with her bright, clashing clothing and seemingly artless ways, had effortlessly outmaneuvered him. Miss Studley, seated with Sir Henry on one side and her chaperone on the other, was now quite inaccessible to him. There would be no private conversation tonight.

Mrs. Price-Jones smiled guilelessly up at Race and patted the vacant chair. "Sit down, my boy, no need to be shy."

Race looked down at Mrs. Price-Jones for a moment and then laughed. "Piqued, repiqued and capotted," he said, shaking his head as he seated himself beside her. The woman was impossible, but he couldn't help but like her.

Mrs. Price-Jones fluttered her eyelashes. "You are too kind, sir. I but carry out dear Lord Salcott's instructions."

"Naturally," he agreed sardonically. She had given *dear Lord Salcott* just such a hard time whenever he'd tried to talk to Izzy alone. She might seem frivolous and scatty, but underneath she was as canny as a general. And unashamedly outrageous.

Wide-eyed, Clarissa leaned forward, peered around her chaperone, who was rather a large woman, met his eye and repeated, "Piqued, repiqued and *garroted*?"

Mrs. Price-Jones chuckled. "Not garroted, dear—capotted," she said. "The terms refer to a defeat in the game of piquet—it's a rather old-fashioned card game—though what on earth dear Lord Randall means by it is more than I can guess. You haven't heard of it? Sir Henry is an expert, aren't you, Sir Henry?" She added with a glint of mischief, "Perhaps you would explain the game to Miss Studley."

"Delighted," the old chap said, and began an enthusiastic description of the game of piquet.

Race went to fetch supper for himself and the ladies. Arriving back with a footman bearing a tray with three glasses of champagne and three filled plates—he was damned if he'd fetch food and drink for Sir Henry—Race almost laughed aloud at the glazed, blandly polite expression on Miss Studley's sweet face. Sir Henry was still waxing enthusiastic about a card game she clearly had no interest in.

She leaned forward and gave Race a narrow-eyed look, as if he were to blame.

He spread his hands in a gesture of complete innocence, but he was laughing all the same. The situation was frustrating, but he couldn't help also finding it amusing.

He passed around the champagne glasses and set down the plates, one for each of the ladies and one for himself. Mrs. Price-Jones immediately passed Race's plate to Sir Henry, who eyed it greedily and said, "Oh, I say, crab cakes. My favorite." Forgetting about the delights of piquet, he gobbled down three crab cakes—Race's crab cakes—in half a minute. Race eyed him balefully. Crab cakes were his favorite, too.

"Not hungry, yourself, dear boy?" the chaperone asked with faux innocence, glancing down at Race's empty place setting.

"No." There was no point going back to fill another plate now. The crab cakes were always the first to go.

Race stepped out into the cool of the night and breathed in deeply. It was a relief to leave. London's air was hardly clean and fresh but the atmosphere at the ball had been stifling with all those expectations and plans. Society events. He rolled his eyes. And the gossip . . .

It was only midnight, still quite early. He could drop in on one of his clubs, play a few hands. Or take a brandy or two with a congenial acquaintance. But he wasn't in a sociable mood. The ball had cured him of that for the moment.

Besides, there were those damned betting books in the

clubs. Irritably he kicked at a stray pebble. Didn't people have anything better to do?

Better to take himself and his bad mood home.

He walked back toward his lodgings, deep in thought, oblivious of his surroundings. She had the wrong idea about him, he decided. That one harmless little remark about his buttons and she'd closed up tight like a sea anemone.

Please don't try to flirt with me, Lord Randall.

And kept him at arm's length for the rest of the evening.

Yet she was attracted to him, he was sure. He knew women, and all the signs were there. Though in her innocence, she might not understand . . .

Did she think he was merely flirting? Or worse, trying to seduce her? Didn't she know he never dallied with innocents?

Of course she didn't. Who would tell her that? On the contrary, she'd probably been warned off him by some blasted busybody. Dozens of them, if he were any judge.

He had to talk to her, let her know his intentions were strictly honorable. And were nothing to do with his friendship with Leo.

He needed somewhere in private, without that wretched chaperone sticking her nose in. He'd planned to tell her at supper, but the chaperone had ruined that little plan. And showed every sign of foiling any future plans he might have.

He strolled on, passing Berkeley Square, which lay in darkness. The mild evening breeze picked up, sending the leaves of the trees whispering and carrying a waft of sweetly scented air: the grass had recently been cut.

He stopped and stared into the verdant shadows. What a fool he'd been. Of course.

His dark mood evaporated.

H e's interested, you know."

Clarissa started. She and Mrs. Price-Jones were in

the carriage on the way home from the ball. It was dark, and she was sleepy. "Who is?"

"Lord Randall."

"Oh, him. I haven't given a thought to him since supper," Clarissa said carelessly. It was a lie. "Why are we talking about him?"

"Because he's interested in you—seriously."

Clarissa's heart fluttered, but she squashed it and managed to say coolly, "Nonsense. Everybody knows Lord Randall takes very little seriously."

"Nevertheless, everybody is talking about his appearance at the ball. It's not his first, either—you will recall he also attended the Arden ball last month, and several since then. Balls which you also have attended."

"Why would that be of interest to anyone?"

"It's not like him, that's why. There's speculation that he's finally decided to take a wife. I believe that wagers have even been made in those horrid betting books in the clubs that gentlemen frequent." Her voice deepened with significance. "Wagers that link your name with his—oh, don't worry, they don't specifically name you—nothing so scandalous. But I'm told they refer to him and a Miss C. S. And you must admit he's been paying you an unusual degree of attention lately."

"Nonsense. He's just being polite while Leo's away. It's a favor, that's all."

"Perhaps."

Clarissa shook her head. "I don't believe the wagers can possibly refer to me and Lord Randall. And even if they did, why would anyone care?"

"To be frank, my dear, there is some degree of surprise that you're the choice he seems to have settled on. It's quite a coup for you."

"Why? Because he's only ever seen with ravishing beauties?" She expected Mrs. Price-Jones to deny it and utter some nonsense about beauty being in the eye of the beholder. Clarissa was fed up with false compliments. She'd been practically drowned in them tonight at the ball.

But Mrs. Price-Jones surprised her. "Yes, that's true, and he's very rich, so it can't be your fortune that's attracting him. But men are peculiar: they might select their, let us call them 'flirts'—"

"You mean mistresses." Papa had made no secret of his various mistresses. Had rubbed Mama's nose in them.

"Very well, mistresses, if we're going to be blunt. They might choose them for their beauty, but when it comes to choosing wives other factors come into play."

"I know. They prefer them rich and beautiful, but when they can't have that, they want them obedient, modest, chaste, dutiful and to be able to provide heirs and run a house," Clarissa said. The depressingly dull virtues. Her mother had drummed them into her. Much good they'd done poor Mama.

"Not necessarily," her chaperone said. "My own dear Price-Jones chose me before many a beauty who'd been setting their caps at him—bless his heart—and you'd have to agree I'm not and never have been a beauty. Nor am I quiet or obedient or even fashionable."

Clarissa nodded. She had to agree.

Mrs. Price-Jones continued, "And I had no fortune—not that he needed one, being full of juice himself, the dear man."

The carriage rattled over the cobblestones. In the distance some revelers in the street shouted and laughed. In the gloom, Clarissa couldn't see her chaperone's face: she seemed to be lost in memories, but after a minute her voice brightened. "He wasn't even the sort of man I thought I wanted, either, being the quiet, thoughtful type, a widower and a complete homebody—he loved his books, you see—and you know how I love a party.

"But we fell in love, and despite our differences we were very happy together. My only regret was that I never had babies, and though he had children by his first wife, they were of an age where they resented anyone taking their mother's place." She heaved a sigh. "But there, that's enough about me—it's Lord Randall we were talking about."

"Must we?"

"Of course we must. He's by far the best of your suitors, and in any case it's clear to me you're far from indifferent to him. You're not, are you?"

Clarissa felt a blush rising and was thankful for the darkness inside the carriage. "It doesn't matter whether I'm indifferent to him or not—he's a rake and I will never marry a man like that. Besides, everyone knows he takes nothing seriously. If there are wagers being made, he's no doubt aware of it and is delighting in fooling everyone. That's the sort of man he is."

They passed a market where even at this time, people worked busily setting up their stalls by the light of lanterns. As they left the busy scene and the carriage interior fell once more into darkness, Mrs. Price-Jones said, "I'm not so sure. Granted, he affects a careless manner most of the time, but I've seen the way he watches you when he thinks no one is looking. He looks like a man bent on courting to me."

Clarissa shook her head, wishing Mrs. Price-Jones would drop the subject. Her chaperone's coy speculation was somehow . . . painful. Clarissa knew perfectly well that everyone, all those gossiping, speculating people who were imagining things about her and Lord Randall, were wrong.

"You're mistaken. He's not courting me at all. He made a promise to Leo to keep an eye on me while Leo and Izzy were away, so if he's doing anything, it's protecting me from fortune hunters and other undesirables. I heard him—Lord Randall, I mean—explaining it to his cousin Lady Frobisher when we went riding the other day."

"Oh." There was a long silence and then Mrs. Price-Jones said, "I'm still not convinced. I think he's serious and you should encourage him."

"Then if you think he's such a catch and I should encourage him," Clarissa said, exasperated, "why did you prevent him sitting next to me at supper?" She knew he'd planned some kind of intimate conversation, which is why she'd been nervous about it. But her chaperone couldn't have known that.

Mrs. Price-Jones laughed. "Oh, my dear, haven't you learned yet? The harder a man has to work at something, the more you deny him, the more determined he becomes." She laughed again. "Besides, wasn't it fun?"

Chapter Six

❧

"No, no and no again, Miss Clarissa! I will not go walking in Hyde Park with you." Zoë faced Clarissa with that stubborn look that reminded her so much of her sister Izzy.

Clarissa eyed the girl in frustration. Since coming to Lady Scattergood's Zoë had not ventured out at all, not even to accompany Jeremiah walking the dogs. She seemed quite content to sit and chat with Lady Scattergood and Clarissa and Mrs. Price-Jones, but she'd refused point-blank to join them in receiving visitors.

And when they were occupied elsewhere, she happily joined Betty and the servants and helped out. She'd shown some interest in Clarissa's use of plants and flowers in making creams and other cosmetic products, but she hadn't even ventured into the garden. Clarissa had begun to wonder whether Zoë might be developing the same affliction as Lady Scattergood's.

"But why not? It's not the fashionable hour—there won't be many people around—and a walk will do you a world of good. And don't call me 'Miss Clarissa.' I'm your sister, and you are *not* a servant. It's just Clarissa."

"I ain't convinced I am your half sister." Zoë lifted a shoulder. "Maybe I'll change my mind when I meet this Izzy you talk about, that everyone says I look like, or when you get some real proof, but until then . . ."

"But a walk in the park—"

"Will cause talk and your reputation will be in danger again."

Clarissa frowned. "Again?"

"Betty told me all about it—what you done for Miss Izzy in bringing her out with you into society. It was terrible risky, she said, but now Miss Izzy is married to a lord so it's all all right. But if people see me with you—"

"They will just think that you are Izzy's and my younger sister. Which you are, I'm convinced. And it's Izzy for you, not Miss Izzy. And 'did for,' not 'done for.'"

Zoë gave her a skeptical look. "A younger sister they've never heard of before?"

Clarissa shrugged. "Why not? You are young; it will be several years before you make your come-out. For all anyone knows you were living back at Studley Park Manor, our former home. Or away at school."

Zoë snorted. "At *school*? Yes, because I'm sooo well educated."

Clarissa pursed her lips. It was true. Zoë was barely literate. She could read, but not well, though reading magazines and newspapers aloud to Lady Scattergood was improving her skills. And though her handwriting was decorative, her spelling and grammar were atrocious. Her mother had done her best to teach her, but not only was she French and unschooled in English, her own education had stopped at the age of eleven when she'd had to flee from the violence of the Revolution. And of course, they could barely afford food, let alone school or a governess.

"Very well then," Clarissa persisted. "We will walk in

the garden at the back of the house. It's quite private—only the residents of the houses that enclose it have access. We hardly ever see anyone there—mostly we see Lady Tarrant and her children. Lady Tarrant is a good friend and a very kind lady. She doesn't go out in society much these days, and in any case, she can be trusted with your story. The little girls, of course, are too young to care."

Zoë considered that, then grudgingly nodded. "If you're sure."

"I am. Now come along, you've been cooped up in the house for too long. Fresh air and a walk will do you good. Fetch your pelisse—the breeze is quite brisk."

"You mean fetch Izzy's pelisse," Zoë corrected her as she hurried away.

Clarissa sighed. She knew the root cause of Zoë's reluctance to embrace her new identity—and Izzy's clothes. It was insecurity. She was certain Clarissa had made a mistake, that she'd be found to be no relation at all and would be sent back to the orphanage. Her anxiety was understandable.

But even if she turned out to be no relation—though Clarissa did not believe it—Clarissa had no intention of casting her off. She'd come to like the girl for herself.

Trust would come with time.

Clarissa penned a swift note to Lady Tarrant, warning her she'd be bringing her shy half sister into the garden, and asking her for understanding—she'd explain later. She gave the note to Jeremiah, Lady Scattergood's young footman-in-training and asked him to race it around to Lady Tarrant.

A few minutes later, she and Zoë exited the back door and entered Bellaire Gardens, the large private garden after which the estate had been named.

"Oh, this is lovely," Zoë exclaimed, looking around. "And the air smells almost like"—she sniffed deeply—"like perfume. You'd never know we was in London."

Clarissa smiled, pleased by her reaction. The garden was her favorite place in the world, now that her former home was lost to her. "At this time of year the roses are at their best, and almost all of them smell wonderful. Whoever planned this garden planted for perfume, as well as beauty."

They explored, taking their time. Clarissa showed Zoë the summerhouse and where the key was hidden. As they strolled, she identified various plants for Zoë, at first a little hesitantly—Izzy liked the garden but had little interest in plant names or varieties of roses, but Zoë seemed quite interested, and asked lots of questions. Or perhaps she was just being polite.

They could hear the sound of children's laughter and, with Zoë's cautious acceptance, meandered slowly toward the big plane tree where Lord and Lady Tarrant's little girls liked to play.

But before they reached the tree a sharp voice exclaimed, "Izzy Studley, what on earth are you doing here? You're supposed to be on your honeym—" The speaker broke off as Zoë and Clarissa turned toward her.

Clarissa sighed. Of all the times for their nosy neighbor, Milly, to come into the garden. Around the same age as Izzy and Clarissa, she was also making her come-out, but had been a thorn in their sides from the very beginning.

"Good morning, Milly," Clarissa said.

Milly ignored her. She came closer, staring at Zoë with a perplexed expression. "I thought you were Izzy, sent home in disgrace when Lord Salcott realized the mistake he made, but you're not Izzy, are you? Though you're wearing her clothes, I see—I recognize that pelisse. Who on earth are you?"

Zoë opened her mouth to speak, but Clarissa touched her arm and said quickly, "As I said, good morning, Milly. Since you ask, let me introduce my sis—"

"*Cousine,*" Zoë said quickly.

Milly frowned. "Koo zeen?" she repeated. Clearly Milly had never learned French.

Zoë lifted her chin. "*Oui.* I am Zoë Benoît, Miss Studley's *cousine*—a distant cousin, visiting from France." The second time, she used the English pronunciation of *cousin*.

Milly narrowed her eyes. "A cousin from France? But you look exactly like Izzy. In fact I thought you were Izzy until you turned around."

Zoë gave a very Gallic shrug. "Can I help what you think?" She looked Milly up and down. "And who might you be to accost us in this fashion? It is hardly polite. But then in *France* we understand good manners."

Milly flushed but her eyes sparked with animosity.

Clarissa hid a smile. So much for her shy little sister. It was a masterly set-down. "Zoë, this is Miss Millicent Harrington, who lives in the house over there with her mother." She indicated Milly's house.

Milly inclined her head graciously, saying, "My mother is second cousin to a duke."

Zoë sniffed, unimpressed. "In France they chop the heads off dukes."

Clarissa smothered a chuckle.

Milly bridled. "Who cares what they do in foreign countries? Everyone knows the French are barbaric." She eyed Zoë thoughtfully. "Besides, I don't believe you're French at all. You're as English as I am, only your accent is straight out of the gutter—an English gutter. I think you're another one like Izzy—one of Sir Bartleby Studley's bast—"

Before Clarissa could interrupt, Zoë let forth with a blast of rapid French. She spoke so swiftly and so heatedly that Clarissa couldn't follow most of it—her own education wasn't impressive, but she did have a smattering of French. She caught some words: *incivile*, uncivil; *impolie*, rude; *arrogante*; *une vache*, which she was sure meant a cow; *je m'en fiche*, which she had no idea of but it was delivered with an emphatic gesture that seemed rather rude; and *salope*—which she was fairly sure was another very rude word.

Milly tossed her dark ringlets and gave Zoë a supercilious look. "I suppose you think you're very clever, gabbling

away like that. It might sound a bit like French, I suppose, but—"

A voice and the sound of clapping interrupted. "Oh, brava,
brava, *ma petite.*" A young woman approached, beaming,
still clapping. "*C'est magnifique*, but really, such an excellent tirade is wasted on one such as this." She turned to
Milly. "And you, Miss whoever-you-are, I heard some of
what you said, and I can assure you, this young lady is indeed speaking French and the very best kind of French at
that." She glanced at Zoë and winked. "Although some of
the words she used were, let us say, less than genteel. Her
accent, however, is perfectly aristocratic."

Lady Tarrant came up behind her. "Oh, Clarissa, there
you are. And this must be Zoë, your young sis—"

"*Cousine*," Zoë said quickly.

"Yes, my cousin from France," Clarissa affirmed. She
felt a little sad that Zoë was so quick to reject their sisterhood, but she could see it was a clever strategy, especially
as Milly had jumped so quickly to the correct conclusion.
Zoë had clearly done some thinking about her situation.
And her French did sound impressively authentic.

"Of course. How do you do, Zoë? Good morning, Milly,"
Lady Tarrant said. "Let me introduce my goddaughter, Lucy,
Lady Thornton, currently visiting from Vienna with her
husband, my nephew, Gerald. He is in the diplomatic service."

Milly muttered a greeting. She glared at Zoë and seemed
inclined to continue the argument, but Lady Tarrant said in
a firm voice, "Milly, I think you've said quite enough."

Milly turned to leave, then turned back. "I don't suppose
you know who has purchased the house near the corner?"
She pointed.

"No, no idea." Clarissa said. For a week now they'd heard
the sounds of workmen banging and hammering and tramp-
ing to and fro. "It's not really our business, is it?"

"I gather the new owner is refurbishing it from top to bottom in the most elegant style," Lady Tarrant said.

"Well, we can see that for ourselves, can't we—but who *is* the owner?" Milly said caustically. "Mama has been trying to find out—she says it's very important that we maintain the exclusive nature of the residents here, and it would be dreadful if the new owner was some vulgar cit or tradesman. But when she spoke to the head workman about it, he was not only common and vulgar but very rude."

Clarissa hid a smile, imagining a workman getting the better of the imposing Mrs. Harrington. "I don't think it matters and anyway, we can't do anything about it, can we? The house is sold."

Milly sniffed. "Mama says we should all band together and let him know his kind is unwelcome here. This is a very select address."

Nobody said anything for a moment, then Lady Tarrant said, "It's time we went in."

"Yes," Clarissa agreed hurriedly. "Isn't that your mama calling, Milly?"

"I don't hear anything," Milly said sulkily.

"You'd better go, in case," Lady Tarrant said. "I would hate your mother to worry."

Milly gave them all a goaded look, sniffed again and flounced away.

As she left, Zoë muttered something in French. Lady Thornton gave a delighted laugh and said, "Indeed, but let us now speak English."

Zoë gave her a sheepish smile.

"And you must both call me Lucy," Lady Thornton continued, "because I know we are going to become firm friends. Now, Zoë, you must come and meet my adorable nieces. I hope you like cats." Linking her arm through Zoë's, and chattering away in French, she led the way back toward the large plane tree that dominated the east part of the garden.

Clarissa followed with Lady Tarrant, who was walking more slowly.

Lady Tarrant gave her an apologetic smile. "Sorry about the slow pace. It won't be long now."

Clarissa hugged her arm. "I don't mind. I'm thrilled for you."

Just then Lady Tarrant's middle stepdaughter, Lina, just turned eight, came rushing up. "I didn't know where you were. You shouldn't go off alone," she told her stepmother severely.

"I was with Lucy," Lady Tarrant said mildly.

Hugging her stepmother's other arm, Lina beamed across at Clarissa and said proudly, "Did you know, Miss Studley? We're having a baby!"

Clarissa smiled at the little girl. Lina's protectiveness toward her stepmother was adorable. "How wonderful. Are you hoping for a boy or a girl?"

Lina shook her head. "Papa says it doesn't matter which, that whoever we get we will love him or her the same." She added, "But I already have two sisters, so I would rather we have a baby boy."

Lady Tarrant said, "Well, I hope whoever it is decides to come along soon. I'm tired of feeling like an elephant."

"You're not like an elephant at all," Lina said fiercely. "You're more beautiful than ever—Papa says so, and Papa is always right."

Lady Tarrant laughed softly, then bent and kissed Lina lightly on the head. Lina, beaming, snuggled closer.

Clarissa swallowed a lump in her throat. Oh, to have a family like this, and a husband like Lord Tarrant, who so openly adored his wife and daughters . . .

"Are your niece—er, your goddaughter and her husband staying long in England?" Clarissa asked.

Lady Tarrant smiled. "She's both my goddaughter and my niece by marriage, but it's confusing, I know. Gerald— that's my nephew—is in the diplomatic service and was summoned back from Vienna. He seems to think he might be being considered for a post in Paris."

"How exciting."

"Yes, he's done very well, I believe. He was in the army before, you know, but sold out once Napoleon was finally defeated."

"And then he joined the diplomatic corps?"

"Yes, he stayed long enough to court and marry Lucy—quite a whirlwind affair it was, too—and then they went off to Vienna. After his years in the army, society life didn't appeal to Gerald—though if you ask me, diplomatic life isn't much different from the ton. It's still all dinners and dances and meetings and boring speeches, but I suppose there's a deeper meaning and a purpose behind everything—a kind of ongoing social chess match. At any rate, they're happy, which is what counts. Now, let's see what those children are up to. I've ordered tea and cakes to be served inside in half an hour."

*B*uongiorno, Lord Randall." Matteo, Leo's majordomo, bowed. "What can I do for you, milor'? You know, of course, that Lord Salcott is still away—"

"Yes, I know, Matteo." Race stepped into the entry hall and handed Matteo his hat. "It's not him I've come about. I want access to the garden."

Matteo looked at him a moment, and then broke into a smile. "Ah, *sì*, of course. You wish to see the young ladies."

Ladies? Plural? Race shrugged it off. Matteo's English was improving in leaps and bounds, but it was by no means perfect yet. "Er, yes. That butler of Lady Scattergood's refuses—"

"Say no more, milor'. Matteo, he know that butler." He rolled his eyes then gestured toward the back entrance. "This way, milor'. And you want refreshments brought to the summerhouse? Alfonso, he like to practice making English-style cakes for the young ladies."

"Some other time, I think," Race said. "Miss Clarissa might not be there."

"She go in the garden most mornings, milord. She like to gather the flowers with the, the . . . morning water still on them."

"Dew."

"*Sì*, that is the word. *Prego*, milor'." Matteo gestured for Race to go ahead.

Race entered the garden via Leo's back gate. It was a sweet setup, this garden, with only the residents of the houses that enclosed it having access. Privacy was precious in this increasingly crowded city.

He glanced around, listening for the sound of voices, but heard only the sound of the breeze in the leaves, the buzzing of bees and the sound of birds. He checked the summerhouse, but it was locked and empty. The rose garden then; he'd heard her say once that roses were her favorite flowers.

Turning a corner, he found her alone, snipping off roses. A basket containing various flowers sat at her feet.

"Stealing flowers, eh?" he said.

She jumped and whirled around. "No, I have permission. And deadheading roses is good for them. It helps to bring on more flowers."

"I was joking," he said, strolling forward. "Good morning, Miss Studley. Isn't it a glorious morning?"

"G-good morning," she stammered. "Yes, very nice. How did you get in? Did Treadwell—"

"No, Matteo."

"Oh. I see." She didn't seem too pleased to see him. She kept glancing around as if expecting to see someone else.

"I came alone," he assured her.

"Oh. Yes. Of course." She bent and picked up her basket. "I should—"

"Allow me," he said, taking the basket from her.

She frowned. "It's not the least bit heavy."

He ignored that. "I wanted to have a private word with you."

She glanced at the basket. "I really need to get them into the drying cabinet."

"I won't take long."

She glanced around again, as if looking for someone, then said, "Very well. Shall we sit over there?" She gestured toward the wooden rose arbor. Which was too open for his liking.

"The summerhouse." Race led the way, trusting she would follow. Of course she would. He was holding her flowers hostage.

He found the hidden key—she frowned at that; it was supposed to be a residents-only secret—unlocked the door and waved her inside.

She chose a seat near the door. It wasn't the delightfully squashy seat he'd seen her use in the past. She sat on the edge of her seat, feet together, hands folded in her lap like a schoolgirl awaiting a trimming by the headmistress, dammit.

It was not the kind of mood he was hoping for.

"What did you wish to speak to me about, Lord Randall?"

"You accused me last night of committing, what was the word? Oh yes, watchdoggery. On Leo's behalf."

"Yes."

"It's not true."

She raised her brows skeptically.

'It's not, I assure you. I admit, Leo did suggest that I could invite you out for an occasional ride, and I assured him it would be my pleasure. But that was all."

"Really?" Her expression made it clear she didn't believe him.

"Yes, really. In fact he actually said that he wouldn't expect me to attend balls and so on, that your chaperone would be perfectly sufficient."

"Protection?"

"Yes."

"In other words, you and Leo were discussing how to protect me."

"Y— No, that wasn't it at all." But it was too late. It was clear her mind was made up.

"Thank you for your concern, Lord Randall, but indeed there is no need to concern yourself about my welfare—"

"It's not that. I am cour—"

"Clarissa! I just seen Lady Thornton's paintings and they were—oh!" A young girl burst into the summerhouse, saw him and broke off.

Race rose to his feet, staring. She was a younger version of Leo's wife, Izzy.

The girl gave Clarissa a guilty glance. "*Désolée,*" she began but Clarissa stood and said composedly, "Lord Randall, this is my cousin from France, Mademoiselle Zoë Benoît. Zoë, this is Lord Randall, a friend of Izzy's husband."

The girl curtsied and greeted him in French.

Race narrowed his eyes. Her French was good—colloquial and aristocratic, but the few words she'd spoken in English had sounded distinctly lower-class.

He bowed. "Delighted to meet you, mademoiselle. What were you saying about Lady Thornton's paintings?"

She gave him a bewildered look, then shook her head as if she hadn't understood. She looked at Clarissa again, said, "*Désolée,* Clarissa," picked up her skirts and fled.

"Forgive my young cousin, she is shy," Clarissa began.

"Young cousin, my foot," Race said pleasantly. "She's another half sister, isn't she? Not only is she the spitting image of Izzy, her English accent reveals at least half her upbringing, and it's less than genteel. The quality of her French, though, is a mystery."

"Her English governess was sadly—"

"Invented?"

Clarissa bit her lip, said nothing for a long time, then sat down with a sigh. "Can I ask for your discretion?"

He inclined his head and resumed his seat. "Of course. It goes without saying."

"Thank you."

"Care to explain?"

She told him how she'd discovered Zoë in an orphanage—an English orphanage, where she had been given the name of Susan Bennet.

"And so, instead of a maid, you discovered a half sister." It explained her jumpiness when he'd asked her about finding a maid the other day.

She nodded. "But Zoë is reluctant to believe it. She insists on proof, and is worried her existence will cause problems for Izzy and me."

"Wise girl." Producing an illegitimate half sister would revive the rumors still faintly circulating about Izzy's legitimacy. Her marriage to Leo had all but quashed them, but society loved a scandal and it would not be hard to reinvigorate this one. And that would affect Clarissa as well.

The girl's caution about embracing this potential sisterhood also impressed him. From the sounds of things she hadn't had an easy life and, related or not, it would be understandable if she jumped at the opportunity to raise her status and increase her security. But it seemed she hadn't.

"I don't care whether it's wise or not. She's my sister and I'm keeping her!" Clarissa declared fiercely.

Race smiled. Of course she was. Loyalty and love were Clarissa's two driving forces. "Then we'd better devise a plan for enabling you to do so."

She frowned. *"We?"*

"Yes of course. I am entirely at your service."

"Oh."

He waited a moment, then said, "It was clever of you to introduce her as a French cousin."

She grimaced. "That was Zoë's idea. I didn't much like it at first, but it will probably be easier to get people to accept it than to convince them that Izzy and I have a younger sister who's been away at school, which is what I'd planned to do."

"A cousin is definitely a better plan. Her French is superb—how did she acquire such an aristocratic accent, by the way? And her grammar is perfect—her French grammar, I mean." But the girl's English was definitely a problem.

Clarissa explained about the girl's mother and her aristocratic background. That made sense to him. "Though the lower-class governess story is less believable."

Clarissa sighed. "I know, but what else can we do?"

"We'll think of something. Now the reason I wanted to speak to you this morning—"

"Tea, Miss Clarissa? Milor'?" Matteo hovered in the doorway, holding a dish of little cakes and smiling tentatively. "Or hot chocolate? Alfonso has baked some little English cakes for you, and—"

"I told you I didn't want any—" Race began, irritable at yet another interruption, but Clarissa jumped up, saying, "Oh dear, the morning has truly flown. I must get these blooms into the dryer. Lady Scattergood is expecting me to join her for luncheon and then I have an engagement to go driving with Mr. Clayborn."

She smiled at Matteo. "Thank you, Matteo, but perhaps you can send Alfonso's cakes over to Lady Tarrant's. The last lot were delicious and the little girls do enjoy them, as does Lady Tarrant and her guest."

Snatching up her basket from Race's feet, she gave him a quick smile. "Thank you, Lord Randall. I did enjoy our little chat."

"But—" He hadn't even had a chance to broach the subject he'd come to talk to her about: his courtship.

But she was gone.

Matteo took one look at Race's scowl and hastily removed himself and his blasted cakes from sight.

Race locked up the summerhouse, hid the key in the usual spot and glared at the garden. Privacy? He snorted.

*   *   *

To Clarissa's surprise, that afternoon when Mr. Clayborn came to collect her for their drive in the park, he didn't come to the door. Instead he sat in the street, in his smart, black-lacquered phaeton and sent his groom to fetch her.

It was odd, and certainly rather poor manners, but when she reached his phaeton he explained. "I must apologize for not coming for you myself, Miss Studley, but to tell the truth, with this wretched leg of mine, it's not a pretty sight, watching me clamber up into this thing. I would spare you it."

She wondered why he'd chosen such a high carriage then, if it was so hard to climb into it. But she supposed men had their own little vanities, so she simply smiled, saying, "I don't mind at all, Mr. Clayborn."

"So gracious of you, Miss Studley. Now, my groom will assist you." He snapped his fingers at the groom, who hurried to help Clarissa up.

"Wait! Wait for me!" Mrs. Price-Jones caroled, and came hurrying down the front steps. Like Clarissa, she was dressed in a carriage dress, but where Clarissa's was pale sage green with several rows of dark green piping around the hem and a narrow band of matching velvet around the high waist, and she wore a simple straw bonnet with a green band, Mrs. Price-Jones's outfit was a rainbow affair in yellow and orange stripes, with wide pleated sleeves in royal blue, trimmed with orange ribbons. On her head she wore a large, broad-brimmed straw hat, lavishly trimmed with yellow and royal blue ostrich feathers.

Both Clarissa and Mr. Clayborn stared. "Ma'am?" Mr. Clayborn said, frowning.

"Mrs. Price-Jones?" Clarissa said at the same time. There had been no mention of her chaperone coming with her on the drive.

Mrs. Price-Jones shrugged. "Lady Scattergood's orders,

I'm afraid. She was fretting about you being alone with a man in public."

"But surely—"

"I know, I know, riding in an open carriage in public—Hyde Park, no less, with all the ton looking on—is quite comme il faut, but Lady Scattergood is insistent. And besides, it's a perfect day for a lovely drive in the fresh air." She smiled at the groom. "Now, my good fellow, help me into this splendid phaeton."

"But, but, but . . ." Mr. Clayborn spluttered.

Mrs. Price-Jones looked up at him, one finely plucked brow raised. "You have some objection to my presence, Mr. Clayborn?"

"No, no, not in the least, dear lady," he said hurriedly. "But my phaeton—it's a two-seater."

Mrs. Price-Jones laughed. "Oh, don't worry about that. It will be a mite snug but I'm sure we'll all fit." She stepped forward.

Clarissa had her doubts, but she took Mrs. Price-Jones's reticule to hold while the lady climbed in. Her chaperone was a lady of considerable bulk, but Mr. Clayborn pulled, the groom pushed and after a few fraught minutes Mrs. Price-Jones was seated beside Mr. Clayborn, puffing but triumphant. She patted the few inches of seat left. "Come on up, Clarissa, don't dally. Mr. Clayborn won't want his horses standing about too long."

Clarissa hesitated. "I don't think I'll fit."

"Nonsense, of course you will. We will be delightfully cozy, won't we, Mr. Clayborn?" Mrs. Price-Jones wiggled even closer to him, and he had to grab the edge of the carriage to maintain his balance.

"Quite," he said, thin lipped.

Clarissa climbed up and did her best to squeeze into the small space left.

"Perfect," Mrs. Price-Jones declared, wriggling a bit

more. She patted Mr. Clayborn's arm. "Now, Mr. Clayborn, let us depart."

With the groom clinging to the back, they headed off. It soon became clear to Clarissa that there would be no opportunity to talk with Mr. Clayborn—indeed, she couldn't even see him unless she leaned forward to see around her chaperone.

Even if she had been able to see him across her chaperone's bulk, the lady's large straw hat and feathers got in the way. Several times Clarissa leaned forward to look, to signal a silent apology, only to see Mr. Clayborn's gloved hand swatting irritably at an ostrich feather that dangled in front of his face.

She sat back, listening to Mrs. Price-Jones happily chatting on, relating this story and that, while Mr. Clayborn's responses became shorter and curter. She struggled not to laugh. Poor man, he obviously had planned quite a different sort of outing. And Mrs. Price-Jones was, seemingly, oblivious of his irritation.

"I will put you down once we get to Hyde Park, Mrs. Price-Jones," he told her firmly as the gates of the park came into view. "You will wish to walk with your friends."

"That would be delightful," her chaperone agreed.

The phaeton swept through the gates and immediately slowed. It seemed that quite a few others had decided a drive in the park would be just the thing on this fine day and there was a line of carriages—phaetons, curricles, landaus, broughams and barouches—all moving at barely more than a walking pace.

The line stopped from time to time, as the occupants of a carriage stopped to speak to people on the ground or others in a different carriage. Some got down from one carriage only to be taken up in another. It was all very leisurely and convivial.

"Let me know where you would like to be put down," Mr. Clayborn said.

"Yes, of course, dear boy. I will tell you as soon as I see my friends."

But strangely, for all the fashionable and familiar ladies promenading in the park, many of whom waved and exchanged greetings, none of them seemed to be someone with whom Mrs. Price-Jones felt inclined to walk.

"Miss Studley, Mrs. Price-Jones, what a surprise to see you here on this lovely afternoon," a deep voice said from Clarissa's left.

"Lord Randall," she responded. He was on horseback, on his beautiful Storm, and his face was more or less level with hers.

"A surprise, is it?" He'd known perfectly well she would be going for a drive here with Mr. Clayborn. She'd mentioned it only this morning.

"A most charming and unexpected surprise," he assured her blandly. His eyes were dancing.

Mr. Clayborn leaned forward and glared at Lord Randall. "Randall."

Lord Randall coolly inclined his head. "Clayborn."

"How delightful to see you here, Lord Randall," Mrs. Price-Jones said. "Finally, someone I'd love to talk to. And I don't even need to get down and walk—I can sit here in comfort. Isn't that splendid, Mr. Clayborn?"

"Splendid," he grumped.

Lord Randall leaned closer and murmured in Clarissa's ear. "In comfort?"

She bit her lip and said nothing. Her chaperone burbled on in the background, apparently intent on finishing a story she'd been telling Mr. Clayborn.

"I'm pleased to see it's not just me whose attempts to converse with you she ruins," Lord Randall said.

Clarissa blinked and looked at him in surprise.

"Didn't you realize?" he said. "Today it's Clayborn she's foiling. Last night at the ball it was me. Does she do it to all your suitors?"

"*Suitors?*" Clarissa echoed, startled. Surely Lord Randall didn't class himself in that group. No, he couldn't. He had no serious intentions toward her, and even if he did, she had none toward him. He was a rake.

"All your gentlemen friends," he amended smoothly. Before she could respond, he said in a low voice, "Prepare yourself, Miss Studley, you're about to meet Sir Humphrey Shelduck, red nose and all."

"Sir Humphrey Shelduck?" she repeated. The duck?

A large gentleman approached, seated on a gray horse. Seeing them he moved closer, lifted his hat and bowed ponderously from the saddle, which creaked. "Ladies, Randall, Mr. um . . ." He gave Mr. Clayborn a brief, dispassionate glance then dismissed him.

"Sir Humphrey, I'd like you to meet Mrs. Price-Jones, Miss Studley and Mr. Clayborn. Ladies, Clayborn, this is Sir Humphrey Sheldon, a fellow member of my club."

After a brief exchange, Sir Humphrey moved off.

"See, told you," Lord Randall murmured to Clarissa. "How could you miss that nose?"

She giggled. It was indeed a very large and very red nose and the man had been rather pompous.

The phaeton moved along, and for the next few minutes while Mrs. Price-Jones engaged Lord Randall in conversation, Clarissa pondered Lord Randall's comment about her chaperone foiling her suitors. She didn't doubt that was true, but what puzzled her was that Lord Randall seemed to include himself in that category. Surely that couldn't be right.

She thought back to the conversation she and her chaperone had had in the carriage coming home from the ball, about Lord Randall being *interested.*

Could he be? She thought about it. He'd been quite attentive lately, taking her riding, inviting her to dance—twice in one evening—and taking her in to supper. And visiting her secretly in the garden. And now, turning up here in the park, when he *knew* Mr. Clayborn had invited her to drive with him.

But she couldn't believe he was truly interested in her that way. On the rare occasions he was seen in public with a lady it was invariably some stunning, sophisticated beauty. Not an ordinary country girl like her, undistinguished in appearance, shy in company and from a family grown rich in trade.

She had tried to accept her looks. Miss Chance had told her more than once that if you felt beautiful people would see you as beautiful. Well, she'd tried that and try as she might, she couldn't feel beautiful. But if beauty wasn't achievable, elegance was, and with Miss Chance's assistance, she could dress elegantly and be stylish and fashionable. And while beauty faded, elegance never did.

And although many aristocrats looked down their noses at people whose family background was in trade, they didn't sniff so loudly if a fortune came with it.

Clarissa's biggest problem was her susceptibility. And her heart. Clarissa feared she had the same kind of constant, loyal heart as her mother: once it was given, it stayed given, no matter what.

So if she didn't want it broken, she had to guard it carefully. And if that meant choosing a husband with her head instead of her heart, so be it. It was what most people did, after all. Her only ambition was to be happy. Her dream was to be loved. Was that too much to ask?

She glanced at Lord Randall, who was keeping Mrs. Price-Jones entertained with some nonsensical tale. He was the very model of a heartbreaker. A bee flitting from flower to flower with never a backward glance.

As she'd told her chaperone that evening in the carriage, he was hardly ever serious about anything. Witness Sir Humphrey Shelduck and Lord Widgeon. No, Lord Randall was handsome, funny and charming company, but he was not a man to be taken seriously—especially not by a girl with a ridiculously susceptible heart.

The truth was, despite her telling him she didn't need his protection, he was still doing it—just as Mrs. Price-Jones was.

And why did that thought not make her feel better? It should.

He was totally ineligible. She knew it, had known it from the start. She needed to get more serious about the list she'd come up with. It had everything she wanted. And didn't want.

Lord Randall, charming as he was—and partly because he *was* so charming—she didn't trust charm—was quite definitely not the man for her.

After the park, Race rode back to the livery stables where he kept his horse. He dismounted, fed Storm an apple, gave him a good pat, and flicked a shilling to the stableboy leading him away. As he emerged onto the street, a phaeton drew up in front of the coach house next door.

It was Clayborn, now with plenty of room to spare. Race's lips twitched as he recalled the way Mrs. Price-Jones had squashed herself in between Clayborn and his target, Miss Studley.

Clayborn was in the process of climbing awkwardly down while his groom held the horses' heads. Race snorted. With a bad leg it was foolish to have hired a high-perch phaeton. Especially when driving with ladies. Better to have hired a barouche or a landau—lower down and more spacious seating.

He nodded as he passed Clayborn and had gone half a dozen steps when Clayborn called out, "I say, Randall," in an imperious voice.

Race swung around. "Clayborn?"

"In the park, earlier," Clayborn began. "I didn't appreciate your interference."

Race raised a brow. "Interference?" he said coldly.

"Miss Studley was with me."

Race inclined his head. "I noticed. As was Mrs. Price-Jones."

"That woman—" Clayborn began angrily, then broke off. "The point is, you monopolized Miss Studley today in the park. Just as you did at the ball the other night."

Race said coldly, "Miss Studley is not a bone to be quarreled over."

"I didn't mean—"

In a hard voice, Race continued, "She is a free agent; free to choose with whom she dances, or takes supper, or to whom she talks. Without anyone criticizing her."

Clayborn flushed. "I wasn't—"

"As for the park today, I would have said I was keeping her entertained. It didn't look as though she was enjoying the drive very much."

"That was the fault of that damned interfering chaperone."

"My point is, Clayborn, neither you, nor I, nor anyone except Miss Studley—and perhaps her guardian or chaperone—has the right to decide who she may or may not talk to or associate with. Is that understood?"

Clayborn muttered something Race didn't catch. Not that he cared what the man said. He went to move on.

"I don't know why it's any of your business. It's not as if you'd be interested in a girl like her," Clayborn said sulkily. "Not seriously."

"What the devil do you mean, 'a girl like her'?" Race clenched his fists. He wanted to punch the stupid, ignorant ass, but you couldn't hit a man who'd been wounded.

Clayborn shrugged. "Everyone knows you're only interested in beauties. Even your convenients are reputed to be absolute high fliers. A plain girl like Miss Studley—"

The man knew nothing. Race made a disgusted gesture and turned to leave.

"Anyway, I do have the right," Clayborn added.

Race turned back and waited for the man to finish.

"The thing is, Miss Studley and I . . ." He swallowed.

"Miss Studley and you . . . ?" Race prompted cynically.

Clayborn took a deep breath and said in a rush, "Miss Studley and I have an understanding. So I do have the right to decide whom she may talk to or not. And I'll thank you to stop bothering her."

Race stiffened. "An understanding?" His voice was icy.

Clayborn reddened slightly and raised his chin defiantly. "Yes. A private one, you understand. With her guardian away . . ."

"I understand you very well," Race said crisply, and strode off, furious.

An *understanding*. What the hell did that mean? Surely she wasn't considering marrying Clayborn? She couldn't possibly. The man was a fool. A blind, pompous ass. Clarissa Studley would be wasted on a fellow like that.

Even if he was pale and handsome and tragic looking and wounded in the service of his country—a war hero. Apparently.

But women seemed to flock around pale and handsome tragic heroes. Especially wounded ones. Dammit!

Chapter Seven

The following morning Clarissa and Betty visited another orphanage and came home with a nice, levelheaded girl called Joan, who was thrilled at the prospect of becoming a lady's maid, and was very grateful to be chosen.

The minute they got home, Betty whisked Joan upstairs to get her settled in and begin training her to be Izzy's personal maid. The first thing they did was to begin going through the clothes Izzy had left behind and deciding what needed to be done to adjust them for Zoë.

Twenty minutes later Zoë came scooting down the stairs in distress. "They're altering all Miss Izzy's clothes to fit me—and she doesn't even know I exist."

Clarissa smiled and patted her on the arm. "Izzy has already taken most of the things she wants—they're over at her husband's house across the other side of the garden, and knowing her, I have no doubt she'll want to purchase more when she gets home."

"But—"

"Don't worry. Betty knows what she's doing."

Zoë shook her head. "I dunno. People get transported to the other side of the world just for nickin' a handkerchief, and this is more—a lot more."

Clarissa hugged her. "Nothing is being stolen, and you're not going anywhere."

Zoë was still doubtful. She glanced up the stairs, and then said, "Would it be all right if I went to visit Lucy, I mean Lady Thornton—she told me to call her Lucy. She's a painter, did you know?"

"No, I didn't."

"She painted these wonderful murals in the little girls' rooms. She showed me the other day. I started to tell you, but then that man was there with you and I didn't know what to do." Her face scrunched as she added, "I made a mess of things with him, didn't I?"

"No you didn't—and it's quite all right. Lord Randall is Izzy's husband's best friend. He knows the truth about you and he will be discreet."

Zoë snorted. "What truth? None of us knows the truth about me, not even me."

"Have faith, little sister, have faith," Clarissa said. "And of course you may visit Lucy. In fact, I'll come with you. There's something I'd like to talk over with Lady Tarrant. I'll just send a note around to see if it's convenient."

Lady Tarrant sent a note back saying she'd be delighted to have some company, so Clarissa and Zoë crossed the garden, waving to the three little girls who were playing outside under the supervision of their nanny, and went in by the back door. Zoë and Lucy immediately took themselves upstairs to look at a new painting Lucy had started.

Lady Tarrant was in a sunny room at the back of the house, knitting tiny garments in soft white wool. Clarissa exclaimed over the fine work and inquired about how Lady Tarrant was feeling. "Weary of waiting, my dear, and excited at the same time. And possibly a little bit nervous—this is my first, you know. And I'm quite old."

Clarissa supposed all first-time mothers were nervous, and she'd heard other women telling Lady Tarrant about the agonies of birth, almost relishing the drama of it, which wasn't at all helpful. "I'm sure everything will go perfectly," she said warmly. "And you'll be a wonderful mother, I know. Look at the way your little stepdaughters adore you."

Lady Tarrant smiled. "They can't wait for the arrival of their new little brother or sister."

Tea and biscuits arrived and the two ladies settled down for a good chat. They talked of many things; the weather, Clarissa's drive in the park with Mrs. Price-Jones and Mr. Clayborn, a new play that was showing, which neither of them had seen, and more, until finally Alice said, "Now, what is it you really wanted to talk to me about?"

Clarissa sighed. "Is it that obvious?"

Lady Tarrant laughed. "Not really, but I can tell something is on your mind. Is it about one of your suitors? I gather you've been seeing a lot of Mr. Clayborn. And also Lord Randall, among others."

Clarissa pursed her lips, not knowing quite how to explain the turmoil of her thoughts.

"You don't have to marry any of them, you know," Lady Tarrant said softly. "Oh, I know everyone is no doubt pressing you to make a choice, but you're not obliged to marry, especially since you are well enough off not to need a husband to support you."

"Yes, I know, but I do want to marry. I want a family of my own, and children. It's just . . ." She shook her head as if to shake it free of the clamor of her thoughts. "It's all so difficult. How does one know whether a man is the right one for you or not? How does one know that the face he shows you is his true one? How can one tell if a man is sincere—especially when one has a fortune? And how can I be sure a man will be faithful?"

Lady Tarrant thought for a moment. The only sound in the room was the clicking of her knitting needles. "It is difficult, I know. And I can't answer your questions. You're quite right: marriage is a gamble and it behooves a young lady to make her choice very carefully." Which wasn't at all helpful.

Clarissa sipped her tea. "How did you find Lord Tarrant?"

"Oh, my dear, I didn't. He found me, and I can confess to you now that I wasn't at all happy about it at first."

"Really? Why not?"

"I had no intention of ever marrying again. My first marriage was . . . not a happy one, and once I was widowed, I was planning on a life of peace and solitude." Shrieks of childish laughter wafting in from the garden made her chuckle. "You see how that plan turned out. And I'm so thankful for it."

"So what happened?"

"James simply refused to give up on me. I suppose you could say he wore me down—oh, don't look at me like that. He didn't push me into anything, far from it. He was very gentle and respectful of my fears and anxieties, and gradually he convinced me that he would be nothing like my first husband."

She finished the row she was knitting and turned the tiny garment around. "And, you know, I couldn't help but like him—well, you've seen how he is with his daughters. And I expect you've noticed that he's very attractive."

Clarissa smiled. Lord Tarrant was indeed a handsome man. And seeing him with his daughters had been a real eye-opener for her and Izzy—that a father could be so openly affectionate.

Lady Tarrant continued, "So gradually he allayed my fears." She glanced at Clarissa and lowered her voice. "If I tell you this, you'll keep it confidential?"

Clarissa nodded. "Of course."

"I asked the advice of an older friend, a lady whose marriage was very happy." She knitted on for a minute. Color

rose in her cheeks. "She advised me to . . . to, um, experiment."

"Experiment?"

Lady Tarrant nodded. "I probably shouldn't tell you
this—it's not exactly proper—but I know you have no older
lady to advise you. Oh, there's Lady Scattergood, of course,
and your chaperone, but I never had the impression that
Lady Scattergood enjoyed her marriage."

Clarissa smiled. "No, not until her husband was on the
other side of the world."

"Exactly. And I don't know your chaperone very well,
so . . ."

"Please," Clarissa said. "I'd be very grateful for any advice you have for me. You mentioned experimenting?"

Lady Tarrant swallowed. "Yes. You see, with my first
husband I'd, um, strongly disliked the marriage bed."

Clarissa blinked. Izzy had told her it was glorious.

"It's not the same with every man, you see, and with my
first husband it was . . ." She shook her head. "So before I
agreed to marry Lord Tarrant, I . . ." There was a moment
of silence, broken only by the distant sounds of the children
playing, then she said in a rush, "I let him take me to bed."

Clarissa didn't know what to say.

"Several times. In fact we spent several days alone together in a cottage in the country."

"I . . . I see."

"Morally reprehensible, I know, but we hurt nobody, and
I have no regrets at all. In fact it made all the difference in
the world to me. Because it was"—she sighed—"wonderful."

There was another short silence, then she glanced at
Clarissa and said, "Have I shocked you?"

"No, not at all," Clarissa assured her, and it was true.
She'd been surprised, yes, but mainly because she hadn't
expected such intimate revelations. But the way Lady Tarrant had described it—dealing with her fears by testing

them out before making a permanent commitment—seemed quite sensible to Clarissa.

"I'm glad, because it changed my life. Not a day goes past that I don't give thanks that I was able to put aside my fears and try again. And so with James as my husband, and the three girls, and now this"—she laid a hand on her swollen belly—"I didn't dream such happiness was possible.

"Now, I'm not advising you to let anyone bed you. That would be most inadvisable for an unmarried girl. You want this"—she patted her belly again—"to be a joy, not a mistake." She smiled at Clarissa. "But a discreet kiss or two in private wouldn't hurt."

Clarissa nodded, recalling that Mrs. Price-Jones had once said to her and Izzy that you had to kiss a lot of frogs before you found your prince. It was not the kind of thing a chaperone usually said, but then Mrs. Price-Jones was not the usual sort of chaperone.

"Thank you, Lady Tarrant," she said, and, feeling a rush of emotion, leaned across and hugged her. "It's so lovely to be able to talk things over with you. I'm so very glad you're our friend."

"So am I, my dear, so am I." She cocked her head and listened.

Clarissa listened, too, but could hear nothing. "What is it?"

Lady Tarrant put her knitting aside and rose awkwardly. "I can't hear a thing, and with children that's generally a sign that someone is up to mischief." Her eyes danced. "Shall we go and see how Nanny is coping with those children of mine?"

After her chat with Lady Tarrant, Clarissa went to one of her favorite spots in the garden, the rose arbor. Zoë had remained with Lucy: the two were still enthusiastically talking painting and drawing. She was glad Zoë had found a friend, even though she was a little sad that Zoë had not embraced her sister quite so eagerly.

But it was natural that Zoë should be drawn to a young woman who had the same interests. Zoë's mother had been a painter and an artist's model, and now, remembering that caricature she'd drawn on the wall of the orphan asylum, it occurred to Clarissa that Zoë was probably quite a talented artist herself. She must buy the girl some art supplies.

Clarissa settled herself on the wooden seat and breathed deeply of the fragrances that surrounded her: roses, lavender and sweet Alice, which was buzzing with bees.

She plucked a leaf of lamb's ear and, stroking the velvety surface meditatively, she considered the conversation she'd just had. Lady Tarrant had dealt bravely with the fears that had been holding her back, and her courage had been richly rewarded.

Clarissa considered her suitors. Really, taking everything into consideration, Mr. Clayborn came closest to the man she'd described on her list. He wasn't a fortune hunter. He was kind, well-mannered and attractive. He wasn't always a good listener, but he did respect her, that was clear. And he was a war hero, which meant he was brave and had risked his life to defend his country, and though that wasn't on her list, it ought to mean something. Best of all, he wasn't a rake.

He was certainly more suitable than Lord Randall.

She thought about what Lady Tarrant had told her. *A discreet kiss or two in private wouldn't hurt.*

Yes. At the next opportunity, she would allow Mr. Clayborn to kiss her.

Race's mind was in turmoil. Had Clarissa Studley agreed to an understanding with Clayborn? Or had the man made it up to save face after Race's dressing-down?

He wanted to call on her and ask her straight out if it was true, but he couldn't.

He'd let himself into Bellaire Gardens via Leo's house the very next morning, hoping to find her in the garden, but though he looked everywhere, there was no sign of her, only a group of little girls playing under the eye of their nanny.

And of course he couldn't just go and ring Lady Scattergood's doorbell, not with that blasted butler.

And it wasn't the sort of question one could put in a note.

He'd asked his cousin to call on her, but it turned out she had another engagement, and anyway, her gleeful curiosity about his motives for wanting her to call caused him to clam up. He was very fond of his cousin, but discreet she was not.

He was walking along in a brown study, not taking much notice of where he was going—his head was full of what Clayborn had claimed—when a voice hailed him. "Randall, well met, old fellow."

He looked up. "Grantley," he exclaimed. "Good lord, haven't seen you in years."

Grantley chuckled. "Away at the wars for most of it. How are you, Randall? Heard your father died. My condolences."

Race nodded. "Years ago now. And how are your parents?"

"Father gone, mother still fighting fit. The grandchildren keeping her active, you see."

"Grandchildren?"

"All ten of them."

"*Ten?*" Race couldn't help but exclaim.

Grantley chuckled. "Not just me—I have two sisters, you know. But I have three of my own—two boys and a girl." He linked his arm through Race's and began walking. "Married a Spanish girl—marvelous woman. Stayed with me through every campaign, didn't turn a hair at the dirt or the danger. A true lady. Ah, here we are."

Race looked up at the building they'd stopped in front of, looked at the discreet brass plate—*The Apocalypse Club*—and halted.

"Join me for a spot of lunch?" Grantley said. "They do a

very good steak and kidney pudding here. Or an excellent grilled flounder if that's your preference."

"Thanks, but I don't think so." He glanced again at the nameplate. "Not my sort of place."

"Why not?" Grantley gave him a shrewd look and then said, "Oh, I know. Expecting it to be full of old war horses reliving their days of glory?"

Race nodded. "Something of the sort." He hated having to listen to former soldiers boasting of their conquests and near misses.

"War's not glorious at all," Grantley said. "You and I know better, don't we? This is a club for real soldiers."

"Then it's not for me. I was barely a soldier at all."

"Nonsense. Not your fault that your regiment was recalled to England after Colonel Grant was wounded. As I recall the 15th Hussars—that was you, wasn't it?"—Race nodded—"were damned successful. Defeated two French cavalry regiments in a single battle. And . . . weren't you mentioned in dispatches? Something about rescuing a fellow whose horse was shot from under him, wasn't it?"

Race shrugged it off. He hated talking about his brief, inglorious career as a cavalry officer. He'd been twenty-three and gone to war full of romantic ideas of glory. The battle Grantley spoke of had been hideous, bloody and ghastly. The weather was freezing: they were all so cold their hands were numb. They'd been ordered to ride their horses in a line at the chasseurs, who'd met them with a hail of gunfire. The sound of screaming horses and men—on both sides— had given him nightmares for several years. The horses in particular haunted him. The men at least had chosen to go to war; the horses hadn't.

He'd lost any illusions he'd had about war that day.

Afterward the 15th had been recalled to England, and for the next two years he'd kicked his heels, bored and frustrated, reading about the battles other men fought from a newspaper. And then his father died, and Race sold his commission to take up his duties on the estate, and in Parliament.

He rarely spoke about his military service, feeling a little ashamed at its brevity and that he came through his only battle quite unscathed, except for a few minor wounds, whereas others . . .

"Come in and dine with me," Grantley urged him. "I promise you, there are no glory hounds here. Just men who've been there, and who want a quiet, convivial meal with good English cooking. I tell you, the steak and kidney pud is superb."

It had been years since he'd seen his old friend so, dismissing his initial reluctance, Race accepted the invitation and entered the club.

Clarissa walked toward the French doors leading out to Lord and Lady Carmichael's garden. It was a fine night and she was tense with nerves. She'd been waiting all night for this moment.

She was about to go outside with Mr. Clayborn and, if he wanted to, she planned to let him kiss her. She'd never been kissed, had never had the opportunity. Until now.

She was shaking a little, but determined on her course.

She recalled what her chaperone had once said: *You need to kiss a lot of frogs to find your prince.* It had shocked her a little at the time, especially coming from a lady who was employed to guard her virtue.

But then Lady Tarrant had told her: *a discreet kiss or two in private wouldn't hurt.*

So emboldened by their words, she was preparing to receive her first kiss. She looked out into the garden. Only a few lanterns had been hung in the trees—not enough to cast light on what was, for the most part, a garden of mystery and shadow. It was an invitation to dalliance: several couples had already vanished into the darkness.

Was she on a quest for romance or was she about to be foolish?

She shivered.

"The breeze is a little fresh. Are you sure you want to step outside?" Mr. Clayborn asked.

"No, it will be refreshing after the heat and stuffiness in the ballroom," she said, making her decision. She wanted to know what it was like to be kissed. Specifically, she wanted to know what kissing Mr. Clayborn would be like.

She glanced at him. Would he even want to kiss her? She had no idea. He'd been perfectly proper in his attentions so far. Was she supposed to signal somehow that she was willing? How? She had the feeling that this sort of thing was generally initiated by the man. Ladies, she had always been taught, were supposed to prevent such intimacies. But nobody had ever tried to kiss her. Yet.

Nothing ventured, nothing gained, she told herself, and stepped out onto the terrace.

"Ah, Clayborn, glad I found you," a voice said from behind. Lord Randall strolled up to them. "Your great-aunt seems to have had a bit of a turn. You'd better go to her."

Mr. Clayborn hesitated, glancing from Lord Randall to Clarissa, but disappointed as she was, there was no question of what he should do. "No, don't worry about me, Mr. Clayborn. You must go at once. Shall I come with you?"

"No need, Miss Studley. Several other ladies are tending to her," Lord Randall said. "But of course she wants her beloved nevvie. Don't worry, Clayborn, I'll look after Miss Studley. You run along."

Mr. Clayborn gave him an irritated glance. "I am so sorry, Miss Studley—" he began.

"Time is of the essence," Lord Randall reminded him.

"I hope it's nothing serious," Clarissa called after Mr. Clayborn as he stomped unevenly away, wincing with each step.

"It's not," Lord Randall told her.

She turned and stared at him. Then narrowed her eyes at him. "You're looking rather pleased with yourself, Lord Randall."

"Who, me?" He smiled. "Why would I not be pleased to be with a lovely lady? I gather you were about to take a walk in the garden. Shall we?" He took her arm and moved forward toward the steps down into the garden.

She shook his hand off. "Was it true, about Mr. Clayborn's great-aunt?"

He shrugged. "Perhaps just a little too much champagne."

"That's—that's outrageous!"

"Do you think so? But plenty of elderly ladies take a few drops too much on occasion. It's not a crime."

"I don't mean that and you know it." She glared at him. "I think you deliberately stopped Mr. Clayborn from escorting me outside."

He gestured carelessly, making no attempt to deny it. "He shouldn't have been taking you outside. He's done it before, and he should know better. So should you, for that matter."

"A harmless stroll in the fresh air?"

"First it's a harmless stroll, then the gossip starts and next thing your reputation is besmirched—"

"Besmirched?"

"Besmirched," he said firmly. "And then before you know it you're betrothed. Whether you want it or not."

"Nonsense."

"It's not nonsense, it's how society works." Tucking her hand into the crook of his arm, he led her down the steps into the garden.

"I don't care about my reputation."

He turned his head sharply. "What? But you must."

She shrugged. "There are half a dozen men in that ball-room alone who would happily marry me even if my reputation were, I don't know—purple. For them, my fortune is the only thing that counts."

He paused and glanced down at her. "And would you want to be tied to a man like that for the rest of your life?"

She wouldn't, of course. She pretended to ignore the question. "This is a pretty garden, isn't it?"

"Because you shouldn't. You should marry a man who loves you, who worships the ground you walk on, a man who would marry you even if you had not a penny in the world."

What a dream. She rolled her eyes. "Oh yes, there are dozens of men like that, I'm sure."

"Not dozens," he said softly. "Just one."

His voice was deep and soft, and sounded sincere, and she wanted, she really wanted to believe him. But he was a known rake. Seductive little speeches were no doubt second nature to a man like him. She couldn't let herself believe him, she just couldn't.

There was a short silence. His words hung in the air a moment then dissipated on the wind. "In any case," she said, gathering her scattered wits and feigning indignation, "it's not your business whether I choose to step outside, with whom, or why. You are not my guardian, or my brother—"

"God forbid."

She gave him a scathing look. "So I will thank you to stop interfering."

"You're very cross still for someone who only wanted a little fresh air. Aren't you breathing in plenty of it now?" He took a deep breath. "Can you smell that? It's rosemary, isn't it?"

The fact that there wasn't even a hint of rosemary in the air added to her annoyance. Lord Randall was playing with her. He took nothing seriously, the wretch.

"It wasn't just the fresh air, it was—" She broke off and, feeling her cheeks warming, looked away.

"What? What was this mysterious reason then, if it wasn't for air?"

Fighting her blush, desperately hoping he couldn't see it in the dim light of the garden, she didn't answer.

A soft breeze soughed through the garden, sending the lanterns swaying and shadows dancing. "Good God, you were going to let him kiss you, weren't you?"

"So what if I was?" she flashed. "It isn't a crime. I'm sure he wanted to, and I've never—" She broke off.

"You've never what? Been kissed? Is that it? Well, all I can say is that with that luscious mouth of yours, the men you've been meeting must be dreadful slow-tops."

"Is that so?" What did he mean, *luscious mouth*?

"Yes, and I consider myself the worst of them. Come along." He drew her into a shadowed alcove.

"What are you do—"

Before she could finish, he drew her into his arms. Clarissa knew she ought to resist, but somehow she couldn't.

"What do you think you're doing?" She was trying for sternness but it came out soft and a little bit breathless.

"Your first kiss shouldn't be with a clod like Clayborn."

Chapter Eight

He bent and kissed her, softly at first, just a bare brush of his lips across hers. Yet it somehow seemed to rob her of breath.

Was that it? It was nice, but—

He kissed her again, more deliberately now, his lips soft but his mouth firm, wonderfully firm and masculine. And at the same time soft.

After a moment he pulled back a little. She swallowed. So that was a kiss. It was lovely, but what should she do now? Thank him? She opened her mouth to thank him and oh— he was in her mouth and it was . . .

She couldn't think straight. His taste, his heat. Sensations, strange and entrancing, swirled and rippled through her. She clung to him, pressing herself against him, too dazed to do anything except to let him do whatever he wanted. And respond . . .

At some stage he released her mouth and leaned back, his arms still firm and strong around her. A good thing, too:

she could barely stand. Slowly, dizzily, her awareness trickled back. So *that* was a kiss. Oh my . . .

She was breathing heavily. So was he. Her hands were pressed against his chest. Was that his heart, beating under her palms?

She gazed up at him. He stared down at her, his eyes dark and unreadable in the shadows.

"Again," she breathed.

He gave a kind of moan and then his mouth was devouring her, possessing her, and she could only cling to him and try to ride the storm, the glorious storm.

"So! This is what you were up to, you villain!"

They eased apart. Lord Randall still held her, one arm around her waist, supporting her.

Mr. Clayborn continued, "I should call you out for besmirching an innocent girl. For sport—that's all she is to you, isn't she, Randall? Filthy rake that you are!"

Clarissa couldn't speak, she was still dazed by the glory of the kiss. She was distantly aware of Mr. Clayborn waiting for Lord Randall's response, but he was silent, still breathing heavily. As was she.

With a disgusted sound, Mr. Clayborn grabbed her arm and pulled her away.

She felt suddenly cold.

Lord Randall made no attempt to stop him. He was staring at her with the strangest expression on his face.

Mr. Clayborn started tugging her back toward the ballroom, saying, "Come along, Miss Studley, you're safe from this villain now. I have you."

Race sank numbly down onto the nearby bench. Well, he thought. Well . . .

She'd certainly taken him by surprise.

He had long admired her, had known he was attracted to her, and had been looking forward to kissing her—

especially seeing as it was her first kiss. He'd expected to enjoy it.

He hadn't expected that it would knock him endways.

He'd kissed dozens of women—possibly even a hundred. But nothing—nothing!—had prepared him for kissing Clarissa. That combination of innocence and passion, sweetness and heat . . . He'd had no idea.

The feel of her in his arms: It was all he could do to keep himself under some kind of control. His body had ached to claim her.

But though she'd been gloriously responsive, she wasn't yet ready for him. There was arousal, but also confusion—possibly doubt—in those beautiful clear eyes of hers. He had to win her trust before he could even dream of winning her heart.

But lord! That kiss had shaken him to his very bones.

He probably shouldn't have let her go off with Clayborn, but he was damned if he'd let her be squabbled over, like a bone between two dogs. And though it was clear that Clayborn was itching for a fight—and while Race would love to punch the man—him and his *we have an understanding*—one simply didn't knock down a former soldier wounded in service to his country.

Besides, it would distress Miss Studley.

Not that he believed for one minute that she had any kind of an understanding with Clayborn. No. She was a loyal little creature—loyal to the backbone—and had there been any hint of an understanding, he was sure she would have refused to go anywhere with him. And she certainly wouldn't have let him kiss her, let alone returned it with such entrancing enthusiasm.

But she hadn't refused, and she'd kissed him with such warmth, such eagerness, such unconscious sensuality—and oh, his heart rejoiced.

Rejoiced.

Race leaned back and took a deep breath of the cool

evening air. He wasn't used to all this . . . emotion. His life had been calm, relatively predictable, and so much easier, until that evening when Miss Studley had walked bravely across a ballroom in clear public support of her illegitimate sister—and the shackles had fallen from his eyes. And his heart.

He sat, staring unseeing at the fresh and lovely garden around him, aware of only one thing: his world had shifted.

As Mr. Clayborn pulled her along the shadowy paths of the garden, heading back toward the ballroom, Clarissa glanced back at Lord Randall. He was seated on the bench, still with that same strange expression on his face.

Didn't he care that Mr. Clayborn had insulted him?

Had he really kissed her just for sport? Probably, she thought with a sinking heart.

Did she care? She did, rather—but she knew she shouldn't. She'd always known he was a rake. Disappointment wrestled with exhilaration.

At least now she knew what it was like to be kissed, *really* kissed. Her mouth—her whole body—still tingled deliciously. The taste of him, the exciting dark masculine taste of him was seared into her very being. She would never forget it.

She'd finally been kissed, and oh, what a kiss. Kisses. She could never go back to the girl she'd been just an hour before. She felt like a caterpillar who, for a brief moment, had felt like a butterfly—beautiful and glamorous.

Still a little dazed, her entire awareness bound up in Lord Randall's kisses, she let herself be towed along by Mr. Clayborn.

Until she became aware of what he was saying.

"—as foolish as to go anywhere with that man. Letting yourself be enticed into a dark corner and used like a whore!"

It was cold water dashed in her face. "A *whore*?" She yanked herself free of the hand that was gripping her arm.

"*I* don't think that, of course," he said hastily. "But it's what people will say. Other people. Ignorant people. Gossips and troublemakers."

She eyed him levelly.

He continued, "You are too innocent to realize it, but Lord Randall is a notorious womanizer with no morals and no scruples. He's an immoral degenerate, not to be trusted with a decent, innocent g—"

She cut him off. "Lord Randall is my guardian's good friend." And she'd seen no sign of degeneracy in him. He'd been considerate and respectful of her. Of course, he probably shouldn't have kissed her but that was not entirely his fault. She'd cooperated. Fully. Invited it, almost.

He snorted. "Some friend, to lure his friend's innocent ward into the shadows and seduce—"

"There was no seduction."

"No, because I rescued you." He tried to recapture her hand.

She evaded it. "You didn't rescue me—"

"I did," he insisted. "What do you think would have happened if people had seen you letting him maul you like that?"

"He didn't mau—"

"You would have been ruined! Or worse, compromised and forced to marry him to save your reputation. No doubt that's what he was counting on, the villain."

She stepped back. "Don't be ridiculous. There was no attempt at seduction, no mauling and though it was perhaps not quite proper, we were very discreet. The place was secluded and quite private. As for his attempting to compromise me . . ." She shook her head. "It was just a kiss. And," she added defiantly, "I was quite willing."

He stared at her in outrage. "*Willing?* You were *willing*? Willing to let that reprobate . . . ?"

Clarissa inclined her head.

He stared at her for a long moment.

"Then in that case—" He grabbed her and mashed his mouth over hers. His fingers dug into her upper arms and her lips were ground unpleasantly against her teeth.

After a moment, he broke off, panting.

"I did not—" she began, but he pounced again, this time thrusting his tongue deep into her mouth.

Clarissa wondered briefly whether she should at least try to give him the benefit of the doubt. But it was unendurable. She tried to end it, tried to withdraw, but his grip on her tightened, his mouth and tongue kept mashing on her, and in the end she was forced to shove him away, hard.

He staggered back, wincing as he landed on his bad leg. He stared at her with an expression she was sure was furious, and wiped his mouth. A frisson of anxiety ran down her spine and she braced herself for some unpleasantness— or worse—but then his expression changed.

"Oh, forgive me, forgive me, my dear Miss Studley. I got carried away. My feelings for you simply overwhelmed me. I was outraged by the way that villain took advantage of your innocence, sullying your purity—and now, I have done the same. Can you ever find it in your heart to forgive a man driven to madness by your—"

She cut him off. "It's getting chilly. I wish to return to the ball." And she wanted a drink to wipe the taste of him from her mouth. She turned and marched toward the lights of the ballroom.

He hurried after her, babbling apologies and excuses, interrupted by small gasps each time he stepped on his bad leg.

Clarissa did not respond. She thought about the advice Mrs. Price-Jones had given her and Izzy when they first entered society: *You need to kiss a lot of frogs to find your prince.*

It had shocked her at the time—chaperones were not supposed to say such things—but now she knew: Lord Randall's kisses were . . . magical, but with his way of life, he could never be her prince.

And Mr. Clayborn, suitable though he was in so many ways . . . He was definitely a frog.

Anxious to leave Mr. Clayborn and his irritating, useless apologies behind she picked up her pace but then, the sound of his agonized efforts to keep up with her pricked at her conscience. She relented guiltily and slowed her pace.

She was angry with him for disappointing her, she realized. She'd been hoping his kiss would confirm that he was the man for her, and instead it had confirmed the very opposite. And his breathless torrent of apologies was just making her crosser—all that nonsense about her purity and innocence!

The moment they entered the ballroom, and he made it clear that he wished to continue the conversation, she cut him off, saying, "I'm terribly thirsty, Mr. Clayborn, could you fetch me a drink, please? Lemonade for preference."

He hesitated, then inclined his head in agreement. He was not the sort of man who footmen and waiters noticed, so after a frustrating few minutes trying to get their attention, he stumped off to fetch the drink himself.

Clarissa heaved a sigh of relief. She needed a few minutes alone to clarify the swirling chaos of her very mixed feelings. So much for experiencing her first kiss. In the last half hour she'd kissed two men—two!—and with very different results. It was terribly confusing.

Why, oh why couldn't Lord Randall have been the frog?

Y our little plot failed, didn't it?" a sardonic voice behind her said.

Clarissa turned in surprise and found a sharp-featured, fashionably dressed lady standing rather close. "Were you talking to me?" she said. The lady's face was familiar but she couldn't recall her name.

The lady didn't respond for a minute. Her gaze raked Clarissa slowly up and down, then she snorted contemptuously. "You haven't a hope, little miss butter-won't-melt. Race Randall isn't the sort who'd let himself be trapped by a dreary little dab like you. He has much better taste than that."

"I beg your pardon," Clarissa began. Lady Snape, that's who she was. Clarissa didn't like the woman's attitude or her tone, and the suggestion that she'd tried to entrap Lord Randall was positively insulting.

Lady Snape continued as if Clarissa hadn't spoken. "Going out into the night with one man and returning with another? Quite the little schemer, aren't you? You must be positively desperate."

"How da—"

The woman swept on. "You'd be better off hanging on to that angelic-looking cripple. You might get him to the altar if you try hard enough. Forget about Race Randall. He isn't the slightest bit serious—he couldn't be. He's the sort of man who's attracted only to the most beautiful women." She preened herself in a suggestive manner. "And I should know. We are intimate friends. In-tim-ate."

Clarissa had no idea what to say.

"A plain little dumpling like you?" Lady Snape's gaze raked her and she snorted again. "You realize you're making a complete fool of yourself, chasing after him as you are."

Clarissa had *not* been chasing after Lord Randall—quite the opposite. Izzy would have snapped back at this nasty creature with something clever and cutting, but Clarissa could never think quickly enough. And when she was angry and tried to be cutting, she invariably messed it up. But she had her own way of handling malicious creatures like this one.

"It's terribly sweet of you to worry about me," she said warmly, "but there's really no need at all."

Lady Snape started at her in blank surprise. "*Sweet?*" she repeated incredulously.

"Yes, indeed, very sweet and most kind of you," Clarissa cooed. "But fear not, I have no designs on Lord Randall, nor he on me. He is only taking care of me while my guardian is on his honeymoon. He's been rather like . . . an uncle to me."

The woman's mouth dropped open. "An *uncle*?"

"Yes. A kind and helpful uncle. Quite stuffy, really, but terribly well-meaning. There's nothing personal in it at all, so you see, you needn't worry that I'm stealing his attention away from you. Or even those beautiful ladies you mentioned that he prefers."

The woman's eyes narrowed.

"But thank you for your *very* kind concern, Lady Snake," Clarissa finished, "even though it was quite unnecessary."

There was a moment's silence, then, "Stupid, too. And the name is Snape, not Snake," the woman muttered, and swept away.

"Oh, I don't think so," Clarissa murmured as she watched her leave. She mightn't be quick with a sharp retort, like Izzy, but responding unexpectedly, meeting nastiness with apparently oblivious warmth disconcerted some people just as effectively.

The woman's darts couldn't hurt her—oh, they had, a little, but as long as the harpy didn't realize it, Clarissa felt she had come out of the encounter the victor.

Now, if only this evening could end. She went in search of Mrs. Price-Jones, planning to claim a headache and ask to leave early. It wasn't quite a lie. She was exhausted.

Race remained on the garden seat, sitting in the dark, his thoughts in a whirl. And the cause? Miss Clarissa Studley.

He hadn't really noticed her when he'd initially met her: she was just Leo's ward, a pleasant, somewhat shy young lady.

Her riding skills had impressed him first. Quiet, unassuming young ladies were generally, in Race's experience, cautious, often barely competent riders, hardly able to do much more than trot tolerably well in the park. But on horseback, Miss Clarissa was not merely capable, but quite dashing. The contrast between her modest and demure social demeanor and her prowess on horseback intrigued him.

Then, witnessing the incident at the Arden ball, where she had publicly stepped forward to defend her half sister— and hang the consequences!—he realized that she was courageous, and amazingly loyal to those she loved.

There was the public Miss Studley—quiet, shy, unassuming—and then there was the private Clarissa, still apparently quiet and shy—but don't ever mistake that for weakness, as some people did. She was full of surprises.

In the last few weeks, in Leo's absence, Race had been thrown more into her company than usual, and as he got to know her, the realization had grown on him that she was beautiful. Oh, it wasn't the obvious arrangement of features that passed for beauty in society—he was well used to society beauties demanding his attention.

Clarissa's was a more subtle beauty, something to do with the softness and purity of her skin, the clarity of those wide hazel eyes and the many expressions and thoughts reflected so candidly in them. There was a sweetness in her that was rare and precious—and he wasn't simply talking about her smile, or that luscious mouth—or that kiss! He shook his head in frustration.

No, no list of features could sum up Clarissa: she was more, so much more than the sum of her parts. He'd been too blind at first to realize it, but now that he truly saw her, he couldn't unsee it. She was beautiful. And warm and loving. And utterly desirable.

He wanted her, he was clear about that. But that one glorious kiss aside, she was proving damnably resistant to his charms.

* * *

D on't suppose you've made any morning calls on Lady
   Scattergood recently, have you?" Race asked his cousin
in what he hoped was a casual manner. He'd dropped in on
the off chance of catching up with his favorite relative. At least
that's what he told himself. They were taking tea together.

Maggie laughed. "Why? Have you developed a tendre
for the old lady? I do find her most entertaining."

Race arched a sardonic eyebrow.

Maggie laughed again and gave him a knowing look. "I
have, as a matter of fact. And in very interesting news, Miss
Studley's chaperone let slip to me that the angelic-looking
Mr. Clayborn is becoming most particular in his attentions.
Most particular. She seemed quite thrilled."

Race set his jaw. Clayborn? Surely she couldn't . . . She
wouldn't . . .

"She gave me to understand that she wouldn't be surprised
if there was an Interesting Announcement in the not-too-
distant future," Maggie continued. "Exciting, isn't it?"

Race said nothing. He hadn't believed in that "understanding" that Clayborn had claimed that time but what if
it hadn't been braggadocio? What if there was some kind of
an understanding and they were only waiting for Leo to
return from his honeymoon to announce it?

It was not to be thought of. But he wasn't going to sit
around and wait for it to happen. He had to act, quickly.

Several society events were being held this evening; a
card party, a *soirée musicale* and a small but very select
dinner at one of the foreign embassies—the Austrian one,
he thought. For some reason Race had received invitations
to all three. He had no doubt his cousin had as well.

"Do you and Oliver have any plans for this evening?" he
said nonchalantly, effecting a change of subject.

"Oh yes, definitely," Maggie said. "You know I like to
keep busy."

"I don't suppose you know . . ." He trailed off. His cousin's expression was that of a magpie spying a glittering treasure. "Oh, it doesn't matter."

"Oliver and I have dinner invitations from the Austrian embassy. You know how Oliver enjoys these political discussions, but if it's too dreary I've told him I'm leaving the moment the dinner is over and will go on to something else more interesting."

"Understandable." His cousin hadn't the faintest interest in politics.

Maggie cocked her head curiously. "Didn't you receive an invitation to it?"

"I did, yes. As well as several others." Lately, since the rumor had spread that he was now in the market for a bride, he'd been inundated with invitations. Curse it.

"And what are your plans?" Maggie asked. "Will you join us at the embassy?"

"No. My plans are undecided at the moment. I don't suppose you know anyone else who might be going?" He couldn't imagine Miss Studley would be invited, but it would narrow down the choices.

"Oh yes, several of Oliver's stodgy friends will be there." Maggie sipped her tea, nibbled on a piece of shortbread and after a few moments said airily, "Miss Studley told me she was planning to attend Lady Gastonbury's *soirée musicale* this evening."

"Indeed?" he said, affecting polite indifference.

His cousin laughed merrily. "You deceive no one with your disinterest, dearest cuz. I made sure I learned Miss Studley's plans for the next week. I knew you'd want to know. She's going to the soirée tonight, and then she'll attend the Peplowes' rout party, and on Wednesday she's going to Almack's—not that you'd be interested in that. I know how you feel about Almack's."

Race stood up. "Thank you for the tea, Maggie. It was very nice."

"Said the man who let his tea grow cold, untouched, and hasn't tasted a single crumb of Cook's delicious shortbread," his cousin said affably. She rose and patted his cheek. "Don't worry, I'll keep you informed of all her activities. We can't let the saintly wounded hero of Waterloo get the better of us, can we?"

Race had nothing to say to that. He didn't want his gossipy cousin to be involved in his courtship at all, but since he could not call on Miss Studley himself—curse it!—he had no choice. But it went very much against the grain. He'd always managed his own affairs in private.

He kissed his cousin's cheek and took his leave of her.

Old Lady Gastonbury's *soirées musicale* were strangely popular with the ton, though why, Race couldn't understand. They were primarily a venue for showing off the talents of her beloved granddaughter. He'd never met Cicely or heard her sing, but rumor held her to be a pleasant girl who couldn't carry a tune to save her life. Apparently neither she nor her grandmother was aware of it.

But Lady Gastonbury was well-liked, and her soirées were famous for the lavish suppers that followed the performances. He supposed that might explain it, though hunger wasn't generally a feature of society life.

Race arrived a little late—he didn't want to appear too eager. As it was, Lady Gastonbury greeted him effusively and his entrance caused a ripple of speculation among the waiting audience. He gritted his teeth. He was prepared for his ears to be tortured in the name of love, but he hated the attention he drew.

He stood in the doorway and surveyed the room. Immediately half a dozen women—both matchmaking mamas and married women seeking dalliance—waved to him, and there was a general shifting of seats as they made room for him to sit.

Miss Studley was sitting on the far side of the room, and luck was with him: there was a spare seat between her and her chaperone. The chaperone was in conversation with another lady. Miss Studley didn't seem to have noticed him yet—she was looking straight ahead of her—but as he watched, her color heightened. She knew.

He made his way between rows of chairs, heading toward her, nodding to various people who greeted him along the way, but when he finally reached Miss Studley, dammit if that spare seat wasn't taken.

He glared at the white-haired elderly dandy who'd stolen his place. The old fellow beamed up at him. "How d'ye do, young Randall? Come to enjoy some fine music, eh? Miss Cicely's a marvel, don'cha think?" He glanced at Miss Studley sitting demurely beside him, and added, "I expect you'd prefer to be sittin' where I am, but when this kind lady invited me to sit with her, well, what sort of a slow-top would refuse, eh? A thorn between two roses, eh? Delighted to be here." He chuckled.

She *invited* him?

Miss Studley smiled politely, but failed to meet Race's eye.

Race inclined his head. "Good evening, Sir Oswald, Miss Studley, Mrs. Price-Jones."

Miss Studley murmured a greeting, but still didn't meet his eyes.

Old Sir Oswald Merridew kept rabbiting on about something, but Race paid him a bare minimum of attention. Why wouldn't she look at him? Was she embarrassed about the kiss they'd shared? Surely not.

But if it had rocked him to his foundations, maybe it had the same effect on her. Had it alarmed her, perhaps? Her first taste of passion.

Or was she really planning to marry Clayborn as the fellow had claimed?

The thought filled his veins with ice. But why else would she refuse to look at him? And invite some jolly old buffer to sit beside her when she must have known he was here and would wish to sit with her.

Lady Gastonbury tinkled a little bell and a hush fell over the audience. By now there were only a few chairs left on the other side of the room. Race took himself to the end of Miss Studley's row and propped himself against the wall, where he could watch her, as well as the performances.

Tonight she was wearing a dress of the palest green, and somehow it made her eyes look almost green. So changeable they were, he'd never get tired of gazing into them.

She was well aware of him, he decided. The music had started—not Cicely yet, some soprano he didn't know; quite good. Miss Studley gave her entire attention to the performance. Her blush had faded a little but it was still there, and she kept darting quick, sideways glances at him and pursing her lips a little.

It was adorable.

She couldn't possibly be thinking of marrying that wretched Clayborn.

The soprano finished her piece, and everyone applauded, then Cicely stepped onto the small stage. Race braced himself—he hadn't ever been to one of these events before, but Cicely's fame had gone before her.

The pianist played the opening bars and Cicely opened her mouth and the noise that came out . . . Lord, but the suppers had better be worth it. He glanced at Miss Studley and almost laughed out loud at the politely smiling rigidity of her expression. Her ears were being lacerated, too.

The song came to an end and she applauded enthusiastically. Race did, too, wondering how many of those clapping were clapping in relief.

But there was more to come. Next she murdered a song from Mozart's *Così fan tutte*, then a Scottish ballad, then it was back to Mozart, who would surely be spinning in his grave.

The concert was endless. Race endured it. What animal was it that could close its ears? Otters? Seals? Whichever it was, he devoutly wished he could close his against the assault they were experiencing.

Finally, blessedly, Miss Cicely finished, and supper was announced. Miss Studley rose, murmured something to her chaperone and they both hurried from the room.

Call of nature, he decided, and sauntered out to the supper room to await her return. Ten minutes passed, then another ten. Where was she? Was she ill?

He waited another few minutes and then took himself to the hall outside the ladies' retiring room. An elderly lady he didn't know was about to enter. "Could you tell me if my er, cousin is in there, please?" he asked her. "Her hair is a soft brown and she's wearing a pale green dress."

A few minutes later the old lady came out. "Nobody else in there at all," she said. "She'll be in the supper room. The Gastonbury suppers are famous. Nobody wants to miss them."

But she wasn't in the supper room at all. She'd left. Understandable—her ears were probably bleeding. But she knew he was here and that he clearly wanted to talk to her. But apart from the murmured greeting when he first arrived, she hadn't spoken a word to him.

She was avoiding him. Why?

"Coming back in, young Randall?" Sir Oswald clapped him on the back. "You'll get a seat this time. Smaller audience in the second half—a lot leave after the supper. Don't understand it, m'self."

There was more alleged music to come? Race was appalled. Murmuring some excuse, he took his leave from Sir Oswald, thanked Lady Gastonbury and Cicely, lied in his teeth about how delightful the evening had been, and how sorry he was that he was expected elsewhere, and fled.

* * *

Would you like me or Joan to make you a nice, soothing tisane, miss?" Betty said in a solicitous voice as she lifted Clarissa's dress carefully over her head.

"No thank you," Clarissa said. It wasn't a soothing tisane she needed, it was a purge, a Lord Randall purge.

"Well, if you're sure, miss. It's no trouble." Betty was helping Clarissa get ready for bed, and at the same time issuing a low-voiced series of instructions to the maid-in-training, Joan, explaining how to wash miss's good silk stockings, clean her shoes and put away her lovely dress—wrapping it in tissue just so, to prevent it creasing. Secrets of a lady's maid.

"Thank you, but no, I just need to sleep." She didn't deserve Betty's concern. She was becoming a liar. This was the second time in a week she'd used an imaginary headache as an excuse to leave a function early. But what else could she do?

The way Lord Randall had lounged against the wall, arms crossed, pretending to listen to poor Cicely's singing, when all the time he was watching Clarissa like a hawk—she could *feel* his gaze resting on her like a warm caress. It made her ridiculously self-conscious. She was sure everyone must have noticed how she was blushing.

Betty finished undoing her corset and set it aside, leaving Clarissa in her chemise. Her nightgown lay ready, draped across the end of the bed.

"Shall I—" Betty began.

"No, that will be all, thank you, Betty—and Joan." She smiled at the new girl. "I want to wash first. I won't need you again tonight—thank you for waiting up."

"You'll need hot water then," Betty said. "Joan—"

"No, no, cold will do very well, thank you. Good night." Cold water was exactly what she needed, in more ways than one.

The maids left and Clarissa washed, using the large ewer of cold water on the marble-topped side table.

She had to find some way of squashing these inappropriate and unwelcome feelings she had for him. She should never have allowed that kiss, that magical, intoxicating, deeply disturbing kiss. She couldn't get it out of her mind.

She smoothed the cool face flannel over her hot cheeks.

What was he trying to do? He never attended things like musical evenings, though people had hinted that he often attended the opera. Not that she ever asked about him, but he was a common subject of gossip among some of the ladies she was acquainted with, and the ladies she'd overheard weren't usually talking directly to her.

The consensus seemed to be that it wasn't the music that attracted him to the opera, so much as the opera dancers. It's what attracted most men, according to the gossips. Opera dancers, Clarissa gathered, reading between the lines, were attractive young women of loose morals. Very loose morals.

She was inclined to believe it. Nobody who loved music would attend Lady Gastonbury's soirées unless they were deaf, fond of the old lady and Cicely, or desperate for a good supper, and in Lord Randall's case she doubted any of those applied.

He must have come because of her—but how did he know she was planning to attend?

She climbed into bed and pulled the covers up.

His cousin. Of course. She had mentioned her intention to Maggie the other day, and Maggie had teased her, saying that her ears would regret it.

He was spying on her, and his cousin was helping him.

It was a very lowering reflection. She punched her pillow into shape and lay down. She'd thought she and Maggie were becoming friends. How disheartening to realize it wasn't true friendship at all, that the lively lady had an underlying intention: to keep Lord Randall informed.

It was more than disheartening, it was infuriating. Leo

must have set Lord Randall to watch over her. He could deny it all he liked: she knew better now.

And in the process, he'd decided to entertain himself by teasing her, and flirting. It was what he was renowned for.

The memory of the way he'd leaned against the wall, watching her, that . . . that look in his eye, as if he and she shared a secret—she could feel herself blushing even now.

She sat up and punched the pillow again. This ridiculous *tendre* she had for a completely unsuitable man—she had to cure herself of it. Somehow. And with that resolution in her head she leaned over, blew out the candle by her bedside and lay staring into the dark. Willing herself to sleep to—what was it?—"knit up the ravelled sleave of care," as Shakespeare put it.

But when sleep finally came—and it didn't come easily—she dreamed of a pair of laughing gray eyes and a tall, lanky and infuriatingly attractive man.

The morning after the *soirée unmusicale* dawned clear and fine, so Race sent a note around to his cousin, asking her to invite Miss Studley to go for a ride. He had to see her, had to discover what she was feeling. Why had she avoided him last night? Was she embarrassed? Did she regret their kiss? Had he upset her in some way?

Half an hour later his cousin responded, passing on Miss Studley's regrets but she was not free to go riding today. "Never mind," Maggie had added. "There's always the Peplowe rout party tonight."

Very well then. The rout party it would be.

Chapter Nine

~❧~

"More flowers from that Mr. Clayborn," intoned Lady
Scattergood's butler, Treadwell, in a funereal voice.
"The biggest bunch yet. He's waiting in the hall." He stood
in the doorway of the back sitting room, gloomily clutching
a large bouquet of hothouse flowers—orchids and lilies and
other rare and expensive flowers.

"Wretched man!" Lady Scattergood exclaimed.

"That's the third bunch in three days," Mrs. Price-Jones
exclaimed delightedly. "And these are even more expensive. The man is wonderfully keen, isn't he?" She beamed
at Clarissa.

"Please inform Mr. Clayborn that I am not at home,"
Clarissa told the butler. She didn't want him to be wonderfully keen, either. She just wished he would go away.

"Oh, but you must speak to him," Mrs. Price-Jones said.
"I shouldn't spoil the surprise, but I believe that young man—
that very smitten young man—has Something of Significance to say to you." She winked.

Clarissa sighed. She knew exactly what Mr. Clayborn was going to say. He'd made it more than clear. Having "sullied her innocence" by allowing his passion for her to carry him away, he was willing, nay, eager to marry her.

He had called, and all but proposed, the day after the ball. She'd felt awkward and embarrassed receiving him—that kiss had clarified all her feelings about him—and she'd done her best to discourage him gently and steer him off the subject of marriage. It wasn't his fault that he turned out to be a frog, and not a prince, poor man.

She thought she'd made her lack of interest clear, but he'd returned the following day with an even larger bouquet—larkspurs, lilies, carnations, stock and roses—and an even more determined smile. But after handing the flowers to her and briefly renewing his offer to marry her—which she'd refused, quite firmly—he'd asked to speak in private to Mrs. Price-Jones. And after that he had taken himself off, which was a relief.

But now he was back—again.

"I don't want to speak to him," Clarissa repeated.

"Quite right," Lady Scattergood said. "Make the fellow work to win you. I made Scattergood ask me a dozen times before I accepted him."

"I don't want him to win me," Clarissa said. "I don't want to see him at all." Ever. It wasn't just the kiss that had turned her off him, it was his persistence in believing—and saying repeatedly—that he'd somehow besmirched her innocence.

But he hadn't: it was just a kiss, and not a very nice one. The worst thing, though, was his attitude to her. It was as if, having kissed her, he now felt he owned her. And had no need to take any notice of what she said. It was infuriating.

Even if he'd never kissed her, the attitudes he'd revealed since would insure she could have no interest in him as a potential husband. His indifference to her repeated responses showed he had no respect for her views, and one thing Clarissa was adamant that she wanted in a marriage was respect. Love was a dream, but respect was a requirement.

"I think you must at least see him," Mrs. Price-Jones said. "When he spoke to me yesterday he explained how dreadful he felt, letting his feelings get the better of him. He feared he had deeply shocked you in your innocence, and he wanted my advice."

The repeated references to her innocence were exasperating. "He didn't shock me. I just don't want to see him."

"Nevertheless, I think you must allow him to apologize."

"He has, repeatedly."

There was a short silence.

"What shall I do then?" Treadwell asked.

"Put the wretched things in a vase, of course," Lady Scattergood snapped. "And keep them out of my sight. I don't know why people send flowers—all they do is die, and who wants to sit around all day watching dying vegetation?"

"I meant," Treadwell said with dignity, "what shall I do with the young gentleman?"

Mrs. Price-Jones leaned forward and put a hand on Clarissa's arm. "Talk to him, my dear. You don't have to commit yourself. I explained to him yesterday that you need your guardian's permission to marry. He told me how he felt he'd compromised you and felt it incumbent on him to offer—"

"*Compromised?*" Lady Scattergood sat up. "Compromised her, did he? The scoundrel! The villain! Toss him out in the street, Treadwell!"

"He didn't compromise me in the least," Clarissa hastily assured the old lady. "Mr. Clayborn is being overly sensitive." Ridiculously so.

Lady Scattergood raised her lorgnette and scrutinized Clarissa's face. "Is that true, gel?"

"Absolutely." If anyone's kiss could be said to be compromising it was Lord Randall's, but Clarissa was determined to keep that a secret.

"Hmph, well, all right then. I suppose it wouldn't do any

harm to talk to him. Put him in the front drawing room, Treadwell—but keep an eye on the fellow."

"But I—" Clarissa began.

The old lady waved her objections aside. "He can't propose without Leo's permission, so talk to the fellow, tell him to stop filling my house with dying flowers, and find out what his travel arrangements are."

"Travel arrangements?" Clarissa repeated, bewildered.

"Of course. How many times do I have to tell you young gels that the secret of a successful marriage is for the husband to head off to the other side of the world shortly after the wedding? Traveling and sending you back delightful gifts from time to time as a token of his regard." She waved vaguely at the clutter of exotic ornaments—valuable and not so valuable—that crammed every surface of the room. "As my dear Scattergood did for the twenty years of our marriage." She gave a fond glance at the cloisonné urn that held her husband's ashes. "So find out what young Claymore's travel plans are."

"Clayborn," Clarissa corrected her halfheartedly.

"Yes, him. And if he has none, make sure you plant the notion in his mind. Now, run along."

"Miss Studley!" As Clarissa entered the front drawing room Mr. Clayborn jumped to his feet, sending his cane flying. "Dear Miss Studley, you have consented to see me." He beamed at her. "Dare I say you have forgiven me my impetuosity?"

"Mr. Clayborn." She picked up his cane and handed it back to him. "Please be seated."

His face fell. "So cold. You haven't forgiven me?"

Clarissa repressed a sigh. "As I have said previously— several times—there is nothing to forgive. Now, I believe you have something you wish to say to me?"

To her horror, Mr. Clayborn clutched his cane tightly in

one hand, and with a groan, attempted to go down onto one knee.

Clarissa leapt to her feet. "Please, I beg of you, stop this at once! There is no need for you to kneel."

He struggled back up. "So kind, so considerate." He took a step toward her. "My dear Miss Studley, you know of my feelings toward you, which grow more powerful each time I am allowed into your charming company. Would you do me the honor—"

"Mr. Clayborn, stop right there," Clarissa said firmly. "I know what you are going to ask, but my answer is still no."

"I know, you must get permission from your guardian. But—"

"This has nothing to do with my guardian. I've already indicated to you—very clearly, I think—that though I hold you in . . . esteem, there is no chance, absolutely no chance of—"

Clayborn reeled back. "Oh, do not say it, you cannot be so cruel!"

Cruel? Clarissa frowned. "I am sorry if you think so, nevertheless as I have told you before, flattering as your offer may be, I will not marry you."

He clapped a hand over his heart. "You have led me on, cruel lady, broken my heart."

She rang the bell for Treadwell, who, having been listening at the door, appeared instantly. "Goodbye, Mr. Clayborn."

"No, no, you cannot send me away like that. Oh, heartless, callous creature."

"Treadwell, please show Mr. Clayborn out."

"Yes, miss." Treadwell bowed, handed Mr. Clayborn his hat, and when the man didn't move, slipped a hand under his elbow and escorted him to the door.

"Oh, cruel, Miss Studley—it's because I'm not a whole man, isn't it? You are heartless, heartless! I fought for my country and yet you spurn me for my . . ." The door shut behind him and his words died away.

Clarissa sank back onto her chair, shaken and shaking. She'd remained firm, at least, but Clayborn's emotional response had distressed her. Had she led him on? She didn't think so. She'd sat out a few dances with him, and allowed him one kiss, that was all. And her refusal certainly had nothing to do with his war injury—in fact she'd honored him for that.

She heard the front door close and heaved a sigh of relief. She would ask Treadwell not to admit him again.

His reaction was upsetting, but the more his accusations echoed in her mind, the more they angered her. She might have considered him as a suitor at the start—she'd considered several men—but at no stage had she ever given him reason to expect that she would welcome him as a husband. One kiss did not amount to an agreement to marry. Especially when she'd made it clear she did not.

She rose to her feet. She couldn't bear to go back into Lady Scattergood's sitting room and face the questions that would await her there. She felt shattered after Mr. Clayborn's accusations, and needed to escape for a short while. Calm down. She slipped out the back door and took herself out into the garden. Being in the serene, lovely garden always made her feel better.

She paced restlessly along one of the garden walks, too wound up to sit. Had she led Mr. Clayborn on? Yes, she had allowed that kiss—not that he'd given her much choice at the time. But both Mrs. Price-Jones and Lady Tarrant had implied, each in her own way, that a discreet kiss or two was acceptable, as long as nobody found out.

No, Mr. Clayborn was being unreasonable and melodramatic. In fact, now she came to reflect on it, she rather doubted he loved her at all. He seemed more angry than hurt.

It was all most disheartening. She'd let two men kiss her and neither one loved her. One was a rake, who might kiss like a dream, but presumably kissed whomever he fancied whenever he liked, and the other was . . . a puzzle.

Why was Mr. Clayborn so angry at her rejection? He barely knew her. And as his great-aunt's sole heir, it wasn't as if he needed Clarissa's fortune, so why the fuss? And she was sure he didn't love her.

Papa had been a very bad loser. She supposed some men didn't take kindly to rejection.

Feeling a little calmer, if no closer to understanding the state of her emotions, she was heading for her favorite seat in the rose arbor when she spotted Zoë seated cross-legged on the lawn. She was all alone, bent over something. Clarissa hadn't given a thought to where her sister might be. She'd just been relieved that Zoë hadn't been witness to the discussion with Lady Scattergood and Mrs. Price-Jones about Mr. Clayborn.

The poor girl was probably bored. She still refused to go anywhere with Clarissa, not even to go shopping. She refused to see people who made morning calls, and spent all day either inside Lady Scattergood's, or in the garden, or visiting Lady Tarrant and the little girls, and Lucy, with whom she'd struck up an instant friendship.

As she drew closer, she realized Zoë's pencil was flying over a white pad. "Good morning, Zoë," she said as she approached. "Isn't this weather glorious? Outside is the best place to be."

Zoë jumped and twisted around, clutching the pad protectively to her chest. "Oh, it's you. I thought it might be that awful Milly. She's forever sneaking up on me trying to see what I'm doing. A right nosy pest, she is."

"I think she's just lonely," Clarissa said. "She doesn't seem to have many friends."

Zoë pulled a face. "Funny way to make friends, sneaking up and spying on people. Anyway, I just talk to her nonstop in French. That soon gets rid of her." She grinned.

Clarissa glanced at the pad Zoë was holding, and the girl flushed and pressed it against her chest. "It's just an old sketch pad I found lying around—nobody was using it, honest, Clarissa. The top pages were all yellowed and grubby. I'm sorry if I did wrong." She jumped to her feet, regarding Clarissa with a guilty expression. "Is the old lady looking for me? I s'pose she wants me to read to her again."

With a pang of dismay, Clarissa realized that Zoë still didn't feel as though this was her home.

"No, not at all. You're free to do whatever you like. And don't worry about taking the pad—you're welcome to it." She smiled. "Now, come and show me what you've been drawing."

Zoë hesitated.

"You don't have to if you don't want to, of course," Clarissa assured her. "I'm just interested, that's all. I remember the clever sketch you did of that woman at the orphan asylum. I can't draw to save myself, so I'm always impressed when others can."

"All right." Zoë was still obviously a bit reluctant but she allowed Clarissa to link arms with her and lead her to the seat in the rose arbor. They sat and Zoë handed the sketch pad to Clarissa.

Clarissa turned the pages slowly. There were dozens of drawings, some quick sketches, conveying their subjects vividly in a handful of lines; others were beautifully detailed. There were delicate drawings of some of the plants and flowers in the garden, and one of a spider in extraordinary detail.

There were lively portraits of Lady Tarrant's little girls—Debo with her cat, Mittens, slung around her neck—several drawing of Lady Tarrant, of Lucy, of Lady Scattergood, one with her beloved dogs, and even some individual drawings of the dogs that were not only recognizable but through some magic of her pencil conveyed their personalities as well. There were also drawings of Betty and Joan, the maidservants, and of Jeremiah, the young footman who tended the dogs. And there was one positively wicked caricature of Treadwell that made Clarissa laugh out loud.

There were also quite a few sketches of Clarissa; she wasn't sure what to think about those. She looked almost . . . not pretty, obviously—as Papa used to say, you couldn't make a silk purse from a sow's ear—but . . . something.

"Zoë, these are good—very, very good," Clarissa said slowly, mentally kicking herself for forgetting she'd decided to purchase art supplies for Zoë.

Zoë hunched an awkward shoulder. "They're all right," she muttered. "I'm still learning."

"No, they're much better than all right. You have real talent." She gave Zoë a quick, one-armed hug. "You should see the dreadful watercolors I tried to paint when I was a girl—truly ghastly. And Izzy's weren't much better." She laughed. "Well, you can't see them: we had to burn the evidence." She handed the sketchbook back.

Her sister should have an art tutor. The poor girl had been laboring through her reading and writing lessons, and she'd been very patient about having her accent and grammar endlessly corrected. Painting and drawing were things she'd actually enjoy. In the meantime Clarissa would purchase drawing and painting materials for her.

She rose to her feet, feeling much refreshed. All thoughts of Mr. Clayborn had been purged by the combination of the beauty and freshness of the garden and excitement over her new plans for her talented little sister.

"Come along. I want a cup of tea, and Cook was baking orange biscuits earlier—a recipe from Alfonso, my brother-in-law's cook—and the smell was heavenly. They should be out of the oven by now."

"Never had orange biscuits," Zoë said. "Ain't never tasted an orange, for that matter."

"Well, we'll have to remedy that, but first a cup of tea and some biscuits. They're made with ground almonds, and oranges of course, and are light and chewy and utterly delicious. Come along, you'll love them." Arm in arm the two sisters headed for the house.

* * *

Lord and Lady Peplowe were popular hosts and their rout party was the kind of fashionable squeeze that insured it was declared a rousing success. Race could have done with a little less attention—the matchmaking mamas were out in force.

Of course they were: he'd forgotten that Penny, the Peplowes' youngest daughter, was still unmarried, and the party was well seeded with eligible young men.

He'd arrived a little late, as was his habit. Not that he often attended this kind of event, but he supposed when a man was courting a young lady it was a necessity.

He grimaced. Courting. He was actually courting. And the whole world seemed to know it, though not whom he was courting, thank God.

He spotted Clarissa, dancing a country dance with some young blade. She was wearing a soft cream and apricot dress that flowed with every movement, caressing her luscious curves in a way that made his mouth dry.

He waited until the dance was over and when the young sprig went off to fetch her a drink, he stepped in. "You are looking lovely, as usual, Miss Studley. That color really suits you and the cut is masterful."

She pursed her lips, looking slightly irritated instead of flattered. What had he said?

He bowed slightly. "May I have the next dance?"

She hesitated, then glanced around as if to check who was standing close by. Then she took a small step toward him. Her skin glowed pure and pearly with a faint flush. He could smell her perfume, a delicate rose scent that was unique to her. It was all he could do not to gather her into his arms.

She raised herself on tiptoe and murmured in a soft voice, "You don't need to dance with me at all, Lord Randall. There are plenty of gentlemen here who don't regard a dance with me as an obligation. But I thank you for your dutiful attention." And with that she turned and hurried away, leaving Race trying not to gape after her.

A dance with her an *obligation*? And *dutiful attention*? What the hell did she mean by that? A dance with her was a damned privilege, not any kind of obligation.

He blinked, shocked by her gentle, but firm refusal. He'd never received a knock-back in his life. In fact it was generally women who made the first move, making it clear his attentions would be welcome—more than welcome.

Had he lost his charm? Had the ease with which he usually attracted women made him lazy? Was he losing his touch? Becoming arrogant? And complacent?

Or was it a tactic on her part? He had to know.

Weaving through the crowd, he found her again and touched her on the elbow. She turned. "I *enjoy* dancing with you, Miss Studley," he told her. "It's not an obligation. Or a blasted 'dutiful attention,' whatever than means."

She glanced around self-consciously. "Please lower your voice. People are looking."

"To hell with people," he said, but he lowered his voice. "I want an explanation."

She looked at him for a moment, then shrugged. "I'm saying that you need not worry about me. I quite understand that you feel an obligation to look out for me on Leo's behalf, but I really, truly don't need it."

"But—"

"And I would be obliged if you ceased bothering me."

"*Bothering* you?" He was stunned.

"Yes. And spying on me. Now good evening." She moved off once more, and soon disappeared into the throng.

Bothering her. Spying on her? It was like a slap in the face.

He wasn't bothering her—he was *courting* her. As for spying—he had no idea where that came from.

Did she have no idea of his intentions? He thought all women understood when a man was interested. He was sure he'd made it clear. She must understand.

So . . . what was it? Could it be that she wasn't attracted to him? And he'd somehow missed all the signs?

The idea appalled him. He'd never forced his attentions on an unwilling or an uninterested woman in his life.

He thought back to that kiss, the way she'd pressed her body against him, the way she'd eagerly returned his caresses. No, she was definitely attracted to him, just as he was to her. Then what was going on? Had someone said something to her to put her off him? But who? And what?

A shocking thought froze him. Had she promised herself to that blasted Clayborn already? If that were the case, she would definitely repudiate Race's attentions, loyal creature that she was. Dammit, he had to find out. He needed to talk to her, privately, away from this crowd.

"Oh, how the mighty have fallen," a sardonic female voice at his elbow said. "That I have lived to see the irresistible Lord Randall given his congé—in no uncertain terms—by a plain little dab of a girl with neither looks nor charm to speak of."

He turned. "Lady Snape," he said coldly. He'd never liked the woman, and these days she hated him. It was a case of Hell having no fury . . .

She laughed. "I heard every word she said. It was glorious."

"Indeed," he said in an icy voice.

"You haven't a hope, you know. She told me the other evening that she regarded you as an uncle—a *benevolent* uncle." She laughed again and turned away, still laughing as she threaded her way like a serpent through the crowd.

An uncle?

He glanced across to where Miss Studley was chatting and laughing with Penny Peplowe and her mother. Protection, he realized. From him?

She'd accused him of *bothering* her. And *spying*. And according to Lady Snape, she thought of him as an uncle. An *uncle*!

He needed to clear that up, and the sooner the better. But he wouldn't approach her again this evening. She'd made herself clear—for tonight, at least. And he needed to get away from the press of over-scented humanity, the sharply speculating eyes and the gossiping tongues.

He needed to go where nobody cared what his matrimonial intentions might or might not be, somewhere congenial. He headed for his club.

Thank goodness. He was leaving. Clarissa hoped she looked serene. Her insides were like jelly, and her hands were still shaking. Thank goodness for evening gloves. She smiled and nodded at something Penny Peplowe was saying, oblivious of whatever it was—some amusing story.

The short exchange with Lord Randall had completely shaken her. It had taken every bit of resolution she had to confront him and ask him not to keep following her around, tell him that Leo had nothing to worry about.

Of course she hadn't been able to explain the real truth of the matter, that his mere presence unsettled her. It was hard enough to battle her inappropriate attraction to him without giving him any inkling of it.

Fatal to let a rake see that little weakness.

And she'd managed—she'd told him, clearly and to his face, that she didn't need him watching over her on Leo's behalf.

And then, look what he did! He'd walked straight off and a minute later was in close conversation with that horrid Lady Snake who had her hand on his arm and was cooing up at him in the vilest seductive manner.

Men. You couldn't trust them as far as you could throw them!

* * *

The pleasantly familiar atmosphere of Race's club surrounded him as he entered, a mélange of fragrances—old leather, woodsmoke, tobacco, freshly ironed newspapers, port, wine and brandy. It was a scent that spelled ease and comfort to masculine nostrils, and was very welcome to his bruised spirit.

Upstairs he found a dim sitting room lit by a glowing fire, and containing half a dozen old gentlemen snoozing comfortably beneath their papers, a couple playing cards and a few sole drinkers brooding silently into their glasses. One of the brooders was an old friend from his schooldays, Barney Temple. He was slouched bonelessly in a red leather armchair.

"Castaway, are you, Temp?" said Race, sitting in the next chair.

"Devil a bit," Barney said gloomily, and lifted his glass in a silent toast. "But I'll get there. What brings you here, Race?"

"This and that. You?"

Barney gestured. "Sanctuary. The mater can't get to me here."

"Like that, is it?" Barney's mother was forever coming up with schemes to marry off her marriage-shy son.

Race ordered a cognac and the two men drank in companionable silence for a while, each one brooding on his own particular problems.

Race pondered the contradictory behavior of Miss Studley, but could make no sense of it. He swirled his glass, eyeing the fire through it. He might as well be shredding one of those blasted daisies with she-loves-me, she-loves-me-not for all it helped.

He felt sure that she liked him, and that she was attracted to him. But was that enough for marriage?

"If you were a woman, Temp, would you want to marry me?"

Barney glanced at him sharply, then leaned away a little. "Sorry, not that way inclined, old thing."

"Not that, you fool. I said if you were a woman."

"Oh, a *woman*." Barney frowned in concentration. "Don't think I've ever considered it. Why would I? I *like* being a man. If I were a woman . . . Lord, I couldn't stand it. All those frills and furbelows, corsets, chaperones dogging your every footstep, can't put a foot wrong without some old busybody pointing the finger and gossiping and—don't shake your head at me—m'sisters had a devilish time of things before they were married."

He took a deep draft of brandy and continued, warming to his theme, "And then there's all the things I wouldn't be able to do: drinking blue ruin with a few pals at Jackson's after an invigoratin' bout or two in the ring and— Lord! I just realized. No opera dancers or anything of that sort! Dammit, Race, you can't ask it of me."

"I'm not, you drunken sot. I was merely asking you if you were a woman, would you consider marriage to me as a desirable prospect."

Barney gazed owlishly at him for a long moment. "A desirable prospect, you say?"

"Yes."

"Depends."

"On what?"

"On the gal, of course. If she wants a title, a fortune and a complaisant husband, then you won't have any trouble—"

"Not that sort," Race said. He was only too well acquainted with that kind of woman. And he wouldn't be complaisant in the way Barney was suggesting, either.

"Oh, you mean the romantic type?" Barney shook his head. "Can't see you married to that sort. No, steer clear of romantic misses, I say. They cling, they sigh, they weep at you, and expect you to dance attendance on them at deadly dull events. *Almack's*," he said in a tone of horror. "And," he added, shaking his finger at Race, "they'll expect you to give up opera dancers! Well, I ask you—is that reasonable? No indeed. Race, my old friend, you stay well away from romantic chits, and avoid parson's mousetrap while you can!"

"Do I understand from that rant that your mother is once more pressuring you to marry?"

Barney groaned. "Been avoiding her for weeks. She has some filly in mind. Some 'suitable' chit she met somewhere or other. Can you imagine me with someone 'suitable'?"

"Not really."

"Me, neither." Barney drained his glass, signaled for another and once the waiter had delivered it, he sat back and smiled muzzily at Race. "This is nice, ain't it? Exchangin' views, givin' advice. Not many people ask me for advice."

"I can't imagine why," Race said dryly. Barney was a good fellow, but deep he was not.

But in his rambling discourse his friend just might have hit on something. Race didn't keep any opera dancers, but his rakish reputation might well be a stumbling block to an idealistic and romantic young woman.

Ironic when he thought about how it had come about . . .

But the conversation, ridiculous as it was, had given him an idea. She and her sister had come to London just a short time ago. No doubt they'd barely tasted all the delights the metropolis had to offer. They had thoroughly enjoyed the outing he'd arranged to Astley's Amphitheatre. Barney had given him another idea.

The next time he saw Miss Studley, Race knew just what to do. "Have you been to the opera lately, Miss Studley?"

She turned to him swiftly. "I beg your pardon."

"The opera. Covent Garden. Mozart's *Marriage of Figaro.* I've heard it's quite delightful."

"I'm sure it is," she said coolly. She seemed oddly prickly.

"I think you'd enjoy it. How about I form a party with

my cousin Maggie and her husband, yourself and Mrs. Price-Jones, and perhaps—"

"No thank you," she said crisply, and sailed away. Actually, *stalked* away was more the word. The gait of a woman in a bit of a huff. What on earth had he said to offend her now?

He went back over the conversation in his mind. Perfectly innocuous. Quite pleasant, actually. An invitation to a pleasant night out.

Perhaps she didn't like music. She did, after all, regularly attend Lady Gastonbury's *soirées musicale*.

Zoë came skipping down the stairs. It was a beautiful day and she planned to visit Lady Tarrant and the children and, most especially, to talk to Lucy about art. It was such a joy to have someone to talk to who really understood, and would happily discuss things like perspective and angles and the light and, oh, all the things that she longed to understand more about. She hadn't heard such matters discussed since Maman died.

And the best thing about visiting Lucy? They talked entirely in French. It was almost like having Maman back. Almost . . .

She made for Lady Scattergood's favorite sitting room first, to ask the old lady's permission, and to check that she didn't want Zoë for anything.

The door was ajar, and she could hear Lady Scattergood talking to Mrs. Price-Jones. Zoë raised her hand to knock before entering when she heard a snatch of conversation that made her freeze.

"Yes, but it was one thing to pass Izzy off as legitimate: it's quite a different case with young Zoë," Mrs. Price-Jones was saying.

Zoë leaned closer to listen.

Mrs. Price-Jones continued, "Even so, Izzy—and with

her, Clarissa—were skating on very thin ice. There are still rumors, and really it was only Izzy's marriage to Leo that caused them to die down—too many people are reluctant to offend an earl. And of course there are plenty who could not believe that a high stickler like Leo would stoop to taking a bastard to wife."

Zoë swallowed.

Lady Scattergood said, "Yes, but they did succeed—the girls, I mean. And Clarissa is adamant that young Zoë is her sister. And I'm inclined to agree. Besides, Zoë is a dear girl and I like her very much. In my opinion, illegitimacy is a piece of nonsense that men invented to control women."

"That's all very well for you to say, Olive, but you won't find many—if any—in society to agree with you. It's the law. Zoë is a dear girl and I like her, too, and I grant you, she is the image of Izzy, but that doesn't change the fact that they're both baseborn. The difference is that Izzy was raised with Clarissa and has all the advantages of a lady's education and training: she looks and sounds like a lady. But Zoë—well, she only has to open her mouth and it's clear she was raised in a London gutter."

There was a short silence. Zoë leaned her head against the wall. Was her accent really that bad?

Lady Scattergood made a piffing kind of noise. "But her French is impeccable, and her accent clearly aristocratic. I have no doubt that her mother was indeed a nobleman's daughter."

"Yes, but English drawing rooms are full of people who speak only the best kind of English and couldn't tell aristocratic-sounding French if it hit them on the nose. Besides that, the child is barely educated. Granted, her handwriting is both elegant and stylish, but her spelling and grammar are appalling."

"Oh, pish! The gel is still young. There is time to remedy that. I've been getting her to read to me."

"I know, and I've been helping, too, and her reading is

improving. But is it enough? I doubt it. And Clarissa still has her head in the clouds about the whole thing."

"Clarissa has a warm and loving heart."

"I agree, but she'll never get anyone to believe that Zoë is her legitimate sister. And if she tries, she won't just fail, it will stir everything up again—all those rumors will spring up afresh and this time they'll be even harder to deny. Clarissa and Izzy—and your nephew Leo, for that matter— will be dragged into a shocking scandal."

Bile rose in Zoë's throat.

There was another short silence, then Lady Scattergood said, "I don't see what we can do about it, Althea. Clarissa is a dear, sweet gel, and generally very gentle and biddable, but in matters such as these she's immovable. Look at the way she defied her father over keeping Izzy. She was a mere child, and Bartleby Studley was a nasty big beast and a bully who should have been drowned at birth!"

Mrs. Price-Jones sighed. "Then what can we do? Personally I couldn't care less about the child's illegitimacy— I don't believe in all that 'sins of the father' nonsense, either. But there's no denying it matters to the majority of people, so I can't just stand by and do nothing while Clarissa courts her own ruin."

Zoë could almost hear Lady Scattergood's shrug. "Well, we'll just have to help young Zoë become a lady. Or at least pass her off as one and hope for the best. She's still young. Now, I think I could do with a cup of tea after all that. Would you ring the bell for Treadwell, please?"

Zoë crept away.

Chapter Ten

❧

It had to be done, Race decided. Little as he wanted to attend, this was the only way to be sure of talking to Clarissa. She'd been avoiding him at every opportunity, and he needed to make something clear. She'd be hard put to avoid him this time. He straightened his neckcloth and stepped forward to ring the doorbell.

"Young Randall again?" a cheery elderly voice behind him said.

Race turned. "Sir Oswald." Of course, it was mainly the elderly who attended Lady Davenham's literary salons. And young ladies and their mothers.

"Didn't know you were a student of literature," the old gentleman said.

"I'm not."

The old fellow chuckled. "*Cherchez la femme*, eh? Good show. Anyone I know? Plenty of pretty young fillies in attendance at these things. Bea—Lady Davenham, that is—loves havin' young people around her. Keeps her young, she says, and who am I to contradict her?"

The door opened and the butler admitted them. Race and
Sir Oswald walked upstairs and entered the large drawing
room in which rows of chairs had been set out in semicircles,
facing a shallow platform. He spied Clarissa seated on the
far side of the room, with her back turned, talking to someone behind her. Her chaperone, as usual wearing an eye-
watering colorful ensemble, was, thankfully, at the other end
of the room, deep in conversation with another old biddy.

Their hostess, Lady Davenham, sat at the front, resplen-
dent in a large turban, from which sprang several bright red
curls. Race swiftly bowed over her hand, and left her chatting with Sir Oswald while he approached Clarissa. As luck
would have it, there was a spare seat beside her. He plonked
himself on it.

She turned. "Lord Randall," she said, unable to hide her
surprise. "I didn't realize you were a reader."

"Oh, I'm full of surprises. Besides, I wanted to speak
to you."

A faint furrow appeared between her brows. "What
about?" she asked cautiously.

"You've been avoiding me."

"Have I?" she said, but her blush betrayed her.

"You know you have. What's more," he added, recalling
a grievance, "you've been going around telling people I'm
like an uncle to you. A *benevolent uncle*, I think were the
words."

She laughed. "Was it Lady Snake who told you that?"

"Lady Snape. Yes it was."

She laughed again. "I prefer my pronunciation. Anyway
I only told her that to annoy her. She was being horrid, and
I wanted her to think her nasty comments were water off a
duck's back. Apparently she believed me. Good."

He stiffened. "What did she say to you?"

Clarissa shook her head. "It doesn't matter."

"It does matter. She's a nasty piece of work and I won't
have her sinking her talons into you."

Clarissa raised her brows at that. "You are not responsible for me, or what other people say to me."

"I didn't mean—"

"Yes you did."

"All right, I did. But—"

"Thank you. When my sister left on her honeymoon, I realized that I had to learn to stand on my own two feet—we'd always been a pair until then, and I'm afraid I let Izzy take the lead in most things. But that can't continue, and so I've been trying to be more . . . more assertive. And dealing with the likes of Lady Snake is part of that."

He frowned, considering her words. "I see," he said at last. "And you're right. I was just angry at the thought that she'd peck at you to get back at me."

"Get back at you?"

He grimaced. "Sour grapes. She doesn't take kindly to rejection."

"Rejection? By you?"

"Several times. But enough about her. I have a question for you: Why are you avoiding me? Have I done something to offend you?"

She gave him a thoughtful look, then shook her head. "No, you haven't offended me. It's nothing like that."

"But you are avoiding me."

She bit her lip. "I suppose I have been."

"Was it the kiss?"

Her cheeks bloomed with color and she glanced around to be sure nobody was listening. "No, it wasn't that. That was . . . very nice."

"*Nice?*" Race stared at her. Cakes were nice. Kittens were nice. His kisses had never been called nice in his life, not even when he was a callow inexperienced youth.

She nodded. "Yes, very nice. But it cannot go any further than that."

He frowned. "What would you say if I told you that my intentions are honorable?"

Her expression turned skeptical. "Even if they were, there would be no point."

"Why not?"

She hesitated, swallowed and then said crisply, "I require fidelity in a husband."

He frowned. "So do I in a wife." Her expression was so skeptical he added, "And you can be assured that once I marry, I will never stray."

She shook her head. "A leopard cannot change his spots."

"I'm no spotty leopard," he said indignantly. "A lion, perhaps, but—"

"Male lions preside over a pride of lionesses—in other words, they have a harem. That's not for me."

He laughed ruefully. "I can see it will do me no good to bandy words with you. So, what shall we bandy? I know, how about kisses?" His eyes danced with roguish invitation.

"Hush! This conversation is ridiculous."

"This conversation is *necessary*. What would you say if I told you I—"

At that point Lady Davenham tinkled a little bell, and people hurried to take their seats. Suddenly he and Clarissa were hemmed in on all sides, and their few moments of privacy were at an end. Curse it. But there would be an interval, surely, for tea and cakes or whatever.

A young woman sitting on a small platform at the front of the room opened a book and announced in a clear voice, "*An Angel's Form and a Devil's Heart*, by Selina Davenport. The beginning of volume two."

"That's one of Lady Davenham's nieces," Clarissa whispered.

Race leaned across to Clarissa and whispered back, "You don't really think of me as an uncle, do you?"

She blushed rosily and shook her head.

The young woman began to read.

Race folded his arms and settled down to wait.

Dammit, he'd been about to declare himself in front of

a gaggle of nosy old ladies. What the devil was the matter with him? He was famed for his sangfroid. He'd always known what to say and when to say it—and to whom. But somehow, when it came to Clarissa Studley, he became a green youth prone to blurting out things, secret things, private things. And in the most inappropriate of settings.

But at least she didn't think of him as an uncle.

He sat through the reading—it was more entertaining than he'd expected—but when an interval was declared and tea and cakes served, he was quite unable to get a private moment with Miss Studley at all—everyone wanted to talk.

The second half of the program was much the same, only with a different niece reading. But when the event drew to a close, and people were leaving, he thought he might have a few moments of private conversation, except her dratted chaperone decided to stick to her like glue.

Race knew when he was beaten.

Yet another ball. Clarissa stood with Mrs. Price-Jones in the receiving line, waiting for Lord and Lady Frampton, their host and hostess, to welcome them. Really, she was getting quite tired of this endless round of parties and receptions and balls. Other people seemed to love this life: not Clarissa.

For once she'd like to spend a week just doing whatever she felt like; reading, getting to know Zoë, playing with Lady Tarrant's little girls, or the dogs, pottering around the garden or working in what Lady Scattergood had taken to calling "Clarissa's stillroom," where she produced her creams and lotions.

She loved making them up, trying out different combinations of herbs and flowers, and in London it was so much easier to obtain the more specialized ingredients she required, as well as some of the rarer ones.

But the season was more than half over, and Mrs. Price-Jones had stressed that it did a girl no good to be left on the shelf by the summer. Not that Clarissa gave the snap of her fingers for that—she wasn't going to get betrothed just for the sake of it.

But Mrs. Price-Jones was employed to chaperone her and help her to find a husband, so here they were again, entering yet another ballroom and wondering who would ask her to dance this time.

The real question in her mind, she acknowledged to herself, was whether Lord Randall would be in attendance tonight. Which was foolish. She'd done her best to discourage him, but the hope that he'd come regardless refused to die.

Her contradictory thoughts about him were driving her mad.

They greeted their host and hostess and entered the ballroom, which at this early stage of the evening smelled of the fresh flowers and swags of greenery with which it had been lavishly decorated. Usually Mrs. Price-Jones preferred to arrive at this kind of event what she called "stylishly late" but for some reason they'd arrived right at the start. The dancing had not yet begun and the decorative chalk pattern on the floor was still crisp and elegant.

"There's Lucy, Lady Thornton and her husband," Mrs. Price-Jones said. "Shall we join them?"

Lord Randall arrived half an hour later, looking splendid in his dark evening clothes, and she tensed, but he'd obviously taken her words to heart and made no attempt to approach her. He simply bowed slightly and inclined his head to her and then strolled off to join a group of other men.

Men—for a change—not ladies.

Clarissa sighed. She told herself it was a sigh of relief that he wasn't going to bother her, but what she ought to feel and what she actually felt were two very different things.

* * *

Three more dances to go before supper. Clarissa was feeling tired. It was exhausting, making conversation with relative strangers and trying to appear vivacious and interesting. For two pins she'd tell her chaperone she had a headache and wanted to leave early, but she'd done that too many times recently. Besides, she didn't like telling lies.

"Miss Studley?"

Recognizing the voice, she whirled around. "Mr. Clayborn. I . . . I didn't expect to see you here tonight." She'd hoped never to see him again, but she supposed that was unrealistic.

"I had to see you. I need to—"

"Please, I have made my feelings clear on several occasions now, and I have nothing further to say to you." She turned away.

"I only wish to apologize."

She half turned to look at him. "You did already."

"But we parted on such bad terms. I behaved disgracefully toward you and I haven't been able to sleep for fretting about it."

He did look a little pale and drawn.

He regarded her with puppy-dog entreaty. "Please grant me just a few moments of your time—just to say my piece and clear my conscience, and after that I'll never bother you again."

She hesitated.

"I promise."

She sighed again. "Very well, say it." *And get it over with.*

"Not here. There are too many eyes on us as it is. And ears." He gestured. "What about over there, in that little anteroom? I could deliver my apology there in privacy and we'd be done in a matter of moments."

There were a few people looking at them, she had to concede. And though she didn't want to spend a single minute in Mr. Clayborn's company, she could see he was determined on it and wouldn't give up until she agreed. Best to get it over with once and for all. "Very well."

He gave her a grateful smile. "Thank you. I'll go first, make sure the coast is clear, and you follow in a moment. That way we won't cause talk."

She nodded. It was all ridiculously cloak-and-dagger, but she just wanted it to be over. And the sooner the better.

He limped away and shortly afterward she saw him enter the anteroom. A few minutes later she followed.

"Thank you for coming." He closed the door behind her and she heard a click. She turned to find him removing his coat.

She gasped. "What are you doing? Stop that at once!"

He tossed his coat aside. "This won't take long." Underneath, his shirt was ripped, one sleeve almost hanging off. He yanked off his neckcloth.

"I'm leaving." She pushed past him and tried the door. It was locked.

"Open this door at—" She broke off. He was unbuttoning the fall of his breeches. The look in his eyes was grim and frightening. "Mr. Clayborn!"

There was a roomful of people on the other side of the door. She opened her mouth to scream for help, but before she could make a sound, he flung himself against her, clamped one hand over her mouth and pressed her against the wall so she couldn't move. She clawed at him with her hands, but he twisted his cravat around them and jammed them behind her against the wall. She struggled, but to no avail. He was too strong for her.

Keeping one hand over her mouth, he used the other to yank at the neckline of her dress. It was well sewn and didn't come away. He swore, and pulled harder at it, once, twice, and finally it ripped, exposing her shoulder and breast.

His gaze fell on her breast and the hold on her mouth

loosened fractionally. Wrenching her head away she screamed as loudly as she could. "Help! Help!"

Almost immediately there was a crash and the door burst open. Lord Randall. Thank God!

He grabbed Mr. Clayborn by the scruff of his neck, pulling him off Clarissa, and almost in the same movement, he swung him around and felled him with an almighty punch. Clayborn collapsed on the floor, moaning.

The doorway was filled with spectators avidly observing the scene and audibly speculating as to what was going on. Mrs. Price-Jones pushed through, and Race shut the door after her, telling the eavesdroppers, "An unfortunate accident. Nothing to worry about."

Returning to Clarissa, he gently cupped her cheek in his hand, tilting her head to look at him. "Are you all right, my dear? Did the swine hurt you?"

"No. I'm all right." She was trying to drag the remnants of her dress up, to cover herself.

"Brave girl," he said softly.

She bit her lip, aware that any more sympathy from him would probably cause her to burst into tears. "He tricked me." Mrs. Price-Jones wrapped a shawl around her. Clarissa glanced past her and saw Clayborn getting to his feet. Lord Randall followed her gaze.

"This is all an unfortunate misunderstanding," Clayborn said in a loud voice, hurriedly buttoning his breeches. "Randall overstepped disgracefully. Miss Studley and I have had an understanding for some time." He wiped a trickle of blood away with his cravat and continued, "And tonight we became betrothed, and in the heat of the moment, our passions overtook us."

Clarissa gasped. "That's a lie. We *never* had an understanding! We are *not* betrothed. He tricked me into entering this room, and then he attacked me!"

Lord Randall turned with a low growling noise. "Attack

a trusting young lady, would you, you cowardly, conniving, sniveling little worm? Try to entrap her into marriage, eh? I'll teach you a lesson you'll never forget." He prowled toward Clayborn, fists clenched.

With a squeak of fear, Clayborn wrenched open the door and wriggled through the press of bodies like a desperate eel. People must have heard, for one woman called out, "Shame!" and another, "Disgraceful." A man said, "A thrashing is too good for him."

Lord Randall gave Clarissa a searing glance. "Are you sure you're all right, Clarissa?"

She nodded, shaky but determined.

"I have her safe," Mrs. Price-Jones assured him, and Lord Randall left in pursuit of Clayborn.

Someone called out after him, "Pistols at dawn, Randall? Need a second?"

Clarissa gave a gasp of fear. A duel? No no no! She didn't want that. Lord Randall could get hurt. Oh, it was all her fault. If only she hadn't been so stupid, letting herself get caught by Clayborn's nasty little plot . . .

Clayborn broke free of the press of bodies clustered around the doorway of the anteroom, and broke into a lopsided run. As he did someone stuck a foot out and he tripped and went sprawling in the middle of the dance floor.

In three paces, Race was standing over him. "Get up, you coward." He didn't care if Clayborn was wounded in the service of his country; the man was going to get the thrashing he deserved. Race would never forget the sight of Clarissa's pale face, desperately trying to maintain some semblance of control, when anyone could see she just wanted to burst into tears—and why shouldn't she, dammit? She'd just been attacked.

He was in a cold rage. He'd seen the torn clothing, the

scratches and red marks on her chest and the dark splotches around her mouth. They'd be bruises in a short while. Clayborn was going to pay for every mark on her. And more.

Clayborn gave him a fearful glance and began to roll around the floor, clutching his bad leg and moaning. "Don't touch me, I'm injured."

"I'll injure you, all right," Race growled. "Get up."

"I can't." Clayborn groaned. "It's my leg, I've broken something. Ow, ow, ow! The pain, the pain!"

"Allow me." A neatly dressed gray-haired man came forward. "I'm a physician. I'll examine your leg."

"No! No, you can't!" Clayborn shrieked. "Don't touch me, it's—it's too painful!"

The doctor knelt down beside Clayborn. "Now, sir, there's no need to be frightened. I'll just remove this boot and then we'll see what the damage is."

"No, no, I'm fine now. Don't touch it." Frantic with fear, Clayborn flailed his injured leg around, trying to avoid the doctor's grasp.

"Oh, for heaven's sake." Disgusted, Race stepped forward and placed a foot on Clayborn's upper thigh, pinning it, and him, to the floor, while leaving the wounded part of his leg untouched. Clayborn swore mightily, and tried with all his might to push Race's foot off, but he couldn't budge it.

"Go ahead, doctor," Race said.

Clayborn shook his head desperately. "No no, don't touch it, I forbid you."

"It's best we get the boot off quickly, sir," the doctor said in a soothing voice. "If your leg swells up, we'll have to cut the boot off, which would be a terrible waste, wouldn't it, sir, such fine boots they are." As he spoke he began to ease the boot gently off.

"No, leave it, I order you!" With his other leg, Clayborn tried to kick the doctor away.

"Oh, don't be such a baby," Race snapped.

A tall young man then stepped forward and coolly placed his foot on Clayborn's other leg, pinning it to the floor. Clayborn lay there like a beached starfish, swearing and batting fruitlessly at their feet with his hands.

"Now, now, Custard," the young man said pleasantly. "Let the nice doctor take your boot off."

Custard? Despite his fury, Race was amused. The tall young man was, as far as he knew, a complete stranger. As he watched, his friend Grantley sauntered forward and joined them. Grantley and the young man exchanged greetings. They were obviously old acquaintances.

"How do you do, I'm Thornton." The young man addressed Race politely, for all the world as if he didn't have a man squirming and moaning and swearing beneath his foot. "Don't think we've been introduced, Randall, but my aunt, Lady Tarrant, and my wife, Lucy, are good friends of Miss Studley's."

"Delighted to meet you," Race responded with a smile. "Appreciate your help."

"Happy to lend a hand. Or a foot, as it were." He glanced down. "Now don't fuss, Custard, you're in excellent hands. Feet." He winked at Race.

"How's it going down there, doctor?" Race asked.

"There." The doctor eased the boot off and set it aside. It fell over and a few little stones rolled out of it onto the floor with a light pattering sound.

"What's this?" the doctor exclaimed. He shook the boot. It rattled. He upended it and half a dozen small sharp stones fell out and scattered on the ballroom floor. "It's gravel," the doctor exclaimed in surprise. "Why on earth would anyone have gravel in their boot?"

Beside him, Grantley swore softly.

Race saw it at once. "All the better to fake a limp with," he said in a hard voice. "Step on some sharp little stones and you won't have to remember to limp. And you'll wince every time they stick into you."

"But that's—that's outrageous," the doctor said.

"It certainly is," Grantley said grimly.

"Take off his stocking," Race said. "Let's have a look at this famed wound of his."

Ignoring Clayborn's resistance, the doctor peeled off his stocking and pushed up the leg of his breeches. Shocked murmurs ran through those who'd gathered in a tight circle, the better to observe the little drama as they pressed forward for a better look.

"So much for his shattered knee. Not a scratch on him." Race glanced at Thornton. "But you knew that, didn't you?"

Thornton nodded. "Served with him in the army—for a very short time. He joined up after all the fighting was over—at least we thought it was over at the time. He didn't expect Waterloo—well, none of us did. I'd sold out by then, along with a lot of my friends, but when Boney escaped from Elba, we all joined up again. But Custard here was horrified at the prospect of actual fighting. Did everything he could to wriggle out of it."

He snorted. "The day before Waterloo, he 'fell' on a broken wineglass and cut his right hand—his fighting hand, he told everyone. Nobody actually saw the alleged injury, mind, but the bandage was huge and he made a great to-do about how devastated he was not to be able to fight. And he didn't. Left Brussels before the fighting even started."

"And yet he's been claiming to have fought at Waterloo, where he received a dreadful injury," Race said.

The crowd murmured and seethed. People didn't like being made fools of.

Thornton made a disgusted face. "Yes, so I've heard. Pretending to be a wounded war hero—trading on the credit and sympathy that other men—far better men—earned. It's utterly despicable!"

"It certainly is. But why 'Custard'?"

Thornton snorted. "That's what the troops named him—Custard Clayfoot."

They stepped away and the crowd slowly dissipated, talking and exclaiming over the exciting events. "Hey, Randall, he's getting away," someone called.

Race turned and saw Clayborn with a hunted expression, scuttling toward the exit, clutching his boot and stocking and limping—genuinely this time.

"I thought you were going to thrash him," a man said in a disappointed voice.

Race said curtly, "I have more important things to do." He desperately needed to see Clarissa.

Grantley said, "I don't." He marched grimly after Clayborn, who, seeing him coming, gave a frightened squeak and fled.

"Custard's been publicly disgraced," Thornton assured Race quietly. "He won't be able to show his face in society again for a good long while—if ever."

"I know. Thanks for your support," Race said. "But now, I have more urgent matters to see to." He shook Thornton's hand, then the doctor's and headed back toward the anteroom.

As Race threaded his way through the crowd, snippets of conversation reached his ears. "Did you see? His breeches were quite unbuttoned . . ."

"*She* followed *him* in—I saw her."

"How far do you think they got before . . . ?"

". . . always thought she was too good to be true."

". . . said they had an understanding . . ."

". . . an heiress, you know . . ."

Race wanted to stop and confront the gossips, but he gritted his teeth and kept walking. Confronting them would just feed the harmful talk about Clarissa.

A small clot of people still lingered around the doorway to the anteroom, several people with their ears pressed to the door.

"Excuse me," he said in freezing accents. "Don't you have better things to do, better places to be?" He raked them with a contemptuous stare until most of them fell back and began to wander off.

He entered, closing the door firmly behind him and paused. He seemed to have walked in on an argument.

"I won't! I don't care if people talk. I don't care what they say," Clarissa was saying in a low, vehement voice.

Her chaperone responded, "You must. And I'm sure he will do it. That man has a soft spot for you. He's very protective."

"I won't ask it of—" Clarissa broke off, seeing him. "You're not going to duel him, are you, Lord Randall? Please tell me you won't."

"There will be no duel," Race said curtly. So, after all that had happened, she still worried about the villain? Surely not? "At least, not with me," he added. Grantley was another matter.

"Oh, I'm glad." Her whole body seemed to relax.

"You did deal with him as he deserved, I hope?" The chaperone smoothed the shawl around Clarissa's shoulders.

"I did. He's gone. You won't see him again." He hadn't taken his eyes off Clarissa. "Are you sure you're all right, Miss Studley?"

She nodded, her smile a little wobbly but heartbreakingly brave. "A bit shaken up, but you arrived just in time. Thank you."

"But her reputation is ruined," Mrs. Price-Jones declared.

"I told you, I don't care about that," Clarissa said quickly. "It doesn't matter in the least."

But it mattered to Race. He'd heard the speculation—curious and malicious—that had arisen in just the last few minutes. It was only going to get worse, as versions of the event were passed around, growing in outrageousness as they went. She didn't deserve to be gossiped about like that.

"Was there an understanding between you and Clayborn?" He had to know.

"No!" she said indignantly. "There was *never* anything like that between us. He did ask me to marry him, I admit, but I refused him. More than once."

Which meant the swine had asked her more than once.

"She needs to be betrothed," Mrs. Price-Jones said with a meaning look at Race. "There will still be a scandal, but a betrothal would make everything better."

"I won't—" Clarissa began.

He stared at the chaperone in outrage. "You mean you would condone her betrothal to that swine?"

The woman rolled her eyes. "Not to him of course! Someone else. Someone respectable." She eyed him meaningfully.

Race frowned. Did she mean him? He was hardly respectable, at least as society saw things.

Mrs. Price-Jones continued. "A betrothal would protect Clarissa from the worst of the scandal. It would direct talk away from the unsavory events that took place in this room, and focus it on the betrothal." She looked at him. "So, Lord Randall . . . ?"

Clarissa shook her head frantically. "No, no, you cannot ask it of him."

"It's the best solution," her chaperone insisted. She gestured. "Out there gossip is already humming like a swarm of wasps, and you—and your reputation, or what's left of it—are at the center of it. We need to replace that gossip with something different, something better." She looked at Race again. "Something that will surprise them all. Don't you agree, Lord Randall?"

Clarissa followed the chaperone's gaze to Race. "I cannot ask it of you. It's not fair. I won't agree. I won't."

"I will do anything in my power to protect you, Miss Studley. It was my fault the swine tricked you into this position. Allow me to make amends."

"How can you say that? You rescued me."

"I should never have let him entice you in here in the first place." He'd seen her follow Clayborn, and his unease at the situation had caused him to loiter outside the anteroom. And when he'd heard her scream . . . He would never forget it.

She shook her head. "No. It was all my fault. I should have been more careful. In any case, I am not your responsibility."

Race took a deep breath. It was not how he wanted this to play out, but when the moment presented itself . . . He took her hand. "Miss Studley, will you do me the honor of becoming my wife?"

Her face crumpled and she snatched her hand back, shaking her head distressfully. "No, I can't," she choked out. "It's not fair that you . . . that you—"

"Nonsense!" Mrs. Price-Jones said briskly. "The man's right. It will solve everything. The minute it gets out that Rake Randall has finally succumbed, everyone will be talking about that." She patted Race on the shoulder. "Don't worry, your lordship, I will deal with Clarissa's fears. You may consider yourself betrothed."

"But I—" Clarissa began, her eyes shimmering with tears.

"Foolish child, you won't have to go through with it. After a few weeks, when the talk has died down and some other scandal has taken the ton's imagination, you can quietly cry off if you want, and no harm done. Isn't that right, Lord Randall?"

"It is," he said curtly. Ladies could call a betrothal off. A gentleman could not.

Clarissa bit her lip and turned a look of entreaty on Race. "Lord Randall, you can't possibly want to do this."

"I do, very much," he assured her.

"Because of the damage to my reputation?"

"And to be of service to you." Which wasn't at all what he wanted to say to her, but he could see she was on a knife's edge of losing her control, and he wasn't going to add any more pressure. She'd endured enough as it was, and was doing an impressive job of holding herself together. So far.

"See?" Mrs. Price-Jones said. "Now, dry your eyes, thank Lord Randall for his very kind offer, hold your head up high as you walk through that crowd, and let Lord Randall take you home, safe and sound."

He frowned. Let him take her home? Alone? The chaperone gave him a meaningful look. "I'll meet you at the front door, after I've spread the good news." Redirected the gossip, she meant.

Clarissa looked up at Race, her beautiful eyes swimming with tears. "Are you sure about this, Lord Randall?"

"Very, very sure. And deeply honored." Race wanted to pull her into his arms and hold her until all doubts faded from her mind. But he couldn't. Not here, not now, especially with that chaperone watching his every move with her beady bright eyes, not to mention the crowd of vultures on the other side of the door.

He handed Clarissa his handkerchief, and she blotted the tears from her face. "I will call on you tomorrow to make arrangements."

She looked up, startled. "What arrangements?"

"Just the official announcement, that sort of thing. Nothing to worry about," he said soothingly. "I trust that butler of Lady Scattergood's will allow me entry to the house this time."

"He'd better." She gave a halfhearted choke of laughter and blew her nose on his handkerchief. "But if he doesn't, go around to the garden—yes, that'll be better. I'll meet you in the garden, in the summerhouse at nine." She glanced at her chaperone. "Where we can be quite private."

"Agreed." He presented his arm. "Shall we?"

Attempting to plaster a wobbly smile over her tearstained face, she pulled the shawl tight about her and slipped her hand into the crook of his arm. Taking a deep breath, she glanced at him and nodded. Mrs. Price-Jones opened the door, and the small cluster of people still loitering outside fell back as the newly betrothed couple emerged.

Lord Thornton and his wife were among them. The wife moved forward as if to comfort Clarissa, but if he was any judge, Clarissa was still teetering on the verge of tears, and sympathy was the most likely thing to set them off, so Race didn't slow, just nodded at Thornton and as they passed, said, "Wish us happy, Thornton, Lady Thornton." A buzz of conversation followed them out.

Behind him he heard Mrs. Price-Jones saying, "Yes, it's quite true. They're betrothed and have been for some time—of course that's what caused Clayborn to panic and try to force the issue. We'd been keeping it secret until Lord Salcott—Miss Studley's guardian—returned to make the announcement officially, but it's out now, so there's little point in keeping it secret any longer."

Chapter Eleven

"What, and then 'e grabbed you?" Zoë was sitting cross-legged on the end of Clarissa's bed. They were drinking hot chocolate and eating fresh pastries. The morning sun was streaming through the window.

"Yes, and with his hand over my mouth, I couldn't scream out and I couldn't get away—he was too strong, much stronger than he looks."

Zoë nodded shrewdly. "You prob'ly thought that because of his limp and his stick."

"I suppose so."

"Why didn't you knee him in the nuts?"

Clarissa gave her a puzzled look. "What do you mean?"

"His balls then."

Still mystified, Clarissa shook her head.

Zoë was incredulous. "Gawd, that's what comes of bein' raised a lady—they don't teach you nothin' useful."

"Anything," Clarissa corrected her. "And I still don't understand."

"Well, you said he opened the front of his britches, right?"

"Yes."

"That's where he keeps his nuts. Or his balls, if you like."

Clarissa wrinkled her nose, trying to understand. "Do you mean his . . . male parts."

Zoë laughed. "Yeah, his 'male parts,'" she mimicked Clarissa's accent. "Or his nuts, his balls or his family jewels, or a dozen other names. The point is, a bloke's nuts are the tenderest part of him. If you give 'em a good hard kick, or jam your knee hard into a man's nuts, he's bound to let you go and double up groanin'. And you can get away."

Clarissa frowned at Zoë's matter-of-fact description. "Have you ever had to do that?"

She shrugged. "Once or twice."

"I'm so sorry."

"It's all right. Where I came from a girl needed to know how to look after herself. I'm just sorry nobody ever taught you that."

"In society there's no need," Clarissa began, but trailed off in the face of Zoë's skeptical expression. "You're right. We're raised to assume we're safe, because in society gentlemen are supposed to be gentlemen, but—"

"Some of 'em ain't." Zoë slipped off the bed. "So now you know. Go for the nuts."

Clarissa smiled. "Thank you for educating me, little sister."

Zoë placed her empty cup on the tray sitting on a side table and, suddenly serious, said, "I hope this Lord Randall is good to you, Clarissa. And that you'll be happy with him."

"Oh, it's not permanent," Clarissa assured her. "This betrothal is just a temporary ruse to redirect the gossip."

"Oh. I thought . . ." Zoë shook her head. "I thought you liked him."

Clarissa fought a blush. "Oh, well, he's quite a charming

fellow, and of course he's my guardian's best friend, so of course I like him. But he's a born flirt and could never be seriously interested in someone like me."

"Why not?"

She said in what she hoped was an airy manner, "He's always seen with the most beautiful women."

"You're beautiful," Zoë said, and when Clarissa disclaimed, she insisted, "Yeah, you are. All the way through."

Clarissa just shook her head. "Besides, he's a rake, and I would never marry a man who is incapable of fidelity. I saw what my father's infidelity did to my mother."

"And mine," Zoë said softly.

There was a short silence. Swallowing the lump in her throat, Clarissa said, "I'm so glad we found each other, Zoë. I can't tell you how thrilled I am to have another sister, and I know when she meets you, Izzy will be just as thrilled."

Zoë said gruffly, "Yeah, well, I want to thank you for all you done for me. You're a good person, Clarissa, and . . . I've been happy here."

Clarissa frowned slightly. It was almost as if there was a *but* coming, but Zoë didn't say anything else. She piled the used crockery onto the tray. "I'll take this downstairs and tell Betty you're ready for your hot water, shall I?"

"Yes please." Clarissa glanced at the ormolu clock on the mantelpiece and flung the bedclothes back. Lord Randall would be here in one hour.

*B*etrothed. To Lord Randall.
After the events of the previous evening, Clarissa had arrived home utterly exhausted but despite that she'd hardly slept. Everything that had happened—Mr. Clayborn's shocking attack, and then Lord Randall's even more astounding proposal—had kept churning around and around in her brain.

She was betrothed to Lord Randall!

She swallowed. Within the hour, he'd be here to discuss that proposal with her.

And even though she'd spent the entire night trying to work out what she felt about it all, and even more important what she was going to do, she still couldn't make up her mind.

Lord Randall's proposal was merely a stratagem to distract the gossips; she knew that. *You won't have to go through with it*, Mrs. Price-Jones had assured her.

That was a relief. The trouble was, Clarissa didn't feel relieved.

He'd said he was doing it to be of service to her. Which sounded practical. And kind. But the look in those smoky gray eyes as he said it was neither practical nor kind. When he looked at her his eyes seemed to burn with sincerity and an unsettlingly intense expression she didn't know what to make of.

Oh, she was fooling herself, letting her own impossible desires carry her away, imagining things that weren't there. They were foolish—worse than foolish. He would break her heart if she let him. So it was up to her to protect herself.

She needed to control herself, stop wishing things could be different, and not let herself . . . dream.

Their betrothal was a pretense, a fiction created to distract the society gossips from the sordid incident with Mr. Clayborn. And it would distract them, she knew. As she dressed, she imagined the conversations: *To think Rake Randall, connoisseur of female beauty and famous evader of marriage, has let himself be caught by a plain little dab of a girl with only her fortune to recommend her.*

And he doesn't even need a fortune . . .

It's too smoky by half. There must be some other reason. Might she be expecting an interesting event?

Chivalry, someone would suggest. *Didn't you hear what happened between Clayborn and that girl? Randall stepped in to save her reputation after she'd shamelessly pursued poor Clayborn. Randall's her guardian's best friend, you know.* The incident at the ball was bound to come up—too many people had witnessed it.

Rake Randall? Nonsense. He's not exactly known for his chivalrous impulses, still less for those resulting in marriage. Clarissa could imagine the cynical laughter that would follow. Because of course the very idea of a chivalrous rake was ridiculous. Even though she knew he was.

I know. It's a mystery.

The girl might yet pull out of it.

And whoever they were speaking to would scoff at the very idea. *Would you? Turn down marriage to the delicious Rake Randall. Don't be ridiculous.*

She looked at her reflection in the looking glass and adjusted the drape of her shawl. The speculation would be vile. But she'd have to grin and bear it. Or try to appear magnificently indifferent to it.

And she *would* turn down the delicious Rake Randall. Eventually. She had to, primarily for her own sake, but also for his. Some repayment for his chivalrous act it would be, to entrap him into an unwanted marriage.

And since he was apparently able to maintain a cool and unemotional demeanor over the deception, she ought to be able to do the same. She looked at the plain, plump girl looking back at her from the looking glass and reminded herself: cool and unemotional.

"So it was all a lie," Clarissa said indignantly. "Even his wound?"

They were in the summerhouse, and Lord Randall had just finished explaining to her how Mr. Clayborn had faked his injury, and even kept gravel in his boot to make him limp convincingly.

She was deeply shocked. All those little gasps of pain that had made her feel so sorry for him . . . Every one self-inflicted. In order to deceive.

She shook her head. "I don't understand his purpose in creating such an elaborate—and quite painful—deception. What was the point?"

He shrugged. "To gain sympathy? Feel more important? Perhaps he thought it would make you more willing to marry him. Who knows?"

She didn't understand it, either. Mr. Clayborn was handsome, pleasant company, and was heir to his great-aunt's fortune. Why fake an injury? "And all those times when he was so becomingly modest about his Waterloo achievements—which everyone believed were prodigious—I suppose they were lies, too."

"He wasn't even present at Waterloo." Lord Randall related the story Lord Thornton had told him.

It was horrid. To think she'd actually imagined—for a short time, anyway—that Mr. Clayborn might make a suitable husband. She shivered. She'd had a lucky escape.

She rose and strolled to the open door and stood in the doorway, gazing out over the garden, her mind teeming. The garden in the morning smelled fresh and lush, the kind of fragrance she'd love to be able to re-create one day, but knew it was impossible. A couple of birds chittered noisily in a nearby bush, squabbling, or perhaps mating. The sound jerked her out of her reverie.

"I don't know Lord Thornton very well," she said, turning, "but I'm well acquainted with his wife, Lucy. They're visiting London and staying with his aunt, Lady Tarrant, who lives over there." She gestured. "Lady Tarrant is a good friend of mine. In fact, you can probably hear her little girls playing in the garden now—her stepdaughters."

He rose and joined her, and she instantly forgot about everything except the sensation of his tall, strong body standing so close they were almost touching. She could sense his warmth, smell the fragrance of his cologne. She took a deep, surreptitious breath, breathing him in, the scent of Lord Randall. Her betrothed? She couldn't believe it. But it could never go any further than that. She leaned a little closer and breathed him in again; the scent of a man. The scent of a rake, she reminded herself.

"I don't hear anything. Just birds," he said.

She frowned. He was right. There was no sound of the usual childish laughter and shouts echoing through the garden, which was strange. She'd seen Nanny McCubbin ushering the three little girls outside into the garden earlier. They'd looked rather subdued, but she hadn't stopped to investigate—she had a meeting of her own to go to.

Clarissa let the moment stretch as long as she could. She was dreading the next part of the conversation—the part their meeting was really about. Their false betrothal.

"You're not going to duel him, are you?" she asked abruptly, and moved back inside.

He shook his head. "It would only make the talk worse, and in any case I wouldn't kill him. Wring his neck, possibly, or beat him to a pulp"—he gave a rueful smile—"but he's a pathetic, cowardly character. In any case, according to my sources he's already left London. Fled in case I did decide to challenge him, I suppose."

"I'm glad. I was worried you might, and though I know you're too much of a gentleman to shoot to kill, he certainly isn't and I don't want you dead."

"Glad to hear it," he said dryly with a smile that did things to her insides.

Flustered, she plopped down without thinking on the nearest seat—the chaise longue. He sat down beside her, close, so that they were almost, but not quite, touching. She was achingly aware of him.

It was on this very chaise longue that Leo had seduced Izzy. Or was it the other way around? She'd never been quite sure.

She ought to change seats but that would look strange. Impolite. As if she didn't want him sitting beside her— which was true. And at the same time a lie.

Lord Randall lounged back, leaning casually against the padded support, one long leg crossed over the other. He was dressed informally, in buckskin breeches and long riding boots. She could smell the leather.

She sat up straighter, folded her hands primly in her lap and tried not to notice how the soft buckskin clung to his hard horseman's thighs.

"I suppose we ought to discuss this false betrothal," she began.

He sat up and faced her. "It's not a false betrothal." His voice was hard.

"But I thought—"

"Our betrothal is genuine and binding—until you decide it's not."

She gave him a troubled look. "Until *I* decide? Why can't you decide to cancel it?"

He relaxed back against the back of the chaise. "Because a gentleman cannot."

"That doesn't seem very fair. Why not?"

"A gentleman's word is his bond. To break it, or to renege on a promise, would be quite dishonorable."

She frowned. "But a lady can? Why is that not just as dishonorable?"

"Because it is the prerogative of any member the fairer sex that she is entitled to change her mind."

"Why? Because women are frippery creatures, too silly and unreliable to understand the concept of honor?" she said crossly.

He shrugged. "I didn't say that, and I don't think that. I didn't make the rules."

"But you abide by them?"

He changed the subject. "It ought to be Leo, as your guardian, who makes the official betrothal announcement, and I expect he'll be back from the honeymoon in the next week or two. In the meantime we should be seen together in public at every opportunity, and let the gossips do the work for us."

"You mean people will be gossiping about you and me, as well as Mr. Clayborn and me?" She closed her eyes briefly. She hated being the focus of people's attention.

"They already are. My cousin Maggie, who wasn't at the ball last night, has already heard. She sent a congratulatory note around this morning."

She opened her eyes. "You mean she believed in the betrothal? On the basis of a rumor?"

"She's been predicting it since that first ride we took together."

"That first ride?" Clarissa almost choked. How could Maggie possibly think . . . She *couldn't* know. She had been perfectly circumspect about her feelings for Lord Randall, she was sure.

He gave her a lazy smile. "She's delighted. Said to give you her warmest felicitations, and to tell you she said, 'welcome to the family.'"

Welcome to the family? Oh, this was dreadful. "Why didn't you tell her it was a false betrothal, a pretense, a subterfuge?"

"Because it's not. As I said, it's genuine and binding until you decide you can't marry me."

"You know I can't."

"Why not?" His voice was deep and low and somehow . . . caressing.

Unable to find the words, she shook her head. "I just can't."

His voice deepened and he leaned a little closer. "That's not an answer, Clarissa. Why do you feel you can't marry me?"

Again, she shook her head and refused to meet his eyes.

"As far as I'm concerned there is only one reason you can't marry me—because you don't love me." He paused. "Is that it, sweetheart? You don't love me?"

Her face crumpled at the soft voice, the endearment, the gentle insistence. "Stop it! It's not fair. You ask me how I feel, but I know you can't possibly love me and—"

"Why can't I?"

She stared at him, shocked at what he was implying. "You can't," she whispered.

"Why not?" He was so close she could feel his warm breath on her skin.

"Because . . . because . . ."

Cupping her chin in his hand, he raised her face and kissed her, gently at first, brushing his lips over hers. The caress was so soft it tantalized . . . and teased. And entranced. She knew she shouldn't, knew she should resist, should push him away from her. Should flee.

But the taste of him was addictive. She wanted more.

She took a deep breath and pressed her mouth against him, opening it in mute invitation. Instantly he responded, and the kiss changed from soft and sweet to hot, spicy and demanding.

Conflagration. Heat, dark and dangerous and exhilarating. She was melting against him, clinging to him like a drowning woman, only she wasn't drowning: she was floating. Gloriously.

Eventually something—some distant sound—pulled her out of the dreamlike state his kisses produced.

She tore her mouth away and rested her face against his shoulder with her eyes closed, her breath coming in shallow gasps as she fought for some semblance of composure. She wanted to burrow into his chest and stay there forever, and at the same time wanted to run from him as fast and far as she could.

He was going to break her heart. If she let him.

He smoothed back her hair, and with one finger lightly caressed the nape of her neck. Delicious shivers ran through her.

Oh, he was so good at this, so skilled, so . . . *practiced*. The word was like a dash of cold water.

She pulled away and sat back. "I don't think we should do this again," she said, her voice shaky and a little husky.

He tucked a curl behind her ear. "Why not, sweetheart? We are betrothed, after all." His voice deepened. "And don't try to tell me you don't like it because I won't believe you."

She couldn't bring herself to deny it, so she changed the subject. "The betrothal is both false and temporary—no, don't argue—and—"

"Wouldn't dream of it." He picked up her hand, turned it over and traced a long finger slowly down a line in her palm. "Strong Heart line," he murmured.

A faint shiver ran through her. Snatching her hand back, she fought for a more businesslike tone. Difficult when her insides had turned to warm, quivery jelly. But he didn't need to know that. "We need to discuss where we go from here."

"I thought we'd decided that. We're going to be seen everywhere, together, right?"

She nodded and rose to her feet. Her legs were distressingly shaky: she hoped he couldn't tell. "In that case I'll see you tomorrow night at Almack's."

"*Almack's?*" he echoed.

She frowned, puzzled by his tone. "Yes. What's wrong with that?" Everyone went to Almack's. If he wanted everyone to see them together and draw the right conclusion, Almack's was the best of all possible places for it. All the ton would be there.

"Nothing." He sighed. "Almack's it is then." He tucked her arm into his, apparently intent on escorting her to her door.

"I'd like to walk in the garden for a while," she said, hoping he would leave so that she could gather her composure before she had to face Lady Scattergood and Mrs. Price-Jones and all their questions.

"Very well then." He turned down one of the paths.

"I," she began, and when he looked at her with a question in his eyes, she said, "Oh, nothing."

They wandered through the lush, fragrant garden, arm in arm but not talking, for which Clarissa was thankful, making their way slowly toward the spreading plane tree that dominated the center of the garden. It was the little Tarrant girls' favorite place to play, but she could hear no shouts and giggles. They'd probably gone inside.

But when they turned the corner, they saw the three little girls sitting in a tight semicircle on the grass, sobbing, with their nanny standing over them, wringing her hands and expostulating, though in a subdued manner.

Clarissa dropped Lord Randall's arm and ran forward. "Whatever is the matter?" She dropped down on her knees in front of the little girls.

"It's Mama," Lina sobbed.

"She—she—she's havin' the baby," Judy added, her face stiff with the effort not to cry. Judy was the eldest and was very aware she was supposed to set an example, but the effort was showing. A tear or two escaped but she dashed them away.

"An' she's gunna diiiie," Debo wailed.

"What? Why would you think that?" Clarissa exclaimed, shocked.

"Sukey and Ethel said so. We heard them."

Clarissa turned to the nanny. "Sukey and Ethel?"

"Two foolish kitchen maids who ought to know better," the nanny said crossly.

Lina wailed. "It's just like the p-poor p-p-princess."

Clarissa sighed. The death of Princess Charlotte in childbirth last year had shocked the nation and many were still in mourning for the poor young princess. Clearly it had made a big impact on these children. She said in a heartening tone, "You can't know that." She looked a silent question at the nanny, who shook her head.

"I certainly never said anything about . . ." She gave a meaningful glance toward the bedroom window where Lady Tarrant was laboring to produce her child. "But they overheard the kitchen maids and worked themselves into a right state, miss. And nothing I say will make them think any different."

Children often knew more than adults deigned to tell them. She and Izzy always knew what the servants were trying to hide. "So there's no reason to think . . . ?"

"No, miss. Nothing at all. But will these bairns listen to their old nanny?" She shook her head in frustration.

Judy threw a fierce glare at the old woman. "Our mother died when she"—she jerked her head at little Debo—"was born, so don't tell us we're worrying about nothing. And Papa's up there with her and everyone knows men only go into a birthing room when . . . when . . ."

"Oh, my dear." Clarissa tried to put her arms around Judy but the child shrugged her off, determined not to be comforted. Debo looked at her, with tear-drenched eyes, her long-suffering cat hugged to her chest, its fur spiky and damp with tears. Clarissa sat down between her and Judy, and put her arm around the little girl. Debo leaned into her.

"Dear me, that is a worry," said a deep voice behind her. The children looked up at Lord Randall, startled. Clarissa had forgotten he was there. "But she's not dead yet, is she?"

They stared up at him, shocked at his bluntness.

He continued, "Your papa might just want to be with your mama when the baby is born. I know when my wife has a baby, I intend to be with her for the birth."

They all stared at him in amazement, Clarissa, too. He smiled. "I promise you it's true." He went on in a brisker tone, "Now, with your mama busy giving you a new brother or sister, and your papa up there with her, supporting her, how do you think they would feel if they knew you were sitting down here weeping, hm?"

Judy stared at him a moment, then straightened her spine, choked on a hiccup and swallowed.

He smiled down at Judy. "Well done. We haven't met, have we, young lady? What's your name?"

"J-Judy."

"Short for Judith," he said. "A fine name. It means 'beautiful and daring'—did you know that? It's a name for a queen—I can't tell you offhand how many queens have been named Judith, but there are lots." Judy blinked up at him. "Do you think you could be brave, Judith, for the sake of your sisters and your mama and papa?"

She swallowed and nodded gamely. Clarissa's eyes misted with tears.

"Good girl," he said softly. Next he squatted down in front of Lina, who was sitting on the end. "Now, sweetheart, we cannot know what the future will bring, but we can decide how we face it. And why worry about a future we cannot possibly know?"

"But I don't want Mama to die." Lina burst into renewed tears.

"No, of course you don't," he said gently. "Come here, little one." He opened his arms. Lina crept forward, and he rose, lifting her up and cradling her against his chest. The little girl clung to him, sobbing into his shoulder, and he just rocked back and forth, rubbing her back and murmuring to her softly.

Clarissa sat with her arm around Debo and, through misty eyes, watched the tall man comforting the distraught child. She had no idea Lord Randall could be like this. So tender and understanding and patient. And he didn't even know these children.

Lina's sobs eventually slowed and Lord Randall produced a handkerchief and dried her face. "Now, what's your name, young lady? We haven't been introduced, you know. I'm Lord Randall, and you are?"

"Lina," she said shyly. "It's short for Selina."

"Ah, from the Greek for 'moon,' I understand. What, you didn't know that?" She shook her head, and he went on, "Selene was a goddess who drove her moon chariot across the heavens, bringing light to the darkness." He gave her a searching look and nodded. "Yes, I think you'd be the very person who would bring light to a dark night."

Lina buried her face in his shoulder again, but Clarissa saw a small, tremulous smile.

He was just as good with little girls as he was with grown women.

Still holding Lina, he looked down at Debo, now leaning quietly against Clarissa, exhausted by her tears. "That's a handsome cat," he said.

"Mittens," she said gruffly.

"An excellent name for a cat. And who does Mittens own?"

She stared up at him a moment, then chuckled. "Me, silly. I'm Debo."

"Short for Deborah?"

She scowled. "No, just Debo."

He nodded. "Well, Deborah was wise woman and a force to be reckoned with, and I can see you are, too." He glanced at the nanny. "Nanny, I don't suppose it would be possible for us to have milk and cookies in the summerhouse, would it? And perhaps if you have it, bring a game of spillikins or something like that as well?"

Nanny beamed up at him. "Bless you, sir, of course it would. I'll be back with them in a jiffy." She hurried off. Lord Randall helped Clarissa to stand and then the two of them and the three little girls—and cat—went into the summerhouse.

Lord Randall began a game of I spy, pulling hideous and ridiculous faces as he gave outrageous hints to those who were too young to spell, and he soon had them all laughing.

"Can anyone join in?" a deep voice said from the doorway.

"Papa!" the little girls shouted. They surrounded him, wrapping him in desperate arms, then fell silent gazing up at him in sudden trepidation.

He smiled, picked up Debo, cat and all, and put an arm around the other two girls. "Girls, you have a healthy little brother."

"And Mama?" Lina asked tremulously.

Lord Tarrant smiled and ruffled her hair. "Mama is fine, darling, just a little tired. She'll be ready to see you in a while and introduce you to your new baby brother, but first you need to deal with these milk and cookies that Nanny has brought you." He stood aside, with some difficulty as his children wouldn't let go of him, and Nanny came through with a laden tray.

Over his children's heads, Lord Tarrant looked at Clarissa and Lord Randall, and said quietly, "I can't thank you enough for what you did for my girls. Nanny explained. I had no idea they were so worried. I'm very grateful, and my wife will be, too."

"It was our absolute pleasure," Lord Randall told him. "Congratulations on the new baby. If he grows up to be anything like his sisters, he'll make you proud. Your daughters are magnificent." He took Clarissa's hand and added, "I only hope we have such wonderful children."

Lord Tarrant gave them a surprised look, then grinned. "You're betrothed? That's wonderful news. Congratulations." He smiled at Clarissa. "I'll tell Alice—she'll be thrilled."

Clarissa opened her mouth to deny it, but Lord Randall squeezed her hand meaningfully, and she swallowed the words she'd been about to say. "Thank you," she murmured, fighting a blush. The betrothal still felt like a lie, even if Lord Randall kept insisting it was real. "Give Lady

Tarrant my love. And congratulations on the baby. I'll visit her in a day or two when she's ready for callers."

They left Lord Tarrant with the little girls, and moved into the garden. "You were wonderful with the children," Clarissa said after a moment. "How did you know what to do? Do you . . . do you have children?" She braced herself for the answer. Rakes were notorious for siring bastards. Her father had begotten two.

That they knew of.

"No, no children."

"Then . . ."

He glanced down at her and winked. "Believe it or not I was a child once."

They strolled toward Lady Scattergood's house in silence. Clarissa felt no pressure to converse, which was a relief.

"Oh, Clarissa, Mama was wondering whether—oh!" Milly, having rounded a corner, came to an abrupt stop. "Lord Randall." She eyed him warily and backed away several steps, as if, being a notorious rake, he would immediately jump on her and ravish her.

"Good morning, Milly," Clarissa said. "What was it your mother wanted to know?"

"Have you learned yet who bought the house on the corner?"

"No."

Milly pouted. "Mama is becoming quite frustrated. She is certain it is some ghastly, vulgar cit."

Clarissa had no interest in Mrs. Harrington's pretensions. "Whoever it turns out to be, I don't think it's any of our business. If that's all, Milly, I'll say goodbye."

"You shouldn't be alone with a man like that," Milly muttered as they turned to leave.

Clarissa turned back. "What did you say?"

Milly shifted uncomfortably. "Well, Mama says he's not to be trus—"

"Your mama talks a lot of nonsense!" Clarissa flashed

angrily. "How dare you refer to Lord Randall in such a manner! To me, he is, and has always been a thorough gentleman. In any case, Milly, he and I are betrothed, so you may tell your mama that!"

Milly's eyes widened. "*Betrothed?* You and that rake?"

"No, this *gentleman* and I!"

"Well!" Milly said. "Well! I don't know what Mama will have to say to that!"

"Why don't you run off and find out then?" Clarissa said. "Come, Lord Randall." And thrusting her arm through his, she marched away, leaving Milly goggling behind them on the path.

"Well, well," Lord Randall said after a few minutes. "Quite the little firebrand, aren't you?"

Clarissa flushed. "Well, but she was so rude about you. And it was so unjust."

He laughed softly. "I don't care what silly girls like that, or their mothers, think of me."

"Well, I do."

He was silent a moment. "So I see."

They arrived at Lady Scattergood's back gate. "So," Clarissa said, trying to appear calm and matter-of-fact, "will I see you at Almack's tomorrow evening?"

He looked a little disconcerted. "Almack's? Ah. Yes, Wednesday, is it not?" He took her hand and bowed, most romantically, over it. His eyes smiled into hers. "Until then, my little dragon defender."

Clarissa slowly climbed the stairs to her bedchamber. She'd seen quite a different side to Lord Randall this morning. The way he'd treated the little girls, with sympathy and understanding—and so gentle. He'd make a wonderful father.

She'd never had a sympathetic or gentle word from Papa in her life.

And then, when Milly had spoken about him in such a

rude and dismissive way, her rarely roused temper had flared. She hadn't been able to stop herself.

His *little dragon defender.*

And yet, Milly's impression of him was exactly what Clarissa herself, not to mention half the ton, had thought about him all this time.

But she didn't feel like that any longer. She paused on the stairs as the realization hit her. She was falling deeper and deeper in love with Lord Randall.

And it scared her half to death.

Chapter Twelve

❧

Almack's. Race gazed up at the imposing edifice on the other side of the road. People were already flocking inside, the ladies in their silks and muslins, the gentlemen, to a man, wearing old-fashioned knee breeches. As was he.

He didn't want to move.

Women had always pursued him. Once he'd made it clear he wasn't interested in marriage, it was only married women and widows who pursued him, and he'd soon discovered that too many of them had motives that had little to do with him, or even the simple finding of pleasure in each other's company.

It was ironic. It was solely for Clarissa's sake that he'd begun to attend society events. But because of that, the rumor had spread that he was finally ready to take a bride—which was, he had to admit, true. But he was not after *any* suitable bride: he wanted only Clarissa.

Still, in society's eyes he'd placed himself firmly on the marriage mart and was considered fair game. And now, since the events of the Frampton ball, he needed to show he was already taken.

For years he'd avoided society balls and routs, especially the ones that the latest crop of newly presented brides-in-waiting attended. Or the second- or third-season hopefuls, who were, frankly, a little unnerving in their desperation.

He'd attended Almack's precisely twice, years ago, very early in his career. He'd lost his father the previous year and, having come into a title and a substantial fortune, found himself the target of ambitious matchmaking mamas and their equally purposeful daughters.

He'd never again darkened Almack's door.

Until—God help him—tonight.

He bent and straightened his knee breeches, took a deep breath, crossed the road and entered.

There was a sudden hush, followed by a twittering of excited speculation.

In minutes he was discreetly but relentlessly mobbed by maidens and matrons, all curious about the incidents at the Frampton ball. And though everyone was agog at what had been revealed about Clayborn, most of their queries, direct and indirect, amounted to the same question: Were the rumors true, that he and Miss Studley were betrothed?

To each, he answered in the affirmative, adding how delighted he was about it. Not a few narrowed their eyes in skepticism and glanced significantly around the room. Where his betrothed was conspicuous by her absence.

Where was she? She'd been very clear that she intended to be here tonight, and that she expected him to attend as well.

He waited and bowed and chatted, and waited and parried intrusive questions, and drank some disgusting beverage and waited as the clock inched with agonizing slowness toward the magic hour: eleven o'clock, when the doors to Almack's were firmly closed against latecomers, no matter what their rank.

Finally, the hour came and Race made his way from the

building. Where the hell was she? Could she still be avoiding him? He didn't believe it. He was sure they'd come to a new level of understanding—of closeness—since the events in the garden, both with the distressed little girls, and again when she'd defended him so fiercely against the very slight insult delivered by that Milly girl. That defense still warmed him.

So where was she? She wasn't the sort to lie, saying she'd do something when she had no intention of doing so.

So something must have happened to prevent her. Perhaps she'd had a headache and gone to bed early. But surely in that case she would have sent him a note.

His brain sprouted all kinds of possibilities. He picked up his pace.

When he reached Bellaire Gardens, he found lights blazing in every window. So nobody had gone to bed early.

He yanked hard on the bellpull. The sound jangled loudly through the house. If that butler refused him . . . He'd never hit a butler, ancient or not—or any servant, for that matter—but there was always a first time.

But when the door flew open it was not the disapproving ancient butler who confronted him, but Clarissa, looking pale and distraught.

"Oh. Oh, it's you," she said in a disappointed voice. She peered around him, looking out into the street, then turned back to him and, with a visible effort, collected herself. "I'm so sorry, I should have sent a note to tell you my change of plan. I gather from your attire you did go to Almack's."

He stepped inside and closed the door behind him. "Yes. Who were you hoping to see just now?"

She swallowed. "Zoë, my little sister." Her face crumpled. "She's gone. Run away."

He drew her into his arms at once, saying, "Hush now, we'll sort this out." Holding her against him, breathing in her essence, he smoothed his hand soothingly up and down her spine and felt her slowly calm.

After a few moments she took a deep, tremulous breath and stepped back, much to his disappointment. "Thank you. I don't mean to be a watering pot, it's just . . . just that . . . she's all alone." She pressed her lips together, fighting for control.

He led her into the front sitting room, which was, thankfully, unoccupied, and sat with her on the sofa. "Now, tell me what happened."

She shook her head. "I don't know. She was here this morning, seeming much as usual. And then, I didn't see her during the day, but that's not unusual—I assumed she was with Betty or visiting Lucy, Lady Thornton, over on the other side of the gardens. She often does. But then when Betty came to help me get dressed to go to Almack's, I discovered she hadn't seen Zoë all day, either." She paused, her forehead crinkling thoughtfully. "And when I thought about it, I realized Zoë has been a little bit . . . odd lately."

"In what way?"

"Yesterday we were talking over breakfast—I told her about what had happened the previous night with Mr. Clayborn—and when we'd finished, she was about to go downstairs and . . ." She gave Race a troubled look. "She thanked me in the oddest way. And then she said she'd been happy here, as if . . ."

"As if that time was coming to an end?"

She nodded.

"So you think she was saying goodbye?"

"In retrospect, yes. Oh, I should have said—we searched the house for her and found a note from her in her bedchamber. I'll fetch it." She hurried from the room and returned in a few minutes with a folded note and some loosely rolled papers tied with a ribbon. She handed him the note.

Dear Clarisa and Lady Skatergood I'm leavin I'm very greatful for all you done for me you bin very good and kind to me but it aint gunna work, me bein yore sister

*Clarisa. I aint no lady and nobodys gunna belive I am and
itull all come back on you and yore sister and I dont want
that to happen so Im goin away. Dont try to find me and
dont worry Ill be all right. Im leavin these pichers as a
little gift as a thank you for all your kindness and so you
dont forget me. Please give Lucy and Lady Tarant and the
little girls the ones of them, with my love and gratitude*

love Zoë

Race folded the note. "I see. You know she's right, don't you?"

She stared at him, shocked. "How can you say that? She's my *sister.*"

"Which hasn't yet been proved." He held up his hand. "No, I don't mean to dispute your claim on her—the resemblance to your other sister is extraordinary. But she's right that people won't believe she's a lady—it shows every time she opens her mouth—and attempting to pass her off as your sister will stir up the illegitimacy gossip again."

"I don't care! I couldn't care two hoots what stupid society gossips say—she's my sister and I want her to live with us, and be s-safe, and know she's l-l-loved." Her face crumpled again, and he drew her into his arms.

"Hush now, I know you don't care what people think. That's one of the things I love about you."

She pulled back and looked up at him in surprise, her beautiful eyes wide and doubting and swimming with tears. But now was not the time to convince her of his sincerity. "Don't worry, we'll find her. Now, dry your eyes and put your thinking cap on. Where might she have gone? What are those other papers?"

Without a word she passed them to him. He unwound the loose piece of ribbon and unrolled the papers. They were drawings, a dozen or so in pen and ink and some in pencil, of Clarissa, of old Lady Scattergood, of Mrs. Price-Jones, of a couple of servants, some dogs, and some others, including the three little girls he'd met in the garden yesterday. Lastly there was a self-portrait of Zoë herself.

"These are very good. Zoë's?"

She nodded.

"She's very talented." He picked up the one of Clarissa and examined it. "She's captured you perfectly."

Clarissa shook her head. "She's made me look pretty and I'm not."

"No, you're not pretty," he agreed. "But you are beautiful, and she sees that beauty in you. As do I." She flushed, and before she could say anything he continued. "She also sees the beauty in Lady Scattergood, see? She hasn't minimized her age or the many wrinkles in her lined old face, but the old lady's inner beauty shines through, don't you see? And the expression . . ."

Clarissa looked at the drawing of the old lady and nodded. "I have to find her and bring her home. She's out there all alone and, and . . . Anything can happen to a beautiful young girl, all alone."

"Don't worry, we'll find her." He tucked Zoë's self-portrait into a pocket. The drawings were beautifully vivid, but they gave no indication of where she might have run to. "Now think—where might she have gone? Would she go back to that orphanage?"

"Never. She hated it there. And she didn't take anything with her—only the clothes she arrived in, which were so shabby." She looked up at him, her face pale and anxious. "I've been thinking and thinking, but I cannot imagine where she'd go. I don't think she has anywhere *to* go."

"What about the place she lived in before the orphan asylum?" Surely she'd head for somewhere familiar.

Clarissa frowned, thinking. "I don't know. I don't think she ever mentioned any particular place—all I know is that her mother was a painter and an artist's model. Maybe Betty will know more. They were friends." She jumped up and sent for Betty, who turned out to be an abigail.

Betty stood in the doorway, wringing her hands on her apron. Another one who was distressed at Zoë's departure. "No, miss, she never told me the place. I don't know London that well, and place names don't mean much to me. Sorry, miss. She never told me she was leaving or I woulda stopped her, I promise you."

"I know, Betty. It's not your fault," Clarissa said softly. "Thank you."

It was a dismissal, but Betty hesitated. "What is it?" Race asked her. "Is there something else you want to tell us?"

Betty bit her lip. "I'm not sure, my lord, it's just . . . She left something with me, asked me to keep it safe for her until she came and fetched it. It was a few days ago, and I was busy and didn't think anything about it at the time. But now, I'm wondering . . . Shall I fetch it?"

"Yes, please," Clarissa told her, and Betty ran off. Clarissa looked at Race. "She didn't mention this before, when we were questioning her. I wonder what it is."

Betty returned shortly with a thick cardboard tube.

"Zoë brought that with her when she came from the orphanage," Clarissa exclaimed. "I didn't like to ask her what it was. She was so prickly at the time, and had so few possessions."

The tube was corked at either end. Clarissa removed one, tilted the tube and a thick roll slid out. She carefully unrolled it. "Paintings!" she exclaimed.

"More of Zoë's work?" Race said.

"No, most of these are proper paintings, in color, and some are on canvas." She leafed carefully through them. "Some are in watercolor and others in oil. Zoë didn't have any paints—I'd been meaning to buy her some, but I kept forgetting," she said distressfully.

"You can buy them for her when we find her," Race said firmly. "Now let's look through these. There might be a clue among them."

The paintings included a couple of watercolors and a

small oil painting of Zoë as a little girl. "Oh, look, her mother must have painted this one. She was so like Izzy, even then," Clarissa breathed.

She set it carefully aside and picked up the next one. It was a watercolor of a castle, a castle in the French style. "I wonder if this was Zoë's mother's home in France." She lifted it to examine it more closely and noticed a sketch pad underneath. "This might contain something that could help us find her." She picked it up and began flipping through it. "No, they're mostly sketches of people's faces, nothing to locate—" She broke off, staring.

"What is it?" Race asked.

Wordlessly she turned the pad around so he could see it. It was a set of three small vivid pen-and-ink sketches portraying an elegantly dressed man with curly dark hair. He looked handsome and arrogant, and very pleased with himself.

Race shook his head. It was nobody he knew. "Someone you recognize?"

"It's Papa," she whispered. "Izzy's and my papa—and Zoë's. It's unmistakable. If this were in color those eyes would be green. Hard, bright green." She looked at Race, her eyes wide. "This proves it: Zoë is indeed our sister."

Race nodded. It at least proved that Izzy's mother had definitely known Sir Bartleby Studley—the sketch was in her style—the same style as most of the paintings and drawings in the tube. And Zoë's resemblance to this man was unmistakable. As was Izzy's.

"Zoë must have seen this," Clarissa said. "So why didn't she show it to us? She must realize this would prove her paternity."

"It certainly adds to the evidence," Race said.

"Maybe it's too painful to look through her mother's things. I know that from my own experience," she told him.

Or maybe she just didn't want to prove she really was Clarissa's sister, Race thought. He didn't understand why that might be, but the girl *had* run away.

Clarissa pondered it a moment, then set it aside. "Let's look at the rest." She started laying out the remaining paintings and sketches.

"Her mother didn't paint this one," Race said, indicating a small oil painting on canvas. "It's by a different hand altogether." It was of a young blonde woman wearing a shabby blue dress that matched her eyes exactly. She was holding a baby on her lap, a modern-day madonna. In the background there was a window through which was a hazy silhouette of several tall buildings, the tallest with three crooked chimneys.

"I think that might be Zoë's mother, and Zoë as a baby," Clarissa breathed. "All these must be very precious to her. Why would she leave them behind?"

Race nodded absently. Where the devil had the girl gone to? London was huge. She could be anywhere.

Betty cleared her throat. "I reckon wherever she was going, miss, she might not have anywhere safe to put them. Better off leavin' them here, where she knows they'll be safe." She gave Clarissa a hopeful look. "Which means, she's intendin' to come back at some stage, doesn't it?"

Clarissa sighed. "Always assuming she can come back."

"Now stop those gloomy thoughts," Race said briskly. He stood up. "Fetch your hat and coat, both of you. We're going out."

Clarissa gave him a surprised look. "Where?"

"We'll start with that orphanage she came from. See if they know anything."

"It's well after midnight," Clarissa pointed out. "And you and I are in evening clothes."

"Ah. Right." He'd forgotten. "In that case I'll pick you up first thing in the morning. Eight o'clock all right? They should be up by then."

"The sooner, the better," Clarissa said. "Oh, I hope she's somewhere safe. I hate to think where she might be. London at night . . ."

"We'll find her," Race said with a lot more confidence than he felt.

"It's that big white building just ahead," Clarissa said, and Lord Randall signaled to the driver to pull up. He looked tired, and was wearing a smart greatcoat, fastened to the throat, which was odd, since the weather was quite mild. There was, however, a fresh breeze.

The other surprising thing was that he'd come in a hackney cab instead of one of his own carriages, quite a shabby-looking cab as well, but she was too anxious to start the search for Zoë to query it. There was room enough for four inside, which was all that mattered to her. A burly, shabbily dressed man clung on behind, apparently on Lord Randall's orders.

Lord Randall alighted first and helped her and Betty down. She'd insisted on bringing Betty in case she had a chance to talk to some of the orphan girls while Clarissa spoke to the matron.

"Are you sure you don't want me to come in with you?" Lord Randall asked.

"Quite sure." She had to do this by herself.

They entered the building and Clarissa asked to speak to Miss Glass. The woman ushered Clarissa into her office, leaving Betty in the hallway, as they'd hoped. Clarissa explained what she wanted.

Miss Glass looked smug. "So she's run away, then? I told you that girl would bring you nothing but trouble."

"There's no trouble," Clarissa said crisply. "I just need the address she was living at before she came here. The address where she was when her mother died."

"That's not possible. My records are private."

"As her employer, I think you owe it to me to provide all relevant details. At once, please. Time is of the essence." Zoë had been out all night, staying God knew where.

Secure behind her big wooden desk, Miss Glass shrugged. "I can't help that. As I said, my records are private. I can't go giving out details to whoever asks for them."

"I'm not any 'whoever,'" Clarissa snapped. "You were perfectly willing to hand over the girl to me when we came here first, so what possible objection can you have for furnishing me with details of her past?"

The woman sat back in her chair and pressed her fingertips together. "Rules are rules."

Clarissa wanted to scream in frustration. The woman was infuriatingly obdurate, and Clarissa knew, she just knew that it was just to be difficult. There could be no possible reason why Zoë's former address should be kept from her.

A shadow darkened the doorway. Miss Glass's eyes widened, and Clarissa turned. Lord Randall stood in the doorway. To Clarissa he said, "I'm sorry, my dear, but I don't like to keep the horses standing about in this wind. Did you get the address?"

"No, because this woman refuses to give it to me."

He looked at Miss Glass and arched an eyebrow. "Introduce us if you please, my dear."

The public endearments surprised her, as did the request. "Miss Glass, this is Lord Randall."

"Miss Studley's betrothed," he added.

Miss Glass rose and came out from behind her desk. "Lord Randall, this is an honor."

"Indeed." He smiled down at her and the woman bridled, smoothing her skirt self-consciously. Clarissa watched. The rake at work.

"Now, Miss Glass," he almost purred, "you cannot provide the address—the former address—of Zoë Benoît, one of your charges—a former charge? Surely you keep records."

"Yes, of course, but there are rules," she said.

"One little address? I could, if you prefer, speak to my friend Sir Cedric Greenspan, who I believe is one of the governors of this establishment—I saw his portrait in the hall. He's a busy man, I know—his son and I went to school together—but of course if there are rules . . ."

Miss Glass compressed her lips. "No, of course, there is no need to bother Sir Cedric over such a small matter." She pulled a heavy ledger from a desk drawer and flipped the pages over. She propped a pair of pince-nez on her long nose and consulted it. After a moment she huffed. "Well, it seems she's not listed here, see?"

She turned the ledger around so Clarissa and Lord Randall could see, and indeed, there was no Zoë Benoît listed.

"Try looking under Susan Bennet," Clarissa said. "Zoë said you claimed her real name was foreign and outlandish and you changed it to Susan Bennet."

The woman gave her a sour look and brought up another page. "Oh yes, here she is," she said, feigning innocence. "Crookneedle Lane."

Lord Randall grimly made a note of it. "Thank you for your assistance, Miss Glass. Come, Miss Studley, let us be off."

They collected Betty and climbed into the carriage. Lord Randall gave the driver directions and climbed in after them.

"That woman!" Clarissa exclaimed crossly as they drove off. "And you! Of course she was all helpful compliance when you swanned in with your title and your charm—*and* your old school friend."

He laughed. "I never met Sir Cedric Greenspan in my life. Or his son, if there is such a person."

She turned to him. "But you said . . ."

"I saw the fellow's portrait in the hall—there was a brass plaque with his name under it, and I took a gamble. It worked, didn't it? Why are you so cross?"

Because she'd wanted to handle it herself, and she'd failed. If it hadn't been for his interference, they would have come away with nothing, so it wasn't reasonable that she was cross. But she was. And she was worried about Zoë.

"Did you find out anything, Betty?"

"Just that she used to talk about artists living there, miss."

Lord Randall nodded. "Yes, that sounds about right. I'll drop you two home first and then—"

"What? We're not going home. We're going to look for Zoë."

"No." He waved the slip of paper with the address on it. "This is a most insalubrious district. It's not fit for a young lady—or her maid."

"Then it's not fit for Zoë, either, and we're going to get her out of there as soon as we can."

"It's too risky. You don't even know she's there."

"Then the sooner we go and look for her, the better. I'm *not* going home. And if necessary I'll walk to this Crook-needle Lane or if it's too far I'll take a hackney cab myself." Clarissa crossed her arms and glared at him.

"Me, too," Betty said.

He rolled his eyes, gave Clarissa a long look, then got the driver's attention and gave him the address. "But you're not getting out of the carriage," he told her.

She shrugged, not committing herself.

"I'm serious, Clarissa. Neither you nor Betty know London very well, and you have no idea how dangerous some of those districts can be. Now, where Zoë lived isn't the worst of them, but it's far from a wholesome environment— no don't argue, I know you don't want her to stay there a moment longer than necessary—if she's even there. Neither do I. But either you promise to obey me in this or I turn the carriage around and head straight back to Bellaire Gardens." He seemed in deadly earnest.

"Oh, very well," she said crossly after a minute. "I promise." But it went against the grain to just sit and wait tamely in the carriage with her maid while Lord Randall ventured into possible danger, searching for her sister.

He leaned forward and took her hands. "I know it's hard, love, but it's bad enough that your sister is lost. I couldn't

bear it if you were lost or put in danger, too." His voice was
low and sincere, and the look in his eyes . . . She felt tears
welling, and looked out the cab window, fiercely blinking
them away.

She sighed. "I'll be good."

The hackney cab turned and suddenly it was almost as
if they'd passed into another country, passing from
wide, fairly respectable-looking streets into a maze of
streets that became ever narrower and dirtier. The carriage
rattled over the cobbles, slowing for handcarts and people
and the occasional dog. The buildings here were ancient
and mean, squashed crookedly together as if they'd grown
there over the centuries, which she supposed they had.

They were not far from the river: Clarissa could smell it.
It was not all she could smell; there was also the odor of
human refuse and rotting garbage that lay in gutters and
piled in corners where rats nosed through it, unperturbed
by the presence of people.

She shivered.

It was a sunny day, but the buildings were so close together and the streets and alleyways so narrow that sunlight
barely touched the people on the ground. They were thin
and ragged looking and somehow hard-faced—or was it
hardship she could see reflected in their faces? She could
see several cripples—returned soldiers by the look of them,
begging in the street. Scrawny children clad in rags ran
about in screaming flocks like wild creatures.

And this was where Zoë had lived as a child? Where her
young mother had come after fleeing the Terror in France.
From some aristocratic mansion or castle to this? However
had she managed?

The carriage slowed, and Lord Randall unbuttoned his
smart greatcoat and shrugged it off. Clarissa blinked at
what he was wearing underneath—shabby, stained buck-

skins and an old, scuffed pair of boots, a coat that was loose and somewhat faded, and a neckcloth tied in a simple knot, instead of his usual sophisticated style.

Catching her look, he said, "It doesn't do to stand out in this part of London."

Judging from the people she could see from the carriage, he would fit right in. Now she understood the choice of the run-down carriage.

The carriage came to a halt in front of a crooked alleyway, barely wide enough for two people to walk abreast. "It's down there, guv'nor," the driver said.

Lord Randall picked up a steel-headed cane that had been sitting unnoticed in the corner of the carriage, and turned to Clarissa. "My man will stay with you and Betty. The driver is in my employ as well, but don't leave the cab." Before she had a chance to respond he kissed her swiftly and jumped lightly down onto the street.

She watched through the cab window as he approached person after person, showing them the drawing of Zoë—to no avail. They had only a street name, so Zoë could be in any one of these ramshackle buildings. Or in none of them.

He approached an old woman sitting on a step and smoking a pipe. Scraggly white elf-locks poked out from under a rag tied around her head. He showed her the portrait, and like all the others, she glanced at it, shrugged and shook her head.

Lord Randall moved on, but as Clarissa watched, the old woman watched him go, then took the pipe out of her mouth, replaced it with two fingers and emitted a shrill whistle. An urchin came running. She said something to him, and he nodded.

Intrigued, Clarissa watched as the boy disappeared through the shadowed doorway behind her. What had the old woman told him?

Minutes passed. Clarissa kept watching. Then the boy peered out of the doorway, looked cautiously around and beckoned to someone inside. A slender figure appeared wearing a shabby hooded cloak, a small bundle clutched to her chest. She darted out into the laneway and Clarissa gasped. She couldn't see the girl's face, but she recognized the way she moved.

In seconds she'd flung herself out of the hackney cab and was running down the street in pursuit. "Zoë!" she cried. "Zoë!"

The figure darted down a skinny walkway.

"Zoë, stop!" yelled Clarissa, following. The figure paused and looked around. "Zoë! It's me, Clarissa."

Zoë glared at her. "What are you doing here, Clarissa? Don't you know it's dangerous—"

Reaching her, Clarissa flung her arms around Zoë. "If it's dangerous for me, it's dangerous for you. How could you leave us like that? I've been so worried—we all have. Don't you know we love you? Come home with me now, please."

Zoë shook her head adamantly. "I'm no good for you, Clarissa. I don't fit into your fancy world, and I never will."

"Do you think I care about that? I care about *you*!" Clarissa hugged her sister again.

"But society people—"

"Pooh to society people!"

"Miss," Betty said in a low voice. "Miss, behind you."

Clarissa glanced impatiently around and saw half a dozen rough-looking men closing in around them.

One of them smiled at her with a mouthful of yellow, rotting teeth, his eyes running over her in a way that made her feel dirty. "Look't the pretty birds in their fine feathers. They'll fetch a good price for us, eh, lads?"

Clarissa looked frantically around for help—where were the men Lord Randall had hired? But the hackney cab was around several corners and out of sight.

Zoë stepped forward, shoving Clarissa behind her. "Leave us be, Jake," she said.

He snorted. "You don't belong here anymore, girlie."

"You think?" Zoë said, and without warning she opened her mouth and let out a shrill, ululating sound. It sent a shiver down Clarissa's back. Before the uncanny sound had even died away, urchins appeared from everywhere. They pelted rotten vegetables and fruit at the men, who swore and ducked and made horrible threats.

"Are these fellows bothering you, Miss Studley?" Lord Randall appeared from behind them. He twisted the handle of his cane and pulled out a sword. His smile was cold as he said, "Now, gentlemen, who wants the first taste of my steel?" He lunged forward, swishing the sword.

The men edged back. "Come on, he's only one man," the leader snarled, wiping a splat of rotten fruit off his face.

"You go first then, Jake," another one said. A chunk of something yellow dribbled down his front.

Seconds later the burly guard appeared, panting, from behind the thugs. He grabbed one of the brutes by the collar, flung him backward hard against a wall and shoved through the gap he'd made in the ring of ruffians to stand with Lord Randall in front of the girls, brandishing a short wooden cudgel. Over his shoulder he said to Clarissa, "Sorry, miss, lost you for a moment there."

"Two of them now," one of the thugs said, brushing rotten fruit off his face. "And I don't like the look of that big bruiser."

"Yeah, s'not worth it," said another.

In seconds the men melted away. The gang of urchins loitered. Lord Randall sheathed his sword-stick, put a hand in his pocket and pulled out a handful of coins. "Thanks for your help." He tossed the coins to the children, who scrambled to collect them.

He turned to Clarissa and snapped, "Into the hackney cab—now!"

"I found Zoë," Clarissa said unnecessarily. She was still holding on to Zoë's hand, worried she might run off again.

"So. I. See." He seemed furious.

They returned to where the cab was standing. "Couldn't leave it untended, milor'. Not in a place like this," the driver began apologetically. Lord Randall impatiently waved his excuses away. He opened the door. "Get in," he told them curtly.

"Just a minute," Zoë said, and ran down to where the old woman with the pipe was sitting.

Clarissa went to follow but Lord Randall caught her arm and stopped her. "If she doesn't want to come, she's not going to stay," he told her. "She'll only run away again, and this time we might not be so lucky."

He was right. She couldn't force Zoë to stay. Clarissa bit her lip as Zoë bent over the old woman. To her amazement, after a brief word, Zoë hugged her. Then she returned to where they were standing beside the carriage.

Zoë stared defiantly up at Lord Randall, who was scowling. "I've known Old Moll all my life. She didn't know who you were and didn't trust you. So she warned me to hide."

Without a word, Lord Randall strode down the alley toward the old woman. Zoë tensed, but Clarissa put a hand on her arm, saying, "It's all right. He won't hurt her."

"How do you know? Din't you see his face? He's bloody furious."

"I know, but he won't hurt her, I'm sure of it." Clarissa didn't know how she knew that Lord Randall would never harm a woman, but she had no doubt of it.

Whatever he said to the old lady was brief, but he flipped something to her that she caught, something that glinted in the light, and then he marched back to the carriage. "Bellaire Gardens," he snapped to the driver. He flung himself inside and the cab moved off.

Chapter Thirteen

❧

Race sat slouched in the corner of the cab, staring unseeing out of the window as they rattled over the cobblestones. His mind kept bringing up the sight of Clarissa, desperately clutching her sister's hand as those filthy jackals closed in on them.

Why the devil had she left the carriage? He'd ordered her to stay—and she'd promised she would!

If he hadn't found them . . .

He'd almost been too late. Anything could have happened to her. The possibilities ate at him.

"What was that sound you made?" Clarissa asked Zoë. "It was quite uncanny."

Zoë laughed. "It worked, din't it? An Arab family used to live above Maman and me, and the girls taught me to make that sound. It's tricky to do—took me ages to get it right, but once I did, we used it to call for help, or warn each other." She darted a glance at Race. "Whistling, too, a sorta code. Which is what Old Moll did to send that warning to me."

Race didn't respond: he didn't trust himself to speak. He was still too angry, and their blithe discussion—as if they hadn't been inches from death or worse, as if it had all been a delightful adventure—infuriated him.

"I wasn't sure anyone would be around who remembered it—I was just a nipper when Maman died and I was taken away—but seems some people remember. I reckon Old Moll heard it and sent the street rats after Jake and his boys." She laughed. "A right mess they made of them."

Clarissa and Betty laughed, too.

Race clenched his teeth and breathed in through his nose. How could they laugh about it so carelessly? Did they have no idea how close they had come? The danger they'd been in? What if he hadn't found them—it was just chance that he'd turned left instead of right, down one of those blasted twisty alleyways, and found them.

The hackney cab rumbled along over the cobbles. Race stared out of the window.

"Where did you sleep last night?" Clarissa asked.

"On the floor at Old Moll's." Zoë gave her a wry look and added, "Didn't sleep much. Seems I've gone soft since I come to live with you. The floor was hard. And dirty. And there were rats."

Clarissa and Betty exclaimed in horror.

"Yeah, it wasn't like that when Maman and I lived there . . . At least . . ." She frowned. "Maybe I forgot what it was really like."

"At least you were safe with Old Moll."

Zoë grimaced wryly. "It wouldn't've bin for free. Always gets her pound of flesh, Old Moll."

Race had a good idea what that pound of flesh might have been. A beautiful young girl in a place like that? Clarissa was too innocent of the world to realize it, but he'd seen the old woman up close, and he'd known the meaning of the dress cut low over a scraggy old bosom and the paint on her face.

Zoë gave him a shrewd look. "And it's not what you're thinking, Lord Randall. I know what Moll's profession useta be, but she was always good to Maman and me, and when Maman got sick, she did her best to help us. She wouldn't have forced me to follow in her own footsteps, but she'd maybe put me to work scrubbing or some such."

"Scrubbing?" Clarissa echoed. "But when we met at the orphan asylum, you said—"

"Yeah, well, I told Moll what I was going to do, and she said she'd give me a week, and if I couldn't make it pay . . ."

"What were you going to do?"

"Drawings. Chalk drawings on the footpath to make people stop and look, and pencil ones for whoever would pay. That's how Maman started." She gave Clarissa a guilty look. "I took that sketch pad and some pencils from Lady Scattergood's."

Clarissa waved that aside. "I'm sure you would have made it pay, as long as you were in the right place to attract people who could afford it."

"Yeah, I had me spot all picked out."

After a few minutes, Clarissa said, "But why did you leave, Zoë? Weren't you happy with us?"

Zoë sighed. "Of course I was happy. You bin ever so kind to me, Clarissa—everyone has. But"—Zoë gave her a troubled look—"I don't fit into your world, Clarissa. Everyone knows it 'cept you."

Clarissa glanced at Race. He'd told her much the same thing. She turned back to Zoë. "I don't care about 'my world.' I never did enjoy going into society, and I only have a few real friends, and they won't care."

Zoë shook her head. "I know some families recognize their bastards, but only if the mothers are highborn."

"Your mother was highborn."

"In France—and nobody here knew her. For all anyone knows she was a prostitute from the stews. She wasn't, but I can't prove it."

"Of course she wasn't. And nobody needs to know you're . . . um, baseborn. Look, let us not worry about all that just now. I'm sure we can come up with a plan."

Zoë's stomach rumbled.

"Oh dear, I didn't think," Clarissa said remorsefully. "You must be hungry. We'll feed you when we get home. But first you must run upstairs and wash and change—if Lady Scattergood sees you in those clothes she'll have a fit. She ordered them to be burned when you arrived, if you remember."

"Yeah, but it's a waste. These clothes might not be new, but there's still plenty of wear in them," Zoë retorted. "And I couldn't wear any of Izzy's fine dresses where I was going. People have been stripped and left naked in the street, just for their clothes, you know."

Clarissa looked horrified, both at the thought of such a crime, and at the matter-of-fact way Zoë spoke of it. "You won't run away again, will you?"

At that point Zoë's stomach gave another loud rumble, and they laughed. "Luncheon won't be long," Clarissa said, "or maybe—good heavens! It's still time for breakfast. We did leave early. With any luck Lady Scattergood and Mrs. Price-Jones will still be abed."

The cab pulled up and the three females jumped down. Clarissa rang the bell and after a few moments the butler answered. Race had paid off his men by then. The women hurried indoors and Race sauntered through the front door after them, repressing a smile at the sour look the butler gave him. Seems he was no longer persona non grata.

"Lady Scattergood wants to talk to you," the butler told Zoë. "She's in the back parlor."

"Me?"

"You. Just you. Alone," he said with a smug expression. Young Zoë was clearly not the butler's favorite person. If he even had one.

Zoë gave Clarissa an anxious look.

"She was worried about you, too," Clarissa assured her. "I expect she just wants to make sure you're all right."

The picture of reluctance, Zoë went slowly toward Lady Scattergood's favorite sitting room.

"Zoë," Clarissa called after her. Zoë paused and looked back. "Please don't run away again. If you don't want to live with me, that's all right—we will sort something out, I promise. Just don't . . . run away. I couldn't bear it if we lost you again."

Zoë stared at her a minute, then rushed back and hugged her. "I won't, I promise. I'm sorry I worried you so. I thought you'd be glad to be rid of me."

Clarissa was shocked. "How could you think such a thing?"

Zoë shrugged. "Since Maman died, I don't reckon anybody cared about me. Maybe Old Moll, but only as long as I could help her out."

Race hoped Clarissa never discovered what price Old Moll would demand for her help. He didn't believe the old woman's benevolence would last until Zoë earned a living. Thank God they'd found her when they did.

Zoë turned to leave, and as Clarissa moved as if to follow, he cupped her elbow in his hand. "A word in private, if you please."

She glanced worriedly to where Zoë was just raising a hand to knock on Lady Scattergood's door, then relented, saying, "Yes, of course." He escorted her into the small private sitting room and shut the door behind him.

She turned to him with a warm smile. "Thank you so much for helping us to find Zoë. We couldn't have done it without you, and I'm so grateful."

"*Grateful?*" he repeated incredulously.

"Yes, very grateful."

"I don't want your gratitude," he growled.

"Oh." Her smile faded. After a moment she said, cautiously, "Are you annoyed about something, Lord Randall?"

"*Annoyed?*" It was hardly the word. He didn't know how he felt, only that he'd never been so damnably stirred up, so frustrated and furious—and so relieved—in his life.

"Yes, you seem rather cross." She tilted her head inquiringly. "What about?"

The blithe obliviousness of her inquiry fanned the embers of his emotional turmoil to flames again. "You dare to ask me what I'm cross about? I'll tell you! You promised me you'd stay in the cab. But you didn't!"

"Yes, I know, because I saw Zoë and if I hadn't followed her—"

"You almost got killed."

"Oh, I don't think so. Those men were very unpleasant, but I don't think they were going to kill us. They were talking about selling something, our clothes probably—they said something about birds and 'fine feathers.' Zoë said people had been stripped of their cl—"

He stepped forward and gripped her shoulders. "They weren't planning to sell your clothes, you little fool—they were intending to sell *you*! To a bordello or brothel. White slavery." He hammered it home.

She stared up at him, wide-eyed, but then smiled and said in an infuriatingly soothing tone, "But they didn't, did they? You and your man and those clever children chased them off, so it all worked out perfectly, didn't it? We found Zoë and have her home, safe now."

It was so tempting to shake her, to make her understand; instead, he let go of her and stepped back. "I'm not talking about Zoë," he ground out.

"But surely she was the whole point—"

"I'm talking about the insane risk you took! What if I hadn't found you? What if Jacobs hadn't arrived in time? A few rotten apples wouldn't have saved you."

She gave him a tentative smile. "But you did find me, and everything turned out perfectly. I don't understand why you are so out-of-reason cross."

"Because if I can't trust you to keep your promises—"

"I do keep my promises, in general," she said indignantly. "It's just that I saw Zoë running off and you were nowhere in sight, and if I hadn't gone after her we wouldn't have found her."

"And so you were that far"—he snapped his fingers under her nose—"from being attacked by those jackals."

"Don't you snap your fingers at me," she snapped.

"I will snap whatever I like!" He glared at her, baffled and furious and . . . aroused. He breathed in a deep breath and tried to moderate his tone. "Look, Clarissa, it is my job to protect you, and—"

She stamped her foot. "No it's not! You are not in any way responsible for me or my safety."

"I am."

"Nonsense! I don't know what Leo asked you to do—"

"This is *not* about Leo," he grated. "We are betrothed, remember?"

She waved that aside. "Pooh! A convenient fiction to distract the ton. What has that to do with anything, pray?"

He stared at her. "What has that . . . ?" he began, and then gave up trying to explain. He pulled her into his arms and his mouth came down on hers, hard. He wanted to punish her, to teach her that she was not to risk herself so recklessly, that in dangerous situations like that she should obey his orders.

Because—God!—she could have been *killed*! Her throat slit with a filthy knife. Dragged off into some hideous dive and raped. Sold into a brothel, never to be seen again.

And did she understand? Did she have the slightest idea of the risks she had taken when she left the carriage?

No she did not! Did she even regret doing it?

No she did not! She was *thrilled* with the result—chattering excitedly all the way home as if she'd done something marvelous!

She'd be the death of him yet.

And, oh God, she was kissing him back with her usual sweet enthusiasm, twining her arms around his neck, and he couldn't bear it. Any minute now he was going to fall to his knees and beg . . .

A man needed to know when to retreat.

He released her and, breathing heavily, stepped back.

"Now do you understand?" Gray eyes blazing, he stormed to the door, yanked it open and turned back. "And for your information our betrothal is *not* a blasted fiction. Nor is it in *any* way convenient! Good day!" He slammed the door behind him.

Clarissa stared at the closed door, then her knees gave out on her. She sank onto the sofa. *Now do you understand?* She didn't understand anything. She knew only that she was in trouble, dire trouble.

This kiss had been different, so different—and yet just as exhilarating. Possibly even more so. She'd tasted a tangled coil of emotions; desperation and fear and possessiveness. Anger and frustration. And relief.

He'd been shaken right out of his usual smooth self-possession.

This Lord Randall was more attractive to her than ever.

"Come in," Lady Scattergood called, and Zoë stepped into the old lady's sitting room. She was seated on her peacock chair, wearing a turban and swathed in half a dozen colorful clashing shawls, surrounded by her dogs. She lifted her lorgnette and stared at Zoë through it for a long, unnerving moment.

"Well, miss? What have you got to say for yourself? Running away, eh? Fretting us all to flinders, worrying about your safety and having to search for you in gutters and stews and God knows where—and for what, eh?" She aimed her lorgnette at Zoë, her beady black eyes glinting. "Why did you run off? Aren't you happy here?"

"Oh yes, ma'am, and I'm sorry."

"Don't we feed you enough?"

"Yes of course."

"Anyone beat you? Make you sit in the cinders?"

Zoë flushed. "No, of course not. You've been very kind and generous. It's just that . . ."

"Just what? Spit it out, gel!"

"I don't belong here."

"Don't belong here? What nonsense! Who says so?"

"Well, you did, ma'am. You and Mrs. Price-Jones."

"Mrs. Price-Jones and I?"

"Yes, ma'am, I heard you talking about me. I think it was Mrs. Price-Jones who said I'd bring Clarissa to ruin, but you agreed. But I don't want that, so . . ."

"Pish tush! What nonsense. Eavesdroppers never hear any good of themselves so let that be a lesson to you, young lady. And I'll wager you didn't hear the whole conversation."

"No, ma'am."

"You think *you* can bring Clarissa to ruin? Poppycock! She is in *my* care! So clear your mind of that bit of nonsense. So, what were your plans, eh? How did you intend to earn your bread and butter—though I'll wager you'd be lucky to get so much as a crust of bread, probably stale, and never a sniff of butter."

"I was going to become a street artist."

"A *what*?"

"Street artist. It's how Maman started, drawing pictures on the footpath in chalk."

"*Street artist?* Good gad." The old lady picked up the drawings Zoë had done of her and the dogs. "You did these, did you?"

"Yes, ma'am."

There was a long silence. "So you think you don't belong here, do you?"

"Yes, ma'am. I don't . . . fit. I'm not a servant, and I'm
never gunna make a lady. And I don't do nothing, nothing
useful, that is."

The old lady gave her an appalled look. "*Useful?* Good
gad, gel, there is more to life than being useful. Pigs are
useful. Chickens are useful. Servants are useful, but most
of the ton, myself included, live utterly useless lives and
still manage to be happy . . . though some are also orna-
mental, I have to admit." She peered at Zoë. "But that's
what you want, is it, gel? To be *useful*?" She pronounced
useful as if it were something nasty she'd stepped in.

Zoë nodded.

The old lady pondered for a few minutes, eyeing Zoë as
if she were some kind of peculiar bird. Then she sat up with
a jerk. "I have it! If you are so determined to be useful, I
shall employ you as my artist-in-residence."

"Your what? Artist-in-residence? There ain't no such
position."

Lady Scattergood raised her lorgnette and said in freezing tones, "You are acquainted with the more rarefied
household cultural practices of the English aristocracy,
are you?"

Zoë flushed. "No, ma'am."

"Very well then. Artist-in-residence you are. Your first
commission is to paint a portrait of me. None of your pencil
or charcoal nonsense. Proper paints, you hear me? And when
you've finished that, you will start on portraits of the dogs.
Understand?"

"Yes, but I don't have any proper paints."

She waved an impatient hand. "Pish tush, don't bother
me with trivialities. Buy whatever you need and get the
shopkeeper to send me the bills. Now, off with you."

"Yes, ma'am, thank you, ma'am." Dazed at the unex-

pected turn in her fortunes, Zoë bobbed a curtsy and turned
to leave.

"And Zoë."

"Yes, ma'am?"

"This time when you remove those appalling rags you're
wearing, burn them."

"Oh, but—

"Burn them."

Zoë sighed. "Yes, ma'am."

A few days later, Clarissa was about to join Zoë in the
garden when she met her guardian, Leo—now her
brother-in-law—entering Lady Scattergood's through the
back door. "Leo," she exclaimed in delight, "you're back!
When did you get back? Where's Izzy?"

He grinned. "We arrived late last night. She's in the garden, looking for you. I was just coming to pay my respects
to Aunt Olive and inform her I'm home. I'm delighted to
see you, Clarissa. You're looking very well."

"Thank you. Welcome home, Leo. Now I'll just go out
and find Izzy. I've so missed her."

Clarissa made to pass him and hurry out to the garden,
but he detained her with a hand on her arm. "My felicitations on your betrothal, Clarissa. I was so pleased to hear
it. Race will make you an excellent husband."

She blinked. "Oh, but we're not really betrothed. It's all
a hum, a scheme to divert the ton from the nasty scandal
Mr. Clayborn tried to cause."

"Yes, I heard about that swine Clayborn. Filthy deception.
But"—he gave her a close look—"that's not how Race explained the betrothal to me. He called on me first thing this
morning. How he knew we'd returned is beyond me. Still
less why he felt he had to call on me at such an unseason-
able hour—we might be back from the honeymoon but—"

He broke off, his color slightly heightened. "I had to receive him in my dressing gown."

Clarissa didn't care about that. "What did he tell you?"

"He seems to be quite serious about marrying you. We briefly discussed settlements—of course the details will be thrashed out later with the legal chaps."

Settlements? She felt suddenly light-headed. "No, he can't be serious. He's just pretending. He's funning you, Leo."

Leo shook his head. "He's not. He's in deadly earnest. He asked for my permission and I gave it. I've drafted the notice to send off to the *Gazette*. I just wanted to show it to you first." He pulled a piece of paper from his pocket.

"No! No, you cannot send it. It's all a mistake, a terrible mistake."

He frowned. "Are you unhappy about this betrothal, Clarissa?"

She shook her head frantically. "It's *not* a betrothal, it's not real. It can't be."

"Don't you want to marry Race? I understood from Izzy that you had feelings for him but if she's mistaken and you're being coerced into it because of that scandal with Clayborn—"

She burst into tears, turned and ran up the stairs to her bedchamber and flung herself down on the bed.

Izzy stepped out into the garden and breathed in the scent of flowers and greenery, tinged with a faint flavor of smoke. She couldn't wait to see her sister. Oh, marriage was blissful, and she'd loved every moment of her honeymoon, but she'd missed Clarissa, missed sharing all her thoughts and feelings with her sister. Leo was a wonderful lover, but he wasn't one for discussing emotions. She chuckled at the very idea.

They'd woken early, as usual, and had made slow, blissful love as a delicate rose and gold dawn broke over the London rooftops. It was her favorite way to wake up, to come to consciousness with Leo caressing her, and then that slow growth of intensity, of feeling . . . Oh, she had no words to describe it.

But oh, the glory that man had introduced her to. She shivered deliciously, remembering. They'd just begun to make love again when Matteo had knocked on the door, saying Lord Randall was downstairs asking to speak to Leo.

She chuckled again, recalling Leo's irritation. He'd groaned, sworn, kissed her, rolled out of bed and shrugged into his gorgeously embroidered heavy silk dressing gown. Then he'd opened the door, looked back at her sitting up in bed in a welter of bedclothes, and marched back to give her a heated kiss that almost left her swooning. "Blast Race. It had better be important," he'd muttered, and stomped off, leaving her to bathe and dress at her leisure.

She looked around. On a beautiful morning like this she was sure Clarissa would be out in her beloved garden. Perhaps the rose arbor. She headed toward it.

Rounding a corner in the path she almost collided with another young woman. "Oh, excuse m—" she began, and stared.

The girl stared back, green eyes wide as she examined Izzy from top to toe.

"Gawd! It's true, then," the girl exclaimed. "I suppose you're Izzy."

"And you must be Zoë. Oh my, Clarissa did tell me there was a strong resemblance—she wrote to me while I was away, you know—but I didn't have any idea how much." Izzy was stunned. It was almost like looking in a mirror.

"Me, too. I didn't expect it to be so . . ." Zoë gestured vaguely.

They continued staring at each other. "I think your hair is a little lighter than mine, not quite as black."

Zoë nodded. "And I'm not as tall as you."

"How old are you?"

"Nearly sixteen."

"Then I think you might have a few more years of growing yet." She gazed at her new sister, almost overwhelmed by the tumble of mixed emotions. Another sister, one just like her, in more ways than she could count.

Izzy bounced up and down on her toes. "Oh, I'm so excited. I want to hug you." She stepped forward. "Would you mind?"

Zoë shrugged and shook her head, and Izzy pulled her into an exuberant hug.

"Good morning, little sister," she said, stepping back but holding onto Zoë's hands. "I'm so very delighted to meet you."

Zoë stared at her, looking bemused. "You don't mind, then?"

"Mind what? That you look like me? No, of course not—you even look like my sister which, sadly, Clarissa doesn't. She looks like her mother while you and I take after our wicked papa."

"No, I meant mind that I'm even here. Once people see me, it's going to cause a bit of nasty talk—especially about you. Bein' a bastard, I mean. Oh, I shouldn't have said that, should I, you bein' one, too? What's the word that proper ladies use?"

Izzy laughed. "Baseborn? A natural child? As opposed to an unnatural one, which sounds much worse." She laughed again. "Proper ladies probably don't even refer to it, but I can see you and I like to call a spade a spade."

Zoë bit her lip. "Yeah, but when they see us, people will talk. And it could ruin you and 'specially Clarissa, and she's bin so good to me, I would hate to—"

"Oh, pish tush!" Izzy declared. "Clarissa and I discussed all this when we first came to London, and if you think either of us would prefer acceptance by nasty-minded society gossips to the company of a lovely little sister, you're very much mistaken. Clarissa refused to give me up when Lord Salcott was trying to make her, and before that when our father wanted to get rid of me, and she'll be exactly the same with you."

Zoë's forehead puckered. "Lord Salcott? But isn't he—"

"My husband, yes." Izzy laughed. "It took him quite a while to succumb, but he did in the end. And he'll stand with us, you'll see."

"Yeah, but you're safely married. And to a lord. Clarissa isn't yet. Though if Lord Randall has his way . . ."

"Lord Randall? You mean he and Clarissa have finally . . . ?"

Zoë grimaced. "Well, they're supposedly betrothed, though it hasn't yet been officially announced—"

Izzy clapped her hands. "I knew it! I was sure Race was keen on her, but I thought Clarissa would never let herself—"

"No, it's a fake betrothal," Zoë interrupted bluntly. "Or at least that's what she keeps telling me. She reckons it's just for appearances' sake."

Izzy frowned. "That sounds complicated. Where is Clarissa? I thought she'd be out here on such a glorious morning."

"Dunno. I expected her to come out, too."

"Then I'll seek her out and discover what's going on. Oh, Zoë, I'm so thrilled to have a new sister. We'll talk later, I promise. I want to find out all about you, but first I need to find my sister—my *other* sister! So exciting to be able to say that! Two sisters! I need to discover what this 'supposed' betrothal of hers is all about. I'll see you later." She hugged Zoë again, and hurried off to Lady Scattergood's house.

She found Clarissa upstairs in her bedchamber, splashing her face with cold water in a vain effort to hide her red eyes and blotchy skin. "Oh, love, you've been crying," Izzy exclaimed.

Clarissa burst into tears.

* * *

An hour later the two sisters were sitting cross-legged on Clarissa's bed, facing each other as they used to do when they were children. They'd hugged, wept a little, laughed a lot and hugged again. And then Clarissa had dried her tears, and over hot chocolate and a dish of delicious orange biscuits they'd talked.

Clarissa sipped her chocolate. "It wouldn't have been so bad if Lord Randall hadn't kept turning up everywhere. Are you sure Leo didn't make him promise to keep an eye on me?"

"Positive," Izzy assured her. "He did ask Race to take you riding, knowing that nobody here can ride, and Hyde Park was too tame for a proper ride. But that's all."

"He did take me riding, and I confess it was lovely to be able to get out of London and go for a proper ride—and he brought his cousin Maggie and I really like her, Iz. And if that was all it was . . . But then he was everywhere—at balls and routs, which everyone knows he never attends—never *used to* attend," she added darkly. "He even went to one of old Lady Gastonbury's *soirées musicale*."

Izzy laughed. "Serve him right. Was Cicely in good form?"

"And he turned up at Lady Beatrice's literary society."

"It sounds as though he really was courting you, 'Riss," Izzy said gently.

"I know, and that's the problem. If I didn't keep running into him everywhere, I wouldn't have—" She broke off and looked away.

"Fallen in love with him?"

Clarissa gave a tragic sigh. "Oh, don't say it, please."

"No point in denying it, love. You were halfway to falling for him even before my wedding and it looks like you've fallen all the way now."

"I haven't. I can't. You know it's impossible, Izzy, you *know* it!" Clarissa scrubbed at her eyes with a damp and crumpled handkerchief.

There was a long silence. Clarissa picked up an orange biscuit and nibbled around the lacy edging. Then she lowered it, saying, "The problem is, he's just too charming. He can make me laugh in the most ridiculous ways. You should have heard him talking about the ducks—and then in the park, I could hardly preserve my countenance when he introduced me to the human version."

She nibbled on the biscuit then continued, "And when I dance with him—and he always asks me and it's impossible to refuse—and you know I'm not that good a dancer, but . . . it's like . . . I feel like I'm floating, and so warm and safe. And happy."

Izzy squeezed her hand and said nothing. She looked troubled.

Clarissa went on, "But that's what rakes are like, aren't they? They know how to do things like that, make people— ladies—feel like that. And when he ki—" She broke off with a guilty look and avoided her sister's eye.

Izzy almost choked on a mouthful of biscuit. "Clarissa Studley! You let him kiss you?"

Clarissa felt her cheeks heat. She nodded.

"Well, how was it? You know what Mrs. Price-Jones said about kissing a lot of frogs—"

Clarissa sighed. "He wasn't a frog." And what an understatement that was. That kiss had haunted her dreams ever since.

Izzy laughed and brushed crumbs off her fingers. "Of course he wasn't. So, you let Race Randall kiss you. That's wonderful."

"I also let Mr. Clayborn kiss me," Clarissa admitted.

Izzy clapped her hands. "You daring little minx! And?"

"A definite frog."

"So it sounds like Race Randall has swept you off your feet with his dancing and his kissing."

"That wasn't all. Oh, Izzy, if you'd seen the way he was with Lady Tarrant's little girls—she's had the baby, by the way. A little boy. They're naming him Ross after Lord Tarrant's late brother."

"Lovely. We'll go and call on them later. Now don't change the subject. Tell me how Race Randall was with those little girls."

Clarissa described how they'd come across the girls and how distressed they were. "If you could only have seen it, Izzy. He knew exactly how to calm their fears and coax them into a happier frame of mind. And the way he picked up little Lina and let her weep buckets into his neckcloth— so patient and kind. I nearly wept myself, watching him."

And because, seeing him so gentle and kind with three small girls he didn't even know, she realized that she was hopelessly and completely in love with him.

"I've never seen that side of him," Izzy admitted. "I've only seen the charming-women side and the way he is with Leo. Leo trusts him completely, you know."

Clarissa nodded. "I'm not surprised. Though men are different with other men, aren't they? If they make a promise to a man—well, their sacred code of honor demands that they keep it. It seems to me their word given to a woman is quite a different matter." She had two illegitimate sisters to prove it.

"He's gallant, too," she continued. "He rescued me from Mr. Clayborn's attack—and it *was* an attack, Izzy—he ripped my dress half off me and he meant to go through with it, I'm sure. He had his breeches open."

Izzy stared. "Good God! I hadn't heard that. What a villain."

"But Lord Randall burst in and dragged him off me. And later he was responsible for exposing Mr. Clayborn's horrid deception with his so-called wound."

"We heard something about it—someone wrote to Leo. Gravel in the boot?—but you can tell me all about it later. Right now I want to hear about what Race Randall did."

"Well, that's when he offered for me, and between them, he and Mrs. Price-Jones convinced me it was for the best, that it would change the nature of the gossip so that it wasn't as damaging to me. And at the time he stressed that I could call it off whenever I wanted. It was all a—a strategy—not a genuine betrothal at all. But I saw Leo downstairs just now and he said Lord Randall had called on him this morning and was quite in earnest about marriage. They'd even discussed settlements!"

More tears came and she scrubbed them away.

When she'd calmed a little, Izzy said, "So what's the problem, 'Riss? You love Lord Randall and it sounds to me very much as though he loves you, too."

Clarissa shook her head. "Even if he does love me—which I'm not at all sure about—he tosses endearments around like—like a farmer sowing seed! He's *a rake*! Just like Papa."

Izzy grimaced. "Not exactly like Papa. Papa would have ignored weeping children and he would no more have offered marriage to save someone's reputation than fly. But I take your point. You're worried he'll break your heart, aren't you?"

Clarissa's nodded. "Rakes aren't generally known for their fidelity, and I couldn't bear it if . . . if . . ." Her face crumpled.

Izzy leaned forward and hugged her. "I know, love. I know."

Chapter Fourteen

❧

I talked to Leo last night about your problem," Izzy said the following morning after breakfast. She'd arranged to meet Clarissa in the summerhouse.

Clarissa blinked. "You discussed me with Leo?" It was a shock to think that Izzy would speak of Clarissa's private problems with her husband, but she supposed that was what happened when people got married: all their previous relationships had to adjust. She wasn't happy about it, but she didn't say anything.

"Oh, don't look like that, Leo won't say anything."

"I know, it's just . . ."

"Leo is your guardian and Race is his best friend. And in any case, it was mostly Race we discussed, not you, goose."

"Oh." Mostly?

"He actually initiated the conversation. He was worried you might be under pressure to carry the betrothal through, against your wishes."

"Pressure from whom?"

"Oh, society in general and Mrs. Price-Jones in particular."

Clarissa sighed. "No, they don't worry me that much. I don't care what society thinks, and though Mrs. Price-Jones is eager to get me married and off her hands, she—"

"Why is that? She's well paid to be your chaperone, and she has no income of her own."

Clarissa chuckled. "Mrs. Price-Jones now has two very rich and eligible silver-haired gentlemen vying for her hand. You missed it all while you were on your honeymoon."

"No!"

"Yes, and she's told them she can't even think about marriage, let alone decide between them, until I'm off her hands."

"The clever old thing. Good for her. I knew she was looking for a second husband—she needs one, having inherited nothing from her first. So who are these silver swains— No, sorry, I don't want to talk about her. It's you we're talking about."

Clarissa sighed. She'd much rather not discuss her problems at all. But Izzy was determined.

"I told Leo I was worried about Race's rakish reputation, and you know what he said?"

Clarissa waited.

"He thinks that Race's reputation is much exaggerated."

Clarissa was skeptical. "Oh, really? In what way?"

Izzy pursed her lips. "That's where Leo became annoying. Said he refused to discuss Race's private affairs, and that if you were worried about his reputation, you should ask him about it."

"Ask him about it?" Clarissa echoed incredulously. "What, just bowl up to him and say, 'Oh, Lord Randall, are you the rake everyone says you are?'" She snorted. "And of course he would say no, of course not and that he was the next best thing to a saint, and then what? I'm supposed to take his word for it?"

"I know, 'Riss, it's not ideal, but what else can you do? You love him, don't you?"

Clarissa pressed her lips together and looked away. She couldn't admit it, not out loud, not even to her beloved sister.

Izzy said in a gentle voice, "So if you love him, you need to fight for him."

"Fight for him? You mean I'm supposed to fight all these beautiful ton ladies who swarm around him whenever he steps into a room?" She formed her fingers into claws and put on a mock-fierce face.

Izzy laughed. "I don't mean physically fight and anyway, I think they'd scratch you to bits—they're much nastier and more ruthless than you could ever be."

"Then what did you mean?"

"I meant that you'll have to confront your own fears and take a risk. If you did talk to him about his reputation, what's the worst that could happen?"

"I'd be totally humiliated." Even the idea of confronting him caused her insides to shrivel in embarrassment.

"Perhaps. But what if it cleared the air and you learned you could trust him more than you do now?"

Clarissa bit her lip. There was a long silence, then Izzy added, "Isn't the possibility of your future happiness worth the risk of making a fool of yourself? In private. With only Lord Randall to witness it?"

Clarissa thought it over, then gave a long sigh. "I suppose so," she admitted reluctantly. But she couldn't imagine actually doing it.

"Well, there's no hurry, just think it over. And now, shall we call on Lady Tarrant and her new baby?"

Clarissa rose quickly, relieved at the change of subject. "Yes, let's. I'm taking her this bouquet of flowers and I also

sewed a little baby gown with embroidery around the neck—
so sweet and tiny. What are you bringing?"

"Nothing I've sewn, for which she must be grateful—
you were always better with a needle than me. I bought her
a music box, which plays—or rather tinkles—the sweetest
little tune. And Alfonso baked some *pizzicati*—delicious
little jam biscuits—for her and the children." She picked up
the small basket she'd brought with her. "Shall we go? What
about Zoë? Will she want to come with us?"

Clarissa smiled. "I suspect she's already there. Most days
she calls on Lucy, Lady Tarrant's goddaughter and niece-
by-marriage, who speaks French to her and they talk painting." She chuckled. "Ever since Lady Scattergood made
Zoë her 'artist-in-residence' she's been working like fury,
and she obtained special permission from Lady Scattergood to paint a family portrait of Lord and Lady Tarrant
and the baby with the little girls." She picked up the vase
containing the bouquet of flowers, and said, "Shall we?"

The visit to Lady Tarrant went off beautifully. She
looked tired but was glowing with happiness, and the
baby was so sweet. They gave her their gifts and each of
them took turns holding little Ross until he started to fuss
and Lady Tarrant announced it was feeding time.

"I'm feeding him myself," she told them proudly. "I know
it's unfashionable and everyone says James should hire a
wet nurse but I never imagined I would be blessed with a
child of my own, and now I have been, I want to experience
everything."

Clarissa, Izzy and Zoë made their farewells and filed out.

As they walked down the stairs the sound of argument
broke out. Judy and Lina were squabbling over something.
"I said—"

"No, you said—*I* said—"

Clarissa and Izzy glanced at each other and chuckled. "Sisters."

"Did you two fight when you were growing up?" Zoë asked.

"Not often, but when we did . . ." They both laughed, then Izzy broke off in midchuckle and went suddenly thoughtful.

"What is it, Iz?" Clarissa asked.

"I've just had a wonderful idea."

"Tell us."

"Not here. The summerhouse, now—yes, you, too, Zoë. Let us hope that wretched Milly isn't around."

"If she is, I'll chase her off," Zoë said confidently. "She's forever hanging around but I just talk nonstop French at her and she goes away."

Chuckling, they made their way back to the summerhouse. There was no sign of Milly.

"Now what's this idea?" Clarissa said when they were settled on their favorite chairs.

Izzy explained.

"It's brilliant," Zoë exclaimed when she had finished. "We did something a bit like that at the orphanage when some of the girls was makin' up nasty lies about another one."

"Clarissa? What do you think?" Izzy asked.

Clarissa screwed up her nose. "I don't like it," she said eventually. "It's like spying, and I don't want to spy on him. And besides, it would be horridly embarrassing—can you imagine asking people something so . . . so . . . ?" She shuddered.

"It's not really spying," Izzy insisted. "And this way you would find out without having to confront him at all."

Clarissa shook her head. "No, I'll just have to find the courage to talk to him about it."

Izzy frowned. "But even if you do find the courage, what if he lies? You said that yourself, if you remember."

"I know, but what else can I do?"

"Follow my plan," Izzy said, exasperated. "It could even be fun."

But Clarissa was adamant. "No, I don't like it. Apart from stirring up who knows what kind of gossip, it's not fair to be going behind his back like that."

"But—"

"No," she said. "I won't do it. Now, I must go and change. I have morning calls to make this afternoon and Mrs. Price-Jones will be waiting."

Izzy and Zoë watched her go.

"She's lovely, Clarissa is," Zoë said. "But she ain't going to do nothing to help herself, is she? She'll do anything to help someone else, but when it comes to sticking up for herself she's like, I dunno, all honey and fluff inside, like a syllabub."

Izzy nodded. "I know. Our father and her mother sucked all the confidence out of her." She gave Zoë a mischievous look. "But if she won't do it, I will. And now I come to think of it, it's better this way. She's unmarried and her reputation is too fragile for something like this—especially since that Clayborn scandal—but I'm a married woman now and can get away with a lot more."

In bed that night, Clarissa thought over the talk she'd had with her sisters that morning. She'd thought and thought and thought, and had come to an uncomfortable conclusion: she had two choices—go on as she had been going, which meant being miserable and torn and uncertain and eventually breaking her betrothal to Lord Randall—or take her courage in her hands and ask Lord Randall about his rakishness. Which would lead to . . . she wasn't sure what. But it would be *something*.

Oh, but the very thought of confronting him about such a delicate subject made her squirm.

But if she didn't . . .

She thought about her visit to Lady Tarrant and her dear little baby. She'd held little Ross in her arms, and he was so tiny and so precious, with his earnest gaze and his tiny starfish hands with their minute, perfect fingernails . . .

She wanted a baby. She wanted to be married and to have a baby of her own. And, she finally admitted to herself, she wanted Lord Randall. She'd tried and tried not to fall in love with him, but it had proved impossible.

She slipped out of bed, turned up the gaslight and fetched the list she'd made so long ago.

1) A man as unlike Papa as possible and *4) Kindness, especially to children. And animals.*

She thought about the way he'd been with the little girls. He might be a rake, but he was nothing like Papa. Lord Randall would make a wonderful father. And even if he was unfaithful, he would be kind to her and any children they had, she was sure.

2) ~~Handsome.~~ Attractive. To me. And interesting.

That went without saying. She was wildly attracted to him, to the extent that every other man she met paled into insignificance.

6) No fortune hunters.

He was rich, so that wasn't an issue.

5) Respects me.

She thought he did, at least he didn't ride roughshod over her opinions like some men did. And he listened to her, truly listened.

She sighed. It all came back to numbers 3 and 7:

3) Fidelity. 7) No rakes.

Ah, that was the rub. He was a notorious rake. Could she trust him to be faithful? And if he wasn't, could she bear it?

8) ~~Love.~~ **Love.**

The ultimate prize. It was a gamble, a risk, but worth it in the end. If she won.

She put the list aside, her mind made up. She had to talk to him, no matter how difficult or embarrassing it would be.

There was no real choice. He might lie to her, but at least
she would have tried.

The following night Clarissa and Mrs. Price-Jones attended a rout with Izzy and Leo. It was Izzy's first public outing since her return from their honeymoon, and she
was keyed up with excitement. She was wearing a new dress
that was part of her trousseau, in vivid emerald silk that exactly matched her eyes. "So good to be out of those dreary
whites and pastels," she confided to Clarissa, who was
wearing a dress in the palest biscuit color. "Won't be long
before you can wear lovely bright colors, too, like Mrs. P-J
and me." She cast a sideways glance at Mrs. Price-Jones's
outfit—red, green and purple—and winked.

"I don't mind soft colors," Clarissa said.

"Yes, but once you're married to Lord Randall, you can
wear whatever you like."

"It's not a real engagement," Clarissa reminded her.

Izzy just laughed.

After greeting their hosts they began to circulate, meeting up with friends and making new acquaintances. After
a while, Clarissa noticed Izzy in close conversation with
Lady Snape. Lady Snake. She hoped that the woman wasn't
being nasty to her beautiful sister. Izzy had been on her
honeymoon when Clarissa had first met that unpleasant lady.
She'd seemed a very bitter, jealous type.

The next time she saw her sister she was talking with the
lady who had warned Clarissa not to fall for Race. Clarissa
still didn't know her name.

A little later she noticed her talking to another dashing-
looking sophisticated woman, and shortly after that, Izzy
fell into conversation with the very elegant, rather daring
Lady Windthrop.

All the women she'd been talking to this evening were
attractive, very modish and with a . . . well, *reputation* was

too harsh a description, but they were certainly not regarded as paragons of respectability. Oh well, her sister was a married woman now, and a countess, and Clarissa supposed it wasn't surprising if Izzy decided she wanted to move in a faster set.

No doubt Izzy had found her pre-marriage society a little . . . tame and was relishing her new freedom. It was inevitable that some changes would occur after marriage. And there was no doubt that Izzy was very happy in her marriage, and that, Clarissa told herself, was all that mattered.

Mrs. Price-Jones was also circulating among a rather younger set than her usual companions, closely followed by her two silver-haired suitors. She smiled, watching each one subtly trying to outmaneuver the other. Then Lord Randall appeared at her elbow—she hadn't even seen him arrive— and informed her that dancing was about to commence in the other room, and she forgot all about her sister and her chaperone.

They danced a country dance, and it was just as well it was one Clarissa knew well, as her mind was wholly occupied with just one thought: how to ask Lord Randall about his rakish reputation.

In the end, she achieved it without finesse, nerving herself to say bluntly at the end of the dance, "Lord Randall, we need to talk."

He raised his brows. "I thought you seemed preoccupied this evening. Is it serious?"

She swallowed. "Very. I need to talk to you in private."

He glanced around at the crowded rooms filled with chattering people. "No chance of privacy here, then. Can I call on you?"

"No, because Mrs. Price-Jones would be sure to sit with us. She did when Leo was courting my sister. Never left them alone together for a minute." Izzy had met Leo in secret, in the summerhouse, late at night. Clarissa didn't want to do that, not for the kind of talk she had in mind. The summerhouse was a place for romance.

Besides, she didn't want Milly or anyone else crashing in on her private talk.

He thought for a minute. "Your chaperone doesn't ride."

"No, but Izzy does and she'd probably want to come with us."

"The summerhouse in the garden?"

"No." Both Izzy and Zoë used it.

"Very well, how about I call for you tomorrow morning to take you for a drive in my curricle. I recall the way your indomitable chaperone squeezed herself into Clayborn's phaeton, but only two can fit in a curricle. And since we're betrothed, a drive in the park in an open carriage is perfectly comme il faut."

She nodded. "Very well then." It wasn't ideal, trying to talk while he drove, but she couldn't think of any other way to be alone with him.

"At ten o'clock tomorrow morning?"

She nodded, feeling slightly sick. There. She'd done it. Set up the meeting. Now all she had to do was get through the rest of the night somehow until ten o'clock. And then . . . She shivered.

But it had to be done. Her future depended on it.

They drove in silence through the streets until they reached Hyde Park. There were already quite a few people around, but nowhere near the numbers that came at the fashionable hour. Lord Randall passed them at a spanking pace, taking them to an area that was quiet and relatively deserted.

Clarissa was glad he hadn't tried to talk while they were moving. She'd been nervous enough at the prospect of the conversation and where it might lead, but when he'd come to collect her and she prepared herself for an undignified scramble to climb into the curricle, he'd simply put his hands around her waist and lifted her—just lifted her—apparently without effort, and she knew she was no lightweight.

It completely scrambled her brain.

The horses slowed to a walk, and when they came to a large tree overhanging the path, he pulled in under it. He secured the reins and turned to her. "Now, is this about our betrothal?"

Clarissa nodded.

"You want to call it off?" He seemed quite tense.

"I'm . . . I'm not sure," she managed. She hadn't slept a wink during the night, thrashing around and tangling the sheets, a turmoil of questions tumbling over and over in her mind, as she rehearsed what she was going to ask him and what she would say if he said this or that. So many possibilities. In the darkness of the night she'd felt quite eloquent: now she could barely think of a word to say.

"You know that I am fully committed to it?"

She scanned his face worriedly. "Really? Are you sure?"

"I am. But you still have doubts? Questions? About me?"

"Yes." She didn't know how to phrase the question, but to her relief he did it for her.

"Is it because of my reputation?"

"Yes." He was making it easy for her, for which she was very grateful.

He nodded, as if in confirmation. "Very well, I promise I'll be honest with you." He fell silent for a moment, then said, "People talk. Gossip. And I'm afraid I've used that to my advantage."

Clarissa looked at him in surprise. It wasn't at all what she expected. "To your advantage? How can gossip be an advantage?"

He gave her a rueful smile. "It's a long story, and not very interesting."

"I'm interested," she said softly. She folded her hands in her lap and waited.

He thought for a moment, then began. "It probably started with my father. After my mother died—I had just turned eleven—he . . ." He shook his head. "I thought they were deeply in love, and perhaps they were, but after she died, he became a byword for . . . womanizing. So much so that even before I'd left school he was known as Rake Randall."

He glanced at her. "Yes, like me. It didn't much affect me—I was at school, and then at university. But then he died . . ."

She laid a sympathetic hand on his arm, but said nothing.

"When he died, I inherited his title and his estates— everything. And when I came up to London, a naive young man, eager to get a taste of the high life, I was . . . hunted. Matchmaking mamas and their daughters. Not interested in me as much as the title and the fortune. But what young man—I was one and twenty—wants to marry and settle down before he's even had a taste of life's possibilities? Certainly not me. So I learned to flirt, but be evasive."

Birds twittered in the tree overhead. Clarissa pretended to look for them while she considered what he'd told her. She could understand his desire not to be tied down at a young age, but how did flirting lead to his being labeled a rake? There was surely quite a difference. She asked him.

"Oh, that was only the start. I began an affair with an older woman—she was not much older than I, except in sophistication. She was an unhappy and very beautiful wife whose husband neglected her shamefully." He grimaced. "At least that's the tale she told me. I certainly fell for it."

"He didn't neglect her?"

He snorted. "Who knows whether he did or not? I realized later that she was trying to spark his jealousy. He caught us together—in retrospect I believe she'd tipped him off. He flew into a jealous rage, and there was a huge scandal and a duel, which we both managed to survive, though I was wounded in the shoulder. I, being the one at fault, deloped, but I think he would have happily killed me. Luckily for me, he was a poor shot."

She gave him a troubled look. It all sounded quite sordid. But he was only twenty-one.

"And B—the woman concerned—wasn't the least bit discreet. She loved all the drama and spread the gossip with great glee. Somehow, through her deliberate indiscretions—and no doubt to needle her husband—I gained a reputation as a superb lover. That, added to my tendency to flirt"—he shrugged—"and I became Rake Randall as well."

Clarissa thought about what he'd told her, then shook her head. "No. There has to be more to it than that."

"Oh, there was, though I never again dallied with a married woman. Nor have I ever seduced an innocent."

Clarissa bit her lip. Could she believe that or not? She wanted to, but . . .

"I'm not claiming to be as pure as the driven snow—far from it—and though I should probably not speak of this to you, I did promise to lay all my cards on the table. I have had mistresses, several over the years, though not at the same time," he added, seeming to read her mind. "Several were widows, not interested in marriage—which was part of their attraction, I confess. I have also maintained a ladybird or two from time to time, who understood exactly what the arrangement involved. Do you understand what I'm saying?"

She nodded. "You forget, my father was a notorious rake."

His expression was somber. "I didn't forget. I suppose he is a good part of the reason we're having this conversation."

She nodded, surprised by his perception.

"Not all rakes are alike."

"I know that," she said quietly, thinking of the way he'd been with Lord Tarrant's little girls. Sunlight drifted through the dappled shade of the leaves. "You said that you used the gossip about you to your advantage. I don't understand."

"Remember those matchmaking mamas? Once my reputation was tarnished, their enthusiasm for thrusting their innocent daughters at me lessened, and when I realized that, I encouraged everyone to think I was more like my father, that like him, I truly deserved the soubriquet of 'Rake Randall.' In fact I deliberately cultivated my rakish reputation. I flirted more, took care never to be seen with the same beautiful lady more than twice, and gave every appearance of being a devil-may-care, unreliable rake."

"You succeeded."

He gave a wry, bitter laugh. "Yes, and see where it's landed me. Betrothed to the only woman I want, but who doesn't believe a word I say."

The only woman he wanted? Could that possibly be true? She wanted to believe it, but . . . "Several ladies of the ton have indicated to me that they are . . . shall we say, intimately acquainted with you. What do you say to that?"

He exhaled in a gust of ironic despair. "I have no answer to that. I have no idea why they would say such a thing— there is no truth in it, though I confess I have never contradicted any rumors that linked my name with some society lady. I don't know who in particular you are talking about, but apart from two widows who shall remain nameless, neither of whom live in London now, I have not taken any society lady as my mistress, not even for one night. I can't prove it, but I swear to you it's true."

He seemed utterly sincere. Clarissa couldn't understand why any lady would deliberately tarnish her reputation, but she supposed if someone was trying to cultivate a reputation for being dashing . . . "Lady Snape?"

He snorted. "I'd as soon bed a viper."

She recalled that he'd told her before that with Lady Snape it was a case of *Hell hath no fury* . . . She thought of several other ladies she could ask him about, but decided it would be demeaning going through a list of names.

She had to make a decision: to choose to believe him, or not.

She sighed and turned away. He was sitting too close for her to think clearly.

"Would you mind if we moved on?" he asked after a minute. "I don't like to keep the horses standing around."

"No, of course not." It was easier when they were moving, with distractions to dissipate the intensity of their conversation.

They came across a cricket match in progress and the horses slowed to a walk. She glanced at him, and saw that the slowing was probably unwitting. His attention was wholly on the players. He tensed slightly as the bowler came running in to bowl. The ball flew, but with a loud thwack the batsman hit it high, right over the heads of the fielders. "Hit for a six. Well done!"

His boyish enthusiasm was endearing. "You're fond of cricket. Do you play?"

Her question seemed to surprise him, and he looked a bit self-conscious. "I did when I was a boy. Lived for it." He sounded almost bitter. He wrapped the reins around his long fingers. The horses came to a halt.

"You lost interest as you grew older?" He clearly hadn't, but she was curious as to what had caused that look, and the odd tone in his voice.

"I don't play anymore," he said brusquely.

It wasn't quite the answer to her question. There was some strong emotion there, tamped down hard beneath the simple statements. "When did you last play?"

There was a long silence. He stared out at the cricket field, unseeing, then he glanced at her and looked away again. Finally he said in a hard voice, "When did I last play? The day my mother died."

She waited.

"Yes, selfish little swine that I was, I chose to play

cricket while my mother was dying." His bitterness and self-hatred were corrosive.

She laid a sympathetic hand on his arm. "Didn't you realize? Did nobody come to fetch you?"

He made a disgusted sound. "Oh, I knew. I was away at school, and my father had sent a message to tell me to come home, that my mother was fading fast." His face quivered with some fleeting emotion she couldn't catch. "But the thing was, it wasn't the first time I'd had that message—far from it—and each time I'd gone home, Mama had rallied, so I pretended I hadn't received the message. We were due to play in the final, and I didn't want to miss it."

"I see."

"Do you?" he muttered.

His bitterness, she decided, was all self-loathing, and not directed at her but at his eleven-year-old self. She let him brood in silence for a few minutes, then said, "Did you win?"

He wrenched himself around to face her and said incredulously, "What has that to do with anything? Yes, we won, but my mother—" His voice broke and he looked away again, his jaw clamped tight. A small nerve in his jaw twitched.

She put her hand on his arm and said quietly, "I think if I were dying, and the choice was having my young son at my deathbed—especially after it had happened several times—or of having him win an important cricket match, I would choose the cricket. Choosing joy for my son, knowing grief was to come."

He shook his head, rejecting her sympathy. "You don't understand."

She didn't contradict him. Nobody could understand another's grief—it was unique to every person, no matter what the situation. All she could do was listen. And empathize.

"Was your mother's a long illness?" she asked.

He stared out over the cricket field. "Years. I'd been called home half a dozen times in the past couple of years, but Mama had rallied each time. And I was sent back to school again."

"But this time she didn't."

"No."

"And you've blamed yourself ever since."

He wrenched himself around to face her again. "It's my greatest shame! Don't you see? If I'd abandoned the cricket she might have . . ."

"Rallied? Yes, she might have, but then again she might not have. You can't possibly know it. And there's no point in torturing yourself about it."

She waited a moment, then added softly, "Don't you think she'd prefer to think of you happy and triumphant on the cricket ground instead of waiting silent and grieving in a sickroom? I know I would."

He didn't respond, but it seemed to her that some of the tension had been released from his body. In silence they watched the bowler deliver the next ball. The batsman clipped it and it flew behind him.

"I loved her," he said heavily. "I thought my father did, too. I was sure of it. But . . ."

"You're thinking of how he became a notorious rake after she died?"

He nodded.

"What if he couldn't bear to lose her and threw himself into debauchery as a way of trying to forget?" she suggested.

He stared at her as if taken aback. "I suppose it's possible," he said slowly.

"What he did after your mother's death does not necessarily reflect on the man he was while she was alive."

"Maybe not." He heaved a sigh. "How did you get to be so wise? Was that what happened with your parents?"

She gave a wry half smile. "No, Papa never cared for

Mama at all—it was all about her fortune for him. And after they'd married and he learned it was still mostly tied up in a trust, he treated her abominably. It made no difference to Mama, though—she loved him until the day she died."

"How old were you when that happened?"

"Eight."

"And you were with her when she died?"

"I sat beside her bedside the entire time she was dying—it took days. She barely even seemed to notice me. All she wanted, all she spoke of in those last days, was my father. He never came, of course."

He took her hand in his and squeezed it gently.

She sighed. "Death so often leaves the living with unresolvable guilt."

"Your father?"

"No, me. I worried for ages about what I should have done for my mother."

"You were eight. And I presume there were physicians where you lived."

"I don't mean medically. She had the best of medical care. I mean to make her love me." He frowned and she added, "She cared for me, of course, but I always knew I was a disappointment to her, and to my father."

"Good God, why?"

She shrugged. "Papa wanted a boy, and Mama wanted Papa to love her and she knew she'd disappointed him by having a useless girl." Especially one who wasn't even pretty.

"They were blind to the treasure they had then," he said softly, and squeezed her hand again. His hands were bare, and the warmth of his skin was comforting.

Touched by the gentle compliment—she'd let the conversation get so melancholy—she forced herself to say brightly, "Oh, you mustn't feel sorry for me. I had a very happy childhood once Izzy came to live with me. And unconditional sisterly love is very precious and makes up for all kinds of slights and unkindnesses." She ached for unconditional husbandly love, too, but she couldn't tell him that. You couldn't ask for love: it had to be given, freely.

There was a cheer from the cricket pitch. A batsman had been caught out, and it startled Clarissa and Race back to the here and now.

She smiled a little self-consciously. "Dear me, we have gone down a melancholy path, haven't we? And it's probably time I went home. But I think we've had some important conversations, don't you?"

He flicked the reins and the curricle moved on. "We've come to a deeper understanding, that's true," he said, maneuvering the carriage around a stationary wagon. "So, have all these grim revelations caused you to want to break the betrothal or not?" He turned and gave her an intense, searching look. "Are you still unsure about marrying me, Clarissa?"

Chapter Fifteen

❧

Clarissa took a deep breath. They'd talked of many things, but she hadn't yet asked him the one thing that mattered most of all.

He gave her a swift sideways glance. "More questions? Should we return to the privacy of the park?"

"No, this shouldn't take long." She cleared her throat nervously. It was the main question. "You've explained that your reputation as a rake is . . . exaggerated. I accept that. I just need to know . . ." She cleared her throat again. "I need to know whether you think you could be faithful to only me. If we did marry, that is."

He transferred his reins to his other hand and took her hand in his. "I don't break my promises, and I would never break my marriage vows." He glanced at her again, raised her hand to his lips and kissed it lightly. "Don't you understand yet that I truly care for you? Because I do, you know. You are the only woman I have ever wanted to marry, and if I were fortunate enough to have you for my wife, I would *never* jeopardize your trust."

There was no teasing note in his voice, no lighthearted tone that indicated he was merely doing the polite thing. Or flirting.

Oh, how she wanted to believe him. The traffic thickened, and he was silent, concentrating on steering his carriage and pair through the chaos.

Clarissa made up her mind. She would probably always have doubts, but if she didn't marry him she would always regret it. Even if she ended up regretting it. She gave a choked laugh at the ridiculous illogic of her thoughts.

If she married him, he would either be faithful, or he wouldn't. Only time would tell, and she didn't intend to live waiting for the axe to fall. Marriage was inevitably a risk, and if she was going to risk her heart on a tall, lanky, wildly attractive charmer, she had to banish any doubts and do it wholly and completely.

He was nothing like her father. He was gentle and kind and . . .

And she loved him. She would give herself to him completely.

She opened her mouth to tell him she would marry him, but before she could say a word, he said, "You don't have to make up your mind now. I don't mean to press you for an answer. Marriage is probably the most important decision you can make in your life, so take your time, and when you do decide, you need to be sure in your own mind that your decision's the right one."

If she'd needed any further encouragement to agree to marry him, that understanding and patience would be it. She opened her mouth to speak again, and he added, "In any case I'll be out of town for the next week or so. Some matters on my estate needing attention. I'll call on you when I return, see if you've made up your mind. Would that be acceptable?"

He glanced at her and she nodded. It wasn't so much that she was relieved at the reprieve, but they were driving through an open market at the moment, and though she'd finally found the courage to tell him, she'd rather not speak the words she'd had locked in her heart for so long surrounded by cabbages and costermongers, beggars, buskers and squabbling stray dogs.

It was hardly the location for a romantic declaration of love and trust.

"Am I interrupting?" Zoë hovered in the doorway of Clarissa's stillroom. It was just a spare scullery that Lady Scattergood had given over to Clarissa to use for the making of her creams and fragrant waters. Clarissa loved it: her own little kingdom.

Clarissa turned, wiping her hands on a towel. "No, not at all. I've just finished mixing this cream, and it needs to set. What is it you wanted?"

Zoë sniffed. "Smells gorgeous. Rose, is it? And something else?"

"Yes, my favorite. And that's lavender water steeping with some herbs I'm experimenting with. Now what did you want?"

"Could I talk to you, please?"

"Yes, of course." Clarissa lifted a small stack of papers off a bentwood chair and gestured for her sister to sit.

Zoë didn't move. "No, in the summerhouse, if you don't mind."

"Of course." It was something private, then. A slender thread of concern coiled in Clarissa's belly. Her little sister looked very serious.

She followed Zoë outside to the summerhouse. To her surprise her sister Izzy was there, already seated and waiting, and also Lucy, Lady Thornton, the goddaughter and niece-in-law of Lady Tarrant. Clarissa glanced at Izzy, who raised her shoulders infinitesimally; she had no idea what this was about, either.

"What's going on?"

"I want"—Zoë glanced at Lucy, who nodded encouragingly—"we want to tell you about a plan we've made."

"Plan?" *We?* Did that mean Zoë had formed a plan with Lucy? And not her sisters?

Zoë nodded. "I know you want to introduce me to society, but you know as well as I do that the minute society people clap eyes on me they'll connect me with Izzy and the whole thing about her bas—her illegitimacy and mine will come up again. And it won't be good for any of us, especially you, Clarissa."

"Don't you worry about m—"

"You know it's true—even that pest Milly could see it at a glance," Zoë said bluntly. "But me and Lucy have a solution, I think. If it's all right with you."

Clarissa blinked, then waved her hand. "Go on then."

Lucy stepped in. "You know my husband and I came to be with Alice for when she had the baby—well, it was why I came, but my husband also came because there's been some talk about his transferring from the embassy in Vienna to the one in Paris."

"How interesting," said Clarissa politely, wondering what this had to do with anything.

"He heard yesterday that he's been given the Paris job."

"Congratulations."

"And that's where I come in," Zoë said eagerly. "Lucy has invited me to go with them to Paris."

"To Paris?" Clarissa exclaimed, dismayed. Izzy took her hand and squeezed it comfortingly.

"Yes," Lucy said. "I understand something of Zoë's position, actually—"

"And you think that taking her away from her family will help?" Clarissa burst out.

"I know it's hard," Lucy said gently. "But I think Zoë will do well, living with me—with us—in Paris. I've talked it over with my husband and he's happy to welcome Zoë into our home, as my young companion. It will give her time to adjust to her new situation in life, and—"

"In a foreign country?"

"Zoë is half-French, 'Riss," Izzy reminded her. Clarissa looked at her in reproach. Whose side was Izzy on?

Lucy continued, "It's not just that. Zoë needs to improve her English reading and writing, and also we need to polish away that unfortunate accent of hers, and her society manners."

"I can help her with all of that," Clarissa said. She'd only just found Zoë and didn't want to lose her.

There was a short silence. "I see that I need to explain to you just why I am the best person for the job," Lucy said after a moment. "But I must ask that you promise to keep my story confidential."

At Lucy's somber tone, Clarissa and Izzy exchanged glances then nodded.

"When I was a girl," Lucy began, "my father, who was— there is no other word for it—a scoundrel, placed me in a series of select boarding schools for the daughters of gentlemen. I say a series, because each time, after he failed to pay the second installment of the very expensive fees, I was expelled." She smiled. "It was upsetting at the time, but it taught me several important things. I did receive an education, even if it was fragmented, and it taught me how to deal with new people—girls who were my social betters, and believe me, they were not kind. My accent at first was, let us say unfortunate, but by the time I had turned sixteen, I sounded like a lady."

Clarissa opened her mouth to speak, but Lucy swept on.

"That was only the start. After school, he left me with a retired Austrian soprano, who taught me German and music and used me as a maidservant the rest of the time. She was very strict, but it paid off: in Vienna I received many compliments on my German, which is not only fluent, but aristocratic sounding."

"Yes but—"

"After her, my father took me to live with a French comtesse, an *emigrée* who fled the Revolution. She also used me as a maidservant, but true to her agreement with my father, she polished my French grammar and pronunciation to the same degree"—she smiled at Zoë—"which enabled me to recognize Zoë's French as that of the aristocracy. And that," she finished, "is why I am in the best position to teach Zoë what she needs to know. Because I've done it myself."

"I . . . see," Clarissa said reluctantly.

"As well, in Paris she can begin to meet people with no fear that her accent will betray her, as she'll be speaking only French in public—even to English people, until I have her English accent perfected. Which will improve her social poise and confidence."

Zoë leaned forward eagerly. "And I've already told people—well, that Milly, anyway—that I'm your French cousin, so you see I can come back here when I'm older, and be your long-lost French cousin. Not your bastard sister. And everyone will exclaim about how me and Izzy look so much alike, but nobody will guess the real reason. Because I'll be French."

"It sounds like a very workable plan," Izzy said, squeezing Clarissa's hand again.

It did. Clarissa couldn't deny it. She'd had no idea that Lucy was anything other than the perfect English lady with the perfect aristocratic background. What an unsettled and difficult upbringing she must have had. But oh, she would miss Zoë—she was only just starting to get to know her new little sister, and she liked her—loved her—so much.

Izzy squeezed her hand again and Clarissa knew what she had to do. "It sounds like an excellent plan," she said, making herself smile warmly at Zoë and Lucy. She rose and gave Zoë a hug, and if it lasted a little too long, and was a little too tight, and if her eyes were wet, well, she couldn't help that.

Zoë was her discovery—well, Betty's—and if she loved

her, she had to let her go so she could learn to fly, away from London's prying eyes and gossiping tongues. But oh, it was going to be so difficult.

She made herself hug Lucy, too, and when she did, Lucy whispered in her ear, "I know it's hard, but I promise I'll take good care of her."

Clarissa tried to think of something more positive to say. "And I suppose you'll have plenty to talk about, with your painting."

"Yes and that's another thing," Zoë said excitedly. "Lucy reckons we might be able to get some painting lessons from some of the best artists in Paris. We might even get to meet Madame Le Brun."

"Who?" Clarissa said blankly.

"Madame Élisabeth Louise Vigée Le Brun," Lucy explained. "She's a French portrait painter and very well-known. She painted many portraits of Marie Antoinette, and other famous people, but fled France because of the Revolution—"

"Just like my maman," Zoë interjected.

"Yes," Lucy continued, "and while in exile, she painted some of the highest in the land in Italy, Russia, Germany and Austria, where I was privileged to see some of her work. I would say she's the French female version of Sir Thomas Lawrence—you've heard of him, haven't you?"

Clarissa and Izzy both nodded. Sir Thomas was the most fashionable portraitist in England.

Zoë looked at Clarissa. "So you won't mind me goin' away with Lucy, will you, Clarissa?"

Clarissa minded it very much, but she could see that this was what Zoë wanted, and more than anything, she wanted her little sister to be happy. "I think it's a wonderful idea, and you're going to be very happy," she said warmly. "But you must write to us often, to let us know how you are getting on."

Zoë wrinkled her nose. "I s'pose it'll be good practice for me grammar and spelling." They all laughed.

"When will you leave?" Clarissa asked Lucy.

"We plan to leave just after baby Ross's christening—I'm to be godmother," Lucy said proudly.

Clarissa swallowed. The christening was to be next week. But all she said was, "In that case we'll have to hurry to make sure that Zoë packs everything she needs. A few new clothes, too, I think. And of course, Zoë will have an allowance while she's away."

"Oh, there's no need—" Lucy began.

"There is every need," Clarissa said firmly. "Zoë is our sister."

Izzy nodded in agreement.

Zoë jumped up and hugged her again. "Thank you, Clarissa. You bin so good to me, I dunno what to say." She hugged Izzy, too, and then she and Lucy left.

Izzy turned to Clarissa and put an arm around her. "You did very well there, 'Riss. I know you don't want to lose her, but it does seem like the perfect solution, especially with Lady Thornton's experience."

Clarissa sighed. "I know. It's just . . ."

Izzy hugged her. "I know. We haven't had her long but already she's in our hearts, isn't she?"

Hah!" Lady Scattergood, in the middle of drinking tea while reading her morning post, snorted loudly. "That explains it!" she declared, wiping the tea from her nose.

"Explains what, Lady Scattergood?" Clarissa asked. Even though the old lady rarely left her home, she kept up a prolific correspondence with friends in various parts of the kingdom, and her morning posts often caused mild exclamations and vague mutters, generally because the letters were crossed and recrossed in tiny writing and she had to pore over them with her magnifying glass. And sometimes she had to ask Clarissa to work something out with her young eyes.

She waved a sheet of paper at Clarissa. "This is from my friend Mariah Pultney. She lives in some godforsaken part of the country—I forget where, but it's not far from where Margery Doulton lives."

Both Clarissa and Mrs. Price-Jones looked at her blankly. "Who?"

"Margery Doulton, as was—what's her married name now? Oh yes, Margery Faircloth, young Clayborn's great-aunt. You remember, the one who was leaving him her entire fortune."

"Oh." Clarissa busied herself with buttering a roll. She had no interest in Cuthbert Clayborn or his great-aunt or her great fortune.

Lady Scattergood cackled and waved her letter gleefully. "Mariah just told me exactly what that grand fortune consists of."

Clarissa added strawberry jam and bit into her roll.

Mrs. Price-Jones glanced at Clarissa, then asked, "What does her fortune consist of, Olive?"

Lady Scattergood cackled again. "A cottage and a cow paddock! That's it! The lot—her entire fortune. Apparently her husband ran through any money they had quite early on, and then he died. She had to sell their home to pay the debts he left and move into this cottage quite a few years ago, Mariah says. Not a large cottage, either, she tells me."

She peered again at the letter. "She didn't say how big the cow paddock was, but it can't be very big, can it?" She set down the letter with a grin. "So, that's the answer to that little conundrum—the wretch was an arrant fortune hunter, and his great-aunt was aiding and abetting him. I never did like her all that much when she was a gel, you know. Had a tendency to embroider the truth even then."

Clarissa stared at her half-eaten roll. So, Clayborn's determined and then desperate courtship was all about her inheritance.

She sipped her tea thoughtfully. She'd known he wasn't right for her, even though she had no idea of his true situation. He was a liar through and through.

And she'd rejected him without knowing any of it. Despite his good looks, apparent wealth to come and tragic injury she hadn't been seduced into accepting him. She'd trusted her instincts. The thought was quite cheering.

She bit into her roll. The jam was delicious.

Lady Scattergood cackled again. "A cottage and a cow paddock! You missed a fine prize there, Clarissa."

Over the following week, Clarissa was drawn into a flurry of social engagements, mainly because Izzy, now returned to London as a newlywed countess, was being invited everywhere, and wanted to enjoy her new position in society. She accepted every invitation that Clarissa had also received and seemed to be making new friends at every event. Some of them were rather fast: daring young matrons, so different from the unmarried girls they were used to mixing with.

It was lovely seeing Izzy so confident and happy—even exuberant at times—but for Clarissa, every event felt strangely flat, and not just because she knew that she would soon be losing her new little sister.

She missed Lord Randall. Missed those gray eyes following her around the room, missed that sardonic eyebrow, silently casting doubt on a far-fetched tale or sharing an amusing moment. And his mobile mouth that conveyed so much with the slightest movement. And when he kissed her . . . Oh my.

She ached for his return.

She wished now she'd told him that she would marry him, despite the market chaos and squalor. Now that she'd finally conquered her fears she wanted it settled.

With days filled by social engagements, visits to Lady

Tarrant and the baby, rides in the park, morning calls, shopping for Zoë, and evenings filled with balls, routs, card parties and visits to the theater, Clarissa barely had time to think.

But her nights, ah, her nights were filled with dreams, dreams of a tall, lean, charming, funny, kind man whose kisses were simply . . . magic.

Race returned to London on Wednesday evening as dusk was falling. He'd come back to London a day early and had hoped to arrive sooner, but an overturned wagon on the London road had held him up by several hours.

Clarissa would, no doubt, be off at some party or other, and even if he did wash, shave and change, he probably wouldn't be able to get a private moment alone with her. Not the way he wished to. That day in the curricle, he was sure—almost—that she'd been about to tell him she was willing to make the betrothal real.

The whole time away he'd gone over their conversation in his mind, minute by minute and . . . he thought . . . maybe . . . There had been that moment when she'd opened her mouth as if to say something momentous . . . and then shut it.

But he still wasn't sure.

Maybe she didn't believe what he'd told her about his reputation. It was hard to believe, he admitted. He thought about the trouble he'd gone to over the years to embellish and embroider the rumors, insuring that his reputation was as rakish as it needed to be. And now it was what stood in the way of his happiness. What an irony.

He was tired and hungry, so he decided to drop into his club for dinner and a relaxing drink. After a hearty meal of steak and kidney pudding, he headed into the reading room. To his surprise he found Leo there.

"Not out escorting your wife to parties tonight?" he said, dropping into a comfortable leather armchair opposite Leo.

"Almack's tonight," Leo said laconically. Race at once understood why Leo had bowed out. Ladies might enjoy the ratafia and orgeat and such stuff that was served at Almack's, but a gentleman needed something stronger to survive an evening in that hothouse environment.

Race ordered a brandy from a club employee.

"Clarissa's chaperone and her two silver swains are escorting them," Leo said once his glass had been filled as well.

"Silver swains?"

"My wife's term." Race smiled to himself at the pride and quiet enjoyment with which Leo said *my wife*. Leo continued, "Apparently Mrs. Price-Jones has two elderly silver-haired suitors vying for her hand. I'm told she will choose between them once Clarissa is married." He raised a quizzical brow at Race.

"Indeed," Race said enigmatically.

"No progress there yet?"

"I have hopes, but no, nothing definite." He took a sip of the brandy and felt it burn pleasantly down his throat. Tomorrow when he spoke to Clarissa he should know more. In the meantime he was living on tenterhooks.

For the next few minutes they talked of this and that; Race discussed a couple of issues that had come up on his estate, Leo told him about a mutual friend who'd lost a pile at the tables and had been forced to sell his horses. But Leo kept shifting uncomfortably, darting glances at Race and then looking away, and Race could tell there was something on his mind.

He was about to tell his friend to spit it out, when Leo said gruffly, "Got a question for you, Randall."

"Yes?"

"People have been talking—well, women mostly."

"Go on," Race said wearily. Women often talked about him. Mostly nonsense.

"Thing is, they've been asking me questions. Intimate and damned embarrassing questions."

Race raised a brow. "Indeed? What have you been up to?"

"Not about me, you fool, about you."

Race put his glass down. "Intimate questions about me? And they're asking *you*?"

"I know! As I said, damned embarrassing. And inappropriate."

"What sort of questions?"

"About . . ." He swallowed. "About the state of your arse."

Race was incredulous. "My *arse*?"

"Exactly."

"What about my arse?"

"Whether the heart-shaped mark on your left cheek is a birthmark or a tattoo."

Race stared at him. "The devil, you say. I don't understand. I don't have any kind of mark on my arse, no birthmark and certainly no tattoo."

Leo frowned. "Are you sure?"

"Of course I'm sure!" Race snapped. Why the hell would anyone be asking about a nonexistent mark on his arse? "What did you tell them?"

"To go to the devil, of course, and that I had no knowledge of—or interest in—the state of your backside! It was a damned cheek asking." And then he added sheepishly, "No pun intended."

"Yes, of course," Race agreed hastily. After a minute he asked, "Who has been asking about this?"

"Women, actually. Some of your better-known flirts, as a matter of fact." He started listing names.

After half a dozen names, Race cut him off. "All right, all right, I get the idea." He shook his head, pondering the mystery. "Why on earth would they be wondering about such a bizarre thing? I don't suppose anyone has asked you about your arse."

"No, of course not," Leo said indignantly.

"Well, don't look at me like that—I didn't start this nonsense. Nor do I like it." A thought occurred to him. "But now you've raised the matter, it partially explains a conversation I had with la Windthrop last week, the night before I left town. We were chatting, and suddenly she leaned closer and in a low voice, right out of the blue, asked my opinion of tattoos—just asked me, straight out, what I thought about them. Which was nothing to do with whatever we'd been talking about."

"What did you tell her?"

He shrugged. "That sailors and others of that ilk were welcome to them. And then she said, 'So you'd never get one?' and I said, 'Of course not,' and she exclaimed 'Aha!' in a *Eureka!* kind of way, and rushed off."

Leo pondered that for a moment. "Odd."

"Damned odd." Worse than odd, it had the potential to be disastrous. He hoped Clarissa never got to hear of such indelicate and bizarre speculations about him. She'd be mortified.

A footman came in, refurbished the fire and refilled their glasses. When he'd gone, Race said, "This blasted speculation has got to stop."

"How are you going to do that?"

"Perhaps when the next person asks whether it's a birthmark or a tattoo you could explain to them that I have neither."

Leo gave him a sardonic look. "If you think that I have any intention of assuring anyone of the pristine state of your arse, Randall, you've got rats in your attic. Big ones."

That same Wednesday evening, Clarissa was getting ready to go to Almack's. Lord Randall had said he'd be back in London by tomorrow. Clarissa couldn't wait.

Izzy appeared at Clarissa's bedroom door. "Are you ready?"

"Yes, almost, but I thought we were meeting downstairs in"—she glanced at the ormolu clock on the mantelpiece—"twenty minutes."

"We are but first I have something to tell you. Something I think you'll want to hear." She turned to Betty. "Thank you, Betty, I'll help my sister with anything that needs to be done now."

Betty ran a critical eye over Izzy and gave a brisk nod. "Did Joan do your hair?"

Izzy smiled and did a quick twirl around. "Yes, it's very elegant, don't you think? You've done a good job training her. I'm very pleased." She gave Betty a quick kiss on the cheek. "Now do run along, dear Betty. I need to speak to my sister."

"All in good time, milady." First Betty picked out a shawl, draped it over Clarissa's shoulders and tweaked it into place. Izzy was practically jumping up and down, but Betty, having grown up with both girls, ignored her as she made a minor adjustment to Clarissa's hair. She was a perfectionist and wouldn't allow Clarissa to go out looking anything less than her best. Finally she wished them both an enjoyable evening, winked at Clarissa and left.

"What is it that couldn't wait, Izzy?" Clarissa was excited herself. She could think of only one thing that would have her sister bouncing in anticipation like this. Was she expecting a baby?

Izzy's eyes sparkled. "Remember my plan to find out the truth about Lord Randall's rakishness?"

A trickle of foreboding ran down Clarissa's spine. "The one we decided not to follow?"

"You decided, I didn't."

"Izzy, you didn't!"

Izzy laughed, clearly delighted with herself. "I did. Oh, don't look at me like that—you need to know whether you can trust him or not. And it worked brilliantly! First I made a list of every society lady who was reputed to have had an affair with Lord Randall."

Clarissa closed her eyes. "Oh, Izzy," she groaned. "How could you?"

"Don't fret, there were only about twelve or thirteen. Anyway I started on the night of the rout, last week. I asked every one of them the same question."

Clarissa sat up, horrified. "You didn't ask them straight out, did you?"

"Of course not. Where's the cleverness in that? Anyway they'd only deny it, only with that knowing sort of look some of them do, you know, denying it in words but their expression telling quite another story, implying all sorts of things."

"Go on." She dreaded to hear what this *cleverness* was.

"We told them it was to settle a wager."

"We? Who's 'we'?"

"I enlisted Mrs. Price-Jones's help—and don't worry, she'll be discreet. And she thought it was great fun." Ignoring Clarissa's moan, she went on, "We asked every lady on the list whether the heart-shaped mark on the left cheek of Lord Randall's bottom was a birthmark or a tattoo."

Clarissa's mouth dropped open. "Izzy, you didn't! Asked them about his *bottom*? And how did you find out about the mark on it in the first place? Did Leo tell you?"

Izzy gave a peal of laughter. "No, of course not. He doesn't know anything about it. He'd have a fit if he knew."

Clarissa knew how he felt. "Tell me the rest then. How did you discover that Lord Randall has a heart-shaped mark on his bottom?"

Izzy's green eyes danced. "That's just it. He hasn't—or at least I have no idea whether he has or not. I made it up."

Clarissa shook her head in bewilderment. "I don't understand."

"We asked each of the ladies on the list whether the mark on his bottom was a birthmark or a tattoo. Giving them a choice of only two, you see. And you know what? Not one of them said they didn't know. Or that he had no mark on his bottom. Not one!"

Clarissa didn't know what to say. It was all too outrageous.

Izzy continued, clearly delighted with her plot. "One of them tried to freeze me out, saying very coldly what a very vulgar wager it was, and didn't I have better things to do with my time than to speculate about a gentleman's birthmark, but see, she answered the question, albeit indirectly. And her color was heightened. All the others happily answered. Most said it was a birthmark but several said now they came to consider it might be a tattoo, after all. So you know what that proves, don't you?"

Clarissa gave her a blank stare. The whole thing was quite mad. And completely, horribly scandalous—and unnecessary—now that she'd decided to trust Lord Randall anyway. Oh, what would he say when he found out? He'd be furious. And who could blame him?

"It proves," Izzy said, "that *none* of those women have been Lord Randall's mistress!"

Which is exactly what he'd already told Clarissa. "Oh, Izzy, I wish you hadn't."

"Why? I thought you'd be thrilled to know the truth at last."

"I asked him about it last week, before he went away, and he explained how his reputation had come to be. I already knew that his reputation was grossly exaggerated, and that most of those society ladies lied by implication— though why I still cannot imagine."

Izzy's eyes widened. "You did? You asked him directly? Oh, Clarissa, how wonderful. I thought you'd never find the courage. So what are you going to do?"

Clarissa blushed. "I was planning to marry him." Now she wasn't so sure. He might not want to have anything to do with the woman who'd indirectly caused such dreadful gossip and speculation about an intimate part of his anatomy.

Izzy flew out of her seat and hugged Clarissa. "I'm so happy for you, 'Riss. When's the wedding?"

Clarissa shook her head. "Nothing's been decided yet."

Izzy gave her a searching look. "Is there something the matter? You don't seem as happy as I thought you would be."

Clarissa forced a smile. Her sister had done what she thought was for the best. She should have been firmer with Izzy about investigating Lord Randall's reputation. "Oh, you know, just so many things to do. I haven't been sleeping well," she prevaricated. "And I have a slight headache. I'm not really looking forward to a night at Almack's."

"Oh, you poor love, why didn't you say so? Shall I fetch you a tisane?" Without waiting, Izzy rang the bell to order a tisane for Clarissa's nonexistent headache.

Izzy was so delighted with her clever plan—and it was clever, she had to admit—but now Clarissa desperately wished she had told him the other day—despite the cabbages and beggars and old turnips—that she loved him and wanted to marry him.

Because now he'd think her decision was because she'd had her sister and chaperone spy on him. And in such an embarrassing way. No doubt half the ton was speculating about this nonexistent tattoo or birthmark.

She pressed her hands to her hot cheeks. Why, oh why did they have to choose his *bottom* to focus on?

He was sure to be furious. Men took their dignity so seriously.

No doubt he'd want to call the wedding off. Which meant she would have to do the calling off, because he was much too honorable to do it.

Chapter Sixteen

When Race returned to his lodgings later that night he found a note from Clarissa waiting for him, asking him to meet her in the garden at his earliest convenience—which was heavily underlined—as soon as he returned to London. And to tell no one. Also heavily underlined.

Earliest convenience? He'd go now, but it was well after one and she'd either still be dancing at Almack's or preparing for bed. First thing in the morning then.

He scribbled a reply saying he'd meet her in the garden at eight in the morning, then paid a servant to deliver it.

As he climbed into bed he wondered what she wanted. It sounded quite serious.

By quarter to eight the following morning he was shaved, dressed in buckskins and high boots, and on his way to Leo's place.

With a knowing smile, Matteo, Leo's majordomo, let him into the shared garden behind the house. Race could have used the other entrance to the gardens, but he wasn't willing to reveal his hand just yet.

It was the kind of morning where the sky was a soft pearly gray, glowing with incipient sunlight that hadn't yet managed to break through. The garden was hushed, motionless, the silence broken only by a blackbird singing joyfully in a tree somewhere.

He quickened his pace.

He glanced into the summerhouse, but it was deserted. The rose arbor then.

His boots crunched on the gravel path as he approached and when he rounded the bend leading to the rose arbor there she was, pacing, looking anxious and adorable in the palest of pinks.

Seeing him, she flew to meet him. He opened his arms to gather her in a hug, but she skidded to a halt and held up her hands as if to ward him off. All color seemed bleached from her skin, her eyes were huge and she eyed him with trepidation. What the devil was going on?

"Miss Studley?"

She swallowed on a gulp, then said, "I'm sorry, Lord Randall, so very sorry. I never meant it to happen. I didn't want it, but my sister—oh, she meant it for the best, but— oh, please don't be angry with her, it's my fault, I should have been firmer. But I didn't know, and I'm truly, truly s-s-sorry." Her voice wobbled and he was troubled to see her glorious eyes were swimming with unshed tears.

"Tell me what has distressed you, and if I can do anything—"

"But that's just it, you can't do anything. It's too late for that."

Race stepped forward to draw her into his arms but she stepped away from him, again holding up her hands as if to rebuff him. "No, you don't know what we—what a shocking thing I have done."

He was feeling more and more disturbed. What on earth could she have done? "Then tell me."

She was silent for a moment, biting her lip, then words

tumbled out of her in a torrent. "It's all my fault. I should have trusted you—I did, but she didn't know that. But I should have been firmer, clearer—braver—because she doubted I would have the courage, you see, but I did, only she didn't know that, so she decided—but if I'd known, I would never— but I should have realized and stopped it. But I didn't and now it's all too late. So you see, it's all my fault."

He didn't see a thing, except that she was too upset to be coherent.

"Come, let us sit down, and you can tell me all about it." He led her to the rose arbor and they sat down. "Now then," he said, "tell me what has distressed you and I promise you, if I can, I will fix it."

"You can't." She drew in several long, shuddery breaths, produced a damp and crumpled lace-trimmed handkerchief and blew her nose fiercely, then turned to him, pale and resolute. Even with her nose all red and her eyes drowning in unshed tears she was beautiful to him.

"It's my fault," she said again. "It was Izzy's idea, but she would never have thought of it if only I had trusted you. And I do, I promise you, though when you hear what I have to tell you, you probably won't believe me. But when she thought of this, I didn't—we hadn't yet had our talk, you see. In the curricle, I mean. Only she didn't know that and so she did it."

"Did what?" he asked gently, cutting to what he hoped was the heart of the tangled speech.

"Began her . . . I suppose you could call it an investigation."

He picked a fallen rose petal from her shoulder and rubbed it between thumb and finger. As soft as her skin. "Investigation into what?"

"Into your rakishness," she said tragically. "And your, your *b-b-bottom*!" One tear rolled down her satiny cheek. She dashed it away and told him a long and tangled story, in which one thing eventually became clear to him—the reason women in society had been speculating about his arse.

"You mean that your sister asked all those women whether I had a heart-shaped birthmark or tattoo on my backside?" he asked unsteadily when she had finished.

"Yes." She gazed at him, her face utterly woebegone. "The left cheek. I'm so sorry."

"And they all said it was one or the other? A birthmark or a tattoo?"

She nodded, biting her lip, the picture of nervous contrition. Braced for his righteous outrage, if he was any judge.

Race couldn't restrain himself any longer. He threw back his head and laughed.

Incredulous, she stared at him. "You think it's *funny*?"

"I do. Preposterous, ridiculous, outrageous and very funny," he managed when he'd brought his mirth under control. There was relief as well as amusement in his reaction, he knew: he'd been sure something truly disastrous had occurred and that she was going to tell him the betrothal was at an end. But this . . . He laughed again. All those women, discussing his arse. It was too ridiculous for words.

"And you're not furious with me? Or with Izzy?"

"Not a bit." She didn't seem to believe him, so he drew a finger down her cheek and added softly, "Stop worrying, sweetheart."

The tears came then, and he gathered her into his arms and murmured soothing things, holding her soft body against him, rubbing her back soothingly. It was strangely peaceful in the quiet of the garden, sitting beneath a cascade of roses, their glorious scent dew-drenched and warming under the morning sun. Essence of Clarissa. She always smelled of roses.

After a few minutes her sobs slowed and drew to a shuddering close. He pulled out a handkerchief and dried her eyes.

She sat up, straightened her dress, and smoothed her hair back off her face. Struggling to regain her composure. Race just watched. After a moment, she darted him a doubtful glance. "You really don't mind?"

"That sister of yours probably needs a good spanking, but no, I really don't mind. Gossip doesn't bother me. I've lived with it all my life. And her little scheme was dam— dashed clever, I have to admit."

She sighed. "You probably won't believe me, but I had decided to trust you before this happened. Because of that talk we had. In the curricle."

"I believe you."

She turned wide eyes to him. "Will you forgive me?"

"I will. On one condition."

"Condition?" she repeated apprehensively.

"That you marry me as soon as possible."

Her eyes widened. "You still want to marry me? After what we did?"

"I do. Very much."

"Then I will marry you, Lord Randall," she said shyly. "I know you care for me, and that will be enough because I love you and I trust you and—"

"*Care* for you? I don't just care for you, you adorable goose. I *love* you, madly, passionately, with every fiber of my body and every drop of blood in my heart. I adore you, I—" He gave up trying to explain—words were so inadequate—and decided to demonstrate.

Cupping her face in his hands he covered her mouth in a kiss. She kissed him back, with all the warmth and sweet eagerness he craved, twining her arms around him and pulling him close, as if she couldn't get enough of him.

As he couldn't get enough of her.

After a while, he forced himself to release her. His body was thrumming with desire and he had to fight for control. Why did this scene have to take place in the middle of a shared blasted garden, where anyone could come across them? On this blasted hard wooden seat. With bees buzzing around him. He surely did pick his moments. So much for the skilled rake.

He glanced down at the woman in his arms and all irritation faded away. Lord, but she was lovely.

Curled into the curve of his body, nestled against his heart, she gazed up at him, her eyes glowing with love and arousal. "You love me," she said softly. It wasn't a question.

"I have loved you almost since the beginning, since the Arden ball, in fact."

She sat up and stared at him. "The Arden ball? When that horrid Lord Pomphret publicly denounced my sister Izzy as a bastard?"

He pulled her back where she belonged, in his arms, snuggled against his heart. "Yes. You marched across that dance floor like a young Boadicea, head held high, and claimed your sister, defying anyone to deny it. You were so beautiful and brave, I vowed then and there that you were the only woman for me, and I'd do whatever it took to win you for my bride."

She let out a long, soft sigh and nuzzled her cheek against him. "I loved you, too, almost from the start."

"Really? But you made it clear that you didn't want anything to do with me."

She gave him a rueful look. "I know. I'm sorry. I tried very hard not to fall in love with you, but I couldn't help it. I was frightened of marrying a rake, you see, because of . . ." She looked away.

"Your father?" He understood now.

She nodded. "He broke my mother's heart, over and over, with his infidelities. And then . . . Izzy's mother . . . and Zoë's."

There was a short silence, then he said in a low voice, "I will treasure and protect your heart for as long as I live." It was a vow.

She eyed him searchingly, then her face quivered slightly and she flung her arms around him, lifted her mouth to his and kissed him.

Something was wrong.

The wedding arrangements were surging ahead with the speed of a runaway coach. What they'd planned as a small, intimate affair with just family and a handful of friends was quickly turning into a Society Event.

Race knew why. He'd heard the talk. And it infuriated him.

Apparently Lord Randall—the famously elusive Rake Randall—had been snared at last, and by a plain dab of a girl of undistinguished birth and substantial fortune. Society was agog, so much so that even he had heard the whispers and speculation.

How had she managed it?

He couldn't possibly want her. Why had he allowed it to happen?

Would he break and run at the last minute?

And of course, everyone wanted to come to the wedding.

Ten days earlier, when he and Clarissa had come in from the garden to announce that the betrothal was now official and the wedding was going ahead, she'd been happy, glowing, excited. Now, the last few times he'd seen her she seemed pale and preoccupied. Oh, she made an effort to appear as normal, pasting on a bright smile from time to time, but she was no kind of actress and he could tell that underneath her general happiness, something was eating at her.

Was it the gossip?

But their entire courtship, such as it was, had been riddled with gossip. And she'd told him several times that she didn't care about gossip. So what was it?

Race led her outside to her favorite spot in the garden, the rose arbor. "What is it, love? You seem worried."

She seemed flustered by the question. "Oh, do I? Sorry. It's just—oh, it's nothing. I'm just being silly, that's all."

"You're never silly. Now tell me what's worrying you."

She looked around as if seeking escape, or rescue, or perhaps inspiration, but finding none, she slumped a little. "It's nothing. I'm just . . . Everyone is talking about what an unequal match this is."

"Unequal? In what way?"

"You're so charming and urbane and handsome and sophisticated and I'm just a girl from the country, shy and plump and plain, and—"

"Stop right there! You're gorgeous and not the least bit plain and if others can't see it, well, I'm happy to keep your beauty a secret known only to a handful of people, people who love you." His kiss was long and lingering. Someday she'd realize she was as beautiful as he knew her to be.

He forced himself to end it. He was aching to make love to her, but this was neither the time nor the place. "Now, is it really the gossip you're worried about?"

She sighed. "Not completely."

"Then what?" He waited a moment then said, "Of course if it's private I won't press you, but if it's something I can help with . . ."

She flushed. "It's just . . . the wedding night."

Was that it? Relief surged through him. Virginal anxieties—he should have expected it, her not having a mother to advise her. Race pulled her hard against him and kissed her again. "Don't be worried, love. You'll like it, you'll see."

"Oh, I know—Izzy explained things to me, and so did Mrs. Price-Jones—and I can't wait, truly I can't. I do want you, terribly. It's just that . . ."

"What?"

"I'm afraid I'll disappoint you."

He kissed her again. "You won't."

But he could see that she didn't really believe him, and that only one thing would prove to her that she really was as beautiful and desirable as he found her.

There was such huge pressure on brides on their wedding day. Everyone watching, everyone knowing what was to come, everyone except the innocent virgin bride, kept ignorant right up until the revelations of her wedding night. It was barbaric.

She sighed, leaning against him. "I just wish it was all over, and we could get on with our lives."

"We could, if that's what you want."

She gave him a startled look. "What? Skip the wedding? But we couldn't. All the arrangements—"

"Not the wedding, the wedding night. We could anticipate it, just the two of us, with nobody else the wiser."

Her eyes were wide. Color came and went in her cheeks as she considered what he was saying.

"It would put your mind at rest," he added persuasively. "Set you free to enjoy your wedding day without any worries about the night hanging over you."

"Could we?" she breathed. "But where? How?"

"Leave it to me."

"Not the summerhouse."

"No, somewhere we won't be disturbed. Leave it to me. I'll arrange everything."

"When?"

She was wound up like a spring, he thought. The sooner they came together and her fears were assuaged, the better. Besides, he could hardly wait, himself. "This evening."

Her eyes widened. "Tonight?"

"Why wait? You don't have any engagements that can't be canceled, do you?"

"No," she almost whispered.

He rose. "Good, then I'll meet you here at eight o'clock." He kissed her briefly and left. He knew exactly where and when he wanted this momentous event to take place, but there were certain arrangements to be made. He wanted it to be perfect.

Clarissa slipped out of the house just before eight. She was wearing a dark gray velvet cloak with the hood up so as to be as inconspicuous as possible. She'd hardly eaten a thing at dinner—a mixture of nerves and excitement and anticipation—and retired to bed early, saying she thought she had a headache coming on, but a good sleep would fix that.

And then, she'd waited until the coast was clear and crept down the back stairs. Oh, but she hated telling lies, even small ones like this. But it had to be done.

She waited in the rose arbor. It was an odd place to meet, inside a wholly enclosed garden, but she supposed it was better than waiting out on the street for him to collect her—and he could hardly collect her from Lady Scattergood's. But where was he planning to take her?

The sun hung low in the sky. A few bees buzzed around the roses, heavy with pollen, getting their last feed before returning to their hive. Where did bees live in the city? she wondered. In the country they lived in the skeps farmers and beekeepers made for them, and sometimes she'd seen hives tucked into a hollow tree, or a fresh swarm hanging in a tree, but she'd never seen a skep or a swarm in London. And hollow trees were soon removed.

Oh, where was he?

"Ready?" The deep voice made her start, even though she'd been expecting him at any moment. He wore buckskin breeches and shiny high boots, a dark gray coat and a plain buff waistcoat. They weren't going anywhere formal then.

Of course not. They were going to . . . to bed.

"Yes." She jumped up. His arms went around her and he

kissed her and she immediately felt better. "Where are we going?"

"Not far." He slipped an arm around her and started walking toward the other side of the garden.

"We're not going out via Izzy and Leo's house, then?"

"No."

That was a relief. She loved her sister, but this was private. "You're being very mysterious."

He smiled down at her. "Do you trust me?"

"Of course."

"Then trust me. It's a surprise."

He led her up to the rear gate of one of the houses that backed onto the garden. She halted. "This is the house that was sold a while back, the one the new owner is refurbishing."

"That's right." He pulled out a key and opened the gate.

She didn't move. "Do you know the new owner?" He inclined his head and she said, "So you have permission to enter?"

"I thought you said you trusted me."

She did, so despite her reservations, she allowed him to lead her inside the house. The late-evening sun shone through the windows, gilding the signs of building works in progress with a gentle glow. The house smelled faintly of paint and plaster dust and sawdust. Tradesmen's tools lay discarded in a corner, and a ladder, bucket and rolls of wallpaper sat at the entrance of one of the rooms.

Uncomfortable with trespassing, even assuming he had permission, she moved toward the front door. "Not that way, up here," he said, directing her toward the stairs, which had recently been polished.

She hesitated. Surely they weren't going to make love here, in this half-finished, empty, stranger's house. She'd thought he'd take her somewhere nice, like maybe a suite in a hotel or something. "I thought—"

"Trust me?"

She sighed and began to climb the stairs, feeling quite

let down. "Very well." But if he expected her to make love among the tradesmen's tools on the floor—even on a dust sheet—he would have another think coming.

But no, surely he wouldn't? She had to trust him.

They reached the first floor and he stopped in front of the closed door. "Close your eyes and keep them closed until I say 'open,'" he told her.

She closed them and kept them closed as he led her inside the room.

"Open."

"Ohhhhh." She looked around her in amazement. The red-gold rays of the setting sun burnished the leaves of the trees outside, the light revealing a fully furnished bedchamber, papered in delicate Chinese-pattern wallpaper in pale blue and gold. The floorboards were polished to a high gloss and a large, soft, blue and cream carpet covered most of the floor. An elegant wardrobe, dressing table and washstand, complete with water jug and bowl sat along the walls, and in the center of the room sat a large, carved wooden bed, fully made up with mattress, plump pillows and a satin eiderdown. The bedclothes had been turned down invitingly, showing snowy sheets. The contrast with the scene downstairs was astonishing.

She turned to him in amazement. "Whose is this house?"

He smiled. "Ours."

"*Ours?*" She glanced around the room again. "Really?"

He nodded.

"But how, Race? When? And why didn't you say so earlier?"

"I wanted it to be a surprise."

"It certainly is that." She wrinkled her brow, thinking back. "You must have bought this house . . . I don't know, weeks ago? Months?" She couldn't remember exactly, but it seemed to her that the sounds of workmen had been ringing across the garden for ages.

His smile deepened. "I bought it three days after the

Arden ball." He let that sink in, then added, "I told you I made up my mind about you back then. I'd hoped to have the refurbishments finished by the time we returned from our honeymoon."

She could still hardly believe it. "You bought this house? For me? Three days after the Arden ball?"

He nodded. "I thought you'd like to have your sister living just across the garden, and Lady Scattergood, too—you seem quite fond of her. And Lady Tarrant and the little girls. And, of course, you'll still have your beloved garden—while we're in London, that is. At other times we'll be at my country estate."

She gazed around the room in wonder. All that time ago . . . "I love it, of course. It's wonderful. Perfect. But what if I'd said no?"

He shrugged. "I was hoping you wouldn't."

Stunned, she sat down on a chair covered in embroidered straw-colored satin. "And this room?" She gestured.

"That I had to pull together today. It was a bit of a rush job, and you can probably still smell the paint. I've had the windows open all day to dispel it."

She shook her head. "It just smells new and clean. But I can't believe you arranged all this today, even the bedclothes. It's all just wonderful."

"The bedclothes were the most important. As to the rest, 'needs must.'"

She gave him a mock-stern look. "When the devil drives? Are you calling me a devil, Race Randall?"

He chuckled. "No, sweetheart, it was my own devil that was driving me, to get this room ready for the most important event of my life."

"Oh." It all came flooding back, the reason why she was here in the first place. "That."

"Yes, my love, that." He prowled toward her.

Suddenly nervous, she rose and moved to the window. The golden glory of the setting sun filtered through the leaves of the trees. She could catch only glimpses of the garden beneath. There were no curtains, but it was very private.

"You won't need this." She felt her cloak slide from her shoulders and for a moment felt like clinging to it. But that was ridiculous. She wanted this, wanted this man. Trusted him. Loved him.

She turned and found herself enclosed by his arms.

"Doubts?" he murmured.

She shook her head, unable to speak. Nerves, yes, a few. Doubts? Only of her ability to please him. She loved him, wholly and completely. He kissed her softly and led her to the bed. He draped her cloak over the armchair, then shrugged off his coat.

Clarissa sat on the edge of the bed. What should she do now? She supposed she should take off her clothes, too, but she hadn't thought ahead sufficiently. Her dress was fastened down the back with hooks: she needed a maid to unhook her. She should have worn a different dress, but all she'd been thinking about was trying to look nice for him. Oh, why hadn't she realized it? Every time she'd thought about her wedding night she'd imagined herself already in bed, wearing the beautiful embroidered silk nightgown that Miss Chance had given her. She gave one to each of her special clients when they got married.

Clarissa plucked at the fabric of her dress with nerveless fingers. Oh, this was so awkward. Any moment now he'd turn around, expecting her to have removed her dress.

He pulled off his boots, then his socks.

She bent to untie the strings of her shoes, but one had knotted. She tugged at it futilely.

"Allow me." Dressed only in breeches and a shirt he knelt at her feet, and without even trying to undo the knot, slipped one shoe off, then the other. She sat there like a doll, feeling foolish, gazing down at his thick, dark hair, wanting to run her fingers through it but unable to move.

He set her shoes neatly aside, then reached for the ties of

her stockings. His hands were cold and she jumped, feeling them on her skin. "Sorry," she whispered. And then confessed, "I need a maid to unhook my dress. I didn't think . . ."

He glanced up, smiled and rose. "I will be your maid tonight." He drew her to her feet. "Now, my lovely," he began.

She grimaced.

He paused, his hands on her shoulders. "Why the face?"

"I've told you before, I don't like false compliments. I know you mean well, but truly, I don't need them. I know I'm not pretty."

"False compliments? You think I'd offer you Spanish coin—false flattery—today, of all days?"

She just looked at him.

"Come here." He led her to the long cheval looking glass. She glanced at her reflection and looked away. She never liked looking at her reflection.

"Almost every woman I've ever known," he told her, his voice soft and deep, "is critical of her looks. Even those who most people think are beautiful will look in a mirror and see only what they consider flaws. But if you could see yourself through a man's eyes, specifically my eyes . . ."

She couldn't speak.

He stood behind her facing the looking glass, his eyes dark and intense. "You have the sweetest face, full of honesty, kindness and strength. And every time we meet I want to do this." He ran the back of his fingers down one cheek, slowly, lingeringly. "Warm silk, and so soft . . . with a hint of rose-petal blush."

She watched her blush rise, and swallowed.

"Your eyes are as clear as a mountain stream, so expressive and lovely I sometimes feel I could happily drown in them. And when you smile, the radiance that shines from them . . .

"Which brings me to your lovely, luscious mouth." His thumb ran gently over her lips and a warm shudder trembled through her. "Utterly delectable."

He turned her around, bent and kissed her, just a brush of lips over lips. It left her hungry, wanting more. She raised herself onto her toes and kissed him back.

He made a low humming noise deep in his throat and sucked on her full lower lip. Her legs trembled, suddenly weak. She clutched at his shoulders with urgent fingers.

He ran his hands slowly up from her hips, caressing her waist, and cupped her breasts lightly. They seemed to swell under the caress. Her nipples, under the layers of fabric, were hard, aching little points. He rubbed his thumb against them and she gasped as heat rippled through her, pooling deep in her belly.

He ran his hands along her spine, and she felt his long, warm fingers at the back of her dress. She shivered. He was unhooking her.

"You can't see this part of you, so pale and satin-velvet it is, but I've been dying to do this every time I've met you. Every single time. And now . . ." Turning her back to the looking glass, he bent and kissed the nape of her neck, his mouth warm and faintly moist against her skin. Shivers of pleasure ran through her. She arched back against him. The heat of his body soaked into her.

He swiftly removed the pins from her hair, his fingers skillful and experienced. He moved her slightly to catch the last rays of sun. "Your hair is like a soft cinnamon cloud, a thousand colors in the setting sun."

She gazed out of the window at the gleaming rose-gilt of the sun piercing the lowering clouds. A whisper of breeze shivered through the leaves of the trees outside the window, making them dance.

"And the fragrance . . ." He buried his face in her hair and inhaled deeply. "You always smell deliciously of roses."

"I make a rinse from rose petals," she mumbled. She was barely able to muster a sentence: his caresses and low, murmured love-speech were washing over her, leaving her weak and dizzy with desire.

She felt her dress slide from her shoulders and pool at her hips. "Even your shoulders are lovely, so smooth and round and creamy soft," he murmured, kissing them. Warm shivers flowed into her wherever his mouth touched.

She watched him in the mirror, entranced by his intense expression, his almost fierce concentration on her. Just her.

He smoothed big hands slowly down her body—she felt them every inch of the way. When her dress dropped to the floor, she was barely aware of it. Without thinking she stepped out of it. He bent and whisked it away, tossed it carelessly over the back of the chair on top of his coat, and slipped his arms back around her.

Clad now only in her fine linen chemise, very aware that beneath it she was quite naked, she turned in the circle of his arms, slipped her hands around his neck and stood on tiptoe to kiss him.

Chapter Seventeen

He pulled her closer so that she was pressed against his strong, heated body. Thigh to thigh, breasts to chest. Excitement shimmered through her as his mouth covered hers, tender yet passionate. And possessive.

He tasted of . . . she couldn't think what. A hint of brandy, perhaps, but most intoxicating was the taste of him, dark, masculine and thrilling.

She pressed closer, opening herself to all that he was demanding of her. She'd given herself morally and mentally to him; now it was physical, all gloriously physical.

She rubbed her fingers along his jawline, enjoying the faint abrasion of his firm, freshly shaven skin. The light fragrance of his cologne mingled with a darker, more masculine scent. She breathed in the scent of him. Spicy, masculine, unique. Addictive.

Still kissing her, he lifted her—effortlessly; she marveled at it—and carried her to the bed. One more kiss and then he stepped back. She felt instantly bereft, but he bent and shoved his breeches and drawers down and kicked them off. All he wore now was his white linen shirt, covering him to midthigh.

She wanted it off him, wanted to see him in all his masculine mystery.

He gazed at her, his eyes dark with desire.

She couldn't bring herself to ask him to remove his shirt. Rendered dumb with a mix of shyness and desire, she did the only thing she could think of: she pulled her chemise over her head and cast it aside, leaving her naked and nervously facing him.

He gazed at her a moment, and she raised her hands to cover herself. He reached forward and caught her hands in his, saying, "Ah, love, don't hide your glory from me."
Glory?

He kissed her hands, one by one and when he released them, she dropped them, nerveless.

He stood back and with one motion, pulled his shirt off over his head and tossed it aside. It floated to the floor and settled over her chemise, but Clarissa wasn't watching. She was riveted by the sight of him.

She'd never seen a naked man before, only statues, and he was so much . . . more than the ones she'd seen. "You are beautiful," she murmured, and reached out to touch him, not the strangest part of him—not yet—but the hard, muscled chest, the broad shoulders and strong, muscular arms.

"Men aren't beautiful," he said, but she gave him a sultry look and said, "Looking through *my* eyes, you are." He laughed softly.

Her eyes devoured that mysterious part of him that looked so hard and erect and fascinating, but before she could look her fill he pressed her back on the bed and joined her there, kissing and caressing her—mouth, eyelids, breasts, stomach, everywhere.

His big, warm hands smoothed, kneaded, and caressed her skin. Clarissa felt desired in a way she'd never before felt. He worshiped her with hands and mouth and body. She tried to caress him the way he was caressing her, but she'd lost all ability to think, only to feel. And to respond.

His hands slipped over her stomach, brushed over the triangle of hair at the base, and caressed her thighs. Her legs fell apart, trembling with need.

He slipped one hand between her thighs and touched her there, in the secret folds of her body. She stiffened at first but then he began to stroke her there, sliding his finger in and out. It felt strange but not at all unpleasant.

Soft shivers of heat began to ripple again and she moved restlessly against his hand, wanting more, but not knowing what. His fingers, his mouth caressed her . . . until she was dizzy with wanting, a trembling mass of heated, helpless desire.

She twisted and writhed, her whole body responding mindlessly to his touch, urgent and aching, helpless in the grip of a force she had never experienced.

Tension rose within her until she felt on the brink of . . . something.

And then his hot mouth closed over her breast. He sucked, hard, and she almost came off the bed as hot spears of ecstasy drove through her body.

She heard a high, soft scream as she arched and shuddered and spiraled into a realm where she'd never been before. Never even imagined.

She collapsed against him, but before she could even begin to gather her senses, she felt him pushing into her; thick, hard, hot. She tensed a moment and he paused, then muttered, "It will be all right. Trust me." He pushed and she felt a swift small stab of pain, not nearly as bad as she'd expected.

So, that was it. She was no longer a virgin.

She lay still beneath him, feeling stretched, and full, and dazed with wonderment. It was all so strange, a little uncomfortable, and yet it felt so right.

She ran her palms over his body, along his ribs and

shoulders, enjoying the feel of his firm, strong body. He felt hard and hot and strangely tense—tense as a bowstring, as if he was holding himself back. From what?

He shuddered under her caresses and slipped his hands between her thighs, where they were still joined. His fingers caressed her there and her body responded, building again to . . . whatever it was. He began to move inside her, then, rocking, thrusting, filling her over and over in a primitive, exhilarating rhythm. She had no control, just clung on to him, wrapping her limbs around him, carried along with his rhythm as they rose together . . . spiraling higher and higher . . .

She heard herself scream again as she shattered around him. As if in the distance, she heard him groan, and with one final thrust, he poured himself into her and collapsed.

When Race came to himself again, it was full dark outside. The moon was in its final quarter and faint moonlight had begun to silver the treetops, letting in just enough light for him to see Clarissa's face as she slept. His chest filled as he gazed at her sweet face and he reached out to gently brush a stray lock of hair from her face.

Her eyelids fluttered open. It wasn't light enough for him to see the expression in her eyes. "How do you feel?" he murmured.

She smiled and stretched luxuriantly. "Wonderful."

He couldn't restrain himself: he leaned forward and kissed her. She was warm and responsive and kissed him back enthusiastically, wrapping her arms around him and cuddling up against him.

"Shall we do that again?" she asked.

He gave a low chuckle. "Not tonight. I think you might need some time to recover."

She pouted. "But I feel wonderful."

He kissed her again, filled with relief that her first experience of lovemaking had been a good one. He was more than ready to make love to her again, but with some difficulty he restrained himself. She'd been a virgin. "By our wedding night you'll be ready to make love several times in a night. But for now, we must practice a little restraint."

"Oh, very well," she said, clearly disappointed. "So, I suppose we must leave now."

"No, it's early yet." He gathered her against him and she snuggled happily up to him, twining her limbs around his and nestling her cheek on his chest. They lay together in the faint moonlight that slowly grew, talking of this and that. He told her about the garden his mother had made at his country estate, and how it had been somewhat neglected.

She told him of the plan her new little half sister had made, to go to France and learn to be a lady. And become a painter. And how she was sad to be losing her, but resigned to it because it was what Zoë wanted.

They talked about the house. She didn't much care about the interior decoration—she was more interested in the garden—oh, and she would want a room where she could make her creams and lotions. But she loved everything about the choices he'd made for the bedroom, and he confessed that he had sought the advice of Leo's Neapolitan major-domo, Matteo, who had overseen the refurbishment of Leo's house.

The whole time she talked, she stroked him, rather like a cat. It challenged his restraint—she was still quite an innocent in bedroom matters—but Race felt like purring. To think that this wonderful woman was going to be his wife.

They discussed the wedding and she confided that she would have preferred something small and intimate, but that her sisters and Lady Scattergood and Mrs. Price-Jones were arranging everything and refused to tell her what their plans were. Mrs. Price-Jones stressed that a small wedding would look like a hole-in-the-corner affair, and after all the scandal, it was necessary to make a splash.

"I would be happy to intervene," Race offered. "It's your day, after all."

She smiled and rubbed her cheek against him. "Thank you. It's tempting, but again I really couldn't. Everyone's gone to so much trouble. I'll just have to endure it—it's only one day, after all." She looked up at him, and the look in her eyes made his heart catch. She added, "And now that I know what will be awaiting me—us—at the end of the day I will have something to look forward to."

He kissed her. She was such a generous soul. He knew she was uncomfortable with crowds, and people looking at her. That would change, he hoped, as she became more confident of her own unique beauty.

"You led me a right merry dance, you know," Race said.

"It was your own fault. I thought you were a conscienceless rake. Everybody said so."

"But I told you I wasn't."

She rolled her eyes. "And of course men never lie to women to get what they want."

He laughed. "Fair enough, but I want you to know that I never lied to you. And I never will."

"I know that now," she said softly.

"Yes, after your sister set the whole of society speculating about the state of my backside."

"I'm so sorry about that—but I didn't know she was going to do it." She patted the relevant body part, and he flinched slightly. "What?" she said. "What did I just do?"

"Nothing, it's just a little, um, tender there just now."

"Why? Did you hurt yourself?"

"Not exactly." He lifted the sheet and turned away from her so she could see the famous backside.

"Oh, Race . . ." she said huskily. "Does it hurt?"

"Only when you poke it. And it will toughen up in a few days. It will be fine by the wedding."

"Oh, Race." Her eyes misted up and she hugged him

tightly. High on his backside a heart had been tattooed, and inside it a name: CLARISSA.

When the moon was the brightest it would be, he judged it was time to go. "It's getting late. Must be almost midnight," he said reluctantly.

She sighed, gave him one last kiss and rolled off the bed. They dressed in silence. Clarissa slipped her dress over her head and then made a small exclamation.

"What is it?"

"I told my maid not to wait up for me. She was to unbolt the back door after the butler went to bed, and then go to bed herself."

For a moment he didn't understand what the problem was. And then he did. "Your hooks?"

She nodded. "I'll never be able to undo them all by myself."

"Then don't do them up."

She looked at him in surprise, then laughed. "If I don't, the dress will fall down around my ankles the minute I take a step."

"Not if we only do up the top ones. You'll be wearing a cloak, after all, and nobody will see. And it's just a few steps across the garden to Lady Scattergood's house." He stepped forward. "Here, let me." He did up the top hook, and then, unable to resist, planted a slow kiss on her velvety nape.

She shivered against him, then turned and kissed him again. "I wish we didn't have to leave."

Oh, but she was hard on his self-control. For two pins he'd take her back to bed . . . but no. She'd been a virgin. She would still be tender. He picked up her cloak and settled it around her shoulders. "Me, too, but in ten days we'll be husband and wife, and can spend as much time together as we want."

As they walked down the stairs, Race began to explain

his plans for the rest of the house, but it was quite dark inside and he soon gave up. "We can come back in the morning and look through it properly if you like." He let her out the back door, then locked it behind him. The gate squeaked as he closed it. "Needs some oil."

The moon was in its last quarter, but the sky was clear and though the moonlight was faint the garden was all silver and shadows. The fragrance of the nighttime garden rose all around them, enhanced by dew.

It surely was a night for romance.

Hand in hand they strolled, stopping every few minutes to kiss. Race couldn't get enough of her.

"Clarissa Studley!" A strident female voice broke into their reverie. Race sighed. The irritating neighbor, Milly something-or-other.

Clarissa sighed, but didn't let go of Race's hand. "Milly, what are you doing out here at this time of night?"

Milly gasped. "What am *I* doing? What are *you* doing out here? Alone. With a man!"

"A man to whom I'm betrothed," Clarissa said calmly.

"Even so, it's not at all respectable behavior."

Clarissa ignored that. "Good night, Milly," she said, and began to move away.

"Did you hear that gate squeak?" Milly said. "It's that place where the rude men have been working. Someone must be trying to get in. Or breaking into the garden, which is worse!" She peered anxiously along the path they'd just come, then paused. She turned and stared at Race and Clarissa. "It was you, wasn't it? You just came from there. You were in that house, weren't you?"

Clarissa shrugged. And then a strange expression crossed her face and she half turned away from Milly and formed a kind of a hunch under her cloak. Race frowned. What the devil?

Milly went on, "Which means you must know who the new owner is. Who is it, Clarissa? Mama is desperate to know."

Clarissa looked up at Race. He couldn't read her expression.

"The new owner," Race said, "is a very respectable fellow, from the north, I believe. He's made his fortune as a very successful manufacturer of"—Milly leaned closer—"sausages, I believe. Pork sausages."

A muffled snort came from beneath the hood of Clarissa's cloak.

"Sausages!" Milly exclaimed in horror. "Mama will be appalled. We can't possibly live next door to a manufacturer of anything, let alone one of sausages!"

"He also does a very fine line in pickled pigs' trotters, I am told, though I haven't yet tasted them myself."

More muffled sounds came from beneath his beloved's cloak.

"*Pickled pigs' trotters!*" Milly wailed. "Mama will die! She'll just die!"

"Oh, nothing so drastic, I'm sure," Race said soothingly. "I believe his manufacturing practices are very clean and healthful. You could eat off his factory floor, I'm told. And she needn't eat the pickled pigs' trotters, after all."

Milly stared at him. "Mama, eat pickled pigs' trotters? You must be mad!" She turned and rushed off down the path to give Mama the appalling news.

The minute she was gone Clarissa exploded into laughter. "You, Race Randall, are a wicked, wicked man," she said between giggles. "Pickled pigs' trotters? I've never even heard of such a thing."

"I'm fairly sure they exist." He added, "But what I'm wondering is why you are standing in that peculiar hunched fashion. Have you hurt your back?"

"No. It's because you didn't do my dress up properly and it's falling down. This is the only way I can hold it up. I was terrified that it would fall at Milly's feet."

Chuckling, he reached under her cloak and did up the first few hooks again. They resumed their strolling.

"Now, all we need is for Betty to have forgotten to un-bolt Lady Scattergood's back door. Or for Lady Scatter-good to be wakeful in the night and gazing out of her bedchamber window," she said. "She does that sometimes, you know. She once spotted Izzy sneaking back in from an assignation with Leo in the summerhouse. She summoned Leo to explain himself the very next morning."

"Then I hope she's fast asleep," Race said. "That old lady terrifies me."

Clarissa laughed and hugged him. "I'll protect you. Be-neath that acidic manner of hers, she's a sweetheart. But she is quite critical of men, I admit."

Race opened the garden gate and looked up at the house. All the windows were dark. "Check the door is unbolted," he said, "and then one last kiss."

Several passionate kisses later—it was simply not pos-sible to stop at one. He didn't want to let her go at all— Clarissa slipped inside. Race waited until he heard the bolt slide home, then he returned to the garden and watched until faint candlelight from her bedroom window showed his lady love was safe.

Ten interminable days until the wedding. It felt like an age.

Epilogue

§

St. George's Church, Hanover Square, London

The organ played softly. Race paced back and forth in front of the altar. Where was she? He pulled out his watch and flicked it open.

"Plenty of time. Besides, brides are always late," Oliver, his cousin's husband, said calmly.

Oliver was Race's best man, and maddeningly placid about the whole thing he was, too. Race would have asked his best friend, Leo, to perform the role but Leo, as Clarissa's legal guardian, was giving the bride away.

"Relax," Oliver said. "Take a pew."

Take a pew, indeed, Race thought irritably. How could he calmly sit when his every nerve was crackling? It was ridiculous, he told himself. Clarissa wouldn't let him down. She'd promised herself to him. She'd *given* herself to him. She wasn't the sort to break faith. He trusted her with his life.

Which was true, and all very well, but *where was she?*

He continued pacing.

There was a stir at the doorway of the church and he whirled around, but it was only Lady Scattergood, who'd been brought right to the church door in her ornate sedan chair. He watched her carefully alight.

She was heavily veiled and wore a large colorful turban. Why the veil? He had no idea. She was an eccentric old bird. Another heavily veiled female guided her to a pew at the front. A servant, no doubt, who led the old lady as if she were blind. Ah, that would be it—Lady Scattergood would have her eyes closed. Blocking out the rest of the world until she was safely inside. Clarissa would be pleased the old lady had made the effort to come.

If she ever came herself.

The two veiled ladies were followed by Clarissa's chaperone, dressed as usual in a rainbow—or an explosion of tropical parrots—and wearing a large feathered and beflowered hat. She also wore an elegant silver-haired gentleman on each arm.

His cousin Maggie entered, waggled her fingers at Race and blew a kiss to her husband. She was followed by that nosy young female who lived on Bellaire Gardens, accompanying a larger, more imposing version of herself; clearly her mother. Lord, how many frills and ruffles could be fitted on one dress? Two dresses.

More and more people entered the church—a surprising crowd, really. He caught himself up on the thought. Clarissa had touched so many people with her sweet nature and kindness.

There were people he recognized from Lady Davenham's literary society, including Lady Davenham herself, accompanied by merry old Sir Oswald Merridew, who sent him a wink. And there was the woman with the granddaughter who caterwauled—he hoped she wasn't going to sing.

An elderly woman dressed in blue entered, leaning on the arm of Clarissa's maidservant, Betty. That would be Clarissa's old nurse. Leo had arranged for her to be brought up to London especially for the wedding, as a surprise. Clarissa had no idea she would be here. The old lady beamed at him, and he nodded back. A sweet-faced old girl.

Lord and Lady Tarrant arrived with their three little girls all dressed in their best. The baby would be at home with his nurse, of course, but why was the smallest girl scowling? Oh, of course; she hadn't been allowed to bring her precious cat into the church.

Lord and Lady Tarrant were accompanied by that fellow who'd helped him expose Clayborn—Thornton, that was it—and his stylish wife.

Half a dozen fashionable ladies filed in, Lady Snape and Lady Windthrop among them. They gave him sour, *Hell hath no fury* looks. A handful of modish, slightly dissolute-looking gentlemen accompanied them, several clearly the worse for drink.

None of them had been invited, of course, but then anyone could enter a church. They certainly hadn't come to wish him and Clarissa happy: bets had been laid that he wouldn't make it to the altar.

So much for that. Here he was, standing proud, waiting for his bride.

His side of the church was filled also, mainly relatives and fellows he'd been to school or university with.

A tall, darkly handsome gentleman slipped into a pew on the bride's side. Vibart! What the devil was he doing here? The villain had had the cheek to court Clarissa—and lost, thank goodness. If the man had a shred of decency he would have taken himself back to whatever hole he crawled from, blast him. Instead he'd had the audacity to come to her wedding. And sit on the bride's side.

Race glared at the elegant rakehell. Vibart caught his glance, smiled and gave the sort of bow that was both insolent and provocative.

Race turned his back on the congregation and looked at his watch again.

"She'll be here," Oliver murmured. "Stop fretting."

Of course she would. Race had no doubt of it. Only *when*?

The organ stopped in midtune. An imposing chord sounded. At last! He turned to face the entrance of the church. And there she was, his love, his life, wrapped in some gorgeous confection of satin and lace. But he had no eyes for her dress; it was the gorgeous woman inside it that mattered.

As their eyes met, she smiled, a smile that stole his breath away. So beautiful and loving. His bride.

Race tried to swallow the lump in his throat. He hadn't particularly cared where the wedding would take place. He'd never been much of a churchgoer, but now, in this hushed atmosphere, with the sun splashing rainbows through the stained glass windows, with the scent of flowers and beeswax and brass polish all around him, and the most precious being in all the world walking down the aisle toward him, he understood that the church was the right place, the only place for a blessing to be bestowed upon him: a blessing called Clarissa.

On Leo's arm, with Izzy following close behind her, Clarissa forced herself to walk slowly down the aisle. There he was, standing in front of the altar, waiting for her, tall and elegant and beloved. He was looking pale and very serious, but oh, the expression in his eyes—if she wasn't careful she'd start crying, and she was determined not to do that.

She glanced at the people seated in the church. She hadn't expected so many to attend. Fashionable London people often skipped the church ceremony, preferring to attend the wedding breakfast instead. But here they all were, so many friends and well-wishers.

Such a short time ago, she and Izzy had arrived in London, not knowing a soul. And now . . .

Her eyes were blurring. She blinked furiously. She would not be married all teary and red-eyed.

She took a few more steps then faltered, spying among the sea of elegant hats, one very familiar straw hat covered with red silk poppies. It couldn't be—but it was! Nanny in her favorite hat. Nanny, who had always refused to travel all the way up to London. Nanny, whom she hadn't seen in an age.

Her face crumpled. Nanny gave her a watery smile in return, and waved.

Leo leaned closer and murmured, "Izzy's idea. She knew you'd want your old nanny here for the day."

"Thank you," she whispered, and put a hand behind her to catch and squeeze Izzy's hand. They continued the long walk down the aisle. She couldn't see Race's face now. He was just a tall, handsome blur. All her friends, and now Nanny.

They reached the altar. She felt a tear trickling down her cheek. She quickly dashed it away, passed her bouquet of roses to Izzy, and held out her hands to him, her beloved husband-to-be.

"I'm sorry," she whispered. "I didn't mean to cry, but—"

"You look lovely." He raised her left hand, kissed it, most romantically, and then kissed the right.

A sigh ran through the watching congregation.

The minister cleared his throat, and they turned to face him. "Dearly beloved," he began.

The wedding breakfast was to be held at Leo's house. It was one of his last duties as her guardian. Their flower-bedecked carriage pulled up in front of his house, and there was Matteo, beaming at the door to welcome them. Clarissa hastily tried to straighten herself—she and Race had been kissing all the way from the church.

Race chuckled. "Don't worry, you still look beautiful." He handed Clarissa down and they entered the house together.

After receiving Matteo's effusive congratulations, they turned to climb the stairs to the reception rooms, but Matteo stopped them. "No, no, this way, milor', milady. *Prego*." He swept out a dramatic arm and ushered them toward the back of the house.

"Is such a beautiful day, we 'ave the wedding breakfast in the garden, no?" He grinned and waved them on.

Clarissa gasped. "In the garden? What a lovely idea."

"Race's suggestion," said Leo, coming up behind them. "He said you would love to have it in the garden, and as you know, Matteo enjoys a challenge."

Clarissa turned and hugged Race. "Oh, it's perfect, Race. I couldn't think of anything nicer." She turned and thanked Leo and Matteo, who modestly waved her thanks away.

They stepped out into the garden. With the spate of warm weather they'd had recently, the garden was in full bloom, heralding the imminent onset of summer. The air was redolent with the scent of freshly cut grass and a multitude of fragrant flowers.

They strolled down the path, turned a corner and found a sea of tables set out on the lawn, each one covered in a white linen cloth and laid with gleaming silver cutlery and crystal glasses. Every table bore several tiny crystal vases containing rosebuds and a collection of other flowers.

A short distance away a raised dais had been set up. On their arrival, a string quartet began to play. Clarissa gazed around. It all looked quite magical.

The other guests started to arrive and soon they were surrounded, exchanging greetings and receiving congratulations and thanking people for their gifts. Under Matteo's supervision, footmen circulated, bearing drinks, and all sorts of delicious-looking dishes.

"Oh, lovey, what a beautiful, beautiful wedding."

Clarissa turned and embraced her beloved old nanny.

Nanny continued, "I could hardly believe it when you walked down the aisle, looking so much like your dear mama."

Clarissa felt a pang at Nanny's words, but Race came up beside her and took her hand, saying, "Her mother must have been a lovely woman, then."

"Oh, she was, she was," Nanny agreed. "I raised her, you know, my lord, and then raised Clarissa and Isobel."

"You did an excellent job then, Mrs. Best." Nanny beamed up at him.

Clarissa was amazed that Race had remembered her old nanny's name, and she could tell Nanny was flattered by his attention.

After a short conversation, Race excused himself and strolled off. "What a handsome and charming man, Clarissa," Nanny declared, watching him chatting with the guests. "I must say, both you girls have done extremely well with your husbands. Lord Salcott has been so very kind to me. Do you know, he sent his own carriage to bring me to London, and oh my, he spared no expense! Every comfort provided along the way."

Izzy joined them, and it transpired that she was going to show Nanny some of the sights of London, and then she and Leo would take her back to the cottage where she lived on Leo's estate.

A short time later, Nanny retired inside to a guest room in Izzy's house. The excitement, she told Clarissa, was wonderful but exhausting and she needed a nap.

Matteo had set up a special reception area for Lady Scattergood and some of her cronies in the summerhouse, and the old lady sat in state there, receiving guests. By now she'd removed her veil, but her mysterious attendant had not.

"Who's the veiled girl with the old lady?" Race asked Clarissa when they had a private moment.

Clarissa laughed and rolled her eyes. "Can't you guess?

It's Zoë, of course. She and Lord and Lady Thornton delayed their departure so they could attend the wedding. I wanted her to be a bridal attendant along with Izzy, but she wouldn't hear of it. Such a stubborn little sister I have. She said she hadn't kept out of sight of the ton all this time only to bring disgrace on me and Izzy at my wedding."

Race eyed her thoughtfully. "She's very protective of you both, isn't she? You know, I think we should do something for her."

"What sort of something?"

"She's going to France, isn't she, for a couple of years with Lord and Lady Thornton? I think we should make her an allowance."

"I did that," Clarissa said. "I gave her part of mine, every quarter, just as I did with Izzy before she was married."

"Very generous of you, love, but I'm talking about a permanent arrangement, something where she won't feel she's dependent on you, or Lord Thornton, for that matter. She's an independent little creature, and she has her pride. I'll tell her it's a normal part of the marriage settlements: an arrangement for a bride's unmarried sisters."

Clarissa hugged him. "That's a brilliant idea. I did wonder what would happen to my inheritance once I was married. I suppose it all goes to you now."

"It does, but I thought we'd put it in trust for our children," he said casually. "What do you think?"

"I like the idea . . . But could we think about it for a while? While I do want any children we have to be well provided for, I wouldn't want any of them to be hunted for their inheritance." As she had been.

"Good point." He glanced over her shoulder and stiffened. "Oh lord, I've just remembered, I have an urgent appointment."

She frowned. "An urgent appointment? On your wedding day?" She turned to follow the direction of his gaze and let out a gurgle of laughter. Two very frilly and determined-looking females were approaching. Mrs. Harrington and Milly. "We're going to have to thank them for that hideous epergne they gave us."

"Ah. You know what a terrible liar I am," Race said earnestly.

"Hence your urgent appointment," she said dryly. "Don't worry, I'll deal with them."

"I knew you'd be the perfect wife," he said, and disappeared into the shrubbery.

The wedding feast had been devoured, the toasts were drunk, the speeches made and the wedding cake had been cut: it was time for the bride and groom to depart.

"Couldn't we just slip away?" Clarissa asked Race. "I'm dreading having to say goodbye to everyone. I'll be sure to cry, and I look dreadful when I cry, all red and blotchy."

"You look nothing of the sort," Race told her. "You've been in tears half a dozen times already today and trust me, you looked beautiful every time."

She gave him a misty smile. "You are such a lovely liar."

"Beautiful," he reiterated firmly, and sealed it with a swift kiss.

They said their goodbyes—she managed not to cry—and a mixed crowd made up of invited guests, local curiosity seekers and street urchins gathered on the footpath outside Leo's house to wave them off and wish them well.

Race tossed a few handfuls of coins into the crowd. The urchins and some of the curious onlookers scrambled to collect them as their carriage drove off.

"That's done then," Clarissa said, leaning back against the seat. She was tired, but so happy. "Where are we going now?"

"Not far."

The carriage turned at the first corner, then turned again at the next, and pulled up outside the house Race had recently renovated. "I thought you'd prefer to spend our first night as a married couple in our new home," he said. "And tomorrow, if you feel like it, we'll travel down to my country home. What do you think?"

She sighed with happiness. "It's perfect. I thought we might be going to one of those big hotels, but this is so much nicer. I always feel a little intimidated in those places."

He helped her down from the carriage. "In that case, Lady Randall—"

"Lord Randall! Clarissa! What on earth do you think you're doing?"

They turned to see Milly hurrying toward them, her face alive with concern. "Clarissa Studley, you're not—you can't possibly be going to visit that dreadful vulgar pickled pig trotter fellow, can you?" She gasped on a sudden thought. "Oh! You didn't invite him to the wedding, did you? Mama would just *die* if he was there, too." She looked at Race. "Mama is second cousin to a duke, you know."

"My condolences," Race said.

Milly frowned. "Condolences? But—"

Anxious to get on with her wedding night, Clarissa cut her off. "Milly, this is Lord Randall's house. He bought it."

Milly's jaw dropped. "Lord Randall *bought* it?"

"Yes," Race said. "The house belongs to me. Now, if you don't mind—"

Milly rushed up to him and clasped his arm. "Oh, thank you, thank you, Lord Randall. Mama will be soooo relieved. And thrilled. And so very grateful. I'm sure she'll take back every unkind—I mean every mistaken thing she ever said about you, now that you've saved us from having that dreadful vulgar pig trotter man as a neighbor. She was considering moving, you know."

"*What* unkind things?" Clarissa demanded.

"You and your mother are most welcome, Miss . . . um," Race said briskly. "Now, if you don't mind." He hurried Clarissa through the front door and shut it firmly behind them.

"I want to know what unkind things they've been saying about you," Clarissa said crossly. "How dare they? I won't have anyone saying unkind things about you, especially Milly and her mother!"

"They won't, my little firebrand, now that I've rescued them from being neighbors with the dreaded Lord Pig Trotters—or should it be Sir Pigly Trotters? No, I think he must be Sir Pigly Trotter-Pickles. Yes, he married well, a rich Miss Pickles, and then was knighted for services to pig trotters. Though," he added thoughtfully, "the pigs might not agree."

"Sir Pigly Trotter-Pickles?" She snorted, then collapsed into giggles. "You truly are wicked, Race."

"I know. And now, my love, let me show you some of the many delightful ways we can be wicked together, now that we're married." He swept her up into his arms and ignoring her protests that she was too heavy, he carried her upstairs and into their bedchamber.

"There," he said, laying her gently on the bed. He took a moment to—quite unnecessarily—close the new curtains; he was a little out of breath and trying not to show it, the dear, sweet man.

He turned. "Now, where were we?"

"You were going to show me some delicious ways we could be wicked together. Or do I mean delightful?"

"Both," he said firmly, and prowled toward her.

It wasn't anything like wickedness, she decided much later, lying boneless and euphoric on the bed. It was pure bliss.

He'd started by simply flipping up her skirt and petticoat and introducing her to what he called the deliciousness.

It had shocked her a little at first—his putting his mouth on her, there. But she was soon dissolving in waves of pleasure and deciding—when she could think at all—that she had no objection to this at all, except that it was wrong to call it wicked.

Slowly she came back to awareness. Her eyes fluttered open and she found him stripping himself naked. She lay, still luxuriating in the last echoes of the sensations he'd aroused, and admired his strong body, his broad shoulders, his long firm thighs, and the small crimson heart high on his left buttock, with her name enclosed in tiny elegant script. It made her smile every time. Along with a small surge of happy possessiveness.

He turned, caught her watching and with a smile, proceeded to undress her, layer by layer, caressing her all the time with lips and hands. And when they were both naked, they moved on to *delightful*, which began rather like their first time, but oh, it was so much more.

Izzy was right: it did get even better.

They dozed for a while, then she felt him stir and get out of bed. She opened her eyes to see him at the window, naked and magnificent, pulling the curtains back and opening the window, letting in the late sunlight and the gorgeous greens and textures and scents of the garden.

She was so lucky—no, she was blessed—to have found this wonderful man. Why had she ever hesitated so long? He made her feel . . . everything. She didn't feel plain and unattractive anymore: he made her feel beautiful. She didn't even feel fat: she felt . . . luscious—his word for her. He respected her, he listened to her. He loved her.

And she loved him, so very, very much.

He turned, saw her expression and hurried to her side. "What is it, love? What's the matter?"

She shook her head; her heart was so full she was unable

to muster a word. She reached up and pressed her palm against his cheek.

His face softened. "Happy?"

"More than happy," she managed as she raised her face for his kiss.

ABOUT THE AUTHOR

Anne Gracie is the award-winning author of the Marriage of Convenience, Chance Sisters and Brides of Bellaire Gardens romance series. She started her first novel while backpacking solo around the world, writing by hand in notebooks. Since then, her books have been translated into more than eighteen languages, including Japanese manga editions. As well as writing, Anne promotes adult literacy, flings balls for her dog, enjoys her tangled garden and keeps bees.

VISIT ANNE GRACIE ONLINE

AnneGracie.com

Ready to find
your next great read?

Let us help.

Visit prh.com/nextread

Penguin
Random
House